I0676451

MOLLY'S MOON

by RON PARHAM

Molly's Moon
Copyright © 2014 by Ron Parham

All rights reserved. No part of this book may be used or reproduced in
any manner, including electronic storage and retrieval systems, except by
explicit written permission from the publisher. Brief passages excerpted for
review purposes are excepted.

This is a work of fiction. Any resemblance to any persons,
living or dead, is purely coincidental.

First Edition
Printed and bound in USA

ISBN: 978-1-940222-42-4

Cover design by Kelsey Rice
Formatting by Kelsey Rice

This novel is dedicated to the two most important people in my life, my son and daughter. My son, Jonathan, was the inspiration for the character of Charlie, and gave me invaluable support during the entire writing process. He is currently studying to become a chiropractor at Palmer Chiropractic College West in San Jose, CA. My daughter, Kelli, was the inspiration for the character of Molly, and was the embodiment of the spirit of Molly's Moon. *She lived with me during the writing of the novel and saw all of my ups and downs, witnessed the many times I almost gave up, and was there when I typed in the last word of the last chapter, when we both wept out of joy and relief. I love them both tremendously and dedicate this work of my heart to them.*

MOLLY'S MOON

by
RON PARHAM

𝓟
Pen-L Publishing
Fayetteville, AR
Pen-L.com

PART ONE

CHAPTER 1

When the speedometer hit two hundred kilometers per hour, Ethan Paxton closed his eyes, opening them just long enough to look at the terrified man sitting next to him in the backseat of the Mercedes. Rob Jamison's knuckles were white when he clutched the back of the driver's seat, the German countryside a blur as the white sedan hummed along the autobahn, like a glider in the air, the only sound the whir of the tires as they barely touched the banked pavement.

"God almighty!" yelled Rob. "Last time I ever tell a German we're going be late for our flight!"

"Relax, Robert," the driver said over his shoulder in his heavy accent. "And please do not rip my seat apart!" The big German seemed to be enjoying his American guest's discomfort. "What is your speed limit in America? Sixty five miles per hour? We back out of our driveway at that speed!" He laughed heartily at his joke, his big belly jiggling.

Ethan stifled a laugh in spite of his terror. He opened one eye to glance at his boss, Henrik van Rijk, a Dutchman used to the high speeds on the German autobahn. He was sitting calmly in the front passenger seat, his arm draped across the back of the driver's seat as though they were out for a Sunday drive.

"We have about twenty minutes, Jost," Henrik said calmly as he looked straight ahead. "Maybe even you can't make it in time."

Suddenly the Mercedes slowed down as it made a sharp right turn, throwing the two Americans in the backseat to the left, then back upright when the car straightened out. Ethan opened his eyes wide as he was tossed about. He saw a sign — *Frankfurt Main Airport*. A few seconds later they were screaming to a stop in front of the departure terminal.

"I'm sorry, Henrik, what were you saying?" Jost Heilemann said, laughing as he got out of the car, opening the left rear door. "Plenty of time, even for Americans!"

Ethan scrambled out the right rear door, grabbing his briefcase. "Someone pry Rob's fingers from the backseat!" he said over his shoulder, glancing at his white-haired friend, noticing the color just returning to Rob's face.

Rob laughed loudly as he got out of the car, slapping the big German on the back. "Damn, Jost!" He bent down and kissed the sidewalk, not once but twice.

"Let's go!" Henrik said, looking at his watch. "We can just about make it if we hurry."

The Dutchman and the two Americans turned and waved to the huge German, who was already speeding away from the departure terminal, still laughing. They began running down the wide sidewalk, dodging other passengers, finally entering the departure terminal with minutes to spare. Boarding passes in hand, they headed directly for the gate. They had started the day in Amsterdam with a seven a.m. flight to Frankfurt It would end back in Amsterdam at four o'clock in the afternoon. The date was Tuesday, September 11, 2001.

Making it to the gate just as the airline attendants were closing the door, Henrik yelled, "Hold the door!"

The three men, breathing hard, handed their boarding passes to the female flight attendant. Hustling down the jet way, they ducked into the doorway of the commuter jet, eliciting frowns from other passengers.

"Please take your seats and buckle up," the blond female attendant said, not smiling.

After stowing their briefcases in the overhead bin, Ethan and Henrik fell into their first-class seats. Rob took the seat on the aisle across from them.

Ethan's chest was still heaving when he noticed the deep frown on Henrik's face. "What's wrong, boss?"

"What? Oh, nothing," Henrik said, forcing a smile. "I don't like having to rush."

"You sure it wasn't because the Dutch soccer team lost again?" Rob said from across the aisle.

"Ha. No, and it's called football over here, as I've told you many times. Real football, not that sissy game you play in America."

"Sissy game?" Rob looked at Ethan. "Are you going to let him get away with that?"

Ethan smiled and shrugged. "You'll never change his mind, Rob. You know that."

The flight attendant came by and checked their seat belts and within two minutes the jet was taxiing out to the runway for takeoff. The three men sank back in their seats, their breathing starting to return to normal.

"Holy crap! Can you believe how fast that damn German was going!" Rob exclaimed as the jet raced down the runway.

"Well, you got him back, Rob," Henrik said, chuckling. "He has ten small gashes in his seat where your fingernails used to be."

The three men enjoyed the back and forth banter while the airplane slowly rose into the afternoon sky. Ethan looked across the aisle at Rob, who was, as always, very animated. He had a naturally ruddy complexion which turned beet red when he was excited. Rob was forty-two years old, the same age as Ethan, but looked older. He owned his own trucking company in California and was usually the life of the party whenever they were together. Ethan smiled and closed his eyes as he thought about the day's events. It was a good day, a successful day, and now they could sit back and relax.

Ethan opened his eyes and glanced at Henrik, noticing the frown again. His boss was a serious man, very intense, always thinking. Ethan knew something was on his mind.

"Everything okay, Henrik?" Ethan said.

The Dutchman turned and looked at Ethan, nodding his head. "Just something I heard in the terminal. Nothing to worry about."

"Well, you seem worried about something," Ethan said. "But, okay. It was a good day, boss."

Henrik smiled weakly. "Yes, it was a good day. I think we need to order some wine."

After the airplane reached its cruising altitude and the seatbelt sign blinked off, the blond flight attendant, smiling now, took their drink orders. The three men ordered white wine and settled back in their seats. After a few minutes of small talk, the wine worked its magic and all three dozed off. Thirty minutes later they were landing at Amsterdam Schiphol airport. They sat in silence as the commuter jet taxied to the arrival gate.

They were tired and quiet as they walked up the jet-way and into the Amsterdam Schiphol arrival terminal. As Ethan opened the door into the arrival terminal he was stunned at what he saw. Everyone had their heads cocked upwards, staring at something. A collective gasp suddenly went up from the crowd, sending a chill down Ethan's spine.

"What the hell?" Rob said, walking behind Ethan and hearing the loud gasp.

They skirted around the edge of the mass of people, unnoticed by anyone. When they were behind the crowd, they craned their necks backwards and saw a television hanging from the ceiling. It was too far away to make out the images, so Ethan began pushing his way to the front, with Rob right behind him. He heard a voice behind him.

"Ethan, what are you doing?"

Ethan turned and saw Henrik standing behind the wall of people. Ethan pointed to the television set, then turned back and looked up at the images on the screen. What he saw didn't register at first.

"What the hell?" Rob said again.

Ethan stared at the television set. "Lots of smoke coming out of a building," Ethan whispered. "Looks familiar but don't know where it is. They're talking in Dutch so I don't know what the hell they're saying."

Many in the crowd were now looking at the two Americans instead of the television, whispering to each other. A few people pointed to them, then to the television set. Ethan jumped when he felt someone grab him.

"Come, let's go," Henrik said sternly, his hand firmly on Ethan's shoulder.

"What are they saying?" Ethan said. "Why is everyone staring at us?"

"I'll explain when we get to the car. Let's go. Now." Henrik began pushing his way back through the crowd.

The two Americans watched the big bearded Dutchman plow through the crowd and head down the long hallway. They hurried after him, glancing back at the television and the crowd of people who were staring back at them. Once free of the mass of people, they began running to catch up with Henrik.

"Whatever it is, it sure spooked Henrik," Rob grunted as he ran.

"It was freaking me out," Ethan said, gasping for air.

The two Americans saw the same scenario play out at each gate they passed, people staring up at the television in silence. Fear began to grip Ethan as they caught up with Henrik in the main Schiphol Airport terminal.

"Henrik, what the hell is going on?" Ethan said, panting.

Henrik didn't reply. He just kept walking.

Ethan looked at Rob, whose face and nearly bald head were turning a deep shade of pink. Rob shrugged his shoulders at Ethan and continued walking briskly, trying to keep up.

As they rushed out of the main terminal, crossing the busy airport thoroughfare to the short-term parking lot, Ethan's mind began racing. *What could make those people so frightened? The looks on their faces . . . .*

Once they reached the black Audi, Henrik finally stopped and turned to his two American friends. His face was ashen.

"Henrik, Goddamn it! What the hell is going on?" Ethan said, out of breath and out of patience.

"Get in the car," Henrik said as he opened the driver-side door.

They climbed into the car, Ethan in the front passenger seat and Rob in the rear seat. Henrik had his hands on the steering wheel, staring straight ahead, silent.

"Boss?" Ethan said, pleading for information.

Henrik cleared his throat. "The World Trade Center in New York has been attacked."

"What do you mean attacked?" Rob said, leaning forward from the backseat.

"Two airplanes have flown into both towers."

Ethan stared at his boss, not comprehending what he was saying.

"It was a terrorist attack," Henrik continued. "Commercial airplanes with passengers on board flew into the buildings about an hour or so ago." He glanced at the two men quickly. "Just about the time we were running through the Frankfurt terminal. I'll turn on BBC so you can hear for yourselves."

Henrik quickly scanned the dial on his radio until he heard an English-speaking voice.

". . . and at 9:37 a.m., eastern standard time, American Airlines flight 77 flew into the west side of the Pentagon in Washington, D.C. The South Tower of the World Trade Center collapsed at 9:59 a.m."

Ethan sat motionless, staring at the radio, the full impact of what was happening beginning to hit him like a blow to the head. *The smoke billowing out of the skyscrapers! The Pentagon! Jesus, America was being attacked!* His mind began to race. He had just left California three days before on a regular business trip to Europe, one he had made many times before. He remembered being upset because he hadn't been able to say goodbye to his two children . . . .

He jerked his head upright. *My children!*

CHAPTER 2

They weren't the normal shouts of a typical workday, but the shouts of frightened people, of people trying to get away from wherever they were. Panic shouts. Molly Paxton watched in shocked surprise as teenagers and adults scrambled all over the school camp site, picking up tools and equipment and putting them in trucks and vans. They weren't scheduled to leave for three more days, but the terrorist attacks of that morning had everyone spooked.

The order to break down the camp had come very early that morning from Mister Sizemore, the Santa Elena Academy's principal. Molly's supervisor, Missus Caldwell, had come into their tent at seven a.m., telling them to start packing up. The group of nearly three hundred teenagers and adults had arrived at the home-building site outside of Tecate, in Baja California, Mexico, on Saturday and had already framed twenty houses. The school, located about an hour north of Los Angeles, had been coming to the Baja area of Mexico for ten years, building nearly two hundred homes for the people in the area since they started. It was something the students, parents and faculty looked forward to every year. This year, they would leave their work unfinished.

"Charlie!" Molly yelled, spotting her nineteen year-old brother on the crest of a hill.

"Hey, kid!" Charlie Paxton said as he turned to look at his little sister running up the hill. "You packing up?"

Molly stared at her six foot tall brother who was covered with grime and sweat. Easily one of the most popular boys at the mission site, as was evident by the number of teenage girls who chased after him, he had an easy smile that captivated everyone around him. He had graduated from the school the year before but had volunteered to come back as an adult worker. School would be starting the week after they got back from the mission trip, and he would be entering his sophomore year at UCLA. Molly was glad he was in Mexico with her, even though she told him otherwise.

She crinkled her nose as she got closer to him. "Whew! You need a shower," she said, backing away.

Charlie tilted his head back and laughed loudly, seeing the disgust in his sister's eyes. "That means I've been working my ass off, sis. Why aren't you packing up?"

"I am, but I need your help. Cindy Lambert is really getting on my nerves because she won't, like, do anything. She makes me so mad! Can you talk to her? She thinks you walk on water so maybe you can light a fire under her lazy-ass butt."

"That's Missus Caldwell's job, not mine. I've got way too much to get done myself without babysitting a little diva. You'll work it out, Moll. Better get back to it so we can get out of here by three o'clock." Charlie gave Molly his best big brother stare, but backed it up with a smile.

"Yeah, okay. Did you call Lupe today to let her know we're coming home?" Molly asked.

"Yep. She said that she was waiting for a call from Dad in Europe so she could let him know."

"Why bother Dad? He's thousands of miles away."

"Because he'll be worried about us. These attacks have the whole damn world scared shitless." Charlie looked around to see if anyone else had heard him.

"What's going on, Charlie?" Molly said, staring at him, the fear creeping back into her mind. Her stomach had been churning ever since Missus Caldwell woke them up that morning. "Do you think they could do something else, even in California?"

"Hell, yeah! They could strike anywhere, anytime. If they can fly airplanes into skyscrapers in New York City, they can pretty much do anything they want."

"I'm scared, Charlie. What if they're at the border?" Molly said with wide open eyes.

"Ah, nothing will happen, kid," Charlie said. "They don't care about a stupid little border town. It'll all be okay, Moll, and tonight we can take showers and watch TV and see what the hell has been happening all morning. Go back and get ready." Charlie dismissed his little sister, then turned back around and said, "Don't worry, sis."

"I wish Mom was here," Molly said, blinking back tears.

"I know, sis, me too. Go on, get packed up."

Molly turned and started the trudge back down the hill to her tent area.

"Charlie?" she said, turning around suddenly.

"Yeah?" Charlie sighed, looking back at her.

She bit her lip. "Nothing. See you later." She began running down the hill.

"Hey, sis!" Charlie yelled after her.

She stopped and looked back at him.

"I love you, Moll," he said, patting his heart.

Molly smiled widely, waved and began running down the hill a little faster.

When Molly arrived back at her tent site, she saw Cindy Lambert sitting on her sleeping bag painting her toenails. She looked inside the tent and saw nothing had been done.

"Cindy! What the . . . !" Molly screamed at her friend.

Cindy Lambert was Molly's best friend, but she was the total opposite of Molly in every way imaginable. Cindy was the typical sixteen-year old: boy-crazy and clueless about life. She was tall, blond and blue-eyed, with pale, freckled skin. Molly was short, olive-skinned, with long dark hair and even darker eyes. She would have passed for one of the local kids in Tecate. Cindy got straight A's without breaking a sweat. Molly worked her butt off to get B's in school. But they were best friends and that's all that mattered to the two girls.

"Do you have any idea what is going on around you?" Molly exclaimed. "People are dying in New York City, terrorists are everywhere and planning God knows what, and we have to get across the border before nightfall! And you . . . you're painting . . . your toenails!" Molly was waving her arms frantically.

"Well, I, like, have to look good when we get to San Diego. What's your problem?" Cindy asked, obviously clueless to why her best friend was mad.

"You . . . you . . . ah, forget it!" Molly yelled as she went inside the tent to continue packing her things. "Aaaaaaaaaaaa!"

"Chill, Moll. Geez" said Cindy.

"Aaaaaaaaaaaaaaaaaa!" Molly yelled from the tent.

"Whatever."

CHAPTER 3

The short, dark-haired man scanned the valley below with his powerful binoculars, then turned and smiled at the woman standing behind him.

"They look like little ants running around down there," the man said. "So many of them, but all I need is three or four."

Natalia Blanco cringed, feeling the bile climbing up her throat again as she stared at the man. Screwing up her courage she said, "Angel, maybe we should forget it since there is such trouble in the U.S. right now." There was very little hope or conviction in her voice.

Angel Rojas lowered his binoculars, turned slowly and scowled at her, his black eyes blazing. "Forget it? Forget it? This is my big chance! They are my ticket, my chance to be somebody. Forget it?" he growled, spitting at Natalia's feet. "Maybe I should forget you?"

"I was just thinking that—"

"Stop thinking! You are a *puta*, you let me do the thinking!" Angel waved her away, muttering to himself. He put the binoculars back up to his eyes and continued to scan the valley below.

Natalia cowered and backed away. *Why did she tell him? What did she think would happen?* She knew his appetite for women, especially younger women. She raised her eyes and looked at him with contempt and hatred. *How could she let him do this?*

"Cesar! Come here!" Angel yelled to one of his henchmen while staring through the binoculars.

"¿*Sí*, Jefe?" a man said, running up to Angel, his gold teeth glimmering in the sunlight. The man was out of breath, the short climb up the hill too much for him.

Angel lowered the binoculars and looked disgustedly at the man next to him. "You fat pig," he said. "Lose some goddamned weight."

The man dropped his head. "*Sí*, Jefe."

Angel shook his head in disgust. "We need to know when they are planning to depart and which road they will take, so send Rafael down to their camp to ask some questions. Make sure he does not raise suspicion. He is to talk only to teenagers, not adults. They should know him by now and feel comfortable seeing him around."

"Sí, Jefe," Cesar said, still hanging his head as he backed away from Angel.

Cesar lumbered back to his group of men and singled out a baby faced kid. Rafael was seventeen years old but looked much younger. He had been a regular fixture at the American school's build site since they arrived, acting like one of the local kids from the Tecate area who visited the Americans every day, seeking money, food or trinkets.

After listening to Cesar, Rafael ran to one of the two black SUVs for the short drive down the hill to the American encampment in the valley below. He kicked up dust as the big SUV sped off.

"Goddamn it, Cesar," Angel yelled. "Can't anyone do anything quietly around here?" He scanned the encampment with his binoculars to see if anyone was looking up at the hilltop.

Angel turned back to Natalia and smiled broadly. "I'm sorry for my outburst, my love. I am just so excited and I owe it all to you. But please do not ever question my decisions again. Come here, give me a kiss."

Natalia shuffled slowly to his side. He drew Natalia to him with his left arm, his right hand dangling at his side, and kissed her roughly, then shoved her away. As he turned his back to her, he looked over at the members of his gang and smiled broadly, his white teeth gleaming in the early morning sunlight. He raised his right arm, his hand covered with a black leather glove.

"La Mano Negra," they said in unison.

Natalia turned away and wiped her mouth with the back of her hand. Her nausea worsened as she realized Angel was going to go through with his plan. She closed her eyes and thought about the nightmare that was about to unfold, and she was helpless to stop it.

CHAPTER 4

Damn Bushmills.

Jake Delgado rubbed his forehead as he walked into the Cozy Hut café, just a few blocks from the bustling Gas Lamp District of San Diego. He had a first-class hangover from the night before, having passed out again at the El Toro Bar and Grill. He rubbed the six-inch scar on his left cheek as he glanced around the small restaurant. Everyone in the cafe was looking up at the television set in the corner, their eyes fixed on something.

Every table was full so he slid into the only empty seat at the counter, his back to the television, not really caring what they were staring at.

"Morning, Jake. Coffee?" asked a small, wrinkled, gray-haired woman behind the counter.

"Yeah, thanks Helen." Jake winced from the pain in his head.

Jake looked up and down the counter to see if there was anyone he knew. Not recognizing anyone, he decided to give the TV a look, just to satisfy his curiosity. He turned sideways on his stool and glanced up at the small TV. What he saw didn't compute in his alcohol-muddled brain at first.

"What the hell is going on?" he said to no one in particular, staring at the TV.

The man sitting next to him looked up. "Are you serious?"

Jake looked at the younger man in the suit and tie. "Yeah, I'm serious. What the hell is going on?" Damn yuppies, always invading his little joint.

The man looked Jake up and down, shaking his head in disbelief. "The World Trade Center has been attacked! Planes flew into them! Where the hell have you been?"

"First of all, it's none of your damn business where I've been, and second of all . . . what the hell do you mean 'planes flew into them?'" Jake took a swig of coffee to ease the pain in his head.

"Airplanes, commercial airplanes with passengers, flew directly into both towers. Hell, it's been on TV for the past two hours!" the man said, staring at Jake's scar.

Jake knew the man was staring at him but decided he wasn't worth it, and turned his attention to the television. He saw large buildings with smoke pouring out of them. *This can't be real—it's a damn movie.* He turned his back on the guy in the suit and looked at an older, gray-haired man on his other side. Not a regular but not a yuppie either.

"Hey, what's this all about?" Jake said, hoping for a straight answer.

The man looked at him in the same way the other man did. "What he said," pointing to the man in the suit. "Damn, mister, you been sleeping under a rock?"

Disgusted, Jake grabbed his coffee, slowly got up from his stool and walked towards the tiny TV in the corner, his head pounding. Words were streaming below the picture. Maybe they would give him a straight answer.

At 8:46 a.m., Eastern Standard Time, American Airlines flight 11 flew into the North Tower of the World Trade Center. At 9:03 a.m., eastern daylight time, United Airlines flight 175 flew into the South Tower of the World Trade Center. At 9:37 a.m., Eastern Standard Time, American Airlines flight 77 flew into the west side of the Pentagon in Washington, D.C. At 9:59 a.m., eastern daylight time, the South Tower of the World Trade Center collapsed. At 10:28 a.m., eastern daylight time, the North Tower of the World Trade Center collapsed.

Jesus Christ! It's true! He looked at the picture on the screen which was showing the collapse of one of the towers. Ash was spewing out and people were running in all directions. Jake stared at the picture, shaking his head in disbelief, which made his head hurt again.

At 10:03 a.m., eastern daylight time, United Airlines flight 93 crashed in a remote area of Pennsylvania, killing all on board. It is believed that the flight was hijacked by terrorists and was heading for Washington D.C., possibly targeting the White House or Capital . . . .

Jake turned around, looking at the clock behind the counter. Eight thirty. He slowly looked around, staring at the people in the café. They were all oblivious to him, all mesmerized by the pictures and words in the little box in the corner. Turning back to the TV he saw the second tower collapse. He backed away, shaking his head. Finally, he turned around and walked out of the café, leaving his coffee and two dollars on the counter. No one noticed.

He walked a block down from the Cozy Hut and opened the door to the El Toro Bar and Grill. It was dark inside, but he knew where everything was so he walked to the end of the bar and sat on his usual barstool. The ancient television behind the bar, with a twenty-inch screen and fuzzy picture, was tuned to CNN. Jake looked at the bartender, who was staring at the small screen.

"Tiny, give me some water and something for my head," he said.

The burly bartender kept staring at the screen, not moving from his spot behind the bar.

"Tiny, goddamn it!" Jake held his head and made a mental note not to yell anymore.

Tiny looked down at Jake and said "Oh, didn't hear you come in, Bull. You want a Bushmills?"

"Hell, no!" *Hell no!* "Water and some aspirin." *Damn, quit yelling.*

Tiny looked away from the television, shaking his head. "Another rough one last night, Bull." It was a statement of fact, not a question.

Jake grunted, holding his head so it wouldn't move.

"Unbelievable, huh?" Tiny said as he put the glass of water and three aspirin in front of Jake. "You been watching this?"

"Yeah, unbelievable," Jake mumbled. He threw the three aspirin into his mouth and chugged the glass of water. *Damn Bushmills.*

"How many?" Jake said.

"How many what?"

"Planes, damn it!" Why was everyone such a smart ass this morning?

"At least four, counting the one in Pennsylvania."

Jake stared at the television behind the bar. "Tiny, when the hell are you gonna get a real TV?"

"That's a real TV."

"That's a toy TV. An old toy TV," Jake said, pointing. "You can't see shit on it."

"You never complained before," Tiny retorted.

"Well, I never had anything I wanted to watch before." Jake said.

Tiny was staring at him.

"What the hell is your problem?"

"You wearing the same damn shirt you wore yesterday?" Tiny said.

Jake looked down at his yellow flowered aloha shirt. "I don't know—maybe."

"Damn, Jake. You ever wear anything else besides those damn aloha shirts? I don't think I've seen you in anything else since you left the SDPD."

"Yeah? So what?"

Tiny just shook his head as he walked back to the other end of the bar.

Jake looked down at his shirt again. *What the hell's wrong with this shirt?* He looked around the bar, waiting for the aspirin to do its job. The El Toro was not just Jake's hang-out, but his office. He was a private investigator by trade, a drunk by choice, which made living in the apartment directly above the bar very convenient.

"Bull, you passed out on the bar again last night," Tiny said as he walked down and filled up Jake's water glass. "It's damn embarrassing, man."

"Yeah, well, that's what you get for having a drunk for a partner." Jake said, rubbing his forehead again.

Jake glared at Tiny, who was laughing, making the folds around his neck jiggle. Tiny was African-American, stood six foot six and weighed around three hundred pounds. He played professional football with the Chargers in the late seventies before he blew out his knee. He opened up the El Toro a few years later and had been there for twenty years. He brought Jake in as a partner when Jake was kicked off the SDPD. He was the only friend Jake had, and the only person that could bust his ass and not get pounded. And Tiny was the only one in nearly five years that still called him Bull.

"What the hell happened last night?" Jake asked Tiny.

"You know Bull, if you'd stay half-way sober you'd know what was going on in here," Tiny said, walking away.

Jake shook his head as he turned his attention to the TV, squinting at the blurry images on the screen.

"Damn it, Tiny. Get a real goddamn TV!"

CHAPTER 5

Ethan was staring straight ahead as they pulled up to the hotel after the one hour drive from Schiphol Airport near Amsterdam to 's-Hertogenbosch, in southern Holland. The three men had remained in shocked silence throughout the drive, listening to the BBC announcer the entire trip.

"If you need anything tonight, just call me—regardless of the time. Okay?" Henrik said, looking directly at Ethan. "Ethan, are you okay?"

Ethan blinked his eyes, finally nodding his head.

Thanks, Henrik," Rob said from the backseat. "We'll be okay."

Henrik nodded to Rob and then turned to Ethan again. "Call your family, Ethan. I'm sure everything is okay."

Ethan looked at his boss. "I can't call them, they're in Mexico." He opened his door and stepped out of the black Audi.

"Ethan . . ." Henrik said, his voice trailing off.

Rob patted Henrik on the arm as he walked past. "He'll be fine. He's just worried about his kids. I'll make sure he calls you tonight. Thanks, Henrik."

"Okay," Henrik said, the concern still etched in his face. "He looks terrible. Make sure he calls me."

Ethan was standing in front of the hotel entrance, staring at the city square. Rob walked up next to him and put his hand on his shoulder. They both turned and watched Henrik pull out onto the cobblestone street, disappearing around the corner.

"Come on, buddy. Let's get to our rooms and get freshened up. You'll feel better after you call home," Rob said, patting Ethan on the back.

"My kids are in Mexico," Ethan said again matter-of-factly. "I can't talk to them."

"I know, but I'm sure they're in contact with someone at home, someone you can call, right?"

Ethan stared at Rob with a hollow look, turned and walked into the hotel lobby, standing silent as Rob asked for the keys to their rooms. The hotel clerk glanced up at Ethan several times, but said nothing. He gave the two oversized keys to Rob.

"I'm sorry for what happened to your country today," the clerk said, looking at Rob, then at Ethan.

"Thanks," Rob said. "It's been quite a shock."

"If we can do anything for you while you are here, please don't hesitate to ask us."

"Thanks," Rob said again, glancing at Ethan, who remained silent.

The two men entered the ancient elevator. It didn't move and began to make a buzzing noise.

"You have to make sure you close the metal gate," the desk clerk said as he closed the noisy gate. "Sorry for the inconvenience, but this is an old hotel."

"Thanks," Rob said, smiling. "I forget every time." Rob glanced at Ethan and saw no reaction, just a blank stare.

They rode the elevator to the third floor in silence. When the elevator door opened, Ethan didn't move, the blank stare still on his face.

"Ethan, it's your floor," Rob said, holding the elevator door open and opening the metal gate.

Ethan blinked his eyes and looked at Rob. "Oh, yeah, thanks." He walked out of the elevator, turning and looking back at his friend.

"I'll call you in about an hour. We'll get a beer in the bar downstairs," Rob said as the elevator door started to close. Rob caught it and said, "Remember to close the gate."

Ethan stood in front of the elevator for several seconds, finally closing the metal gate when it started to buzz. He glanced right, then left, trying to remember which direction his room was located. He finally turned right, trudging slowly down the narrow hallway.

When he entered his room, Ethan threw his briefcase and jacket on the bed and walked into the small bathroom. He stared at the haggard face in the mirror, the dark circles beginning to form under his blue eyes. He brushed salt and pepper hair back from his forehead and splashed water on his face and watched as it dripped from his chin. He toweled off and stared at his image in the mirror. *What was happening? The world has gone mad!*

He trudged back to the bed and turned on the television set. It was just after five p.m., so he calculated that it would be eleven a.m. on the east coast of the United States. He channel surfed until he found an American station.

Sitting on the edge of the bed, he listened to the American announcer and watched the images for the first time.

"The death toll now is estimated at over three thousand people in the World Trade Center and Pentagon attacks," the television commentator said. "The North Tower collapsed around ten-thirty eastern daylight time, so the full extent of the damage and death toll cannot be determined. The images you see now, of people jumping out of the towers to certain death, are difficult to watch. The immense heat generated by the fire inside the tower is overwhelming to the people trapped on the upper floors."

Ethan watched in horror as one tower collapsed, then the second. Images of the Pentagon being attacked, and then news of another commercial airplane, supposedly headed for Washington D.C., crashing somewhere in Pennsylvania after kidnappers had taken it over. He was filled with sadness, anger, and disbelief. He held his face in his hands for several minutes, his mind numb.

When he raised his head he looked at the clock on the bedside table. It was five-fifteen. Quickly doing the calculations in his head again, he knew it was eight-fifteen in the morning in California. Picking up the telephone, he began dialing his home number. He was praying that his live-in housekeeper, Lupe, had heard from his children.

"Hello?" the voice on the other end said in the familiar choppy accent.

"Lupe, it's Ethan," he said.

"Mister Ethan!" Her voice was strained, but excited. "I was hoping you would call. How are you?"

"I'm fine, Lupe," he answered. "Have you heard from Charlie and Molly?"

"Yes, Mister Ethan, Charlie called me thirty minutes ago. They are okay."

"Are they coming home from Mexico?" Ethan asked anxiously.

"Yes. He said that they were crossing the border this afternoon."

Ethan blew air out of his lungs, the tension releasing like a helium balloon. He bent over at the waist and then stood up again.

"Are you okay, Mister Ethan?" Lupe said.

"I'm fine, Lupe. How about you? What have you heard about the terrorist attacks in New York?"

"It is awful," she said. "I am afraid."

Ethan thought about his housekeeper being all alone in his house, with no one to talk to.

"Call Sherry or Monica if you need someone to be with you," he said, referring to his two sisters-in-law who lived close by.

"Okay, Mister Ethan. I will be okay, I think. I cannot wait for the children to get home."

There was several seconds of silence before either of them spoke again.

"Mister Ethan? Are you coming home?" she said.

"I'm going to try, Lupe, but with this madness going on it may be difficult."

"Why?"

He held the phone away from his mouth as he let out a slow sigh, not having the patience to explain to Lupe. "Because they may shut down the air traffic in the U.S." He knew that Lupe would have a hard time understanding this.

"Why would they do that? It happened in New York, not California."

Ethan rubbed his eyes. "I don't know, Lupe. I'll try to get on a plane as soon as I can." He pinched his nose. "I'll let you know once I know something."

"Okay. I will tell Charlie and Molly that you will call them."

"Lupe, I can't call them. Charlie's cell phone . . . . Just have Charlie call me when you hear from them. Will you do that?" His frustration due to the language barrier was rising, as it always did. "Grab a pen and I'll give you the number of my hotel."

"Okay, Mister Ethan. Just a moment."

Ethan could picture the heavy-set woman shuffling to his office to find a pen and piece of paper, then shuffling back to the phone, slowly.

After what seemed like several minutes, she came back on the phone. "Okay, Mister Ethan, I am ready."

Ethan sighed again and gave her the phone number of the hotel and reminded her to have Charlie call him as soon as he and Molly got back into the United States.

"Tell him not to worry about the time over here when he calls. I want to hear from him and Molly just as soon as they cross the border," he said again. "Okay, Lupe?"

"Yes, I will tell him."

"Thank you, Lupe. Everything will be fine," Ethan said, with as much confidence as he could muster. "And Lupe?"

"Yes?"

"Thank you for taking care of things at home. It's a big help and comfort to me."

"You are welcome. Goodbye, Mister Ethan."

"Bye, Lupe."

Ethan gently put the phone on the cradle and shook his head. He leaned back on the bed, resting on his elbows, staring at the wall. His mind began racing. He had tried calling Charlie's cell phone on Sunday when he arrived in Amsterdam but got no connection. He knew it was fruitless to try until they arrived back in the U.S. He had to wait.

Connie. He thought about his dead wife. He missed talking to her, especially when he was away on business trips. She was always so calm and steady. *God, how he missed her.*

Memories of the past six months began flooding his mind. He and Connie had been married for over twenty years. She had been a beautiful, fiery Hispanic woman, his rock and his guiding light, always available whenever he called from whatever corner of the globe he was in at the moment. Connie had died of cancer in March of that year after a prolonged and painful battle with the disease. It was devastating to him and to the children, but they somehow got through the last six months. He knew that the children had to be missing her right now. Connie had gone on the home building mission with them the previous year, before she began her battle with cancer. She had been so energetic and full of life, always wanting to help people. *And now she was gone. Forever.*

Lupe had been their housekeeper for several years and had agreed to stay on to help take care of the children after Connie died. One of Connie's sisters had volunteered to live with them but Ethan said no. Lupe was loyal and dependable and he had needed that, especially when he was on one of his frequent business trips. And the children liked her, almost like a second mother.

His son, Charlie, was nineteen and had taken his mother's death hard. But he was very mature and was slowly getting over the pain and loss. He was a sophomore at UCLA and was becoming a man. Ethan knew that he could count on Charlie if anything happened.

Molly, his sixteen-year old daughter, was a completely different story. She internalized her feelings, rarely letting him or anyone else know how she was feeling. She looked fine on the outside but Ethan worried about how she was coping with the loss of her mother on the inside. She was fiery and independent, just like her mother, and she was a teenager, with teenage ideas about life.

Charlie and Molly had left very early Saturday morning for the mission trip with Molly's high school. Ethan had a flight to Amsterdam that same afternoon so the children didn't wake him to say goodbye, knowing he had a long flight ahead of him. He had had an argument with Charlie the night before about some stupid thing that meant nothing now. *He should have gotten up when they left. If only he'd been able to say goodbye . . . .*

The ringing phone jarred him from his thoughts. He cleared his throat as he picked the phone up.

"Hello?"

"Ethan, it's Henrik. How are you doing?"

Ethan cleared his throat again. "Just a little numb from everything."

"Have you called home yet?"

Ethan hesitated. "Just got off the phone with . . . Lupe," he answered. "My housekeeper." He couldn't remember if he had ever told Henrik about her.

"Has she heard from your kids?" Henrik asked.

"Yes, she did. They're leaving Mexico today, hopefully."

"That's good, Ethan," Henrik said. "I know how rough it's been since Connie died."

Ethan pinched his nose with his fingers. "Yeah, thanks boss."

After some hesitation, Henrik continued. "I've got some bad news. The FAA has closed all air traffic into and out of the U.S. You're going to be stuck here for a while."

Ethan rubbed his red eyes for the umpteenth time. "Not a surprise," he said.

"Get some rest, Ethan. You guys go out and enjoy yourselves tonight, have a nice, relaxing dinner. Your children are headed home so nothing to worry about, right?"

"Right," Ethan said with little conviction.

"I'll call you tomorrow."

"Okay. Thanks, boss."

Ethan hung up the phone. *Nothing to worry about? You've got to be kidding. The whole damn world is falling apart and you want me to relax?* He fell back on the bed and closed his eyes. His mind was full of visions of smoking skyscrapers, of airplanes flying into buildings, and of the poor souls jumping from the twin towers. *Madness! Pure madness!*

CHAPTER 6

Ethan sat up straight when the phone rang, having dozed off with his feet dangling over the side of the bed. He rubbed his eyes and glanced at the big red numbers on the bedside clock. Six p.m. The phone rang again.

Ethan reached for the phone. "Hello?"

"Ethan, you okay?" It was the familiar voice of Rob Jamison.

"Yeah...yeah. Just dozed off for a few minutes. What's up?" Ethan was rubbing his eyes again.

"You want to meet in the bar for a drink?"

A drink, or two or three, sounded pretty good to Ethan. "Sure. I'll meet you in the bar in five."

"You got it."

Ethan hung up the phone and shook the cobwebs out of his head. He threw some water on his face, combed his hair, and swished some mouthwash. After putting on a clean shirt, he walked out of the tiny room, heading for the elevator. As Ethan exited the elevator into the main lobby he heard laughter coming from the bar. *Rob's there already.*

"Hey, did you start without me?" Ethan said as he walked up to the bar.

"Damn right!" Rob answered, slapping Ethan on the back. "Just discussing the day's events with Hugo here. Hugo, this is my good friend Ethan Paxton!"

"Hi, Hugo. A pleasure," Ethan responded. "We haven't seen you in the bar the last two nights."

"The pleasure is mine," Hugo answered in his heavy Dutch accent. "I work on Tuesday and Wednesday nights only. Your friend has already ordered you a beer."

"Ah, thank you. Cheers, Rob!" Ethan clinked his beer glass with Rob's and they both downed half their glass in a couple of gulps.

"You look better than you did an hour ago," said Rob. "I was worried about you. Family okay?"

"Yeah, thanks. My kids are still in Mexico but they're headed for the border. They should make it across in a couple of hours."

"It has to be tough as a single dad," Rob said. "Sorry, Ethan, I know Connie's loss is still fresh."

Ethan forced a smile. "Don't worry about it. It's tough, but my housekeeper is a jewel, really keeps things running, you know?"

"That's great, Ethan. This terrorist crap has everyone scrambling back home. We might have a tough time getting home ourselves."

"Henrik called and said that they've shut down all air traffic in and out of the U.S."

"Damn!" Rob said, shaking his head. "What a nightmare."

"It looks like we'll be here for a while, old buddy."

"You heard from Pete?" Rob asked.

"Pete?" Ethan hit his forehead with his palm. "Hell, I forgot all about him! He was touring Amsterdam today with Henrik's secretary. I'll call Henrik—"

"No need, old pal."

Ethan looked up at the sound of the familiar voice. Pete Cruz was walking into the lounge dragging his suitcase, a big smile on his face.

"Pete! You sorry son-of-a-bitch!" yelled Rob, pouncing on Pete with his patented back slap.

"Forgot all about me, Ethan?" Pete had a mock look of hurt on his face.

Ethan shook his friend's hand. "Sorry, Pete. With everything going on . . . you know. It's good to see you."

"Don't worry about it. Good to see you gents, too," Pete said, a broad smile on his well-tanned, handsome face. "Wasn't sure what was going on for a while there. What a mess, huh?"

"What happened, why aren't you up in Amsterdam?" Ethan said.

"Marta called the airline and they said all flights into the U.S. were canceled until further notice. Rather than staying up near the airport by myself I decided to drive back down here with her and stay with you guys. We may be here awhile."

"So we've heard," said Ethan.

"The hotel where I was booked tonight jacked their prices up by double. Marta gave 'em some crap and they backed down and let me cancel. They'll make a killing over the next few days, so they don't need my money."

"She's one tough lady. Do you have a room here tonight?" asked Ethan.

"Marta called while we were on the road and booked a room." Pete looked at the beers on the bar. "I see you guys have started without me."

"Time for another!" Rob said, pounding the bar. "Hugo, three more and keep 'em coming!"

"We've got lots to talk about," Ethan said, downing the last of his beer.

"That we do. Let me down this beer and get checked in, then we'll see what trouble we can get into tonight." Pete threw back his Amstel in two gulps. "See you guys in a few." He walked back down the hallway to the reception area.

Ethan smiled as he watched his short, pudgy friend walk out of the bar. Pete worked for another transportation company that Ethan's company did business with. They had met nearly five years before when Pete made a sales call on Ethan at his office in California. They immediately hit it off and had been traveling the world together for the past few years. They worked hard and played hard, and always had a good time together. Pete had traveled to the Netherlands at Ethan's request, as did Rob. Ethan began to feel guilty about putting his two good friends in a tough situation, thousands of miles away from their families with little chance of getting home anytime soon.

"Hugo, can you turn that TV to an English news channel?" Ethan asked the bartender.

"Sure, no problem."

Hugo changed the channel from a Dutch station to CNN. The Americans were the only ones in the tiny bar so no one else was around to complain. For the next twenty minutes Ethan and Rob watched the events unfold on the tiny screen. They watched the twin towers falling once again, watched and listened to the United flight 93 story, then they got the official news they were dreading.

"The Secretary of Transportation has confirmed that all commercial and private air traffic in the U.S. has been grounded, effective immediately. The only air traffic allowed in the U.S. skies will be U.S. military aircraft," the CNN announcer said. "No timetable was given on when this order will be rescinded."

"Well, there it is," said Rob. "We're officially stuck here for days, maybe weeks."

Ethan nodded. "Well, I guess it could be worse. Just think about the people that were half way over the Atlantic or Pacific. They'll have to return to where they came from or divert to someplace else. If we're going to be stuck somewhere, I can think of much worse places than Den Bosch."

"Very true, buddy."

Ethan glanced at his long-time friend. Rob Jamison and he had traveled together many times before, but this was Rob's first international trip with Ethan. It was like traveling with a little kid because everything was new to Rob and he got excited over the smallest thing. Ethan was an experienced traveler and had been traveling internationally for nearly fifteen years. Rob had re-energized him on this trip, made him see things he had taken for granted. Ethan, Rob and Pete had arrived in the Netherlands two days before, on Sunday, and they'd been to a couple of restaurants and bars and had gotten to know several people around the city square. The employees of the hotel were getting used to seeing the three Americans in the bar or in the square.

"Is it just me, or are people looking at us differently?" Ethan said, noticing a few restaurant patrons staring at them.

"I noticed it, too", said Rob. "Don't know if it's out of curiosity, sympathy or something else."

"It is empathy," said Hugo, the bartender. "Everyone in Holland is sad for Americans today. You've been attacked in the most horrendous way and the Dutch people feel badly for you."

"Why empathy? It didn't happen to them," Rob asked.

"Terrorism is becoming very common around the world, unfortunately, and no one country is alone in this fight. We have many Muslims in the Netherlands and it could happen here just as it happened in the U.S. I believe the world will stand behind you on this."

"Even when we unleash our military might to find and destroy the bastards that did this?" Rob said.

"Yes, to a point. Like everything America does, sometimes you go too far. But you have everyone's support right now."

"Very well put, Hugo. You sound like an educated man," Ethan said.

"I am an industrial engineer, or I should say that is what I studied at University," he replied. "Bartending is something I do to pay the bills."

"Good for you, Hugo my man!" Rob exclaimed as he raised his glass.

Hugo smiled at Rob. "You know, if you go out to the bars tonight you may not be able to buy a beer."

"Why's that?" asked Ethan.

"Everyone will want to buy you one, so I'm afraid you may return to the hotel tonight a little drunk," he said, smiling.

"Outstanding! What are we waiting for?" Rob said, waving his arms. "Let's get this party started!"

Ethan looked at Rob and didn't comment. His enjoyment was tempered by the thought of the thousands of dead Americans, the families who had to deal with this tragedy, and, of course, his children who were still in Mexico. The border situation could change at a moment's notice and they could be stuck down there. He wouldn't be able to enjoy much of anything until he knew for sure that Charlie and Molly were safe. It was going to be a long night.

Pete walked back into the bar, rubbing his hands together. "Let's hit it, gentlemen!"

The three Americans said goodbye to Hugo, leaving him a large tip, and walked out the front door which opened onto the city square, an old-fashioned cobblestone area that had alleys and side streets jutting out in every direction. They had learned that the city was one of the oldest in the Netherlands. The name 's-Hertogenbosch meant "The Duke's forest", named after Henry I, Duke of Brabant, who lived around 1185. The Dutch called the city Den Bosch, similar to Den Haag, or The Hague in English. The square was bustling with activity.

"Where to, gents?" asked Pete. "I'm thirsty and hungry."

"How about a big, juicy steak at that restaurant near the church?" Rob said.

"De Kroner," said Ethan. "Just down the alley from St. John's Cathedral."

"Let's go!" said Pete. "A juicy steak and red wine sounds great."

The three Americans walked several blocks until they were in front of the huge St. John's Cathedral, one of the oldest in Europe. They all glanced up at the massive spires that reached into the sky and wondered at the ornate stonework on the old cathedral.

"This is a pretty impressive place," Ethan commented, still looking up at the church.

"That it is," answered Pete. "Not too many like this in the U.S."

Several alleys and streets jutted off from the cathedral square like spokes in a bicycle wheel.

"Which way?" asked Rob.

"This way," said Ethan, pointing to one of the middle alleyways. They walked two blocks down the narrow alleyway, passing several bars and restaurants. Ethan stopped in front of a brick building with a quaint sign saying "De Kroner" hanging over the door.

"Good job, Ethan. I'd be wandering around all night looking for this place," said Rob. "Too many little streets and alleys in this town."

"Good evening, gentlemen!" said the gray-haired maître d with an air of familiarity.

They had eaten here two nights before, their first night in Den Bosch. He led them to a center table. The décor was dark wood everywhere, with candles on every table. The restaurant was crowded and noisy, but a hush fell over it when they walked in, several of the customers recognizing them from before.

Ethan looked around the small restaurant and smiled nervously. All eyes seemed to be on him and his two friends. Almost everyone smiled back, somehow knowing they were Americans.

"Looks like we're the top attraction tonight," he said to his friends.

"Gentlemen, I will take the liberty of opening this bottle of red wine, on the house," the maître-d' smiled. "The same one you had the other night. Shall I pour?"

"Absolutely!" Rob exclaimed. "What's the occasion?"

"May I say, we all are so very sorry for the terrible tragedy befallen your country today. We know how sad and anxious you must feel. Please relax and enjoy yourselves." He bowed graciously and left them to look over the menus.

"Wow! That was classy," said Pete as they sat down.

"Hell yeah! And free wine!" answered Rob, a broad smile on his face.

"I love the Dutch. They're outspoken, but honest and friendly," said Pete. "Some of the best people I've met anywhere in the world."

"And the women are all smokin' hot!" exclaimed Rob. "Cheers!"

"Cheers," said Ethan as he raised his wine glass to clink with Rob and Pete. "To one hell of a day."

"One hell of a day," said Pete in a somber tone.

"Amen," Rob said.

The three Americans ordered their steaks then sat back and drank their wine and began to discuss the day's events. Ethan looked at his two friends and saw the emotional strain in their faces. In spite of the jovial atmosphere, he knew they were struggling, just as he was.

"How are your families coping with everything?" he asked.

"My wife is freaked out," Rob said. "She thinks California is next. Not much I could say to make her believe everything was okay, 'cause I don't know if it is."

"Does she know you can't make it home right away?" Ethan asked.

"No, because I didn't know it when I talked to her. I probably have a message on my phone in the hotel. I told her I'd call her back later tonight."

"My family seems to be holding up okay," said Pete. "My son is a little freaked out, but he's only twelve, so it's all unreal to him. I told my wife that all the flights into the U.S. were canceled so at least she knows."

"Well, my situation is a little tense, as you guys know," said Ethan. "My kids are still in Mexico on their mission trip and are supposed to be crossing the border in a couple of hours. I worry about them making it across okay. The borders must be tighter than hell right now."

"No kidding," said Rob. "At least they're part of a big group crossing at the same time, right?"

"Yeah, and they supposedly have security people with them so they should be okay. I'll just feel better when I get that call from my son tonight."

The steaks came and the three Americans enjoyed their meal for the next hour, talking about the day's events and what lay ahead of them. After the last of the dishes had been collected they ordered after-dinner drinks. The cognac burned on the way down but tasted good to Ethan.

"Wasn't that something about the plane that went down in Pennsylvania," Pete said. "Talk about heroes! They said on CNN that the terrorists had it headed towards Washington D.C. Can you imagine if it hit the White House or the Capitol building?"

"That was unbelievable," Rob said. "What guts it had to take for those passengers to rush the friggin' terrorists, knowing they would all die!"

"The image of those people jumping out of the towers is what I can't get out of my head," Ethan said. "I heard CNN say that one person on the ground died when one of the jumpers fell on him."

The three Americans were silent with their own thoughts for several minutes. When Ethan looked up, he saw an older gentleman walking toward their table. He was well-dressed in a suit and tie, gray hair on top of a weathered but handsome face. An attractive well-dressed woman followed behind him. They both must have been in their late seventies or early eighties.

"Excuse me," the man said. "I'm sorry to bother you, but my wife and I wanted to give you our sincere condolences. My name is Henk and this is my wife Gaby. We are truly sorry for what your country is enduring right now."

"Thank you," Ethan said. "We appreciate it very much. I'm Ethan, and this is Pete and Rob," he said, pointing to his two friends.

"Please, sit down," said Pete as he grabbed another chair from the next table. Rob grabbed one also and offered it to the woman.

"Well, thank you very much. We don't want to bother you as we know you must have much to discuss. Can I buy you another bottle of wine?"

"I think we've probably had en—" Ethan started to say. He stopped talking when the smiling maître arrived with a bottle of port. He opened the wine as another waiter brought five glasses.

"This is from Mister De Groot," the maître-d' said, nodding to the older gentleman. "He is a very famous man in this area."

"Really?" asked Rob, leaning forward with interest.

"I think I can explain that a little better than my husband," said Gaby in a dignified, refined voice, her English impeccable. "He is very shy and humble. My husband was the mayor of Den Bosch for many years and retired a few years ago. But his local fame is due more to his exploits in World War II. I know he doesn't look old enough," she said with a chuckle, "but Henk was a resistance fighter in the war. He has many stories he can regale you with if you ever have the time."

The three Americans nodded their heads and looked at the man with renewed respect.

"Oh, I don't think these boys want to hear an old man's ramblings about a war over fifty years ago," Henk said, smiling. "We just wanted to pay our respects to you gentlemen. The Americans were very kind and friendly to us after the war and we have always had a special place in our hearts for the U.S."

Henk then raised his glass of port. "I'd like to propose a toast, if it's all right."

The Americans raised their glasses in unison.

"To the United States of America, may she endure through this struggle and overcome as she always has."

Ethan noticed that many of the other diners were raising their glasses at the same time.

"Thank you so much," Pete said.

"Very kind words. Thank you," said Rob softly.

Ethan glanced at his friend, who was usually loud and demonstrative. He noticed a tear streaming down Rob's cheek. Ethan was beginning to choke up himself, so knew he had to respond quickly.

"Our country has changed today. We're at war against an unseen enemy. In World War Two you at least had an enemy you could see and identify. I'm afraid the world as we knew it has changed for the worse. We are so proud of our country, and are glad we have friends like you in the world." Ethan felt embarrassed and felt his face grow red.

"Thank you, young man. You put that very well." Mister De Groot looked intently at Ethan, embarrassing him even more. "I believe that America will do the right thing and that my country and most other free nations will stand behind you."

Ethan looked up at the old man with tear-filled eyes. He nodded, unable to respond.

"Gentlemen, I am so sorry to interrupt your dinner. Please enjoy yourselves in our fine city. I pray that your families will be safe. God Bless America," Henk said as he stood up. "Come, sweetheart. Time for us old folks to get home."

Henk took Gaby by the arm and lead her out of the restaurant, looking back at the Americans and waving as he walked out the door. He locked on Ethan's eyes and smiled. Then they were gone.

After several minutes of silence, Ethan cleared his throat. "Very kind people," he said.

"Very," said Pete.

"Did he call us 'boys'?" Rob said. "It's time to take this party elsewhere!"

They all broke out in laughter.

Ethan knew that his two friends would be drinking the rest of the night. But his mind was on Charlie and Molly, far away in Mexico. The tightness in his gut wouldn't go away until he knew they were safely across the border.

CHAPTER 7

Thirty cars, vans and pickups were lined up all the way out to the main road, with people standing next to their car peering back at the end of the convoy. There were some shouts, some honking, everyone connected with Santa Elena Academy impatient to get on the road to the border crossing.

Squawk! "Julie, are you ready yet?" *Squawk!*

Molly Paxton heard Mister Sizemore's perplexed voice in the walkie-talkie and watched as Missus Caldwell answered.

"Hello, George," the teacher said into the little box. "We're waiting for one last student. She's in the bathroom, I think."

Squawk! "Well, hurry her up. We have a lot of impatient people waiting for you." *Squawk!*

"Okay. It shouldn't be more than a minute or two." Missus Caldwell sighed as she threw the walkie-talkie into the van, continuing to look around the camp. "Cindy, where are you?" she yelled.

She looked at Molly. "Molly, run down to the latrine to see if she's in there."

Molly shook her head in disgust. "Okay."

She ran down to the port-o-potties set up at the bottom of the hill. All the doors were unlocked except one. She knocked on the door. "Cindy, are you in there?"

"Yes! Hold on! Geez!" Cindy said from behind the plastic door.

"Hurry up, you freak! Everyone is ready to leave and we're waiting on you!" Molly yelled. She had been pushing Cindy all morning and afternoon to get ready and now she was holding up the entire caravan.

The door opened and Cindy walked out, frowning at Molly. "Can you, like, get off my case already?"

"When we cross the border and are in the U.S., then I'll, like, get off your case, but until then get your ass up the hill! Aaaaaaaaaaaah!"

"Whatever, Moll!" Cindy said with a wave of her hand as she trudged up the hill to the waiting caravan.

"Finally!" Missus Caldwell said. "Cindy and Molly, get in the car so we can get on the road."

Picking up the walkie-talkie, she said, "Mister Sizemore, we're all ready." *Squawk!* "Okay, finally. Thanks for holding all of us up, Julie." *Squawk!*

"Asshole," Molly heard Missus Caldwell say. She knew her teacher was not a big fan of the principal.

Molly closed her door and watched the line of cars and vans as they slowly began to move. Mister Sizemore, in the lead car, had given walkie-talkies to several people throughout the caravan in order to communicate during the drive to the border crossing at Otay Mesa. Even though it was only twenty miles, it was on a hilly, isolated road and he didn't want to take the chance of anyone getting lost or left behind. He had instructed all of the adult drivers to keep in visual contact with the car in front of them.

"Okay, we'll keep our eyes on the brown van in front of us, girls," Missus Caldwell said. "Next stop, the United States!"

Molly looked around the deserted, litter-strewn camp as their white Toyota van finally began to move. It was always sad to leave, but this time it was worse. They didn't even have time to pick up the trash and litter. Molly felt a twinge of guilt, but knew that their safety was the most important thing. There were several local children standing close by, waving to the departing Americans. Molly rolled down her window and waved to them.

"*¡Adios* Carolina!" she yelled to a little girl with almond-shaped eyes she had befriended. "*¡Adios* Carlos!" she yelled to another little boy.

Tears welled up in her eyes as she looked at their sad faces. She always got attached to the children and it never got any easier to leave. As she looked behind her to wave goodbye she noticed two black SUV's on top of the adjoining hill. Two men were standing next to the trucks, watching them. She recognized one of them as a teenage boy named Rafael that had been in and out of the camp over the past few days. Something about him made her nervous. *Something's not right.* Molly thought about telling Missus Caldwell but decided to forget about it. They were going home anyway.

As they pulled out onto the main road, Molly turned her thoughts to her brother, who was in one of the lead cars. He had come over to talk to her right before the caravan departed. He'd told her to keep her cell phone on and if anything happened between the camp and the border, to call him on his cell. She'd been worried ever since their conversation about the terrorists earlier that morning. He had even told her that he'd ride in her car if she wanted him to. She'd tried to be brave and told him it wasn't necessary. All she needed was to have Cindy Lambert tell everyone that she needed her big brother around. Now she wished she would have asked him to ride with them. Her stomach grew tighter after seeing the two SUV's on the hill.

"Well, girls, we should be at the border in about thirty or forty minutes. Everyone okay?" asked Missus Caldwell.

"I'm sooo glad we're leaving!" moaned Cindy. "I need to take a long shower, like, so bad!"

"You okay, Jenny?" Missus Caldwell asked the pudgy girl sitting next to her in the front passenger seat.

Jenny was very shy and quiet, never saying much of anything. She nodded yes.

"How about you Molly?" Missus Caldwell said, looking in the rear-view mirror.

Molly again thought about mentioning the two SUV's. "Missus Caldwell, why are we the last car in the caravan?" Molly said, leaning forward.

Missus Caldwell was a plump but attractive woman in her mid-thirties and one of the most popular teachers at Santa Elena Academy. She was more a friend than a teacher to the teenage girls riding in her white Toyota van.

"Well, ask Cindy. She just couldn't seem to get her act together back at camp," Missus Caldwell answered, nodding her head at Cindy, who was sitting next to Molly in the backseat. "Is it bothering you that we're bringing up the rear?"

"No, I guess not," said Molly. *Yes, I'm scared!* "Will the other cars stop if we have to stop or if there's a problem?"

"Well, that shouldn't be a problem because the border isn't that far away. There's hardly any traffic so we'll stay close to the brown van up ahead. I have the walkie-talkie if we need to talk to Mister Sizemore. Don't worry so much, Molly."

Molly felt embarrassed and sat back in her seat. She took another glance through the back window and saw nothing. *It's foolish to worry, there's nothing behind us.* She began to relax and started thinking of getting back to the U.S. and taking a hot shower.

CHAPTER 8

Natalia was in the passenger seat of the black SUV, watching the first SUV ahead of them, where Angel was riding in the front passenger seat. They had waited until the last of the American caravan left the camp site in Tecate and now were on the lonely, winding road leading to the Otay Mesa border crossing. It had been thirty minutes since they left the hill above the campsite and she knew they were getting close to the last car in the convoy. She had seen three teenage girls, two blondes and a brunette, climb into the white van that was bringing up the rear of the convoy. She closed her eyes and silently prayed that something would go wrong with Angel's plan.

"What are you doing?" the man driving the SUV said as he stared at her. It was Cesar, the man with the golden teeth.

"Nothing. Mind your own business," she said, glaring at him.

Cesar laughed. "You stupid *puta*! You feel sorry for them, don't you?"

Natalia continued to glare at the fat man, the disgust flowing out of her. She said nothing.

"I saw a pretty dark-haired girl in the white van. I think Angel will want her first," Cesar said, chuckling loudly. "As for me, I want the skinny blonde girl. Yumm."

"You pig," Natalia said through clenched teeth. "You stay away from them or I will cut your fat, hairy balls off!"

Cesar laughed heartily, his big belly bouncing against the steering wheel.

"Hey, *pinche perra*. You talk to Angel that way?" He laughed again, even louder.

Natalia turned and gazed out the side window at the desert scrub brush. Her stomach was boiling in a mass of acid and bile, threatening to come up through her throat at any time. *How can I stop this? I have to do something!*

Cesar was still laughing when they reached the crest of a hill. Natalia peered down the road ahead of them and saw the white van about a mile away. She choked as the bile finally reached her throat.

CHAPTER 9

"Missus Caldwell, I have to go to the bathroom." Cindy was bouncing up and down in the backseat like a ping pong ball, in obvious distress. "Like, really bad!"

"Oh, Cindy, we're almost at the border. I thought you went at camp? Can't you hold it until we get across?" asked Missus Caldwell.

"No, I'm sorry, I can't wait! I had too much water before we left."

"You can hold it, Cindy. No way we're stopping out here!" said Molly. She turned around and looked through the back window. There was nothing but empty road behind them. *But still . . . .*

Missus Caldwell looked into the rearview mirror and saw how much pain Cindy was in and decided to pull over to the side of the road. It was a deserted desert road with plenty of scrub brush she could hide behind.

"Okay, Cindy, but hurry. Molly, go with her will you? I'll let Mister Sizemore know on the walkie-talkie that we are stopping for a couple of minutes."

"Okay," Molly sighed, jumping out of the car and running after Cindy. Cindy was already squatting behind a big brown bush, the relief on her face forcing a laugh from Molly. "You should see your face! It's hilarious!" Molly said to her friend.

"Hurry up!" Missus Caldwell shouted from the car.

"Yeah, hurry up you dork!" Molly echoed.

"Okay, I'm done!" Cindy shouted back, shooting Molly a dirty look.

The two girls ran back to the car and got in.

"Sorry, Missus Caldwell, but I was, like, bursting!" Cindy exclaimed.

"No harm done, Cindy. We'll catch up with the others once we get to the border crossing." Missus Caldwell slowly pulled out onto the road and began to accelerate.

Molly glanced back and froze, seeing the two black trucks behind them and coming up fast. She turned to look at Missus Caldwell, then back at the black trucks, getting bigger and bigger.

"Missus Caldwell, can't you go any faster?" Molly said, pleading. "Did you tell anyone on the walkie-talkie that we stopped?"

"I'm going to contact Mister Sizemore right now," Missus Caldwell said as she looked in the rear-view mirror and saw the two black trucks approaching.

"Mister Sizemore, come in please," she said, the urgency in her voice sending shivers down Molly's spine.

Squawk! "Yes, Julie." *Squawk!*

Missus Caldwell pressed the button on the walkie-talkie. "George, we stopped for a couple of minutes for a bathroom break, but we're back on the road."

Squawk! "Okay, Julie. Please catch up as soon as you can. We're almost to the border." *Squawk!*

"Where did they come from?" Missus Caldwell said loudly as the black trucks caught up with them.

Molly turned and all she could see out the rear window was black, and a shiny chrome bumper. They were so close she couldn't even see the driver. Her stomach tightened into a knot as she let out a silent scream.

Missus Caldwell pushed the walkie-talkie button as she stared into the rearview mirror. "George, there are two black trucks right behind us."

Missus Caldwell opened her side window and began waving the two SUV's around. "They don't have to drive so close," she muttered. "Go around!" she shouted out the window.

Squawk! "What's that about two trucks, Julie?" *Squawk!*

The first SUV began to pass the white van on the left. Molly looked up at the man in the front passenger seat, who was looking directly at her, smiling. He kept his gaze on Molly until they had passed the van. The second SUV was right behind and Molly saw a woman in the front passenger seat, staring straight ahead. The two trucks continued on up the road. Molly watched them disappear over a hill.

"That was bizarre," said Missus Caldwell. "You girls okay?"

"Yeah, but, like, why did they get so close?" said Cindy.

"George, never mind, they passed us," Missus Caldwell said into the walkie-talkie. "We'll be caught up in a few minutes. See you at the border."

Molly thought about telling the teacher about seeing the trucks when they left the build site, but the walkie-talkie crackled before she could get it out.

Squawk! "Okay, Julie. See you at the border." *Squawk!*

As their van came to the crest of the next hill, Molly saw the two black SUV's parked on the side of the road at the bottom of the hill.

"Missus Caldwell!" Molly screamed, pointing ahead.

"I see them."

Missus Caldwell gripped the steering wheel so tight that Molly could see her knuckles turn white. The teacher pushed down on the accelerator as far as it would go, trying to pass the black trucks as fast as possible. Molly saw her glance down at the walkie-talkie but she kept her hands on the steering wheel. Molly leaned forward and grabbed for the walkie-talkie but it fell to the floor near Jenny. She was jolted back in her seat when one of the SUV's began to pull out onto the road. The SUV was going very slowly, causing Missus Caldwell to begin slowing down. There weren't any cars coming in the opposite direction on the paved road so she started to pull into the oncoming lane to pass.

Suddenly the second SUV pulled out into the road almost on top of the white van, causing it to swerve to the left onto the shoulder of the road. The first SUV then moved over in front of the van. The van was now surrounded in front and on the right by the two SUV's. The van made a sharp turn onto a dirt road jutting off to the left, but the SUV's followed. Missus Caldwell continued driving down the dirt road until one of the SUV's pulled in front of her and slowed to a stop. The white van was now trapped between the two black SUVs, exactly what they had wanted her to do.

Molly looked back up the main road and saw the brown van disappear around the bend. She pulled her cell phone from her purse and immediately speed-dialed her brother's number.

"Please pick up, Charlie," she said, whimpering. She glanced at Cindy who was sitting in frozen silence, her eyes wide and her mouth open.

"Pick up, Charlie!"

Molly watched Missus Caldwell grab for the walkie-talkie on the floor and put it to her ear, but it was ripped out of her hand by a man in a black hood. When the teacher tried to resist, the man slammed his fist into her face, spraying blood onto Jenny and the passenger-side window. Molly saw Missus Caldwell go limp and watched in horror as they dragged her teacher out of the van and threw her roughly into the first SUV.

"Charlie, pick up! Pick—"

Molly stopped in mid-sentence when the car door opened next to her and another black-hooded man began pulling her from the car. As she was dragged out she dropped the cell phone on the floor of the car, kicking it under the driver's seat. Molly and the other girls screamed and fought as they were roughly thrown into the back of one of the SUV's. Molly saw the woman whom she had seen on the road staring back at her from the front seat. Strangely, tears were streaming down the woman's face.

"Charlie!" Molly screamed as the rear door was closed. Duct tape was slapped onto her mouth and a black hood thrown over her head as she felt the SUV speed down the dirt road. *Charlie! Charlie.*

CHAPTER 10

Charlie Paxton was in the fourth car as the Santa Elena caravan approached the Otay Mesa border crossing. The lines were long, as they expected, but they seemed to be moving.

"Looks like every American in Baja is trying to get back across the border," Charlie said to no one in particular. He was in a large van with six other people, mostly young adults like himself that had volunteered their time and services for the mission. Charlie was in the front passenger seat and had a birds-eye view of the border crossing mess ahead of them.

"This will take hours!" complained someone in the back of the van.

"Damn, I wish we had a walkie-talkie," said Charlie.

He glanced back at the convoy of cars and vans and wished he would have insisted on riding in Molly's van. He grabbed his cell phone to call her when he noticed "voicemail" on the readout screen. *Oh crap!* They had been talking so loud inside the van he missed a call. Fear began to grip his throat as he pulled up his voicemail. It was from Molly. He froze in terror as he listened to the voicemail from his sister, dropping the phone.

"Stop the car!"

"What the hell?" asked the driver, a parent of one of the boys in the van.

"Stop the car! I have to talk to Mister Sizemore!" Charlie screamed as he opened the car door.

He began running to the front of the convoy. Mister Sizemore's car was four ahead of Charlie's van, going very slowly due to the traffic approaching the border. When he spotted the blue van with the Santa Elena Academy sign on the door, he ran up to the passenger side and pounded on the window, startling the middle-aged man in the van.

"Mister Sizemore! Stop!" yelled Charlie, out of breath.

George Sizemore rolled down his window, irritation written all over his face. "Charlie, what's going on? Quit yelling, son," he said, glancing around.

"Mister Sizemore," Charlie said, trying to catch his breath, "I just got a call from my sister in the rear of the convoy. All I heard was shouting and screaming! Something's wrong! Can you call them on the walkie-talkie?"

"Okay. Okay. Hold on," the principal said nervously. He grabbed the walkie-talkie and pushed the call button.

"Missus Caldwell, are you there?" *Silence.* "Julie Caldwell, are you there? Answer please." *Silence.*

"Oh shit. Something's happened!" yelled Charlie.

"Hold on, Charlie. Maybe they couldn't hear us," said Mister Sizemore, trying to calm Charlie down. "Let's not jump to conclusions, son."

"No, it was screaming! She screamed my name and then I heard a car door slam shut! I heard something like someone getting hit and another car door shut!"

"It was voicemail?" Mister Sizemore asked.

"Yes!"

"Let me listen to it, son."

"I . . . I dropped my phone in the van. I'll go get it!"

Charlie sprinted back to his van, retrieved his cell phone and ran back to Mister Sizemore's van. By this time other cars were honking at them as they were stopped in the middle of the road. Charlie doubled over, trying to catch his breath again.

"Here. Listen!" Charlie pleaded with Mister Sizemore, handing the cell phone to him.

Sizemore listened to the voicemail and his face became ashen. He listened to Molly's message one more time to make sure he heard everything, and then handed the phone back to Charlie.

"Keep that phone on you, Charlie, and don't make any calls. Molly may call back so you need to keep it on and open."

"What are we going to do?" asked Charlie, his voice cracking.

"Missus Caldwell called me on the walkie-talkie about fifteen minutes ago, so they couldn't have been more than a couple of miles behind us." Mister Sizemore checked his clipboard quickly. "The closest walkie-talkie to Missus Caldwell's car is the Mason's. Hold on." He grabbed the walkie-talkie.

"Bob Mason, come in!"

Squawk! "Bob here. What's up, George?" *Squawk!*

"Bob, we have an emergency. Julie Caldwell is not answering her walkie-talkie and . . . ." He hesitated and looked at Charlie. "And Charlie Paxton got a very disturbing voicemail from his sister, Molly. She's in Julie's car. Can you send someone back there to see if they are anywhere close?"

Squawk! "I can see the Johnson's in their brown van about eight to ten cars behind me. Julie was right behind them, but I don't see her white van." *Squawk!*

"Have one of the older kids in your car run back to double check, please!" said Mister Sizemore.

Squawk! "Okay, right away!" *Squawk!*

"Charlie, when did Molly call you?"

Charlie pushed some buttons on his cell phone. "About fifteen minutes ago!"

Mister Sizemore sat silent, staring straight ahead.

"Mister Sizemore, we have to go back!" Charlie said, the panic in his voice getting worse.

Squawk! "George, come in!" *Squawk!*

"George here," Mister Sizemore said into the walkie-talkie.

Squawk! "Julie's van is not behind us anywhere. I can't see it in any of the lanes around us either." *Squawk!*

George Sizemore glanced at Charlie. "Thanks Bob."

"Okay, Charlie. Let's get in your van and drive back down the road."

Mister Sizemore turned to the driver of the van and said, "Ted, can you lead the convoy up to the border? All the documents are on my clipboard. I'm going with Charlie to see if we can find Julie's van. I'll leave the walkie-talkie with you and will grab the Mason's when we drive by them. Let's go, Charlie."

Mister Sizemore and Charlie ran back to Charlie's van. Mister Sizemore climbed into the front passenger seat and Charlie climbed into the second row. Mister Sizemore looked at the driver and said, "We need to turn around, Russell."

The driver of the van looked at the principal. "I can't turn around. We're surrounded on all sides by other cars."

"Bloody hell!" Mister Sizemore exclaimed.

"We can run back to the Mason's van! They're towards the end of the line!" said Charlie.

"Okay, let's go. Thanks, Russell."

Mister Sizemore and Charlie got out of the van and began running back down the line of cars until they came to the Mason's red van.

Sizemore, an older man in his late fifties, was out of breath. "Bob, we need to turn your van around and go look for Missus Caldwell's van." he said puffing.

"We don't have much room to turn, George," Bob Mason said, looking around.

"Please, just do it!" Sizemore's voice rose as he climbed into the front seat. Charlie squeezed into the backseat next to a teenage girl.

Bob Mason had just enough room next to him to turn the van around but he had to drive over a median to get in the lane heading back to the road. The traffic was very light coming from the U.S. so they had a clear shot to the main road, Highway 2D. As they passed the cars in line for the U.S. border they checked for any white vans. They didn't see one so got back on the main road, headed towards Tecate.

"What's going on, George?" asked Bob Mason.

"Hold on. Let me use your walkie-talkie to see if Missus Caldwell answers."

Sizemore held the walkie-talkie to his ear. "Missus Caldwell, come in!" Nothing. "Julie, come in please!" *Silence.*

Sizemore turned to Bob Mason. "Charlie got a voicemail from his sister which was very disturbing. Lots of screaming and shouting, and doors slamming." Sizemore glanced at Charlie. "I'm fearing the worst."

"Holy God!" said Bob Mason. "Where do we look?"

"They had to be only a couple of miles back, so we need to be looking on both sides of the road now. Look for their white van."

"We could have missed them and they might be sitting in the border crossing line right now," Bob Mason said.

"It's possible. Let's hope so," said Sizemore.

Charlie Paxton continued looking out the window, hoping to see a white Toyota van, the sounds on the voicemail screaming in his head. The last thing he heard on the voicemail was the frantic sound of his sister screaming "Charlie!" Fear engulfed him as he thought of the ugly possibilities.

"Mister Sizemore, did Missus Caldwell say anything when she called you on the walkie-talkie?" Charlie asked.

"Just that they had to stop to let one of the girls go, uh, to the bathroom," he said, not looking at Charlie.

"Why didn't we stop the caravan?" Charlie said, his voice rising.

"She told me not to, that they would only be a minute or two." Sizemore's voice belied his nervousness.

"Did she say anything else, anything about other cars being around?"

Sizemore glanced quickly at Charlie then back to the road ahead. "No, she said nothing."

Charlie stared out the window, frantically looking for the white van. *Molly! Molly.*

CHAPTER 11

Natalia Blanco watched the white van enter the old Tijuana warehouse first, followed by the other black SUV, then hers. A hooded man rolled the huge metal door shut as soon as her SUV was clear. She sat in the front passenger seat, still stunned by what had just happened.

"Hey, let's go!" Angel Rojas yelled at her, opening her door. "*¡Vamanos!*"

Angel had been in the first SUV, the one with the teacher. Natalia had been in the second one, with the three teenage girls. She heard them whimpering in the back. They had been hog-tied at their ankles and wrists, a piece of duct tape had been put over their mouths, and black hoods had been thrown over their heads. The duct tape had stopped the screaming and by the time the forty-five minute drive from Otay Mesa was over, they were lying still, all three whimpering softly.

Angel and his men were pulling the three girls out of the van, each one thrown over the shoulder of one of the men, carried like a sack of potatoes. They were taken to a dark room at the back of the warehouse where four filthy mattresses were laid out on the floor. The girls were dumped onto a mattress, each crying softly and moaning in pain.

"Angel, tell them to not be so rough," said Natalia, realizing that this might bring Angel's wrath down upon her.

Instead he surprised Natalia. "Hey, Cesar! Don't play so rough! Take it easy!" He smiled at Natalia and kissed her on the hand. "Whatever you say, *mi amor*. Now they are all yours. Take good care of them. If they cause any trouble, I will let my *amigos* handle it, and you don't want that, eh?"

Natalia glared at him, nodding. She walked into the dark room and ordered the men out. They looked at Angel, waiting for his orders, ignoring Natalia.

"*¡Vamanos!*" she yelled. "Get out!"

She saw Angel nod to his men, who took his cue to leave the dark, smelly room. Natalia closed the door behind them, seething at their arrogance.

She knelt down close to the girls and spoke softly in English. "No one is going to hurt you. I need you to lie still while I untie your feet. If you are good, I will be good to you. Do you understand?"

Two of the three girls nodded their heads. The dark-haired girl did not. Natalia bent down close to her ear.

"*¿Comprende?*"

The girl finally nodded her head.

"*Bueno,*" said Natalia.

Natalia began untying the ankles of the two blond girls, rubbing them after taking the twine off. She purred soothingly, like a mother to her children. The two blond girls continued to whimper. The dark-haired girl didn't make a sound when Natalia untied her ankles, but when she tried to massage them, the girl pulled away. *This one will be a problem.*

She then took out three needles from a black bag that she had carried into the room. She injected the first needle into a small vial and drew out a clear liquid. She took the needle and went up to the first blond girl, the heavier one.

"I am going to give you something to help you sleep. Do not struggle or you may cause harm to yourself." She said this matter-of-factly, with little emotion.

She rubbed alcohol on the girl's shoulder then jabbed her with the needle, injecting the drug. "Lie back and rest," she said.

She did the same thing to the other blond girl, the thin, freckled one, and watched both of them grow limp and silent. She took the hoods off and then gently removed the duct tape from their mouths. Natalia noticed that the thin one was very pretty, with long blond hair. She knew that Angel would like this one. The other one was chubby and homely. She closed her eyes as she thought about the fate of these two girls.

Natalia then glanced at the dark-haired girl and walked over to her. "Please don't move. I am going to give you something to help you sleep. It won't hurt you."

She began to rub the girl's arm with alcohol. The girl pulled away. Natalia grabbed her arm and jerked it back. She held it firmly as she injected the drug into the girl's arm. Unlike the other two, she rubbed the spot where the needle had been.

"Go to sleep, *mija,*" she said gently, not knowing why she used the term of endearment with this one.

Natalia watched the dark-haired girl grow limp and quiet. She took the hood off of her head and very gently took the duct-tape off of her mouth. She stared at the girl for a long time, noticing her beauty immediately. She had olive skin, so unlike the other two. Her hair was jet black and long, like many of the young girls in Tijuana. She gazed at the girl for several minutes, tears welling in her eyes. She began to brush her hair softly, like a mother would her daughter. *This one is special. Very special.*

Natalia grabbed three thin wool blankets and covered the girls. She kept their wrists tied, but loosened the knots. They would be out for eight or nine hours and then she would clean them up and give them food. They were hers now, to watch over and to protect against the animals outside. She heard the men laughing just outside the door, the grotesque laugh of men about to make their conquest. She heard a woman moan and knew it was the plump teacher. Natalia didn't want to know what they were planning to do with her. All she knew was that she would protect these three girls, especially the dark-haired one, like a mother lion protects her cubs. The hyenas outside would not sink their teeth into them. Natalia began humming softly, brushing the hair of the dark-haired girl.

CHAPTER 12

Ethan woke with a start when the phone rang, prying his weary eyes apart. He tried to clear his mind as he looked at the clock on the bedside table. Somehow during the night he had taken his clothes off and had slipped under the covers. The room was completely dark, with the bright red numbers on his bedside clock showing 4:02. The red button on his phone was the only other light in the room. He reached for the phone, clearing his throat of god knows what. In the darkness he hit the phone and knocked the receiver off. Cursing under his breath, he picked it up.

"Hello?" he said, still lying in bed.

"Dad?" a familiar voice said on the other end. "Dad, is that you?"

Ethan's eyes opened wide and he sat straight up in bed. "Charlie?"

"Yeah . . ." There was several seconds of silence. "You sound weird," his son said.

Ethan cleared his throat again. "Sorry son, I had a late night last night. It's four in the morning here, so I'm a little groggy."

"Oh, sorry Dad. I didn't know what time it was over there," Charlie said hoarsely.

"Did you make it across the border?" Ethan said, swinging his legs onto the floor, his head pounding. "Did you and Molly make it across the border okay?"

There was silence.

"Charlie?" Ethan said.

"Dad . . ." Charlie said, stopping in mid-sentence. "Molly is missing," he finally said, his voice cracking.

Ethan sat stunned. He covered his right ear so he could hear better. "Missing? What do you mean missing?"

"Dad," Charlie said, his voice cracking again. "I think she's been kidnapped!"

Ethan stood up next to the bed, eyes wide. He quickly turned on the lamp next to the bed.

"Dad, did you hear me?"

"Hold on son," Ethan said, clearing his throat.

"Dad? It was on the way back from Tecate, just before we got to the border."

"Why do you think she was kidnapped?"

"We've been searching for the car for two hours, plus there's her voicemail."

Ethan couldn't speak.

"She called me on my cell phone while it was happening. I've listened to it a hundred times," he choked.

Ethan stood in shocked silence. "What . . . what did she say?"

"I'll play it for you, hold on."

The shouts and screams came out loud and clear, although he couldn't make out what was being said. Ethan heard screams from young girls and shouts from grown men in what sounded like Spanish. But it was the last scream that hit Ethan like a sledgehammer. He recognized his daughter's voice and could hear her terror as she screamed "Charlie!" After that he heard several car doors slam shut and engines revving and then sounds of cars driving on a rough road. Then silence.

"Charlie." Ethan cleared his throat. "Play it again."

Charlie played the voicemail again for his father. Ethan choked back a scream by putting his fist to his mouth. *Get it together.* Several seconds passed before he could put the receiver back up to his ear.

"Charlie, tell me everything that happened."

"Okay, Dad. I'll try."

Charlie proceeded to tell his father the entire story from the point when he first heard Molly's voicemail up until he and Mister Sizemore left the San Diego police station just a little less than an hour before. He told him about the drive back to the camp site, about talking to some locals around the camp sight to see if they knew anything or had seen anything. He told him about Mister Sizemore organizing a search party out of the remaining cars and vans that had not yet crossed the border and searching the entire area between the camp site and the Otay Mesa border and about telling the U.S. border guards and how they dismissed it, claiming that a national emergency took priority and that we would have to report it to the San Diego police. About calling the San Diego police as soon as they crossed over into the U.S. and going in and giving them a statement.

"Dad, the police are not going to do anything. They claim that the terrorist attacks have caused chaos and that they have all available officers working on that. They told us that Molly and the others had to be missing for twenty four hours before they would consider them missing."

Ethan rubbed his tired eyes vigorously. "How many were with Molly?"

"Two other girls and a teacher, Missus Caldwell. Four total."

"Has anyone heard from the . . . from the . . . ?"

"Kidnappers? Not that I know of," said Charlie. "I just got to the motel where everyone is staying and no one has heard anything."

"What about the parents of the other girls? Has anyone talked to them?"

"Mister Sizemore called them. None of them are down here, they're all back home. He said that they haven't heard anything either."

Ethan began pacing back and forth in the small hotel room, his head swimming. "How are you doing, son? Are you holding up okay?"

"Yeah, but it's been tough, Dad. I keep hearing Molly scream my name and I wasn't there to help her!" Charlie began crying into the phone. "I should've been there, Dad!"

Ethan bent forward as he heard his son begin to cry. He waited until Charlie's sobs became sniffles. Fear was beginning to smother him like an ocean wave.

"Charlie, you can't blame yourself," Ethan said, his voice raspy. "You had no idea that this was going to happen."

"Her car was the last one in the convoy, Dad. Mister Sizemore feels terrible, said over and over again how he should have taken the time to organize the convoy better instead of trying to get out of camp so fast."

Ethan held his head, anger starting to invade his mind. "Well, we have to deal with the reality now. Have you tried calling Molly's cell phone?"

"Yeah, but I don't get any connection. What are we gonna do, Dad? The police won't help. Mister Sizemore is concerned that the border police may not let us back into Mexico because of the terrorist threats. What should we do?"

Ethan held the phone away then put it back to his ear. "I don't know, Charlie. Give me a little time to think about it. Are you at your motel now?"

"Yes, I checked in a little while ago."

"Give me the phone number and your room number. Don't call anyone on your cell phone. Keep it on in case . . . in case Molly calls . . . or in case someone else calls. Since they probably have her cell phone they may call your number to give us their . . . their demands." Ethan tried to keep the ugly thoughts at bay. "And . . . and keep it charged."

"Okay, Dad." Charlie gave his father the phone number of the motel and his room number.

"I'll call you back in thirty or forty minutes, son. In the meantime, call Lupe on your motel phone and tell her you talked to me. Tell her to stay by the phone in case . . . in case someone calls. Okay?"

"Okay, Dad."

"Charlie, we'll get your sister back," Ethan said, knowing that the reality was that he was stuck in Europe and didn't have a clue about what to do.

"I love you, Dad."

"I love you, too, son," Ethan said. "Be strong. I'll call you in thirty minutes."

Ethan heard Charlie hang up, dropped the phone to the floor and ran to the bathroom and threw up.

CHAPTER 13

After several minutes of eliminating whatever was left in his stomach, Ethan threw water on his face and cleaned himself up. He looked at himself in the mirror and just shook his head. He trudged back to the bed and sat down, his head resting on his hands.

I have to do something. Think, Paxton! Think! He thought about waking up Pete and Rob but knew they would still be sleeping off last night. Henrik? No, it's too early in the morning. *Think, damn it!*

He began to think through the sequence of events and lay out the facts that Charlie had given him. Molly was kidnapped only a couple of miles from the border. Charlie and the principal searched for her van but came up empty. The San Diego police couldn't or wouldn't do anything. The terrorist attacks had the border on high alert and it could close at any time. He was six thousand miles away with no way to get home for days or weeks. His son was holding up, but for how long? The school didn't seem to be doing anything. He needed outside help. But who?

Who does he know in San Diego? He sat on the bed and forced himself to think through the cobwebs. He didn't have any work contacts in the San Diego area. How about old Air Force buddies? It came to him suddenly, like a bolt of lightning. *Jake Delgado!* Jake was an old friend from the Air Force who became a San Diego cop after being discharged. Jake and he had played some football together while they were stationed in Japan and had become pretty good friends. He hadn't talked to Jake since they were in Japan together, over twenty years ago. It was a chance. A very slim chance, but at least a chance. *How do I contact him? I don't even know if he's alive.*

Ethan paced around the room for several minutes until it hit him. *Munson!* Mickey Munson was Ethan's best friend from the Air Force and had kept in contact with just about anyone and everyone that they had known. If anyone would have Jake's number it would be him. Ethan knew his friend's phone number by heart and dialed it. He looked at the clock while the connection was being made and calculated the time in California. It would be 7:20 p.m. *Come on, Mickey. Pick up!*

"Hello?" the familiar voice said. There was background noise and Ethan knew that he was in a bar, as was usual in the evening.

"Mickey!" Ethan said. "Damn, I'm glad you answered."

"Ethan? I thought you were in Europe?"

"I am. I am. Damn, I'm glad you answered!"

"Yeah, you said that. What's going on?"

"I need a number."

"What?"

"Remember Jake Delgado, the big redheaded quarterback in Japan?"

"Jake Delgado? What the hell you need to talk to him about? It's been over twenty—"

"I know, but I need his help," Ethan interrupted, trying to keep his voice under control.

"Why do you need his help? You in some kind of trouble?"

"Yeah, Mickey, I am," Ethan said, taking a deep breath.

"What the hell . . . ?"

"Mickey, Molly's been kidnapped," Ethan said, his voice wavering when he said the word.

Silence for several seconds. "Say again?"

"My daughter was kidnapped yesterday in Mexico while her school mission group was traveling to the border . . . ." Ethan dropped his head into his hand.

"Damn," Mickey said. "Damn, Ethan."

"I don't have time to explain. I'll tell you later, but right now I need Jake's phone number. Do you have it?"

"Jesus . . . uh, let me check. I'm not at home but I might have something in my book."

Ethan had seen 'the book' many times while sitting with his friend in a bar somewhere. When Mickey Munson got to drinking he liked to call old Air Force buddies and reminisce. He had all their phone numbers in a small little address book he kept in his back pocket.

"Ethan, the last number I have for him is pretty old. I haven't talked to him in years."

"Give it to me. Maybe he kept the same number."

"You know he's not a cop anymore. He got kicked off the San Diego force five or six years ago."

Ethan cringed at this news. "How do you know?"

"I was talking to Paul Boyer a couple of years ago. He was pretty close to Delgado. He told me that Jake got into some kind of fight and got kicked off the force. I think he's a private investigator now."

Ethan's mood brightened. "That's good. That's great, if he's still in San Diego."

"Well, like I said, this number is pretty old."

"Give it to me," Ethan said, getting a pen and piece of paper from the nightstand.

"Mickey, do me a favor and call around to see if anyone has a more recent number for Jake, in case this one doesn't work. I have to get in touch with him as soon as possible."

"Okay. You want me to start looking for PI's in the San Diego phone book?"

"Yeah, that would be great, in case I can't reach Jake. Thanks, Mick."

"Okay. I'll make some calls and see what I can find out."

Ethan gave him the hotel phone number.

"Hang tough, Ethan, and I'll find out what I can."

"Thanks, Mickey."

Ethan hung up, staring at the number on the note pad. He was nervous as he dialed the number that Mickey had given him, having little hope that it would be any good.

"El Toro," a voice said.

Ethan heard lots of noise in the background. "I'm looking for Jake Delgado?"

"Who?"

"Jake. Jake Delgado," Ethan said, ready to hang up. "Did I get the wrong—"

"Hold on." Ethan heard someone shout, "Bull! Telephone!" After several seconds the man came back on the line. "Yeah, he'll be right with ya. Hold on."

"Uh, who's . . . ?" He heard the phone clunk onto a table or bar. He tried to contain his growing excitement as he waited. Maybe the guy misunderstood him. *Who the hell is Bull?*

"Yeah, El Toro Investigations," a scratchy voice said on the other end. "What can I do for you?"

"El Toro . . . what?" Ethan said, putting his hand to his right ear. "No, I'm looking for Jake Delgado."

"You found him, pal."

Ethan's heart raced and he nearly dropped the phone. He cleared his throat. "Jake . . . I'm not sure if you'll remember me. We were stationed in Japan together."

"Japan? Hell, buddy, that was a long time ago. Who the hell is this?"

"Ethan. Ethan Paxton."

There was coughing. "Say again?"

"Ethan Paxton. We were stationed in Japan together back in '79. We—"

"Ethan! Jesus!" More coughing. "Had to blow the cobwebs loose there for a second. Damn, it's been a long time."

The coughing became worse, causing Ethan to hold the phone away from his ear. When the coughing died down, Ethan put the phone back to his ear.

"Yeah, long time. Listen, Jake, this isn't a social call. I've got a big problem and I need your help."

"Oh, hell. Wife cheating on ya?" Jake asked.

"What? No. No." Ethan shook his head. "My wife . . . . No."

"Oh, sorry. I usually do cheating husbands, that kind of stuff. Pays the bills."

Ethan shook his head again. "Jake, let me explain." Ethan wasn't sure if he could bring himself to say it, so just blurted it out. "My daughter's been kidnapped."

Silence. "I'm, uh, sorry," Jake said in between coughs.

"Can you help me? It happened in Mexico, across the border from San Diego."

"Damn, Ethan, I haven't worked on a kidnapping since . . . shit, I've never worked a kidnapping. Not sure if I can help you. You contact the police?"

"Jake, just listen. I'm stuck in Europe and can't get home because all the flights into the U.S. are canceled due to the terrorist stuff. The San Diego police won't do anything and they're saying she has to be missing for at least twenty four hours. I don't know what else to do or who else to call. I remembered that you lived in San Diego and used to be in law enforcement."

Silence again.

"Jake? You there?"

Coughing. "Yeah, I'm here. I gotta tell you, Ethan. I don't do that kind of stuff anymore. I chase assholes that cheat on their wives, not kidnappers. Plus," he said, coughing again, "I drink. A lot."

Ethan felt a pain in his chest and knew his chance was slipping away. He had to make a decision.

"Jake, I know the kind of person you are, or at least used to be, and I know you are stubborn as hell. You never gave up on anything when we were in the Air Force together. I just need someone to start digging around while I try to get home. Just do some investigating. Can you do that, Jake, for an old friend?"

"I . . . I don't know. I haven't had to do any real investigating..."

"Jake! Damn it! Some Mexican animals have kidnapped my little girl, and I can't help her!" Ethan was yelling into the phone. "You've got to help me! Please."

Ethan bent over in frustration, holding the phone to his ear. *He was pleading with a drunk. Talk about desperate.*

"Hold on Ethan."

Ethan heard Jake yell. "Tiny, a Bushmills!"

After a few more coughs, Jake came back on the phone. "Okay, I'll do what I can. But I can't promise anything."

"I understand," Ethan said excitedly. "I just need someone to be out looking for my daughter until the police.." He shook his head. "If I was in the States I'd do it myself, but I'm not." Ethan's voice cracked. "I need some hope, Jake."

More coughing. "I don't want you to get your hopes up too high, Ethan. It's been a long time since I've done any real detective work. Plus, we have this little problem of terrorist attacks going on. Not sure what that may do to the border."

"I understand, Jake," Ethan said, listening to more coughing. "Jake, you okay? You don't sound too good."

"Ah hell, I'm fine. Just been drinkin' a little more than usual today because of the damn airplanes falling out of the sky. I'll be fine."

"I'm counting on you, Jake. My little girl is counting on you. You sure you can do this?"

"Guess we'll find out." More coughing. "Now, I need to know what I'm dealing with here."

Ethan proceeded to give Jake a summary of his daughter's kidnapping. He mentioned the voicemail and the fact that his son was in San Diego and the lack of interest or cooperation from the SDPD and Border Patrol.

"Typical SDPD bullshit," Jake said. "Course, this terrorist shit adds a huge unknown factor. The border is probably a mess."

"You probably have contacts across the border in Tijuana, right?"

"I used to, but haven't had to use them in a few years. I'll do some checking tomorrow."

"Can you start tonight? I don't know how much time my daughter has."

"Yeah, I can make a few phone calls tonight. What about the other girls and the teacher. Anyone working for them?"

"I don't know. My son will know. He can fill you in tomorrow. You can talk to the school's principal, a Mister Sizemore. He's in San Diego."

"Okay, Ethan. Send your son over first thing in the morning, say nine o'clock. In the meantime, I'll contact a couple guys I know."

"Great! Give me your address and I'll give it to my son, along with your phone number."

"Tell him to meet me at the El Toro Bar and Grill, in the Gas Lamp district. That's my office."

"Really?" Ethan stared blankly at the phone. *What the hell am I doing?* "Okay. He'll be there tomorrow at nine."

"Uh, Ethan," Jake said, hesitantly. "I'll need an advance for expenses. Can your son handle that?"

"I don't have access to my money right now. How much?"

Jake cleared his throat. "Two grand should get us started."

"Okay. Okay, I'll do what I can. I'm in a tough spot here, Jake. Can you get started and I'll work on getting you the money."

"Okay, should be okay. Let's see where this takes us before we talk about my fee. How old is your son and what's his name?"

"Charlie, and he's nineteen."

"Shit, he's still a kid himself. A lot to lay on a kid, Ethan."

"I don't have much choice, Jake. While you're working with my son, I'm going to try to get out of here and into Mexico. I don't know how, but I'll get there."

"Well, good luck with that. Matter-of-fact, good luck to us all, 'cause we're sure as hell gonna need it."

"Jake, thanks again. I . . . ."

"I know, Ethan. Just get your ass over here as fast as you can. See ya."

Ethan hung up the phone and sat on the bed, staring blankly at the wall. He closed his eyes. *God help us.*

Ethan called Charlie back and gave him Jake's information. Charlie was understandably hesitant but agreed to meet with the PI the next morning.

"Charlie, he's not your typical private investigator so don't expect too much," Ethan said to his son.

"Well," Charlie said sarcastically, "he works out of a bar, he got kicked off the police force, he's a drunk, and you haven't seen him in twenty years. I'd say he's a huge longshot, Dad."

"That's true son, but he's the only shot we have right now."

CHAPTER 14

Jake sat staring at his Bushmills, swirling the ice around in the glass, coughing and cursing under his breath. *Damn rummy! Worthless drunk is all you are.* He started to take a drink, but sat the glass back down on the bar in front of him.

"What's wrong, Bull? You haven't touched your Bushmills in a while," Tiny said, standing in front of Jake. "Not like you."

Looking up at the bartender, Jake pushed the glass of Bushmills away. "Don't want anymore."

The big bartender stared at his friend. "What the hell's eatin' at you, Bull?"

Jake loved Tiny like a brother, but sometimes he could be nosy as hell. He shoved his barstool back, where he'd been sitting since nine o'clock that morning. He bent backwards, trying to relieve the stiffness in his back, then moved his head back and forth, trying to get some feeling in his neck. Nothing was working.

"Just don't want anymore, Tiny. I'm gonna take a walk."

"This got anything to do with the phone call you got tonight?"

"See you later, Tiny," Jake said as he shuffled his way to the door, continuing to move his head back and forth.

"Okay, Bull," Tiny said, shaking his head. "Be careful out there."

Jake walked out of the dark bar into the twilight, the sun just disappearing over the horizon. Jake looked up into the night sky and took a deep breath. He looked left, then right. He couldn't remember the last time he'd left the El Toro this time of night, especially half way sober. But the call from his old friend, Ethan Paxton, had sobered him up quickly. He turned right and began walking towards the Gas Lamp district, a few blocks from the El Toro.

He slowly trudged down the sidewalk. *Damn, Jake, what the hell are you doing?* As he got closer to the main drag he began to hear the noise and laughter. *How can people be laughing and having a good time? Didn't they know what was happening?*

The lights almost blinded him as he turned the corner onto 6th Street. His little corner of the world, the El Toro Bar and Grill, was only three blocks away, but it might as well have been in a different state. Hardly anyone other than locals and regulars ever ventured that far away from the lights and action of the Gas Lamp. Jake couldn't remember the last time he had walked down the main drag. It looked, smelled and sounded much different at night. He began to walk north along 6th Street, dodging people entering and exiting the many bars and restaurants. *Damn yuppies.*

His mind was fuzzy from too many Bushmills and from watching too much terror on the little television in the El Toro. Jake rubbed his red, burning eyes as he walked, stretching his back to try to relieve the soreness.

My old friend needs someone who knows what the hell he's doing, not some drunk who gave up on life years ago.

"Hey, watch where you're going!" said a college-aged kid walking out of a bar, nearly running into Jake.

Jake glared at him, but said nothing. Normally he would've cursed the kid out, but he let it pass.

What's the plan, Bull? Who you gonna call? You told Ethan you had contacts. Shit! You haven't talked to anyone from the force since they kicked you out. What now, big man?

He continued walking up 6th Street, then got tired of the crowds and the noise so took a right onto A Street. The crowds began to thin out, the noise getting further and further away. *Hell, why did I say I would help him? Ethan's a good man, or at least he was twenty years ago. He's in trouble and needs a real investigator, not some damn drunk.*

Jake headed back towards the El Toro, the fresh air not helping him at all.

Maybe Tiny can help me with some contacts I can call. He knows everybody.

Jake looked up at the familiar sign above the door: *El Toro Bar and Grill.* He always wanted to ask Tiny where the Grill part came in. The only food they ever served in the little hole-in-the-wall joint was stale peanuts and beef jerky that would break a tooth in a second. But it was his little hole-in-the-wall joint and he felt at home here. He opened the door and walked back into the darkness of the bar.

CHAPTER 15

Ethan turned on the shower and let the hot water pour over him as his mind raced.

How am I going to get out of here? Can I trust Jake Delgado? Will the kidnappers call? My daughter . . . .

After a fifteen-minute shower, Ethan shaved, got dressed, checked the clock—5:15. It was too early to wake up Rob and Pete. They were in pretty bad shape when they got back to the hotel around midnight, so he knew they were still sleeping it off. Thank goodness he'd taken it easy on the drinking. Even now he felt guilty about being out with his friends when his daughter was . . . who knows where.

Ethan shook the thought out of his head. He had to be productive, do something to try to get to Mexico, if Mexican air space was still open. He decided to call Henrik, who was well-connected with the airlines in the Netherlands. He checked the clock one more time—5:16. *Sorry, Henrik.*

Picking up the phone, he dialed his boss's home number. He was hoping Henrik was already up, getting ready for the day.

"Hello?" said a female voice, speaking softly in Dutch.

"Hello, Renate. I'm so sorry to wake you. It's Ethan Paxton."

"Ethan?" she said groggily. "Hold on, I'll get Henrik."

Ethan heard some rustling and whispering, and then someone picked up the phone.

"Ethan? Are you okay?" Henrik said, yawning.

Damn, I woke him up. "Sorry to wake you up, boss, but I need your help."

"What time is it?"

"It's about five-twenty," Ethan said, wincing.

"Uh, okay, let me go to the living room. Hold on."

Ethan heard some more whispering and then heard a door open and close.

"What's wrong, Ethan?" Henrik said, speaking normally now.

Ethan began to tell him about his daughter but his words got stuck in his throat. He held his hand over the phone and cleared his throat.

"Ethan?"

"Sorry, Henrik." Ethan closed his eyes. "My . . . my daughter's been kidnapped." Just saying the word was almost more than he could stand.

"Kidnapped?" Henrik repeated.

"Yes, in Mexico."

"Dear God," Henrik said. "How? When?"

Ethan proceeded to tell Henrik the entire story, just as Charlie had explained it to him. He also told him about hiring Jake Delgado.

"Henrik, I need to find a flight out of Amsterdam into Mexico, or as close as I can get. Can you help me?"

"Of course. I'll start making calls right away."

"Thanks, Henrik. I—"

"Ethan," Henrik interrupted. "Has anyone heard from the kidnappers?"

Ethan paused. "No, nothing yet."

"Have you thought about the possibility that it's not a kidnapping for ransom?" Henrik said.

Ethan hesitated. "What do you mean?"

Henrik cleared his throat. "Well, I hope this isn't the case, but three young teenage American girls are quite a prize in the sex-trafficking market. It's a big problem here in Europe and Asia."

Ethan felt a sharp pain in his temples and sweat began to form on his forehead. He hadn't thought about this possibility and it caught him completely off guard.

"Ethan? I'm sorry, I shouldn't have mentioned that."

Ethan was beginning to panic for the first time, unable to speak or move. This new possibility hit him like a sledgehammer.

"Ethan, you okay?"

Ethan cleared his throat. "I hadn't . . . thought about that," he said, his voice hoarse.

"Listen, Ethan. I'll begin working on getting you a flight out. I'll charter a plane if I have to. I don't want you to worry about that. I wish I could take back what I said, but... You stay strong for your daughter. Let me worry about getting you home, okay?"

"Okay."

"Call me back at . . . nine o'clock. It may take me a couple of hours to rouse people up."

"Okay, nine o'clock," Ethan repeated.

"Ethan . . . I'm so sorry," Henrik said. "I'll get you home."

"Thanks, Henrik."

Ethan hung up the phone and stared off into the dark room. It was eerily quiet at that time of the morning, everyone in the hotel still asleep. He fought against the thoughts that were beginning to creep into his head, but they wouldn't go away. *Sex trafficking*. He'd held it together until now, but the tears finally came in a flood as the fear and terror engulfed him.

CHAPTER 16

"Tiny, one more," Jake said from his perch at the end of the bar. He'd been sipping on the same Bushmills for an hour, his mind beginning to clear. It was time to get some help.

Tiny walked down the bar with the bottle of Bushmills Irish Whiskey in one hand, a fresh glass with ice in the other. He silently poured the whiskey into the glass and slid it in front of Jake.

"Taking it easy tonight, Bull?" he said.

Jake looked up at the bartender, and then looked down the bar at the other customers. He looked behind him to see if anyone was sitting at one of the tables. They were empty. He turned back to Tiny.

"I need to talk to you about something, Tiny."

"Fire away. What's going on?"

Jake took a sip of his drink, sat it down on the bar, and leaned closer to Tiny. "I'm in deep shit."

Tiny stared at his friend for several seconds. "I'm listening."

"The phone call tonight? It was an old friend from my military days," Jake said. "He needs my help."

"What kind of help?"

"His daughter's been kidnapped and he wants me to find her."

Tiny's eyes grew wide. "No shit? Damn, Bull."

"Thing is, he's stuck in Europe because of the terrorist crap. The girl was taken in Mexico, just over the border."

"Holy crap, Bull."

"Yeah, my thoughts exactly," Jake said, shaking his head. "I need some help. You know of any ex-cops down there? My contacts are long gone ever since I left the force."

Tiny thought for a few seconds, and then his face lit up. "Yeah, your old partner, Manny, lives down in Rosarito Beach. He tried to contact you for months after you left the force, but you didn't want to have anything to do with anybody back then. He calls me every now and then. I think I have his number."

Jake's face brightened when Tiny mentioned Manny Rodriguez, his partner for two years on the SDPD. "When did he retire?"

"Couple of years ago. He moved down to this enclave in Rosarito Beach where other retired cops bought condos. There's a bunch of them down there."

"Get me his number, Tiny."

Tiny nodded and walked back down the bar. Jake took another sip of Bushmills and for the first time in a long time, smiled. Manny Rodriguez was the best partner he'd ever had. He'll know what to do. Jake dropped his head back and finished the rest of the whiskey.

"Tiny!" he yelled. "I need another one." Jake's smile turned into a grin as he looked down at the big bartender.

Tiny brought the bottle of Bushmills back with him, along with a piece of paper.

"I haven't seen a grin on your face in years, Bull. Here's Manny's number. I'm just gonna leave the bottle. I'll bring the phone down. Say hi to Manny for me."

"Thanks, Tiny."

Jake poured some Bushmills into his glass and gulped it down. He glanced at the phone number just as Tiny put the phone in front of him. He punched in the numbers and waited. After three rings, someone came on the line.

"Hola," a masculine voice said.

"This Manny Rodriguez?" Jake said, not recognizing the voice.

"No, this is Eduardo. Hold on, I'll get him."

Jake took another sip and gave Tiny a thumbs up.

"Hello. Manny here," an older male voice said.

"Hello, Manny," Jake said.

There was a pause. "Bull? Bull, is that you?"

"One and the same," Jake said, smiling at the sound of his nickname on the force.

"I'll be goddamned!" Manny said excitedly. "How the hell are you, you old cocksucker?"

"Gettin' by," Jake said. "You living south of the border now, huh?"

"Yeah, for a couple of years now. It's cheap as hell and I have a little place right on the beach. Life is good down here."

"Sounds like retirement suits you." Jake took a deep breath. "Manny, I need your help."

"Okay, Bull." Manny's voice became quiet, measured. "What kind of help you need?"

Jake took another deep breath and blew it out. "I have a client, an old friend from my military days."

"Okay."

"His daughter went missing in Mexico today. My client thinks she was kidnapped."

After a few seconds of silence Manny said, "Holy shit. Whereabouts?"

"Outside of Tecate, close to the border crossing at Otay Mesa," Jake replied. "You know the area?"

"Yeah, it's about forty five minutes east of Tijuana. What was she doing there?

"She was on a school mission trip. Bunch of kids and teachers building houses for poor folks. Her car was hijacked, her and three other girls, just a couple of miles from the border."

Manny whistled into the phone. "She's probably toast, Bull. Hate to say it, but the odds aren't good."

Jake felt a pain in his stomach when he heard this. "I promised my client, my friend, that I would try to find her, Manny. Can you help me?"

Manny paused, then said, "Let me put it this way, Bull. There are about ten ex-SDPD guys living down here that sit around drinking beer all day and tequila all night. We're all bored out of our minds. So, yeah, I think you can get as much help as you need on this. What do you want us to do?"

"Do you or any of the others have any contacts at the TJPD?"

"Yeah, I know a guy."

"The SDPD has shoved this under the rug, claiming that the terrorist crap has all their attention right now. We need to keep this quiet. Do you trust your TJPD guy?"

"Yeah, I'll vouch for him. You want me to call him and get him to put some feelers out?"

"Let's start there. Can you and I meet tomorrow sometime?

"Hell, yeah. How about Lily's on the Avenida. You remember that place?"

"Yeah, I remember Lily's. Big cop hangout."

"What time do you want to meet?" Manny said.

"Well, I'm meeting with my client's son tomorrow morning. He was with the mission group and has a voicemail from his sister that could help us. How about tomorrow afternoon, say around five?"

"Sounds good. It'll give me a chance to get into TJ."

"What about the border? You heard anything about how tight it is since the attacks?"

"No, but I can find out. Can I reach you at the El Toro?"

"Yep. Thanks, Manny. See you tomorrow at five."

"Good talkin' to ya, Bull. Hang in there, old buddy."

Jake hung up the phone and poured another drink. He lifted his glass and finished it off. He looked at the bottle of Bushmills in front of him and thought about pouring another glass, but shoved the bottle away. He looked at the clock on the wall. Nine-thirty.

"How'd it go, Bull?" Tiny said from the end of the bar.

Jake held his thumb up in the air, a smile on his face. "I'm going home, Tiny. Big day tomorrow." Jake slid his barstool back and stood up, arching his stiff back and swiveling his stiff neck in a circle. He started walking towards the door.

Tiny smiled at his old friend. "Good to see you back, Bull."

CHAPTER 17

Molly heard the voice before her eyes would open. The same voice that she heard before the blackness overtook her. She tried to open her eyes but they were so heavy. She felt something wet and warm on her face and she drew away. She winced when she felt the twine around her wrists.

"It's okay, *mija*. Just a warm washcloth, to help you wake up. Let me help you."

The voice was right next to her, patting her face with the washcloth. It felt good, so Molly allowed the woman to continue. Finally, her eyes opened into small slits. Everything was blurry at first and then became clearer. The woman sitting next to her was pretty, with medium-length dark-brown hair. Molly noticed her eyes, which were big, wide open and dark, and they seemed kind. Molly kept staring at her.

"Feeling better, little one?" the woman asked, her accent heavy.

"I have to go to the bathroom," Molly said, her voice barely audible. She felt like she had cotton in her mouth and kept licking her lips. "And I need some water."

"Okay. Let me help you to the bathroom first. Be careful, your legs will be wobbly."

Molly struggled to her feet with the help of the woman. She almost toppled over, but the woman steadied her. They began walking towards a small, dark, smelly room. For the first time, Molly saw her surroundings. It was a large dark, musty room with a single light bulb hanging from the ceiling, casting shadows around the room. There was a small skylight above the light, but it was dark outside. She noticed someone lying to the right of her and saw blonde hair. *It's Cindy.* She looked to her left and saw a plump blonde lying on her side on a filthy mattress. *Jenny.* Both of the girls were lying motionless, their arms tied behind them.

"Are they okay?" Molly said in a raspy voice.

"Yes. They are fine. They will wake up soon. Come, here is the toilet."

The woman led Molly into the small, dark room. She almost gagged at the putrid smell.

"I'm going to throw up," she said, putting her head over the toilet. She gagged but nothing came out. She gagged a second time and again nothing.

"The drug will wear off and you will feel better," the woman said behind her. "I'm sorry I can't leave you in here alone, but I will turn my head while you go."

"Can you untie me?"

The woman looked at her closely. "Okay, but if you struggle it will bring the others in."

The woman approached Molly and untied her wrists. Molly rubbed them, trying to get the circulation back. She unbuttoned her jeans and slid them down, watching the woman carefully. She had turned away as she had promised. Molly sat on the toilet, relieving herself. When she was done the woman gave her some toilet paper. Molly pulled up her panties and jeans and buttoned them. She noticed a shower in the corner of the room.

"Can I take a shower?" she asked the woman.

"Maybe later. You feel better?"

"I need some water."

"Okay, turn around. I have to tie your wrists again."

"No, please! It hurts so bad," Molly pleaded, backing away.

"I will tie them loosely, so they don't cut into your wrists. I must or I will get in trouble."

Molly continued to back away but knew it was useless. She turned around while the woman retied her wrists, loosely as she had said, but not so loose that Molly could slip them off.

As they walked back into the main room, Molly looked around again. It was large but with no furnishings except the mattresses and a wooden chair sitting next to a metal door. The door was closed. No windows. It was hot and humid and hard to breath. She noticed the empty mattress.

"Where's my teacher?" Molly said, staring at the empty mattress.

"I don't know. Outside."

Molly turned and glared at the woman, who was averting her gaze. "What are they doing to her? Where is she?" Sweat was beginning to trickle down her face.

"Lie down and you will be cooler."

Molly sat on the mattress but did not lie down. She continued to glare at the woman, waiting for an answer. The woman was dressed in tight fitting jeans that showed a well-shaped body. She had on a tee-shirt that said 'San Diego' on the front. She was about Molly's height. She had no shoes on.

"Where is she?" Molly repeated, her voice getting louder.

"Keep your voice down or they will come in."

"Where is she?" Molly said quietly, but forcefully.

"She is outside, in the other room."

"Why? What are they doing to her?" Molly said, tears beginning to well up.

"I don't know," the woman said, hanging her head. "What's your name, *mija*?"

Molly looked at her but said nothing.

"Please, we are going to be here a long time together. I would like to know what to call you."

"Molly."

"Molly? You don't look like a Molly."

"Why would you say that?"

"You are *Latina*, no?"

"No. I mean, yes. My mother . . . was Hispanic." Molly cursed under her breath for saying too much. *Keep your mouth shut, Molly.*

The woman's eyes got bigger. "Oh, that explains it."

Molly saw her looking at her more closely, a strange look on her face, almost like she recognized her. The woman reached over to brush Molly's hair but Molly pulled away.

"My name is Natalia. I won't hurt you, Molly. And I will make sure no one else hurts you."

Molly looked at Cindy and Jenny, who both were beginning to show signs of life. She noticed Natalia looking over at them.

"Why did you kidnap us?" Molly blurted. "What are you going to do to us?"

Natalia looked at her sadly. "No one will hurt you, *mija*, I promise."

"Answer me! Why did you kidnap us?"

"Please," Natalia said, looking at the door. "You must be quiet or the others will come in."

"Tell me why," she pleaded, the tears beginning to run down her face.

"Oh, *mija*. I'm so sorry," Natalia said softly.

Molly looked over and saw Cindy staring at her. She was lying on her side with her head tilted up at an awkward angle. Molly glanced over at

Jenny and saw movement. She watched Natalia walk over to Cindy and wipe her face with a washcloth.

"Molly?" Cindy said, barely audible.

"I'm here, Cindy. It's okay, she won't hurt you." Molly glared at Natalia.

"Do you have to go to the bathroom?" Natalia asked Cindy, with none of the same gentleness that she had shown Molly.

Cindy nodded her head and rose up on her elbows, looking at Molly in bewilderment.

"It's okay, Cindy," Molly said softly.

Natalia looked at Molly and smiled. "Yes, listen to your friend. I will help you." Natalia stood Cindy up and untied her wrists. "Do not struggle," she said. She led Cindy into the bathroom, keeping the door open so she could watch Molly. After Cindy relieved herself Natalia retied her wrists. They walked back and Natalia helped Cindy back down on the soiled mattress.

"Where are we?" asked Cindy, beginning to get her voice and senses back.

"In some smelly, hot dungeon," Molly said, staring at Natalia.

Natalia's smile disappeared. "You are safe. No one will hurt you, as long as you are quiet and do not struggle."

Molly looked at Jenny, who was on her elbows staring at them. She didn't say a word, but her eyes were moist and red.

"Jenny. Are you okay?" Molly asked her friend.

Jenny continued to stare at Natalia, then Molly. Tears were now streaming down her face.

"Do you need to go to the bathroom?" Natalia asked the girl. She didn't wipe her face with the washcloth as she had Molly and Cindy.

"Wipe her face!" Molly said angrily.

Natalia stared at Molly, grabbing the washcloth.

"Clean it off first, with warm water." Molly stared back at Natalia.

Natalia went into the bathroom and ran warm water over the washcloth, all the while staring at Molly. She came back out and rubbed Jenny's face, the gentleness gone. She untied Jenny's wrists without saying a word and led her into the bathroom. The entire time she stared at Molly, who stared back at her. When Jenny was done relieving herself, Natalia tied her wrists again and Jenny winced in pain.

"Loosen them, like you loosened mine!" Molly said sternly. She knew she was close to crossing the line with Natalia.

Natalia loosened the twine on Jenny's wrists and led her back to her mattress. "Lie down," she said harshly.

There was a loud knock on the metal door, so sudden the girls all gasped. Natalia snapped her head towards the door, looking back at the girls. "Everyone lie down and keep quiet!" she said, looking at Molly. "For your own good."

Natalie walked to the door and knocked twice.

Molly heard a loud noise on the other side, like a dead bolt being unlocked. She watched as the heavy metal door slid sideways, a ray of light sending a beam into the room. Molly realized that she didn't even know what day it was or what time it was or how long she had been out. She saw a man poke his head through the opening, looking around at everyone in the room.

"*¿Que tal andas?*" the man asked Natalia.

"*Aqui nomas,*" she answered.

The man handed Natalia a basket and a bottle of water. Molly saw him look at her and smile, gold teeth gleaming in the small slit of light.

"*¡Pendejo! ¡Vete a la chingada!*" Natalia said.

"*¡Ay, pinche perra!*" the man said with a sneer before sliding the door closed and locking it from the outside.

Natalia walked to the girls and showed them the contents of the basket. Molly saw several tortillas and a bottle of water. Natalia tore the tortillas into three pieces and fed them to the girls. They were so hungry they chewed vigorously. Natalia put the bottle of water to each of their lips and let them drink as much as they could. The water dripped down their chins and onto the mattresses.

Molly wiped her chin on the mattress and then looked at Natalia. "What did you say to him?"

"Nothing, just told him to get out."

Molly stared at Natalia for a long time, trying to decide who and what she was. Why was she being kind?

"What now?" asked Molly, still staring at Natalia.

"Now you go back to sleep."

"Wait, what time is it?"

"It's almost one a.m."

"What day?"

"Wednesday."

"We were out for eight hours?" Molly said, her eyes moist.

"Yes. Now it is time to sleep again." Natalia stood and walked to a bag lying next to the chair. She reached into the bag and pulled out a needle and vial and turned to look at Molly. "This will be for your own good, *mija.*"

"No, please. Let us stay awake a little while longer," Molly pleaded. "Please."

Natalia looked at Molly, then at the other girls. "No, it is too dangerous. They are right outside."

Molly looked over at Cindy and Jenny as Natalia swabbed her arm. They had tears streaming down their cheeks as they looked back at her. She tried to smile, to reassure them, but the smile turned to a grimace when she felt the needle go into her arm. She stared up at Natalia as the blackness began to overtake her again. She felt Natalia brushing her hair and heard her humming softly as she faded into sleep.

CHAPTER 18

Ethan walked out of the hotel into mostly darkness, the sun just beginning to show itself in the east. The air was cool for a September morning. He looked out over the empty town square where he and his two friends had stumbled through on their way back to the hotel just six hours before. He had half-carried Rob, who was mumbling something about Henk, the old man at the restaurant. Ethan felt a pang of guilt as he thought about being out with his friends while his little girl was living a nightmare. He fought against the tears, pulled his jacket collar up around his neck, and began walking.

The fresh, crisp air felt soothing, the sting on his face felt real, healing. He walked across the square, noticing a man on a bicycle skirting the edge, disappearing down a side street. The only sound was the click clack of his shoes on the cobblestone. He smelled bread baking as he walked down a narrow alley towards St. James Cathedral, the one landmark that he knew well. He walked quickly, trying to stay warm. Once in front of the massive church he stopped. There was no one around, but he noticed a light shining through the front door. Walking up the steps, he opened the heavy, wooden door a few inches and peered inside. There was just enough light to see the altar far off in the distance. *I could use some help right about now.* He slid through the crack in the doorway and stood in the vestibule, looking around. With no one in sight, he walked quietly down the main aisle, toward the altar. He saw the crucified Christ hanging from a cross, the crown of thorns on his head.

Ethan moved silently into a pew and sat down, staring at the cross, his eyes becoming moist. He was a spiritual man, but hadn't been inside a church since his wife had died. He put his hands on the pew in front of him and bent his head down, closing his eyes. He began to pray silently, his lips moving but no words coming out.

Ethan jerked his head up when he heard a voice. He looked at the altar but saw no one. Suddenly, a hand was on his shoulder. Ethan turned with a start and stared with eyes wide open at a priest standing next to him, a warm smile crossing his face.

The bearded man said something to Ethan in Dutch.

"I'm sorry, I don't speak Dutch," Ethan replied.

"American?" the priest said.

"Yes."

The priest smiled and patted Ethan on the shoulder. "May I join you?"

Ethan hesitated. "Yes. Please." Ethan slid over to make room.

The priest was a heavyset man and was dressed simply, a brown robe draped over him. He had silver hair on top of a pinkish face covered by a full white beard. He looked to be in his sixties or early seventies. He looked up at the altar and made the sign of the cross before he sat down.

"Are you praying for your country, son?"

Ethan hesitated. "No," he said as he looked squarely into the eyes of the friendly priest.

"No?" the priest said in surprise. "Your country is going through quite an ordeal right now."

"Yes, it is," Ethan replied. "And I'm so sorry for all the victims and their families, but . . . ."

The priest stared at him, a quizzical look on his face.

"But I was praying for my daughter."

"Your daughter?"

Ethan nodded and gazed up at Christ on the cross. "She was kidnapped yesterday," he said, his voice cracking.

The priest's eyes narrowed as he put his hand on Ethan's shoulder. "Oh, my son. I'm so sorry."

Ethan continued to stare at the altar. "Father . . . should I call you Father?"

"If you wish. My name is Father Maarten."

"Father Maarten, could.. you pray.. with me for.. my daughter?" Ethan said, the words coming in uneven spurts.

"Yes, my son," the priest said, bending down. "What is your daughter's name?"

"Molly."

"And your name?"

"Ethan."

The priest dropped his head on his right hand, his left hand on Ethan's shoulder, and closed his eyes.

Ethan looked at the man, then bowed his head and closed his eyes.

For the next few minutes the priest prayed for Ethan and his daughter. He prayed for Molly's safety, for her safe return to her family. He prayed for Ethan to find peace and comfort and faith. At the end of the prayer he put his hand on Ethan's and squeezed. When he opened his eyes he made the sign of the cross again.

"Thank you, Father," Ethan said quietly, reverently.

"I will continue to pray for you and Molly, son. I am so sorry," the priest said as he stood up. "Please, stay as long as you like." He put his hand on top of Ethan's head and then backed out of the pew, walking back up the aisle.

Ethan sat motionless for several minutes, his head bowed, saying his own silent prayer.

When Ethan returned to the hotel, he splashed water on his face and looked at his haggard reflection in the mirror. The bags under his eyes looked darker, the lines in his face seemed deeper. A knock on the door startled him. He glanced at his watch. Eight o'clock. Thinking it was the maid he opened the door and was surprised to see Pete standing there with two cups of coffee in his hands. He was all cleaned up and immaculate as always. Pete was an expert at shaking off a hangover and getting on with his day.

"Morning, Mister Paxton!" Pete exclaimed cheerfully, handing a cup of coffee to Ethan. "Room service."

"Ah, thanks buddy. I need this," said Ethan, taking a big gulp of the hot coffee. It was typical Dutch coffee, much stronger than American colored water. "Damn this tastes good!"

"You don't look so good. You feeling okay?"

Ethan glanced at his friend, shook his head and said, "Sit down. I've got something to tell you."

He proceeded to tell Pete about his daughter's abduction, the phone calls with his son and Jake. He felt somehow better after telling his friend everything.

"Holy shit!" said Pete, staring at Ethan with bulging eyes. "I don't know what to say."

Ethan nodded. "Have you talked to Rob yet?"

"No, I thought I'd give him a little longer to sleep. He was pretty well toasted last night. Not that I was much better, but Rob's an old fart and doesn't bounce back like I do." Pete paused. "What next? Are you going to call Henrik?"

"Already have. He's working on getting me a flight out of here. I'm hoping he can find something into Mexico City or somewhere close. I don't know how much time I have . . . ." Ethan's voice trailed off as he gazed into the distance.

Pete put his hand on Ethan's shoulder. "I'll call my Amsterdam office and have them start looking, too. Between the two of us we should be able to find something leaving today. If we can arrange it, I may decide to go with you."

This last remark surprised Ethan. "The best we can hope for is something into Mexico City. That's still sixteen hundred miles from the U.S. border. You sure you want to risk that?"

"Well, it's closer to home than I am here, plus I think you could use some help. You've got a couple of rough days ahead of you."

"I'd definitely welcome the company but I don't want to put you at risk. Parts of Mexico are pretty dangerous. You might want to check with your wife before making a decision, if there's a decision to make.

"If I have time to call her, I will. But if not, I'll just make the decision and live with it. Mexico isn't a place you want to travel in alone, Ethan. Plus, I speak a little Spanish so I may be able to help in that area."

Ethan nodded. "It's eight-thirty now, so let's meet downstairs around nine, maybe grab some breakfast. I'm starving."

"Okay. Maybe by that time Rob will be alive again. See you in a bit," Pete said, walking out into the hallway. He stopped and held the door. "Stay strong, Ethan."

Ethan nodded at his friend as he dialed his boss's office number.

"Hello," a female voice said in Dutch. It was Marta, Henrik's administrator. No one got to Henrik without first going through Marta.

"Hi Marta. It's Ethan Paxton."

"Oh, hi Ethan! How are you? Henrik's been expecting your call." There was a moment of silence. "Are you doing okay?"

"Well, it's been a long night but I'm okay. I need to talk to Henrik urgently, Marta. Can you patch me through?"

"Absolutely. Hold on."

He could tell by Marta's voice that Henrik had not told her about his dilemma. After only a few seconds Henrik was on the line.

"Hello, Ethan," he said.

"Hi, Henrik," Ethan replied. "Any news?"

"I've been on the phone for the past two hours and have a couple of possibilities, but nothing confirmed yet."

"Okay," Ethan said. "Pete and I are going to grab some breakfast so I'll call you back in about an hour. That okay?"

"Sure," Henrik said. "You doing okay?"

Ethan didn't answer immediately, the tension evident in both men's mind.

"Ethan?" Henrik said.

"I'm okay. I just don't know what to do. Everything seems to be crumbling around me . . . ."

"I understand, Ethan. We'll get you home. In the meantime, get some breakfast and I'll keep working the phones."

"Thanks, boss." Ethan hung up, shaking his head. *It's going to take a miracle.*

CHAPTER 19

Ethan had eaten half of his breakfast while Rob and Pete had gobbled everything down.

"Ethan, you've got to eat. You have a long day ahead of you," Pete said.

Ethan looked at his two friends and gave them a weak smile. "Thanks guys, but I can't eat anything right now. My stomach is in knots. I have to call Henrik back in a few minutes so better head up to my room."

Rob was staring at Ethan, concern and sorrow on his expressive face. "I am so sorry, Ethan. I can't even imagine what you're going through. But Pete's right, you've got to eat to keep your strength up."

Ethan grabbed a piece of toast and began nibbling on it.

"My Amsterdam office is still working on finding something into Mexico. Mind if I come up with you when you talk to Henrik?" Pete asked.

"Sure, come on up. You too, Rob, if you want."

"Thanks, but I think I'll take a walk around the square to get the juices flowing. Still feeling a little queasy from last night. Is there anything I can do, Ethan?"

"No, but thanks. I just need to get my ass on an airplane heading for North America. Anywhere close."

"Well, between Henrik and Pete, they should find something. I'll stay close by in case you have to leave in a hurry. Good luck, buddy."

"Thanks Rob. Let's go, Pete." Ethan stood up from the table after signing for the tab. "See you later, Rob."

Ethan and Pete took the elevator to the third floor in silence. Walking into his room, Ethan saw his message light on. He immediately went to the phone and punched the button for messages.

"Ethan, it's Henrik. Call me as soon as you can. Very important."

Ethan disconnected from the message and after getting a dial tone, dialed his boss.

"Hello?" Henrik answered.

"Hi Henrik, it's Ethan. I'm not used to you answering your own phone. Where's Marta?"

"Out. I found you a flight out of Schiphol. How soon can you get ready to go to the airport?"

"I can pack my bags and be ready in fifteen minutes. What did you find?"

"You've got a choice to make, but very little time to make it. I got two seats on a charter cargo flight out of Schiphol into Mexico City, departing at one o'clock, arriving in Mexico City at six tonight. Or, KLM has a flight departing at seven thirty tonight, non-stop to Mexico City, two first class seats, but it arrives after midnight."

Ethan didn't stop to think about it. "The charter. I have to get there as early as possible."

"Hold on. The seats are probably uncomfortable at best, very little if any food, and it's a charter, so no guarantee of takeoff or arrival time. The KLM flight is first class, guaranteed two seats, plenty of food and wine. Here's the kicker. If you miss the cargo flight at 1 p.m., the seats on KLM will probably be taken, so your next option would be tomorrow afternoon at the earliest. We have at least an hour and a half drive to Schiphol, so you'll be cutting it pretty close with the cargo flight. Plus, the security lines are long as hell because of the terrorist attacks. You'd be taking a pretty big gamble."

"The next few days are going to be one big gamble, Henrik. If I don't get into Mexico City until midnight I won't be able to get a flight to Tijuana until the next day. If I arrive at six tonight, I may still have time to get something closer to Tijuana. I don't know how much time my daughter has, so no choice here. It's got to be the cargo flight."

"What about Pete or Rob? I only have one other seat available."

"Pete's right here with me, and I have you on speaker. Pete, what do you think? This is my problem, not yours. I don't want you to suffer because of me."

Ethan saw Pete doing calculations in his head. "Let's do it," he said. "I'm with you, whatever you decide."

"Cargo or first class?" Ethan asked.

"Well, I do love the wine in first class, but the cargo flight gets us there faster."

Ethan stared at his friend and smiled. "Book us both on the charter, Henrik. We'll be downstairs in fifteen minutes."

"Great. I'll pick you up myself in fifteen. What about Rob? "

"He's taking a walk in the square. We'll try to find him and let him know."

"Ask him if he wants the KLM flight tonight."

"Okay. Thanks, boss. I owe you."

"See you in fifteen."

Ethan hung up and gave Pete a high five. "Let's roll!" he said.

Pete dashed out of the room. "Downstairs in five minutes so we can look for Rob," he said over his shoulder.

"Got it."

Ethan began throwing his clothes into his soft-sided suitcase, not caring if he mixed clean clothes with dirty. He collected his toiletries from the bathroom, threw them into the suitcase and closed it. He unplugged his laptop computer and put it in his computer bag. He picked up the phone and told the front desk that he was checking out in five minutes. After one last check around the room, he walked out the door and headed for the elevator, his heart racing wildly.

After checking out and leaving their bags with the bellman in the lobby, Ethan and Pete walked out into the city square to look for Rob. They had eight minutes before Henrik would arrive. They scanned the familiar city square looking for a balding, white-haired American. It was mid-morning so the square was filled with bicyclists and pedestrians.

"You see him?" asked Pete.

"No," Ethan replied, "I don't see him any—"

"What the hell are you two jokers looking at?" said a voice behind them.

Ethan and Pete turned around and saw Rob sitting at the coffee shop next door to the hotel, a cup of coffee in front of him.

"Had to get some more caffeine in me to wash out the alcohol from last night," he laughed.

"Rob, so glad we found you," Ethan said, walking over to his friend.

"You didn't find me, I found you," Rob said.

"True. Well, I hate to leave you alone, but Henrik found a cargo charter flight into Mexico City with two seats available. Henrik asked for a third but no luck. He can get you on a KLM flight tonight into Mexico City if you want it. First class."

"That's great, Ethan! Why aren't you taking the KLM flight?"

"The charter gets in earlier, giving us time to find a connecting flight to Tijuana or somewhere close."

Rob nodded his head. "As far as me flying into Mexico, I think I'll pass. I'll take my chances on getting a direct flight home from here. Don't worry about me, I'll be fine."

"You sure?" Ethan said. "It may be days before you can fly into the U.S."

"Yeah, I'm sure. I like it here and think I'll look at it as a holiday. May never get back to Europe, so, you know."

Ethan nodded, smiling at this friend.

"Stay out of trouble, you old fart," Pete said. The two friends hugged and shook hands. "Wish I could stay to keep you company, but I think Ethan needs my help more than you do."

"Absolutely! Wish I could go with you, but I'll get out of here soon enough. I'll be praying for you guys."

Ethan reached his hand out and shook Rob's hand. He pulled him in and gave him a hug, Rob giving Ethan his customary slap on the back.

"I'll miss you, my friend," Ethan said.

"Good luck and safe flight. I hope everything turns out okay," Rob said quietly. "Get your daughter back."

Ethan nodded. "Hey, Henrik said you can ride up to Schiphol with us and he'll bring you back, if you want."

"No. Think I'll hang out here and stretch my legs. I don't need a two-hour car ride right now."

"Okay. I'll tell him. Take care, Rob," Ethan said.

"You guys be careful in Mexico," Rob said. "It's a dangerous god-damn country."

Ethan and Pete waved goodbye as they headed for the hotel lobby. Henrik was waiting for them.

"Good morning, gentlemen. Rob coming?" he asked.

"No. He's going to pass on the KLM flight, too. He had a rough night last night," Ethan answered.

"Okay, let's go," Henrik said as he walked through the door to his idling car. "Your bags are in the car."

Ethan told Pete to take the front seat as he climbed into the backseat. As they pulled away from the hotel Ethan looked back and saw Rob standing outside the hotel, his hand raised. Ethan waved to him and turned back around.

"I'll keep working on something for Rob," Henrik said. "I'll come over tonight and take him to dinner."

"He'd like that, boss. Thanks," Ethan said.

"Be careful. He'll want to take you out drinking afterwards," Pete said. "Believe me, you don't want any part of that."

"I'll try to bring a little culture into his life tonight," Henrik said, smiling.

"Good. He needs it," Pete answered. "Oh, by the way, we met the ex-Mayor of Den Bosch last night."

"Really? Mister De Groot? He's a very famous man around here."

"So we heard. A very classy guy," said Ethan, remembering the older man from the previous night.

"He was quite a war hero, they say. I met him once at a function several years ago," Henrik said.

"If circumstances were different," Ethan replied, staring out the window, "it would have been nice to spend a few more days here."

"Yeah. Great city, great people," Pete said.

"Well, when you come back next time, we'll see if Mister De Groot can join us for dinner. Quite a storyteller, I hear," Henrik said. "And you *will* come back, both of you." He was looking at Ethan in the rearview mirror.

Ethan smiled at him. "So Henrik, it's ten thirty now and the flight leaves at one. Can we make it?"

"Depends on traffic. You never know on the A2," he said, referring to the main north-south highway dissecting the Netherlands. "I'm more worried about security at Schiphol. I heard that the lines are long and slow since yesterday. I'm having Marta give the cargo line a call to see if they can have someone meet you at the departure terminal. Maybe you can avoid the lines. Don't know if the cargo airline will hold the plane for you, but if needed, I'll call them."

"Thanks, boss. I'm glad you're connected around here," Ethan said.

Ethan grew quiet, thinking of the long flight ahead of him and what he had to do once he landed in Mexico. It was going to be a very long day, indeed.

"Ethan, is there anything you need before getting on the plane?" Henrik asked.

"Well, yes, now that you mention it. I was going to buy a cell phone today so that I could communicate with my son and the private investigator. I don't know how the phone system works in Mexico so I'd rather have my own phone."

"You don't have to buy one, use my private cell phone." Henrik reached into his glove box and grabbed a Motorola cell phone and charge cord. "My wife and two sons are the only people that have the number so all

I need to do is tell them to call my work phone. It's all programmed for international calling. Use it as much as you need and just give it back when this is all over."

"Thanks, boss. This is very generous," Ethan said as he took the phone and charge cord from Henrik.

Henrik's business cell phone rang.

"Henrik here," he said. "Hi Marta, what did you find out?"

Ethan watched his boss nod his head as his administrator talked on the other end of the phone.

"Thanks, Marta. Great job," Henrik said before disconnecting. He looked at Ethan in the rearview mirror. "The charter company will have someone meet you at the entrance to the departure terminal. They can take you through immigration and security without standing in line. Have your passports ready and just follow his lead."

"Whew! That will help big time!" said Pete.

"Tell Marta thanks for me," Ethan replied. "Who the hell could say no to her?"

"Not me! She'd kick my ass!" Pete said.

The three men rode in relative silence for over an hour until the traffic stopped dead on the A2. Ethan glanced at his watch as the minutes slipped away.

"What's going on?" Ethan said, looking at Henrik.

"Probably an accident. Usually is. This is not good." Henrik glanced at his watch and then at Ethan and Pete. "It's noon already and we're half an hour from the airport with no traffic. Not looking good."

Ethan gazed out the window and saw a large windmill, the blades slowly moving in a circle, two cows munching grass in the field around it. He had never stopped to look at the Dutch countryside before, but it was pleasant, idyllic. A bicyclist came pedaling slowly down the frontage road.

"That guy on the bicycle will make it before we do," Ethan said absently. He glanced at his watch, his stomach starting to tighten again.

Finally, at twelve thirty, after twenty five minutes at a dead stop, the traffic began to move. Slowly at first, then picking up speed.

Ethan shot a worried glance at Henrik. "We're not going to make it, boss."

"I'll call Marta and have her call the charter company to tell them we'll be late," Henrik said. "They don't like it when passengers are late."

As Henrik called his secretary, Ethan glanced at Pete in the front seat. He was sleeping, completely unaware of the circumstances. *Damn guy can sleep anywhere.*

"Okay, Marta will call them. It's going to be close, so be ready to move fast when we get to the airport," Henrik said. He glanced over at Pete. "You'd better wake him up."

Ethan shook Pete's shoulder. "Pete. Wake up."

Pete slowly opened his eyes. "We there?"

Ethan smiled weakly. "No, about a half an hour away, but we'll have to hustle when we do get there."

"Okay, wake me up when we get there." Pete closed his eyes again, falling to sleep immediately.

"Wish I could do that," Ethan said, shaking his head. "Sometimes I wonder if he has a care in the world."

Henrik cleared his throat. "Ethan, I want to again apologize for bringing up that subject we discussed this morning. I should have thought before opening my mouth."

"It's okay, Henrik. It was a shock, but I have to face the possibility," Ethan replied, looking at Henrik in the rear-view mirror and seeing the worried look on his face. Ethan had seen the look many times before. Ethan turned and looked out the window as his stomach began its incessant churning.

"Do you want me to call anyone for you, let them know where you're headed?" Henrik said, turning to look at Ethan.

"It would be great if you could call my son on his cell phone," Ethan said . He wrote the phone number down and gave it to Henrik. "Please tell him I'll be out of communication until I land in Mexico and that I'll call him then. And can you give him my cell phone number? Thanks again for letting me use it. It will make life much easier once we land in Mexico. It's the middle of the night in California so you might want to wait to call him until later tonight."

"I'll call Charlie tonight before I leave the office."

Riding the rest of the way in silence, the men finally saw the sign for the airport. Ethan poked Pete in the shoulder. "We're here, Pete. Get ready to move."

Henrik took the turnoff to Schiphol Airport and they pulled up to the departure terminal exactly at one o'clock. He put the Audi into park and got out. Ethan and Pete were already retrieving their bags from the trunk.

"You have to move fast, so get going," Henrik said.

Henrik shook Pete's hand. "Have a safe journey, my friend. Be careful in Mexico."

"Thanks for everything Henrik," Pete said. "Take care of Rob for us."

Henrik nodded and turned to Ethan. Ethan reached out to shake Henrik's hand but the big Dutchman grabbed his shoulders and gave him a hug, something he had never done before. Feeling the emotion building, Ethan turned around and began walking quickly towards the terminal. As he was about to go through the revolving door into the terminal, he heard a shout behind him.

"Ethan!"

He turned and stared at his boss standing next to the black Audi.

Henrik had his fist raised. "Get those sons-of-bitches!"

PART TWO

CHAPTER 20

The two Americans spotted the man with the sign as soon as they entered the departure terminal. Ethan and Pete walked quickly to him.

"Hi," Pete said to the short, blond man. "We're Paxton and Cruz."

"I am Arnold," the man said. "We have to hurry. Let's go."

Arnold took off in a sprint through the crowded terminal. Ethan and Pete hurried after him, carrying their suitcases, their computer bags slung over their shoulders. They had to run just to keep up with the short Dutchman, all the while dodging other passengers. They were both soaked in sweat by the time they stopped at a small office next to the main immigration area.

"Your passports, please," said Arnold, who took them and gave them to an older man who had stepped out of the office. The man looked at them, glanced at Ethan and Pete carefully. The man said something to Arnold in Dutch, pointing to the sweat on the two American's faces.

Arnold explained to the man in Dutch, then turned to Ethan and Pete. "He wants to know why you are sweating," he said with a grin. "I explained to him that we are late for the flight."

After glancing at the two sweating men one more time, the man stamped the passports, waving them through the line. Once on the other side of the immigration line they began running again.

They looked at the long, winding security line, which snaked through the departure lounge, and realized that they never would have made it without Arnold's help. Ten minutes later he stopped at another small office next to the security area. A man unlocked the door and motioned them into the office and closed the door. He asked them several questions and had them open their suitcases and computer bags. After looking at their passports he told Arnold to take them out another door into a private hallway which skirted past the main security area. They found themselves on the other side of security looking back at some very angry people staring at them.

Arnold then began running down the carpeted terminal past gate after gate, with Ethan and Pete huffing and puffing after him, still carrying their suitcases. At least twenty gates later, after dodging many passengers along the way, they finally stopped at the last gate at the end of the terminal. It was marked "Holland Air Cargo." It had no gate number.

"This man will take you to the airplane," Arnold said, breathing heavily.

Before the Americans could thank him, Arnold was gone, off to his next emergency.

"Mister Paxton and Cruz?" said the man at the gate.

Out of breath, they just nodded. The man lead Ethan and Pete through the gate, down some stairs and out onto the tarmac, where a 747-200 was parked. The cargo doors were closed and it was evident that it was ready to depart. The man pointed to the metal stairs. Ethan and Pete saw a man standing at the top of the stairs, frowning and looking at his watch. They scrambled up the stairs, lugging their heavy suitcases, sweat pouring from them like water off of a duck.

"Give your suitcases to the man near the stairs," the red-headed man said sternly as they reached the top. "And get up the stairs quickly."

Another man took their suitcases and pointed to a ladder, which was straight up and down. Ethan looked quickly around the cargo hold and was surprised to see several horses munching on hay.

Ethan glanced at Pete, who was bent over in exhaustion. "You okay, buddy?"

"Damn I need a drink," Pete said, taking deep breaths, sweat cascading down his face.

"Almost there, Pete," Ethan said, patting his friend on the back.

They put their computer bags on their shoulders and climbed up the ladder. Once they were in the bubble, they saw comfortable-looking seats configured two by two in ten rows. Three people were sitting towards the rear of the cabin, an older couple and a younger woman. The couple was staring at them, frowns on their faces.

"Take any seat and buckle up and get ready for departure," the male flight attendant said, the same man who had met them at the top of the stairs. He was still frowning.

"No champagne, no orange juice, no heated nuts?" Pete said to Ethan, still breathing hard.

They took seats in the second row and buckled themselves in, the sweat streaming down their faces. They both took deep breaths, trying to slow their breathing down. Within a few minutes the big 747-200 began to back away from the terminal.

Pete's laughter broke the tension.

"And to think we gave up first class for this!" Pete said, in between gulps of air.

"It's not too bad up here, but those horses down below might bring us a nasty surprise when the plane takes off," Ethan said, glancing at his watch. Twenty five minutes past one. They had run the entire course of the airport in less than twenty five minutes.

He closed his eyes and took several deep breaths as the jumbo jet gradually taxied to the main runway. A few minutes later the giant plane began lumbering down the runway. No warning from the pilot, no admonition from the flight attendants to ready for takeoff. It took the entire runway for the big jet to begin lifting, but once it did it made a smooth, steady climb into the Dutch sky. It banked left, giving them a good view of Amsterdam, and then was immediately out over the North Sea.

"Gotta love these 747's," Ethan said, his breathing finally returning to normal. "I've been on probably a hundred of them and they are the smoothest airplanes in the sky. Loud, but smooth."

"We must be really loaded down because it took everything they had to lift this sucker into the air," Pete responded. "Maybe we put it over the weight limit."

Suddenly a smell came wafting up from the cargo hold below. It was the unmistakable smell of horse manure, powerful enough to cause both Ethan and Pete to hold their noses.

"Good God!" exclaimed Pete. "Do we have to put up with that the entire flight?"

The flight attendant poked his head around the seat in front of them. "Just at take-off," he said, smiling. "Horses get very nervous at take-off but settle down after we level off." Obviously enjoying their discomfort, he turned back around.

Ethan and Pete looked at each other and shrugged their shoulders, broad grins crossing their faces when they looked at each other holding their nose. They each stifled a laugh, thinking about the absurdity of the situation.

After the aircraft leveled off, Ethan saw the red seatbelt light go out and watched as the flight attendant unbuckled his seatbelt and stood up. He turned to them and smiled.

"My name is Jan. Sorry I was so abrupt when you boarded. We were ordered to hold the plane for you and I had to listen, and smell, the horses down below while waiting. I guess this is what you Americans call payback," he said, a big grin on his face.

He was a tall man with brownish red hair. He had a thick Dutch accent, but spoke English well, and had a blue uniform on, just like a regular flight attendant.

"Are you gentlemen thirsty? Orange juice, champagne, heated nuts?" Jan said, smiling at Pete.

Pete laughed. "Ouch. Nice to meet you, Jan. And, hell yes we're thirsty!"

"What would you gentlemen like to drink?"

Ethan looked at Pete and they both smiled. "White wine for myself, and some nose plugs," said Ethan.

"Same here," said Pete.

"Coming up, except for the nose plugs," Jan said.

Jan walked back to the other three passengers and began talking to them in English. Ethan looked behind him at the others who were eight rows back. The man and woman seemed to be in their mid to late fifties, attractive and well-dressed. Across the aisle from the couple was an extremely attractive woman who looked to be in her late twenties. She had long black hair tied up in a ponytail. Ethan was immediately taken by her beauty. He felt his face turn red as she smiled at him before she turned to talk to Jan.

"Wonder who they are?" Ethan said. "Nice looking couple."

"Couple my ass," Pete said, looking back at the woman behind them. "You're looking at the gorgeous thing sitting across from them. Don't try to bullshit a bull shitter, son. Think she'd want to sit up here with someone more here own age?"

Ethan glanced at Pete. "She's probably their daughter. Don't embarrass me, Pete," he said, shaking his head.

Pete took one more look and turned back around, grinning. "Can't wait for that glass of wine."

Ethan glanced at his watch again. It was six thirty in the morning in Mexico City, which meant it was four thirty in California and Tijuana. This thought jolted him back to reality. He began to think about what would transpire over the next eleven hours while he was in the air. Suddenly, he didn't care about wine, food or anything on the airplane.

He thought about the chaos and tragedy in New York that seemed so far away now. About Jake Delgado and whether he had made a mistake hiring him. About his son Charlie, wondering if he and Jake would be able to work together. But most of all he thought about his baby girl and the unimaginable things she must be going through. Ethan closed his eyes and remembered the priest in the cathedral that morning. He said another silent prayer.

CHAPTER 21

"Shut the damn door!" Jake roared as sunlight flooded the dark bar. Through the blinding light he saw a young kid at the door. "Shut the goddamned door, kid!"

"Sorry," the kid said quietly, blinking his eyes in the darkness. "I'm looking for someone."

"Who might that be, son," Tiny the bartender asked.

"Jake Delgado."

"Who the hell wants to know?" growled Jake from the end of the bar.

"Uh, Charlie. Charlie Paxton." The kid squinted his eyes as he peered down the bar, trying to see who was growling at him.

Jake looked at the clock behind the bar, which said 9:05 a.m.

"You're late, kid," he said.

"You Jake Delgado?" Charlie replied.

"Yeah, but don't tell the big guy behind the bar because I owe him money," Jake said, looking at Tiny. "Tiny, me and the kid are goin' to the back of the bar. C'mon, kid."

"Stop calling me kid," Charlie said loudly.

Jake peered at Charlie Paxton through the darkened bar. He was tall, much taller than he expected, and thin. He had brownish blond hair on a good-looking face. He didn't look anything like Jake remembered his dad looking, but that was over twenty years ago.

"Oh, excuse me. Please join me in the rear of the establishment," Jake said sarcastically, grunting as he got off his barstool. He arched his back, trying to shake off the soreness, and trudged to a table in the back of the bar. Damn kids these days. No sense of humor.

Jake watched as Charlie slowly walked to the back of the bar and stood in front of him.

"Sit down, ki . . . uh, Charlie."

Charlie scraped an old wooden chair across the floor and sat down.

"Damn, kid! Easy on the noise." Jake quietly pulled another chair out from the table and sat down with the back of the chair in front of him. He looked at Charlie for a few seconds. "How old are you?"

"Nineteen."

"Hell, you're the same age your dad was when we were in Japan together. I don't remember your dad being so damn tall, though."

Charlie just stared at him, a slight smirk on his face.

Jake felt him staring at his scar, so decided to get it over with.

"You wanna touch it?"

"Touch what?"

Jake ran his finger down his scar. "This."

"No."

"Well then, take a picture and stop staring at the damn thing."

Charlie looked away for a second, but then looked back at Jake. "How'd you get it?"

"None of your business," Jake snarled. "You heard anything more about your sister?"

"No."

"Heard from your dad?"

"No."

"You always talk this much?"

"No."

Jake chuckled to himself, thinking about Ethan Paxton. His son was cut from the same cloth, except the kid didn't smile nearly as much as his old man. But then, he didn't have much to smile about right now.

"Well, Charlie, we've got a lot to talk about. Want something to drink?"

"Yeah, a beer."

"I meant coffee, soda? It's nine o'clock in the morning, son." Jake raised his cup of coffee and showed it to Charlie.

"Corona."

Jake looked at Charlie and smiled. The kid had an edge to him. "Want a lime with that, son?"

Charlie shrugged his shoulders.

"Tiny, bring the kid a Corona. With a lime!" Jake yelled to the bartender.

"He got ID?" Tiny yelled from the bar.

"Just bring the kid a Corona, damn it." Jake looked at Charlie and said softly, "I have pull in this joint."

Charlie looked around the dark, smelly bar. "Yeah, I bet."

Jake stared at Charlie and shook his head. Another smartass.

"My dad said you drank a lot. Doesn't look like it," Charlie said.

"Yeah, I drink a lot, but right now we have a lot of ground to cover and not much time to do it. Your dad didn't tell me you were a smart ass."

Tiny brought the Corona over, with lime, and loudly plopped it on the table in front of Charlie, all the while staring at Jake.

"Thanks Tiny. Put it on my tab," said Jake.

Tiny grunted, "Yeah, right."

Jake looked at Charlie and watched him guzzle half the bottle. Jake shook his head and drank his coffee.

"You ready, son?"

Charlie shrugged his shoulders again and took another swig of the Corona.

Jake leaned forward on the table, his head a foot from Charlie. "You got a problem with me, son? 'Cause I'm starting to have one with you."

Charlie stared at him, then let loose. "Yeah, I do actually. You work out of a bar, you're a drunk and you got kicked off the police force. Why my dad hired you I have no idea!"

Jake glared at Charlie, the scar getting red from the blood rushing to his face. He began to say something, then stopped. He leaned back and took another drink of his coffee. He smiled at Charlie.

"All true, son. All true. I don't know why your dad hired me either. Believe me, I've got a million other things I'd rather be doing—"

"What, getting drunk?"

"Listen, son—"

"Stop calling me son! I'm not your son! And I'm not a kid! My name's Charlie!"

Jake looked at the young man sitting in front of him and saw himself at nineteen. Ready to take on the world, pissed off at everybody. Just as Jake had reasons when he was nineteen, Charlie had his own reasons. Jake backed off and drank the rest his coffee. He put it down on the table softly, turned his chair around and leaned back.

"Charlie, I'm sorry. I know how you must be feeling right now. You've been through some rough shit the past twenty four hours and probably haven't slept since all this happened. Your dad called me last night because he didn't know who else to call. If he had a choice, I doubt if you and I would be sitting here right now. But he didn't have a choice and he asked me to help him, so here we are. I have a ton of respect for your dad, even though I haven't seen him in over twenty years. I wouldn't do this for just any Joe Blow off the street. But for your dad, and for you, and especially for your sister, I'm willing to bust my ass. Can we work together to get your sister back?"

Charlie's shoulders relaxed, the fire went out of his eyes. His lips began to tremble and tears formed in his eyes. "Can you help us get Molly back?"

Jake saw the pain in Charlie's face. "Charlie, I'll go to hell and back to get Molly home."

"Why?"

"Because I knew your dad and know what kind of man he is. I see a lot of him in you. And for the first time in many years, someone needs me. That's why."

Charlie's lip stopped trembling, he wiped the tears from his eyes, and for the first time he smiled. "Then what are we waiting for?"

Jake smiled back at Charlie, ordered himself and Charlie a cup of coffee, and pulled out his notebook. "Now we're talkin'!"

"How did you get it?" Charlie said, pointing to Jake's scar.

"Funny enough, I got it right here in this bar. I'll tell you the story sometime. Now let's get to work. You got a picture of Molly?"

Charlie pulled his wallet out of his back pocket and took out a small school picture. "This was her freshman picture from last spring."

Jake looked at the olive-skinned girl with the big, dark eyes and dark flowing hair. "She's a beautiful girl. Looks nothing like you or your dad. Stepsister?"

"Adopted. But she looks like my mom. My mom is . . . was Hispanic."

Jake looked at Charlie intently. "Your mom's . . . ?"

"Dead. Yeah, she's dead." The tremble returned to his lips, the tears to his eyes.

"Damn, I'm sorry. I didn't know."

Charlie wiped away a tear. "She died six months ago. Cancer."

Jake looked down at his coffee and shook his head. When he looked up he saw Charlie staring at him.

"Don't you dare feel sorry for me! Just help me get Molly back!"

Jake nodded his head. "We'll get her back, Charlie."

A single tear ran down Charlie's cheek and he wiped it away. "So now what?"

Jake cleared his throat. "Okay, you said that Molly was adopted, that she's Hispanic?"

"Yeah, so?"

"Hmm." Jake wrote in his notebook, then said "This may add another wrinkle to things. You have any other pictures? Maybe some full body pictures?"

"No, not with me. What do you mean 'a new wrinkle'?"

"Well, she's a Latina, or at least looks Latina. She's not blond and blue-eyed like most American girls. I don't know if this will mean anything, but it could."

"Like how?"

"It could possibly help her or it could hinder her. All depends on her kidnappers. Do you have your cell phone?"

Charlie pulled it out of its holder and handed it to Jake.

"That's okay. I want you to play Molly's voicemail for me."

As Jake listened to the voicemail he watched Charlie's face. He saw the pain in the boy's face, the agony when his sister yelled 'Charlie!'.

"Play it again," Jake said. He listened intently for anything being said. He heard men shouting in Spanish, but couldn't make out the words. "Has anyone translated this?" he asked Charlie.

"Yeah. They're telling them to be quiet and get out of the car. Hurry! Stuff like that."

"You speak Spanish?"

"Yeah, a little."

"Play it one more time."

This time Jake listened for the background noise. He heard the car doors open, scuffling of the girls being dragged out of the car, and then a sound that was unmistakable to him, because he'd heard it many times. *Whack!* The sound of someone getting hit in the face.

"What was that? What happened right there?" he asked Charlie.

Charlie looked at him and hung his head. "I think it was Missus Caldwell getting hit," he said.

"Who's Missus Caldwell?"

"The teacher driving the car."

"How old is she?"

"I don't know, maybe thirty, thirty five."

"Attractive?"

"I guess, for an older lady. A little on the heavy side."

This made Jake chuckle to himself. To a nineteen year old, thirty five would be old. "Why do you think it was her?"

"Well, Mister Sizemore said that she was probably resisting, trying to protect the girls. I don't know if it was her or not, but I didn't hear her voice on Molly's voicemail."

"What about the other two girls. Were they friends of Molly's?"

"Yeah, one of them, Cindy, was her best friend. The other one was a friend but not real close."

"Good looking girls?"

"Cindy was pretty cute, long blond hair and stuff. The other one, Jenny, was a little pudgy and real quiet."

"Fat?"

"No, not fat. Just a little heavy. Nice face though. Why are you asking what they look like?"

Jake glanced at Charlie, hesitating. "The prettier they are, the harder it's going to be for them." He looked at Charlie for his reaction but didn't get any.

"Has anyone talked to you about what the possibilities are?"

"What do you mean?"

Jake took a deep breath and let it out. "Everyone thinks this is a kidnapping for ransom, right?"

"Yeah, what else could it be?"

"When teenage girls get abducted it could be a kidnapping for ransom, but more than likely it's a kidnapping for another reason." Jake looked at Charlie again. The boy was frowning, waiting for him to go on. "You've heard of human trafficking—sex trafficking?"

Charlie's eyes got big and Jake saw the fear invade his mind.

"It's only a possibility, but the longer we go without a ransom demand, the bigger this possibility becomes. We have to proceed with this as the primary possibility until we hear otherwise."

"What will happen . . . I mean, Molly . . . ." Charlie stammered, not knowing what to say.

"Charlie, that's why time is so important now. We have to find Molly and the other girls before they can be moved. If we get a ransom demand before we find them then we'll change our tactics, but until then we move as fast as we can. Understand?"

Charlie nodded in stunned silence.

"Okay, what about at the camp where you were building homes. Did anything happen there that was unusual? Any suspicious people hanging around?"

"I don't think so, but I was so busy I didn't really notice. Kids from the local town came in and out of the work site all the time. Most of them pretty young. But, I do remember this one kid that kept hanging around. He was older than the others, and he acted much older. You know, like he was looking for something. He asked a lot of questions."

"Did you tell anyone about him?"

"No, I didn't think much about it at the time. Like I said, I was always too busy to think about much."

"Do you remember his name? Would you recognize him if you saw him?"

"I don't think I ever heard his name, but I'd definitely recognize him."

"Okay, that's a lead. Once I get across the border I'll drive over to your camp site and fish around. It had to start there."

"Okay. When do we go?"

"Whoa, wait a minute. Who said you were going? This is going to be dangerous and I don't think your dad would appreciate me taking you across the border."

"You have to take me! How else are you going to know where to go? And how would you recognize the kid I saw?"

Jake sat back in his chair, took a swig of coffee and thought about this. Charlie had a point. Jake would be fishing in the dark without someone with him that knew the camp and the kid.

"What about your principal, or one of the other adults. Did they see this kid?"

"I don't know, but who cares? I did! You gotta take me with you, Jake!"

"Okay. Okay. We have a lot to do before we get to that point. I need to talk to your principal and others in your school group, then work on getting across the border. No promises, kid." Jake winced when he said the word 'kid' but couldn't take it back. He looked at Charlie, waiting for his youthful wrath.

"Okay, let's go!" exclaimed Charlie, suddenly excited.

Jake looked at the kid stand up and head for the door. *Christ, what did he get himself into?*

"Hey, don't forget your cell phone," Jake said, groaning as he got up from the hard wooden chair. "And give your cell number to Tiny."

"Tiny, you can reach me on the kid's number. I'll be working on his case for the next few days."

"Congratulations," said Tiny. "Glad to see you working again."

"You don't know the half of it. And if anyone calls me here, give them the kid's number," Jake said as he and Charlie walked out into the blinding sunlight.

CHAPTER 22

Natalia jerked awake when she heard the knock on the door. She was lying on the empty mattress, trying to get some much needed sleep. She jumped up and ran to the door, glancing back at the three girls, who were still out. She knocked twice, the signal that everything was okay.

The dead bolt squealed against the rust as it slid open. The door slid open slowly, showering the dark room with light. Natalia hid her eyes with her hands as the light blinded her.

"How are our little *chicas*?" said Angel Rojas as he sauntered into the room. Two men were behind him, carrying a limp body. The men dragged the body of the teacher to the empty mattress and threw her down roughly. Natalia gasped at the sight of the woman. Her face was unrecognizable, covered in blood, with both eyes black and swollen shut.

"What did you do to her?" she said, looking at Angel.

"She was a fighter, so we had to rough her up a little," he said, smiling. "She's worth nothing to us, so what does it matter?"

"What do you mean she's worth nothing? She can bring money just like the others."

Angel threw his head back and laughed. "Not now! She's too old and too fat—and now, too ugly." Angel looked at Natalia with scorn in his eyes, daring her to argue with him.

Natalia glared at him but said nothing.

"Clean her up before the girls wake up. And keep them quiet! If I hear one scream I will send my *muchachos* in here to take care of them." He smiled, showing his gleaming white teeth.

Natalia looked at the other two men standing behind Angel. Cesar was smiling and nodding, showing his gold teeth. The other one was looking at the young girls lying at their feet, lust evident in his eyes.

"*Okay*, Angel. I'll keep them quiet," she said.

"*Bueno, mi amor.* It will be happening very soon. We have to keep the *chicas primo* for our customer."

"Customer? What do you mean customer?" she said, startled.

Angel smiled again and patted Natalia softly on the cheek. "Awe, my little mama hen is getting attached to her brood?" He grabbed her by the hair and pulled her to him, kissing her roughly. "Don't get too attached, my love. Your little chicks will be gone by tomorrow night."

She pulled back and began to wipe her mouth, but instead lowered her hand. "What do you mean sold? What about the ransom demands, like we talked about?"

"That is one option, but I like the other option better. Much cleaner and less risky."

"But you said . . . ."

Angel glared at her, his eyes blazing. He grabbed her hair again and forced her to her knees. "Ayy! Don't you see? We would be taking a big risk if we try to get a ransom. The American *federales* would make our lives hell, and then they would force the Mexican *federales* to hunt us down. We would never see the money. The other way, we sell them without anyone knowing who we are. They just vanish!"

She moaned and grabbed his hand. He let loose of her hair and backed away. Natalia glanced over at Molly.

Angel saw her look at the olive-skinned girl, her black hair splayed on the mattress. He reached down and brushed the girl's hair, then turned her face upwards so he could see it more closely. He brushed the back of his hand over her cheeks, feeling the flawless, smooth skin.

"*Muy bonita.*" He looked up at Natalia and, still running his hand over Molly's cheek, said, "You take care of this one. She will bring us the most."

Natalia wanted to reach out and scratch his eyes out. How dare he touch her!

Angel stood up, still looking at the dark-haired girl. "*Muy bonita.* She looks like a *latina.*" He looked at the two men, who were staring at the girl, smiling. "*¿Latina. No?*"

"*Sí, jefe,*" they said in unison. "*Latina.*"

Angel looked back at Natalia. "Have you spoken with them yet?"

"A little," she said. "But they were too drugged to say much."

"When they wake up, let me know. I want to talk to this one," he said, pointing at Molly. "She is very interesting." He smiled as he gazed over the girl's body.

Natalia nodded, not looking at Angel.

"I have neglected you. Do you want to . . . ?" He moved his hips up and back suggestively, smiling at Natalia.

Natalia didn't look at him. He repulsed her now. "No, I have to clean up the woman."

Angel stood and stared at her with his piercing jet black eyes of pure evil. "Do you not love me anymore?" he pouted with a fake frown. He moved closer to her, grabbing her by the throat. "Do you love me?" he whispered, his mouth next to her ear.

She cringed and tried to move his hand away. "*Sí*, I love you."

His grip on her throat tightened. "Do you love me?" he whispered again.

Natalia's eyes grew big as her breathing was cut off. "*Sí*, Angel. I love you," she said, gagging.

Angel loosened his grip and rubbed her cheek gently. "When this is over we can go away together, just you and I. Would you like that?"

Natalia glared at him, the hatred oozing out of her. She looked away. "*Sí*."

He stopped smiling and stepped back. He glanced at the dark-haired girl again, then back to Natalia.

"*Vamos, amigos*," he said to the other two men.

The men walked out the door ahead of Angel. He walked to the door and looked back at Natalia. "You know, she looks like you. She could be your long lost daughter." He laughed at this, a mocking laugh, designed to hurt. He stepped out of the room and the heavy door was rolled shut, the dead bolt sliding into place.

How she hated the man. He had turned into this wild animal that she despised, just like all men. They use you and then cast you away. He didn't care about her. Why didn't she realize this before she got caught up in this mess? These poor girls, their lives forever ruined. She looked at Molly. *Angel said she looked just like me. She could be my daughter*. Natalia bent down and brushed the girl's hair, caressed her face as a mother would her daughter. She is so beautiful, so innocent. At that moment, Natalia knew what she had to do. She had to protect these girls from their fate, from a life worse than death. It was her calling, her destiny. She would find a way to get them out. Especially Molly. She would save her and then she would have the daughter back that she gave up long ago. They would go far away and live the rest of their lives in happiness.

Natalia bent down and kissed the girl on the cheek. "I will protect you, little one. We will escape from these animals and run away. Far away."

She continued to stroke Molly's hair, humming softly.

CHAPTER 23

The turbulence woke him up but the smell kept him awake. Ethan pinched his nose with his fingers. The turbulence had gotten the horses all riled up and nervous, he guessed. He'd been sleeping for several hours after they were served a big, mostly tasteless, meal by Jan. Several glasses of wine put them over the edge and both he and Pete had slowly drifted off around the same time.

He looked at his watch, which was set to Mexico City time. Almost noon. That would make it ten a.m. in California. He looked over at Pete, who was still sleeping and oblivious to the smell and bouncing of the airplane.

"Please make sure your seatbelt is fastened," said Jan, who was walking by holding the seatbacks as he walked. "And your friend's seatbelt, too."

Jan had a glum look on his face. Probably just woke up himself, Ethan thought. He watched as the flight attendant walked back to the other three passengers to check on them. Ethan lifted Pete's blanket and checked his seatbelt. It was attached. Another jolt of turbulence made him tighten his own seat belt.

He opened the window shade and looked outside. They were headed southwest from Europe, across the Atlantic Ocean. He looked back towards where they had come from and saw shards of sunset far in the distance. It was six p.m. in Den Bosch. Henrik and Rob would be having dinner together right about now. He smiled when he thought of Rob trying to talk Henrik into going drinking later on. Two immovable objects, Rob and Henrik.

Still staring out the window, his thoughts turned to what lay ahead in Mexico. They were about six hours from arrival in Mexico City, which was in the middle part of the country. He knew that several major cities, Guadalajara, Monterrey, and Chihuahua, were in the north. He'd try to get a flight into Tijuana as soon as they arrived, but would have to find a flight to one of those other cities if they couldn't fly direct to Tijuana. Probably have to rent a car and drive all night, which was dangerous anytime, but driving at night was almost suicidal.

His thoughts turned to Jake and Charlie. They should have met by now. Did they hit it off or would Charlie refuse to work with him? Charlie wasn't too happy about hiring Jake and he could sometimes have a hot temper. From what he remembered about Jake, so did he. He would call Charlie as soon as they landed in Mexico City.

Jake. The stranger that he had brought into his personal nightmare. He wasn't technically a stranger, but he might as well be. He hadn't seen Jake in over twenty years. Jake was a year older and had many more worldly experiences than Ethan when they first met on the football practice field at the Air Force base in Japan. Ethan had only been in country for a week, arriving in early September in 1978. Just a year before that Ethan had been the star running back on his high school football team, a pimply-faced kid.

Jake was the quarterback on the squadron team, a tall, husky redhead with arms like tree trunks. He could've been a lineman or tight end, but he had a cannon for an arm. He was at least four inches taller than Ethan and about the same difference in width. They won the base championship that year with an undefeated record. Jake and he became good friends and spent many nights together in the bars surrounding the base. Jake had gotten into several fights, usually ending them with one punch from those tree trunk arms. He got busted a few months later when he put an officer in the base hospital. Ethan wasn't with him when it happened, and he never saw Jake again.

Then he thought of Molly. His beautiful daughter, so innocent and trusting. *What nightmare is she living right now? Is she alive?* Ethan shook the thought out of his head, refusing to think about all the possibilities that might be facing his daughter. He had to keep his focus on moving forward, on getting to Tijuana. He couldn't allow himself to get bogged down with pity or remorse. He had to keep moving, and hoping. He tried to fight off the fear that was growing in him, but how long could he continue to fight it? He felt helpless, sitting in a flying sardine can half way over the Atlantic, his daughter . . . .

A loud yawn suddenly yanked him out of his thoughts. He looked over at Pete, who was stretching and pinching his nose.

"Holy shit! Who woke up the horses? Whew!" Pete said, waving his hand in front of his nose. "What the hell got into them? I know what came out of them!"

"You missed the best part, old buddy. It's just about gone now," Ethan said, chuckling.

"Glad I slept through it, then. The gift that just keeps on giving," he laughed. "How long you been awake?"

"Not long. We had some pretty good turbulence earlier but you slept through that, too."

"Hey, that's how I keep my girlish figure and good looks. I can sleep through anything."

"That's the truth," Ethan said, smiling.

He wondered if Pete had a serious bone in his body sometimes. Everything was a joke or punch line to him. Many times he had wished he had the ability to shake things off like Pete, but Ethan was a worrier, a thinker, always analyzing things. Sometimes this stole the enjoyment from his experiences, but not when Pete Cruz was around.

"What time is it?" Pete asked.

"Around noon in Mexico City," Ethan answered. "We've been flying for about five hours. Another six to go."

"Almost half way already. Not bad. When do we eat?"

"You'll have to ask Jan. He's back there with the other people."

"Well, I have to see a man about a dog."

Ethan watched Pete get up, wobble just a bit, and trudge towards the bathroom in the front. Ethan turned and looked at the back of the plane. The couple was still talking to the flight attendant. Suddenly, the older man looked up at Ethan and locked on his gaze, and then turned back to Jan. Jan turned and looked at Ethan, a serious look on his face, and then turned back around when he saw Ethan looking at them.

Wonder what that was about? Ethan turned back towards the front when he heard Pete return.

"Okay, now I'm ready to eat," Pete said as he plopped into his seat next to Ethan.

Before Ethan could respond he saw Jan standing next to them. "Mister Paxton, the gentleman in the back would like to pay his respects. Would you mind following me to the rear?"

"Pay his respects?" Pete said.

"Yes, he knows of Mister Paxton's circumstances and would like to talk to him. Mister Paxton?"

"How the hell does he know of my circumstances?" asked Ethan, a little annoyed.

"When Mister van Rijk booked these seats for you and Mister Cruz he explained your situation and the urgency of you getting to Mexico. This is a charter flight and Mister Calderon has purchased part of it."

"Oh, okay," Ethan said, softening. "Sure, I'd be glad to meet him."

"Mister Cruz, you can join us too, if you'd like."

"Thanks Jan. Think I will."

Ethan and Pete got up and followed Jan to the last row of seats where the couple was sitting. The man stood up when he saw them coming. He was well-dressed in dark slacks and a white shirt, with a bolero tie around his neck. Grayish wavy hair was on top of a very well-tanned face.

"Mister Paxton, a pleasure to meet you," he said in a heavy Spanish accent. His English was excellent, if a bit formal. He held out his hand to Ethan.

"A pleasure to meet you, too, Mister Calderon," Ethan said, shaking his hand. "Please call me Ethan. This is my friend, Pete Cruz."

Mister Calderon shook Pete's hand. "My pleasure, Pete. And please call me Arturo." He turned to the woman sitting next to him. "This is my wife, Alexandria."

Ethan and Pete nodded to the attractive older woman, who was still seated and did not offer her hand. She had a serious look on her face, as though she and her husband had had an argument or disagreement. She was also well-tanned and elegant, even after flying for five hours. Ethan was impressed with her beauty, especially for an older woman.

"And this is my daughter, Victoria," he said, pointing to the younger woman across the aisle.

Ethan turned and was immediately struck by the younger woman's natural beauty. She was nearly as tall as Ethan and dressed in white slacks and a loose-fitting sweater. Her skin was flawless and her smile electrified him. He felt his face becoming flushed.

"Hello, Victoria. It's a pleasure to meet you," he said nervously.

"The pleasure is mine, Mister Paxton," she replied, shaking his hand and bowing slightly.

Her touch sent a jolt through him. "Please, call me Ethan."

"Hi Victoria. Pete Cruz," Pete said, pushing Ethan out of the way while holding out his hand. "You're quite beautiful."

"Oh, thank you," she said, an embarrassed look on her face.

Ethan stared at Pete. *Don't embarrass me, Cruz.*

"And call me anything you want, but I'll answer to Pete," he said, smiling at Ethan.

Victoria laughed. "Okay. Ethan and Pete. Please call me Vicki."

They heard someone clear his throat behind them. Ethan turned to look at Arturo Calderon, who was looking at them with amusement.

"Victoria always seems to draw the attention, especially from the younger men," he said, laughing. He smiled at his daughter, who waved her hand at him.

Ethan shot an embarrassed look at Victoria. "Jan just told me that I have you to thank for letting us tag along on this charter," he said to Arturo.

"I purchased just a part of the charter. Those are my horses below that have caused you such discomfort," he said, smiling. "We are returning from several quarter horse shows in Europe. I'm afraid I didn't make the decision to let you ride along. That was the charter company." Arturo put his hand on Ethan's shoulder. "But I'm glad we could help you."

"Well, thank you, in spite of the horses."

Everyone laughed.

"I was made aware of your circumstances by Jan just a few minutes ago." Calderon took his hand off of Ethan's shoulder. "I hope you don't mind him telling us. It must be heartbreaking what you are going through."

"It's very difficult, yes."

"I know there are despicable people in my country, as there are in all countries. I hope you find your daughter and bring her home safely."

"Thank you," Ethan said.

"How are you getting to Tijuana once we arrive in Mexico City?" Vicki asked him.

He turned to face her. "I'll have to see if I can get a flight to Tijuana when we land," Ethan said. "Everything happened so fast we didn't have a chance to do much planning, unfortunately."

"That could be a problem," she said. "Because of the terrorist attacks in the U.S., they have restricted many flights into Tijuana."

"Why's that?" Pete asked.

"Because the airport is so close to the U.S-Mexico border, the U.S. government has asked Mexico to restrict flights into Tijuana and other border cities, I suppose to eliminate the threat of hijackers flying into the U.S."

"I was afraid of that," Ethan said. "I'll have to look at other options, I guess."

"Maybe I can help you in that regard," said Arturo. "My wife and I will be taking another charter to my ranch near Chihuahua. It's a much smaller aircraft but you are welcome to join us if you like. Chihuahua is still a long way from Tijuana, but it's in the north of Mexico and will get you much closer."

Ethan looked at Pete, who was nodding. "That would be fantastic!" Ethan exclaimed. "Are you leaving tonight?"

"Yes, the flight is scheduled for eight-thirty and should arrive in Chihuahua around ten-thirty this evening, barring any unforeseen problems." He smiled at Victoria and said, "And my daughter is the pilot."

Ethan and Pete looked at Victoria in surprise. "A pilot? That is very impressive," Ethan said, smiling.

"I'd be happy to help you," she said, returning his smile.

The two continued to look at each other until Ethan heard Pete clear his throat. He glanced at Pete and, embarrassed, turned back to Arturo, who was smiling.

"That would be perfect. How can I repay you for this kindness?"

"Please sit down and let's order some wine. I have a story to tell you," Arturo said, motioning to the seats across from him. He looked at Alexandria and said, "Is it okay, Alex?"

Alexandria looked at her husband hesitantly, sadness evident on her face. She nodded for him to continue.

Pete sat down in the aisle seat one row in front of Victoria. Victoria moved over and offered Ethan her seat. Ethan sat down and accidently touched Vicki's arm. He glanced at her. She was smiling.

Arturo waved Jan over and ordered a bottle of cabernet and five glasses.

"This is from my personal collection. I love California cabernets. Are you familiar with this one?" he asked, pointing to the label on the bottle. Pete and Ethan recognized the label.

Pete whistled. "Yes, one of my favorites," he said, smiling broadly.

Jan brought the bottle and five glasses and began to pour. Once finished, he bowed and said, "Enjoy."

"Excellent! *Salud*, gentlemen!" he said as he raised his glass.

Pete and Ethan raised their glasses and they all took a sip of the full bodied red wine.

Arturo glanced at Alexandria and she nodded again.

"This is very painful for us, but it is important that we share our story with you in light of the circumstances." He looked at Ethan. "I must start by saying that we have been very fortunate in our lives. We got married very young, had four beautiful children," he said, smiling at Victoria, "and grew a very successful horse breeding business in northern Mexico. God has been good to us, no question. Our children were all healthy, intelligent and ultimately successful in their own right. All except our youngest daughter, Gabriella." He stopped and looked at his wife again, who was looking down at her lap.

After several uncomfortable seconds, he continued. "Gaby was a beautiful girl of fifteen and looked just like her beautiful sister, Victoria, who was twenty at the time."

Ethan turned and looked at Vicki, who smiled weakly as she brushed back a tear.

"She was abducted while attending a horse show with us in Cuidad Juarez, which is across the border from El Paso, Texas. As a successful businessman in Mexico, I was a prime target for kidnappers. The kidnappers demanded a ransom, which I was willing to pay." He cleared his throat. "But the *Federales* said that they could get her back without it. They did not want to negotiate with the kidnappers for fear of more of them in the future. Against my better judgment, I listened to them."

Arturo hung his head and put his hand over his eyes. Alexandria put her arm over his shoulder. The pain was obvious in both of their faces.

Ethan glanced at Victoria and saw the tears beginning to well up in her eyes.

"Then . . . ." Arturo said, stopping in mid-sentence, his voice cracking.

"The kidnappers killed her," Alexandria said, finishing the story. She put her head on her husband's shoulder.

Ethan sat in shocked silence.

"God, I'm so sorry," said Pete.

"I wish I would have followed my instincts. My beautiful daughter might still be alive," Arturo said haltingly. "I am not telling you this to scare you or to gain your pity. But I needed to share with you our tragedy so that you know we understand your pain and your fear. That's why we are so anxious to help you in any way we can, to help you avoid what we have been through. We believe that God has put us in your path to help you, but also to help us with our guilt."

"I don't know what to say," Ethan finally said. "Thank you."

Arturo was obviously a proud man, a successful man. But Ethan could tell that the guilt he felt about his daughter's death had broken him.

"What is your daughter's name?" asked Alexandria, wiping away her tears with a handkerchief.

"Molly," Ethan replied.

"A beautiful name. Do you have a picture that we might see?" she asked.

"Yes." Ethan pulled out his wallet and the picture of his daughter. "This was taken in April of this year. She's sixteen."

Arturo and Alexandria looked at the picture of the olive-skinned, dark-haired girl. They blinked in surprise, looking at the picture then back at Ethan.

"I know. She doesn't look much like me. My wife is . . . was Hispanic. We adopted Molly at birth. Her birth mother was from Mexico."

"I'm sorry for my reaction. She is so beautiful, stunning actually. You're right, she doesn't look anything like you," Alexandria said, smiling. "How old was she when you adopted her?" She passed the picture to Victoria, who looked at it carefully before handing it back to Ethan.

"Six weeks old. The birth mother was living with an aunt in the U.S., close to where we lived, until she had the baby. My wife knew someone who knew the aunt and one thing led to another. The birth mother was only seventeen when she had Molly."

"Mexico is a very Catholic country, so being pregnant and unwed, especially at such a young age, must have been traumatic for her," Alexandria said. "Did you meet her, the birth mother?"

"No, we never met her. After she had Molly, she went back to Mexico and we never heard from her again. We had some contact with the aunt, but the birth mother just disappeared. Her aunt hasn't heard from her in twelve years."

"That is so sad. But happy, also. I'm sure Molly has had a wonderful life with you and your wife," Alexandria said.

"Yes, she has had a very good life and we couldn't have loved her any more if she were born to us naturally. She is . . . ." Ethan's voice started to crack.

Arturo cleared his throat. "Your wife . . . you said . . . ."

Ethan looked at Arturo and Alexandria and then at Victoria. "She died six months ago, of cancer."

Alexandria put her hand to her mouth, trapping the gasp that was sure to come out.

Ethan felt a touch and looked down to see Vicki's hand on his. When he looked up he saw the sorrow in her eyes.

"I am so sorry, Ethan," Arturo said. "I can't imagine what you must be going through."

Ethan nodded, fighting against his emotions. He felt Vicki's gentle squeeze on his hand.

"Ethan, our resources are at your disposal. Once we arrive in Chihuahua we will help you find a way to Tijuana. Mexico can be a very dangerous country, even for our own people. We will help you in any way we can," Arturo said.

The two men stood up and hugged each other. Alexandria slid across her husband's seat and stood up. She hugged Pete, then Ethan.

"Our prayers are with you, Ethan. We pray that Molly gets home to you safely."

Victoria stood and put her hand on Ethan's arm. "I understand what you are going through. I lost my baby sister and think about her every day. I will do whatever I can to help you find your daughter, Ethan."

Her touch excited him and sent a jolt through his body. "Thank you, Victoria."

"Please. Vicki," she said, removing her hand.

He nodded at her, staring into her dark eyes. "Thank you, Vicki," he said softly.

Arturo coughed and said, "All right. Now let's finish the wine and order another bottle!"

"I'll second that," exclaimed Pete. "And some food!"

CHAPTER 24

When Jake and Charlie arrived at the Holiday Inn in Chula Vista, most of the kids and adults from Santa Elena had left for home. Several adults, including Mister Sizemore, had stayed behind. The fathers of Cindy and Jenny had arrived that morning. Charlie and Jake had driven from the El Toro bar in one of the school vans that Sizemore had let Charlie use. The motel was a mile from the San Ysidro border crossing and was the usual stop-over point for the school when their home-building mission was over. It was where they relaxed, took showers and washed off the stink and grime of five days in the Baja desert. Sizemore was outside the motel talking to two men when they pulled into the motel parking lot.

Walking up to the van, Sizemore said, "Hi, Charlie. Did you have any trouble finding Mister Delgado?" He poked his head into the van, looking at Jake and giving him a full body scan with his eyes.

"Not really. Just a lot of traffic," Charlie said. "Jake, this is Mister Sizemore, the principal of Santa Elena Academy."

Jake held out his hand to the middle-aged, gray haired man. "Hi."

"Nice to meet you, Mister Delgado," Sizemore said, with obvious disdain.

"Call me Jake."

"Okay. Jake. You can call me George. Why don't you two come on into the lobby so we can talk?" George Sizemore walked back toward the lobby of the motel. As he passed the two men, he made a motion with his head towards the van.

"He sounds like a prick," said Jake, as he and Charlie got out of the van.

"He's okay, but, yeah, he's a prick," Charlie answered. "Those two men are the fathers of the other two girls, Cindy and Jenny."

As Charlie and Jake walked toward them, one of the two men stuck out his hand.

"Charlie, I'm Dick Lambert, Cindy's father," the first man said, grabbing Charlie's hand and shaking it vigorously. "Molly and Cindy are best friends."

"Yeah, I know," Charlie replied. "I'm sorry."

"Molly has been over to our place many times," Lambert said. "We think of her as our daughter. She's such a sweet . . . ." The man's voice trailed off as he hung his head.

"Charlie, I'm Dave Carter, Jenny's dad," the other man said, extending his hand.

"Hello," Charlie answered, looking at Mister Lambert and feeling uncomfortable.

Jake stood behind Charlie, watching the meet and greet with interest. Both men seemed a little dazed and tired. He noticed Mister Lambert wiping tears from his eyes.

"This is Jake Delgado, the man my dad hired to . . . find Molly," Charlie said, pointing to Jake.

"Gentlemen," Jake said, nodding his head, not offering his hand. Jake noticed that both men were staring at his scar, which he had become used to.

"We heard that your dad hired a private investigator," Mister Lambert said, staring at Jake. "Not exactly sure why, since the police will be handling this, uh, situation."

"The police aren't doing sh—" Charlie began to say, his voice rising.

"Gentlemen, it was nice meeting you," Jake interrupted. He knew he had to get Charlie away from the two men as quickly as possible. "Charlie, let's go inside," Jake said, grabbing Charlie by the arm.

They walked into the lobby of the motel and saw Sizemore sitting at a table in the lobby area. He had his legs crossed and his arms draped around the back of a chair, looking confident and superior.

"There's coffee and juice if you want some," the principal said.

"No thanks," said Jake. "Where's everyone else?"

"Most of the kids and adults left this morning to go back home. Everyone is concerned about what's going on with the terrorist situation and wanted to be home with their families." Sizemore looked at Charlie. "I see you met Cindy and Jenny's fathers."

"Yes. What about your family?" Jake asked.

"They're fine. Right now, my only concern is Molly and the others," he said. "Charlie told me a little about you, Jake. I have to admit, I'm not in favor of bringing on a private investigator right now."

Jake saw him staring at his scar, but decided to let it go. "Well, that's the Paxton's decision. I'm here to help Charlie and his family find his sister."

"I understand, but Charlie really doesn't have the auth—"

"His dad does, and he's the one who hired me," Jake said, knowing where the man was headed. *What a prick.*

"Yes, but Mister Paxton is thousands of miles away, so . . . ."

"Listen, George. You may not like me or approve of me, and you may not like my scar, but I don't give a rat's ass. I'm here to help Charlie find his sister, and I'm helping an old friend. What you think or say means nothing to me."

The principal sat up straight, his face turning pink. "Well, I didn't say I didn't like you, Jake. I just don't think it's necessary to bring someone like yourself into this at this point."

"Someone like myself? What exactly do you mean, George?"

"Well, I meant . . . well, a private investigator."

"Again, not your call. Now we can sit here and chit chat and waste valuable time, or you can tell me what you know so I can do my job. What's it going to be?"

Charlie had been watching the jousting and finally chimed in. "Mister Sizemore, my dad thinks it's important to have Jake out looking for Molly, and I agree with him. If the cops were any help, then maybe we wouldn't need him, but they're worthless. If we're going to find Molly, we'll have to do it ourselves."

Jake looked at Charlie and smiled. The kid was growing on him. "There you go, George. Now, what can you tell me about the past twenty-four hours?"

Sizemore glanced at Charlie and gave him his best 'I'm the principal' look, then turned his attention to Jake. "Okay, Jake. Let me get a cup of coffee then we can begin."

As Sizemore walked to the coffee maker, Jake slapped Charlie on the shoulder. "Thanks, kid."

Charlie frowned. "Don't call me kid."

"Sorry—just habit."

"Okay, let's get started," Sizemore said, sitting down across from Jake, crossing his legs as though he were in a faculty meeting.

"How much have you told the SDPD about the abduction?" Jake started.

"Nothing. They refused to talk to us last night because . . . well, because of the attacks . . . and, the fact that the girls hadn't been missing for at least twenty-four hours."

"They didn't take a report, listen to your story?"

"No. It was chaos at the police station. We were virtually invisible to them."

"Are you planning to talk to them today, once the twenty-four hours are up?"

"Of course. We need their help."

Jake looked at the man and mumbled something under his breath. "Okay. Tell me about yesterday, from the beginning."

"We left the Tecate campsite at three o'clock yesterday afternoon with a convoy of about thirty cars and vans. I was in the first van, with a walkie-talkie. I gave walkie-talkies to four other people in the convoy, including Julie Caldwell, the driver of Molly's van. They were bringing up the rear of the convoy, but were within sight of the other cars at all times." The principal said this with an air of confidence, almost arrogance.

"Why did you let a woman and three girls bring up the rear of the convoy?" Jake asked, looking up from his notebook.

"Well . . . we wanted to depart for the border while we had plenty of sun left. Julie had some trouble with one of her girls getting ready so they just . . . well, they were the last to leave." The arrogance was eroding quickly.

Jake glanced at the man, who was visibly nervous. "Okay, so why didn't you have at least one male adult with them?"

"As I said, we were in a hurry. In hindsight, I probably should have taken some extra time to think it through." Sizemore glanced at Charlie, but quickly turned his gaze back on Jake.

"Did you have any security with you?"

Sizemore sat up a little straighter in his chair, obviously uncomfortable. "Well, no, not at the time. They had left earlier that day, since we were going home."

"Were they American or Mexican security?" Jake said, leaning forward.

"Well, we had one American with us the entire time but," Sizemore coughed, "he left early to get things ready at the border crossing—to pave the way, so to speak."

"That was it? No security with the convoy?"

Sizemore cleared his throat. "The Mexican security company left that morning, so no, we had no security with the convoy."

Jake stared at the man in silence, until Sizemore finally looked away. The cockiness was long gone.

"Okay. Was there anything at the campsite that made you suspicious, any strange men hanging around, maybe someone asking lots of questions?"

"No. Not that I remember. I did hear from several people, including Charlie, that one of the local boys was hanging around the day we left. He was a little older than most of the local kids."

"Was he asking questions or did he seem a little too curious?"

"Again, I didn't see him myself. I was told this by several people after the, uh, kidnapping happened." Sizemore was looking down at his hands, obviously very uncomfortable.

Jake glanced at Charlie and saw him staring at Sizemore, eyebrows furrowed.

"When Charlie told you about his sister's voicemail and after you listened to it, what did you do?"

"Well, I knew it was not good. The screams and shouts. It was horrible." He said this calmly, without a hint of emotion.

"Were you worried, upset . . . what?"

"Yes, of course I was worried, and, uh, upset," Sizemore said with a hint of indignation.

"And you did what?"

"Charlie and I and several other men turned around from the Otay Mesa border crossing and went back to look for Julie's van. I tried to contact her on the walkie-talkie but there was no answer. We drove all the way back to the campsite and then back to the border again, but didn't see the van anywhere."

"Did the teacher..." Jake looked at his notes. "Julie. Did she call you at any time on the walkie-talkie before you got to the border the first time?"

"Yes. Yes she did. She contacted me to let me know that she was stopping to let one of the girls go to the bathroom, but that they would only be a couple of minutes and to not stop the convoy."

Jake looked up from his notebook. He noticed Charlie looking at Sizemore with wide eyes.

"You never told me that!" Charlie exclaimed. "When did that happen?"

"Right as we were approaching the turnoff to the border crossing. I'm sure I mentioned that, Charlie. We couldn't stop because of all the traffic, and Julie told us not to stop."

"Jesus Christ!" Charlie yelled. "That's when it happened!"

"We don't know that, Charlie," Jake said, trying to calm him down. "But it does sound like the logical point, if the kidnappers were following them."

"No shit!" Charlie yelled, staring at Sizemore.

"Julie said everything was okay," Sizemore said nervously. "She didn't sound scared or concerned on the walkie-talkie."

"But if you would have stopped the convoy anyway, or had someone in the back of the convoy stop and check on them . . . ." Jake's voice trailed off, letting the pause sink in with the principal.

"They would be here with us now!" said Charlie, getting ready to blow.

"Well, that's..that's possible, but we don't know for sure that's when it happened!" Sizemore said, beads of sweat popping out on his forehead.

"Okay, let's stay calm," Jake said, grabbing Charlie's arm. "Charlie?"

Charlie was breathing hard, his breaths coming in spurts.

"Charlie?" Jake said again.

Charlie looked at Jake and back to Sizemore, then down at his feet. His breathing slowed down as he continued to stare at this feet.

Jake let Charlie get his composure back before continuing. He watched as Sizemore wiped the sweat from his brow with his handkerchief.

"Okay, let's suppose the kidnappers had been following the convoy. Unless someone stopped somewhere along the way, how would they have cut someone out from the convoy? It would have been nearly impossible unless the last car fell too far behind the next car. Did you ask the next to last car if they had a visual of Julie's car the entire trip?"

"Yes, I did," Sizemore said confidently, regaining some composure. "They said that Julie was always in sight right up until they, uh, they . . . ."

"They what?" asked Jake.

"The road made a sharp right turn just before Otay Mesa. They lost sight of Julie's van when they rounded the turn. But they told me later that Julie was not more than half a mile behind them at the time."

"Who is 'they'?"

"The Johnson's. They were in the next to last van."

Jake made some notes in his notebook. "Did the Johnson's say whether there were any other cars on the road behind them?"

"Umm, let me think." He put his hand on his forehead as though he were thinking very hard. "Yes, they remember passing a couple of trucks sitting on the side of the road."

Jake stopped writing and looked up at Sizemore. "Were those trucks still there when you went back to look for Julie's van?"

"Well, I . . . I don't know. I can't remember."

"No, they weren't!" Charlie said. "There were no cars of any kind on the side of the road when we went back to look for them!"

Jake and Charlie looked at each other, realizing that the two trucks were probably the kidnappers.

"Did the Johnson's say what color the trucks were?" Jake asked the shaken man.

"I believe they said they were black."

"Jesus Christ! Jesus Christ!" Charlie said, rocking back and forth in his chair. "We could have been looking for two black trucks! Didn't you think that was important, Mister Sizemore?"

"Well, in hindsight—"

"Fuck hindsight! You killed my sister!" Charlie lurched out of his chair and grabbed the stunned principal by the collar, knocking him to the floor. He was about to slam his fist into the man's face when a tree trunk-sized arm stopped him.

"Charlie! Get up! Get up, son!" Jake yelled at him.

Several people in the lobby of the motel were looking at the three men in astonishment, including the fathers of Cindy and Jenny. Jake saw the desk clerk reach for the telephone.

"Let him up, Charlie. Now!" Jake said.

Charlie let loose of the man's collar and stood up, his entire body shaking.

"We're done here," said Jake. "Let's go son, before we have more trouble than we can handle."

Jake helped the principal up and straightened his shirt. The man's face was beet red. Fear was all over his face. Jake leaned into the man, his mouth next to the principal's ear.

"You'd better hope we get Molly and the other girls back, George. We're borrowing one of your vans to go find them. By the way, I wouldn't mention this to anyone, especially the police. You don't come out looking too good in this story." Jake let go of the man's shirt, smoothed it out, and smiled as he walked out the front door with Charlie in tow.

CHAPTER 25

Jake watched through the window as Charlie quickly packed his duffle bag in his motel room. He was sure the desk clerk in the motel had called the police when Charlie almost popped his principal. *Good thing Charlie graduated last year.*

"Make sure you get the cell phone charger. We're gonna need it," he told Charlie.

"I've got it."

"Okay, let's get out of here before you're sent to detention," Jake said, chuckling.

They climbed into the same blue van that Charlie had driven to meet Jake at the El Toro. It was a Toyota mini-van with the 'Santa Elena Academy' logo on the side doors. Plus, it still had valid Mexican insurance for a few more days and had already been into Mexico and back, all things that Jake had checked on while driving to the motel with Charlie. He knew it would make it easier to get across the border into Mexico.

Charlie backed out of the motel parking lot and turned right towards the border crossing.

"Will we get in trouble for taking the van?" he said nervously. He was still shaking from the events in the motel lobby. "And for my assault on Mister Sizemore?"

"No, I don't think George will file a complaint. He wants Molly and the others back probably more than anyone now. He knows he blew it. He's not going to do anything but pray we find them." Jake tried to sound confident but he knew that Sizemore could make trouble for them.

"I almost clocked him! If not for you, I don't know what I would've done. I've never lost it like that before."

"Well, welcome to the club, Charlie. I've been there a few too many times. Nothing good ever comes from losing it like that. Wish I would've had someone around to stop me back in the day."

"Thanks, Jake," Charlie said quietly.

"You're welcome, kid. We need to stop at this gas station over here so I can make a call. You got your passport with you?"

"Yeah, in my bag. We crossing over?"

"If they let us. We aren't going to accomplish anything on this side of the border. You ready?"

"Hell yeah!" Charlie said excitedly.

"Kid, this isn't an adventure. This is serious shit. We're heading into the unknown and I need to make sure we have some back-up and help."

Charlie pulled into a gas station a couple of blocks from the Tijuana border crossing. He handed his phone to Jake, who looked at it like it was radioactive.

"You dial the number," Jake said.

Charlie stared at Jake. "You ever used a cell phone?" he said.

"Just dial the damn number," Jake said as he read the number to Charlie.

"Hello," the voice on the other end said.

"Manny, it's Jake."

"Jake, what's going on?" Manny said.

"Me and the ki . . . uh, Charlie, are going to be crossing over in a few minutes. You have any info on what's going on at the border?"

"Yeah, I checked with my sources. It's open, but tight as a duck's ass. San Ysidro is a mess. You got all the docs?"

"Yeah, we're good. We're gonna cross at Otay Mesa instead of San Ysidro. I want to backtrack the entire route so we can determine where the kidnapping took place."

"Good plan. I've talked to a couple of guys and we'll have some help for you when we meet tonight."

"Thanks, Manny. We should be in TJ around five."

"Jake?"

"Yeah?"

"You packing?"

"Hell no," Jake said.

"Thought so. I'll have something for you when we meet tonight."

Jake thought about this before answering. "We'll talk about it when we meet. Manny, one more thing."

"What's that, Bull?"

"Can you check with your sources at SDPD to see if anyone has, uh, filed a complaint against me and the kid?" Jake shot Charlie a glance, shrugging his shoulders.

"Yeah, I can do that. What happened?" Manny said.

"I'll tell you when I see you at five," Jake said, pushing the red button on the phone to end the call.

Jake handed the phone back to Charlie. "Let's take highway 905 to Otay Mesa and cross there," he said.

Charlie's eyes lit up, a broad smile all over his face.

"Damn it, Charlie," Jake said, shaking his head. "Your dad would kill me if he knew I was taking you across the border with me."

"He won't care as long as we find Molly," Charlie said defensively.

Jake sighed. "Then let's go find Molly."

CHAPTER 26

Molly was the first to wake up from their drug-induced slumber. She leaned on her side, her hands no longer tied behind her back. She shook her head, trying to get the cobwebs out. Her eyes would hardly open, so she closed them and opened them again, trying to get rid of the blurriness. Gradually the dizziness wore off and things began to come into focus.

She blinked her eyes several times and looked around the room. The windowless room was dark except for the one dim light hanging from the ceiling. She noticed the chair next to the door was empty. She looked towards the bathroom. It was dark. *Where's the woman?*

She looked at Cindy and Jenny and saw that they were still sleeping soundly. Then she noticed the dark form on the fourth mattress. She raised herself to a sitting position and blinked her eyes several times, trying to get accustomed to the poor light. She could make out the form of the person lying on the mattress. *Is that Natalia?* She blinked again and squinted her eyes to see better. It wasn't Natalia. *Oh God! Missus Caldwell!*

She got on her knees and gradually stood up, balancing herself after almost falling over. She stood still for several seconds, letting the dizziness pass. She took one tentative step towards the woman, stopped and got her balance. She slowly shuffled over until she was standing over the woman, who was lying on her side. Molly couldn't see her face, so she bent down and shook the woman on the shoulder. When she got no response she rolled the woman over onto her back. She recoiled when she saw her face. She stumbled backwards, almost falling over Cindy's sleeping body. She put her hand to her mouth to stifle the scream. *Oh, my God! What did they do to her?* She could hardly recognize her teacher. Her face was beaten, bruised and bloodied beyond belief. Her eyes were swollen shut. Molly bent down and put her ear next to the woman's mouth. She felt breathing, but in slow, short bursts. Molly reached over and gently shook her. Nothing. She shook her again, this time harder. She heard an almost imperceptible moan come from the woman's mouth. She shook her again and felt the woman move her arm.

"Missus Caldwell," she said quietly, her face next to the woman's face. "Missus Caldwell, can you hear me?"

The woman groaned, this time louder, and moved her head.

"Missus Caldwell, can you hear me? Move your hand if you can hear me."

Molly saw her hand move slightly.

"Missus Caldwell, it's Molly Paxton."

"Mo . . . Mo . . . lly," the woman whispered, barely audible. She could barely move her lips, which were swollen and parched.

"Yes! It's Molly!"

"Molly." She breathed heavily. "Molly," she said again.

Molly stared at her, the tears flooding her eyes. "I'm so sorry."

Suddenly, Molly heard a loud noise on the other side of the metal door. She heard the deadbolt beginning its slide. She stood up and quickly walked to her mattress, lying on her side, facing the door. Her heart was beating through her chest. She wiped her tears on the filthy mattress.

The metal door began to open, showering the dark room with light once again. Molly put her head in the mattress to shield her eyes. When she glanced back at the door to see who was entering she saw Natalia, carrying a basket and a bottle of water. She was alone.

Natalia put the basket and water on the chair next to the door and slid the door shut. When she turned around Molly was sitting up.

"What did they do to her?" Molly said, tears still streaming down her face.

Natalia glanced back at the metal door. "Shhh. You must be quiet. They're outside."

Molly glared at her, her eyes demanding an answer.

Natalia walked quickly over to Molly and bent down. "I'm sorry, *mija*. I didn't know that they would hurt her so badly."

"So badly? She's almost dead," Molly said through clenched teeth.

"I'm sorry. Let me take care of her," Natalia said, walking to the teacher.

Molly watched Natalia wash the face of Missus Caldwell, gently dabbing her bruises and eyes with a warm washcloth. She watched as Natalia wet the washcloth with the bottled water and put it to the woman's mouth. Missus Caldwell licked her lips as the wet washcloth touched them.

"Why did they do this to her?" Molly said quietly.

Natalia didn't look at Molly, but continued to wash the blood from the teacher's face.

"Tell me. Why?"

Natalia turned and looked at Molly, glancing at the other two girls, who were still asleep.

"She must have resisted," she said quietly. "They are animals, Molly."

Molly stared at the woman, the hatred for her and the men outside beginning to consume her.

"When did you wake up?" Natalia whispered.

"A few minutes ago. Did you untie my hands while I was sleeping?"

"Yes, I didn't want the twine to cut into your wrists."

Molly looked over at Cindy and Jenny and saw that their hands were free also. "Thank you."

"You're welcome."

Molly looked at Missus Caldwell. "She's barely breathing."

Natalia bent over the teacher and listened to her breathing. She glanced at Molly as she put her hand on the woman's wrist, feeling for a pulse.

"She's dying," Molly said.

"I know," answered Natalia.

"Why? Are they going to kill all of us?"

Natalia took her hands away from the teacher and walked over to Molly. Staring into Molly's eyes she said, "No! No, they will not kill you! On my life, they will not kill you."

Molly stared at her, seeing the pain on her face up close. And the fear.

"She needs a doctor," Molly said, looking away.

Natalia shook her head. "He won't allow it."

"Then she'll die, and it will be on your head."

Natalia hung her head. "Yes, I know."

Molly saw the remorse, sadness, and the guilt in Natalia's face. She knew she had to act quickly.

"Natalia, you have to get us out of here."

"I can't. We would have to go through that door and they are right outside."

Molly looked at the heavy metal door and her heart began to sink. They were in a prison cell, with no way out. Her shoulders slumped and she fell back on the mattress. She stared at the dirty, gray ceiling. Suddenly, she sprang back up to a sitting position.

"You will have to distract them somehow," Molly said.

"There are too many of them. His entire gang is outside, maybe ten men. They have guns, knives." She looked at Molly and began to brush her hair. Molly pulled back.

"You have to do something, or we will all die," Molly said sternly. "You have to get us out of here somehow."

Natalia just hung her head, not answering.

"Have they contacted my dad yet?" she asked.

Natalia blinked, wiping away a tear. "What?"

"My family. Have they been contacted for a ransom yet?"

Natalia stared at her. "No."

"How long has it been since they kidnapped us?"

"About twenty hours or so."

Molly thought about this, doing calculations in her head. They were abducted around three thirty in the afternoon the day before, so that would make it just after noon. She had been here for over twenty hours! *Why haven't they called with ransom demands?*

"What are they waiting for?" she asked Natalia.

Natalia stood up and walked to the metal door, making sure no one was on the other side listening. She walked back to Molly and knelt down, putting her face close to hers.

"There will be no ransom."

"No ransom? But, what . . . ?"

Molly suddenly realized what Natalia was saying. She looked at Cindy, then Jenny, and put her hand to her mouth to stifle the scream. She was never going home. They were going to kill her . . . or sell her. She looked up at Natalia, the tears beginning to flood her eyes.

"How much . . . time do we have?" she said, her words coming in spurts.

Natalia had her head buried in her hands, sobbing quietly. After several seconds, Natalia's sobs stopped. She dried her eyes with the back of her hand and looked down at Molly, the sadness covering her face.

"It will happen tomorrow."

CHAPTER 27

After another bottle of wine and a meal that tasted like cardboard, and after more conversation with the Calderon's, Pete and Ethan moved back to their seats in the front of the cabin. Alexandria Calderon had begun to yawn, a clear sign that she needed sleep, or was bored, or both. They would see plenty more of the couple once they landed in Mexico City.

"Nice couple," Pete said, after taking another drink of his wine. "And Victoria! What a knockout."

Ethan looked over at his friend. "Yes they are a nice couple. But it's heartbreaking what they went through with their daughter." He stared out the window, thinking of his own situation.

"I noticed you and Vicki had a moment back there," Pete said, a mischievous smile on his face.

Ethan smiled at him but didn't say anything, just turned and stared out the window.

"You're going to get Molly back, partner. Keep thinking positive," Pete said quietly.

Ethan nodded, smiling weakly at Pete. "The closer we get, the more anxious I get. Not knowing and not being able to talk to anyone is the hardest part."

"Tell me about this guy you hired. What's that all about?"

"It was just a wild hair of an idea that popped into my head this morning. I felt so helpless when Charlie called me about Molly. I had to think of something because I felt useless being six thousand miles away. I don't know if I made a mistake or not. Guess we'll find out when we get to Tijuana."

"Well, just like you told Charlie. It may be a long shot, but at least it's a shot."

"Yeah, I've got to hold on to that, I guess. You know, he was one hell of a football player back in the day. I've never seen anyone with thicker forearms. He could throw a perfect spiral sixty, seventy yards and put it on your fingertips. He told me once that his goal was to throw it further than I could run. We made quite a team back then."

"What was he like, as a person I mean?"

"He was a larger than life kind of guy, a living legend in Japan. He could be friendly and funny when he was feeling good, but he could turn nasty in a split second. His fights were legendary and so was his temper. He didn't have many close friends, but for some reason he and I hit it off. I think it was because I didn't judge him, just accepted him the way he was. Sad that we become so jaded as we get older."

"Life does it to us, makes us mistrust people," Pete said. "The terrorist attacks yesterday will just make most people more jaded and cautious."

Ethan nodded. "He saved my butt one night back in Japan. It was shortly after we won the base football championship. Jake and I had been hanging out quite a bit, but I could see a change in him. He was becoming more and more withdrawn and surly. One night I was down in the *machi* . . . ."

"*Machi?*"

"Sorry, Japanese word for town. Whenever I think of my time in Japan, some of the old words and phrases pop into my head. Anyway, I was in this small town outside the air base, which was in northern Japan. They had an area about two blocks from the main gate we called AP Alley." Ethan saw a blank look on Pete's face. "You know, because the Air Police patrolled it all the time. Lots of bars, drinking, brawling, stuff like that. It was after our last day shift so everyone in my squadron was downtown bar hopping, because we had four days off. We usually spent our entire paycheck in one night and then had to stay on base the rest of the break."

"I would've stayed on base and read a book," Pete said with a straight face.

"Right. Anyway, it was close to midnight and I'd been downtown for a few hours, so was pretty drunk. I'd found a *jo-san*, a bargirl, at one of my stops. Nice looking gal, very young and very popular. Don't know why she ended up with me."

"No kidding."

Ethan smiled. "I was sitting in a bar called The New Tokyo, in a booth way in the back. We were having a good time—"

"Now we're talkin'!"

"Four guys from another squadron came in, full of piss and vinegar. They'd just gotten off the swing shift and were downtown to drink as much as they could before the bars closed. They must've hit every bar between the main gate and New Tokyo, because they were toasted when they stumbled in."

"Kind of like us last night?"

"Well, like you and Rob. Anyway, they started messing with the *jo-san* behind the bar, so I knew they were drunk because she was old and homely. Then they saw me in the back. One of them, a big guy with an attitude, walked up to me and said, 'that's my girlfriend, asshole'. I didn't say anything, just tried to ignore him. He said it again. 'That's my girlfriend, shitface', or something to that effect. It was obvious he either wanted the girl or he wanted a fight. Probably both."

"Was she his girlfriend?"

"Maybe. Those girls had one or two boyfriends on every squadron. There were four squadrons at the Security Wing where I worked and three were working when one was on break, so the *jo-sans* could have a different boyfriend every few days. They just rotated through when they were on break. It was great for them, but sometimes the boyfriends crossed paths like they did that night."

"That sucks."

"Yeah, it did. His three friends walk back and I know I'm in big trouble. I'm the only one in the bar from my squadron and I'd been drinking for hours, so I was pretty far gone. Plus, I wasn't a fighter. Never have been. Usually, I was fast enough to run away from a fight."

"Coward."

Ethan poked Pete in the ribs. "So this boyfriend grabs the *jo-san* and begins to pull her away from me. I pulled her back and said, in a very manly way, mind you, 'I don't think so'. That was all she wrote. The guy grabbed me by my collar and dragged me out of the booth. He was just about to start pounding on me when I heard a loud bang in the front of the bar, like someone had just busted through the door. I was praying it was the Air Police, but it was better—it was Jake Delgado. He'd been bar hopping all night and was smashed. I don't think he knew I was in the bar."

"What happened?" Pete said, leaning closer.

"When he saw the four guys in the back and saw me in the grasp of this poor sucker, he shot back to where we were, didn't ask any questions, and began wailing on these poor bastards. They went down one by one. One punch each. The last guy, the one that had hold of me, got the bonus. He got two shots. All of them were out cold, just lying on the floor of the bar."

"Damn."

"He grabbed me and slurred, 'Let's get outta here, rookie'. I wasn't about to argue, because I knew the Air Police would be there any second. The *jo-san* behind the bar was still on the phone when we walked out the front door. Fortunately, no one knew our names or what squadron we were on, so we never got into trouble. The other guys were so drunk they couldn't remember what I looked like, and they never saw Jake—just his fist."

"What about the girl?" Pete asked.

Ethan looked at Pete and laughed. "Leave it to you to worry about the girl. She survived. Probably went home with one of the guys after they woke up. They didn't care, as long as the guy had money."

"I would've gone back for her."

Ethan grinned and shook his head.

"Jake and I never talked about it after that night. It was pretty normal for him. I don't think he ever lost a fight while he was in Japan. Then toward the end of his tour he went into a really dark period. He and I stopped hanging out and he became a loner. One night he got drunk and hit some officer, a captain or major or something. They didn't wear their uniforms downtown so you never really knew who was enlisted and who was an officer. The base commander decided to make an example out of Jake and threw him in the brig and demoted him. He got discharged shortly after that and I never saw him again. Never talked to him again until this morning."

"Damn, he sounds like one mean SOB."

"He was, but he was a great guy if you were on his good side. He saved my butt from a first-class ass-whipping, that's for sure."

"I could do that."

Ethan nodded and smiled at his friend.

"He's a long shot all right. You sure you want this guy working with your son?"

Ethan stared out the window. "There's nobody I'd rather have on my side right now—as long as he's sober. My son was supposed to meet with him this morning so I can't wait to hear how that went. Charlie has a temper, too, so I hope they get along okay."

"Well, we'll find out soon enough."

Ethan nodded, closing his eyes. "I just hope it's not too late."

CHAPTER 28

Jake and Charlie left the gas station and backtracked north on Interstate 5, then headed east on State Highway 905 to the Otay Mesa border crossing. It was about a thirty minute drive and Jake didn't know what to expect because of 9/11. As they approached the border he saw that the traffic lines were light heading into Mexico.

As they passed the U.S. Customs checkpoint, Jake saw several heavily-armed border cops patrolling the check-point, as well as some heavier artillery sitting off to the side. Jake assumed that it was the same all along the U.S.-Mexico border. Normally they wouldn't have had to stop at U.S. Customs on the way into Mexico, but these were not normal times.

"I didn't know what to expect, but it doesn't look too bad," Jake said to Charlie. "Just be cool and show them your passport. They may ask us some questions, so let me answer."

Charlie nodded at Jake nervously. "This brings back memories of yesterday," Charlie said. "It was less than twenty four hours ago that I was here. Seems longer."

Jake reached over and patted his shoulder. "You okay?"

"Yeah, let's do it."

They pulled up to the U.S. Customs agent, who leaned down and looked at them, then glanced at the back of the van, scanning everything with his eyes.

"Passports," he said, looking at Charlie. He glanced at Jake in the passenger seat and lingered on the scar a little too long.

Jake handed his passport to Charlie, who handed both of them to the agent.

"You were just here yesterday?" the agent said to Charlie. Jake noticed the agent looking at the SEA logo on the door.

"Yes."

"What's the reason for your return?"

"We're going back to our home building site in Tecate to pick up some tools we left behind," Charlie lied.

"How about you sir?" the agent said to Jake, again looking at the scar.

"Just helping him out," Jake responded.

"You coming back across today or are you staying in Mexico?"

"Not sure. We may stay one or two nights to finish some of the construction we started," Jake said, glancing at Charlie.

"It's probably not a good idea to stay in Mexico right now," the agent said. "The border could close at any time. You have a place to stay in Mexico?"

"I have a friend in Rosarito Beach, if we end up spending the night," Jake responded.

Jake caught the agent looking at his scar again and waited for a comment. None came.

"Okay. Drive on through. Be careful down there," the agent said, waving us on.

They drove a short distance to Mexican customs, where they were waved through without being checked. They were in Mexico.

"That was the easy part," said Jake. "The hard part will be coming back. U.S. Customs will be much more stringent than they ever were before. That's if the border is even open."

"I don't even remember how it was yesterday," Charlie said. "I was in a fog when we finally crossed."

They drove past the spot where Charlie first listened to Molly's voicemail the day before.

"This is where it all started yesterday," he said, pointing to the traffic waiting to cross into the U.S.

"Okay. Take me back on the same route you took yesterday. I want you to point out anything that you think I should know."

"Well, we take a left onto Highway 2, which goes all the way into Tecate, but we turn off onto a back road about a mile up from here."

"Is that the road you took yesterday?"

"Yeah. Highway 2 turns into a toll road, called 2D, about a mile up. The road the convoy took forks off to the right, which takes us south of Tecate, where our build site was located. It's about twenty miles to the campsite on that road."

Jake got his notebook out and began taking notes. "Where approximately do you think Molly called you?"

"I don't know, but it couldn't have been more than a mile or two from where the road forks. Mister Sizemore said the Johnson's lost visibility when they turned right, just before the border crossing turnoff."

Jake was looking at the terrain. It was high desert-type terrain with sage brush, cactus and rock outcrops. Easy to hide someone taking a leak. They came to the fork and turned right, leaving Highway 2. The road curved left sharply about five hundred yards up the road.

"This must have been the turn where the Johnson's lost visibility. Lots of high rocks on the corner that would hide anything behind you," Jake said, peering up the road after the sharp left.

After driving about half a mile, Jake noticed a dirt road that veered off the main road.

"Stop! Let's check out this road right here," he said to Charlie.

"Why?"

"It shoots off into the desert and would be an easy get away for the kidnappers. You said the black trucks were not around when you and Mister Sizemore drove back this way, right?"

"Right."

"Where did they go? Did they continue on this road towards Tijuana, or did they take another road so that they wouldn't be noticed?"

"I don't remember passing any black trucks when we came back this way yesterday, but I wasn't looking for them either."

"Let's stop here and see if we can spot anything," Jake said.

Charlie pulled over to the side of the road, about fifty feet past the dirt road turnoff, and they got out. Jake was looking at the dirt and sand on the shoulder, looking for footprints or signs of shuffling feet. Or tire tracks. It was mostly loose dirt and dust, so any tracks could have been blown away by the wind.

"Check the other side of the road for any tire tracks, footprints or any kind of activity. I'll check this side," he said to Charlie.

Jake walked up the left shoulder, towards the dirt road, looking for any clue of activity in the area. As he approached the entrance to the road he saw several tire tracks. Two of the tracks were similar, as if they were the same kind of vehicle and tire. There was a third track that was narrower than the other two. The three tracks seemed to intersect, then separated a short way down the road.

"Charlie! I got it!" he yelled.

Charlie ran across the road to where Jake was standing.

"Look at these tire tracks. What do you see?"

Charlie looked down and said, "I don't know, some tire tracks?"

"Three sets of tracks, meaning three cars."

"Looks like two of them are about the same," Charlie said, getting excited. "The other one is narrow, maybe a smaller car?"

"Bingo! Two trucks and a smaller car or van. What does that tell you?"

"Two black trucks and a white van!" Charlie exclaimed.

Jake smiled at Charlie and gave him a high five. "Now, let's see if there is anything else, like footprints or scuffling marks."

The two men scoured the area, walking up the dirt road. Charlie was the first to see the footprints.

"Jake, look here! Looks like three or four sets of footprints. The dirt has covered most of them, but definitely footprints," he said excitedly.

Jake bent down and looked at the prints closely. "Looks like pretty big feet, probably men's prints. I don't see any smaller prints, though, like those of a woman or girl."

Charlie looked disappointed, then brightened. "Wait! If the men pulled the girls from the van and carried them to the truck, there wouldn't be any prints!"

Jake looked up and smiled at Charlie. The kid was really growing on him.

"I think you've got it, son. Looks like three or four men scrambling around this area, but no smaller prints. I like your idea. This had to be where it happened."

Charlie was beaming, a smile from ear to ear as he looked at Jake.

Jake wrote down some notes, then took his Polaroid camera out of the van and took some pictures of the tire tracks and footprints.

Jake then walked around the area to get his bearings. He looked for a natural marker that he could use as a reference point later. He saw a large boulder on the right side of the main road. He took a smaller rock and walked over to the boulder. With the smaller rock he rubbed a large 'X' on the boulder, just visible enough for him to recognize.

"Now let's see where this road goes," he said, climbing into the van.

The two men started down the dirt road slowly, looking for the tracks or any indication that the trucks may have pulled off the road. Jake looked up at the horizon and saw the road continue over a rise.

"Let's drive up to that rise and take a look."

Once on the top of the rise, they looked around and saw nothing but emptiness and desert. The road continued on into the desert.

"Let's follow it to see where it goes," Jake said.

They drove several miles to a point where the road ended at another road, going north and south.

"They had to turn left or right," Jake said. He looked left and saw the road continue on into some hills. He looked right and saw it continue on where it seemed to intersect with another, bigger road. "Let's go right."

They turned right and drove for about a mile, looking up in surprise when they saw Highway 2 ahead of them. The same road they had taken when they came out of the border crossing. As they approached the main road, Jake looked to the right. In the distance he saw the border crossing. He now knew the escape route of the kidnappers.

"The road bypasses the border crossing and swings around to intersect with Highway 2 right here. From here, they turned left and drove to Tijuana. That's why you didn't see any black trucks when you drove back from the border crossing," Jake said.

"They took them to Tijuana?" Charlie asked.

"It sure looks like it."

Charlie started to pull left onto Highway 2.

"Hold on! Where you going?"

"To Tijuana! That's where Molly is!"

"First things first. Let's go to the campsite in Tecate and see if we can get some information."

"What kind of information? We know what happened."

"I know, but we might get a name, a description, anything that will give us a lead as to where to look in Tijuana. TJ is a big place so we need as much info as we can get."

Charlie looked at him and nodded. He turned the van right onto Highway 2, towards Tecate. They passed the Otay Mesa border crossing on their left and kept driving east.

It took them thirty minutes to reach the school campsite in the barren hills south of Tecate. Charlie pulled into the parking lot where just yesterday there were nearly thirty cars and vans full of kids and adults. Now it was empty, except for one car parked near a small house at the end of the lot.

Jake looked at the campsite, which was still littered with paper and other remnants of a small city. He could see where the tents had been set up.

"How many people were here?" he asked Charlie.

"Probably three hundred or more. I'm not sure."

"Everyone stayed in this area?"

"Yeah, except when we were at the build site, which was most of the time."

"Where did the local kids hang out, here or the build site?"

"The build site."

"Let's go there."

Charlie turned the van around and drove less than a mile to a large area where homes were scattered around the hillsides. The area was in a valley, with medium-sized hills on each side. It was hard land, with scrub brush and rock outcroppings on the hills. Jake saw the area where twenty homes were in the middle of construction. The frames were up on all twenty homes and some had walls partially constructed.

"Is this where you were building?" he asked Charlie.

"Yep. Another two days we would've been done with all twenty homes."

Jake saw several small boys rummaging around the site, looking for nails or anything that they could use or sell. He looked at the hills surrounding the site. They were not imposing, but high enough to discourage someone walking up or down them.

"You ever see anyone on those hills?"

"Yeah, all the time. Mostly kids hiking or playing."

"You ever see any cars or trucks up there?"

"Yeah, every now and then. I think there are roads that come up from behind the hills. Why?"

"The kidnappers had to have a vantage point, either over the build site or the campsite. Probably both. These hills provide a perfect vantage point without being noticed much."

"Yeah, I guess I can see that. I was always too busy to notice."

"That's my point. Everyone was too busy. Let's go talk to some of the kids over there," Jake said, walking to the partially built homes.

Charlie began asking the local kids some questions in Spanish.

"Where'd you learn Spanish?" Jake asked.

"Yeah, well, both my mom and housekeeper spoke it all the time so you pick stuff up. I'm not fluent, just words and phrases I picked up along the way. I asked them if they saw anyone that didn't live around here while the Americans were here. Someone that didn't seem to belong."

"What did they say?" Jake said.

"They said there was one boy, older than most of the kids around here, that wandered around asking questions. He wasn't from this area. They said he sounded like he was from the city."

"Meaning Tijuana, maybe?"

"Maybe. I asked them if they knew his name and one said 'Rafael'. I asked for a last name and he didn't know. Probably the same kid I heard about. Some of the kids in my group said there was an older boy, a teenager, that was hanging around asking questions. Nobody paid much attention, though, 'cause there are so many people coming and going, hammers banging, people talking. Easy to blend in around hundreds of people."

"Yeah, maybe for the Americans. But these local Tecate kids noticed him and knew that he was an outsider. That may be our guy."

"Rafael."

"Yeah, Rafael."

"Ask them what he looked like and the last time they saw him," Jake said.

Charlie talked to the kids in Spanish for several minutes and walked back to Jake.

"He was average height, dark hair, and had what they called a *baby* face," Charlie said.

"A baby face," Jake said, nodding. "That's why he could move around so easily with the other kids."

"Yeah. And they last saw him yesterday right after our caravan left—around three o'clock." Charlie stopped and smiled at Jake. "And guess what?"

Jake lifted his hands up, palms up, and said, "What?"

"He was on top of one of the hills with another man—standing next to a big, black truck," Charlie said proudly.

Jake grinned at this news and slapped Charlie on the back. "You might have a career ahead of you, Charlie. Good job. Rafael is our guy, no question now."

Jake looked at the surrounding hills. "Which hill did they see him on?"

The kids were standing right next to the two Americans by this time, interested in the big man and his scar. One of them was pointing to Jake and saying something, his eyes as big as saucers.

"What's he saying?" Jake said, starting to get annoyed.

Charlie grinned. "The kid said that you looked like a gangster because of your scar."

Jake looked down at the Mexican kids and gave them a scowl and a growl. They backed away.

"Now ask them which hill," he said, grinning at the kids.

Charlie asked them to point to the hill where they had seen Rafael, which they did.

"Okay, let's go up there and see if we can find any tire tracks. If we're lucky, they may match the ones from the road," Jake said.

Charlie turned to the kids. "*Gracias, muchachos.*"

Jake and Charlie got in the van and drove to the back of the hills overlooking the build site where they found a dirt road to the top. They drove up the road and once on top of the hill, they got out and gazed down at the build site below.

"This must be it. Perfect vantage point from here," Jake said.

"Jake. Look here. I think it's the same tread as on the road," Charlie said, pointing to a tire track.

Jake bent down and looked at the tire imprint in the dirt. He looked at the Polaroid of the tire track that he had taken on the road and then looked back at the track in front of him.

"I think you're right. They were here. They were watching your camp yesterday, watching you break down the camp."

"So what does that mean?" Charlie said, looking down at the half-finished homes below.

"It means that the kidnapping was planned. We're up against someone who knows what he's doing. Let's look around up here and see if can find anything else that might help us."

They walked around the hilltop looking for any sort of clue or information.

Jake saw something white in the scrub brush behind the hilltop and picked it up. It was an empty cigarette box.

"This is a Tijuana brand," he said to Charlie. "Not much, but another bit of intel pointing to Tijuana."

Jake looked at his watch. It was four o'clock. They had been in the area for almost two hours.

"Time to head to Tijuana. We have to meet Manny in an hour, and it's been a while since I've been to TJ, so it might take us some time to find Lilly's. Let's go," Jake said.

Jake saw Charlie looking at the build site and empty campsite below. He knew what thoughts were going through the kid's head.

"Jake, Molly's been with those animals for twenty-four hours," he said, his voice quivering. "Will I ever see her again?"

Jake saw the pain in his eyes. "I don't know, Charlie." He put his hand on Charlie's shoulder. "But one thing I do know. We have to find her before another twenty-four hours go by."

CHAPTER 29

The cabin in the bubble of the 747 was dark except for the lights near the cockpit. Ethan, the only one awake, was staring off into the night sky, alone with his thoughts. They were an hour away from landing in Mexico City, an hour away from the next leg of his unknown journey. It was six o'clock in Mexico City and the sun was just beginning to set in the west. He had tried, but sleep wouldn't come.

Ethan looked around the dark cabin one more time, hoping to see anyone awake so that he could talk to someone, to take his mind off of the nightmare that had invaded his life. There was no movement anywhere in the cabin, the only noise the hum of the jet engines outside.

He closed his eyes again, random thoughts invading his mind. He remembered reading to his children at bedtime when they were small. Charlie liked books about fire engines and airplanes. He wanted to be a fireman when he grew up. He memorized all the pictures and quoted them back every night. He knew what an aileron was on an airplane, for crying out loud! He once asked where the automatic pilot sat, bringing a smile to Ethan's face. So innocent, so happy.

Reading to Molly was a different story, literally, every night. She liked to hear stories that Ethan made up, and got such a huge smile on her face when he mentioned a little girl named Molly in the story. He used the stories to teach her about being careful of strangers, her eyes getting so big when he mentioned the bad men. She knew what kidnapping was when she was five . . . .

He looked out the window of the aircraft and saw the moon in the half-lit sky. It was not quite a half-moon. It made him think back, when Molly was three or four. They were standing in the backyard, looking up at the stars in the sky, his wife, Connie, standing between them. 'You know what that is?'

she asked Molly, who was looking at the sliver of a moon in the sky. 'That's your toenail moon.' Molly looked up in amazement, smiling from ear to ear. 'Oh yeah, my toenail moon,' she repeated. From that moment on, whenever they saw a sliver of moon, it was Molly's toenail moon. It eventually became just 'Molly's Moon'.

Ethan stared at the half-moon in the twilight sky outside the airplane. He sucked in a gasp, glancing over at Pete anxiously. He took short, halting breaths. *He had done everything right.* He taught both of them to be careful, to never, ever talk to strangers. And now, his little girl...

He jumped when he felt a hand on his shoulder. Turning, he saw Victoria Calderon standing in the aisle. She was leaning on the back of Pete's seat, a concerned look on her face.

"I couldn't sleep and saw that you were awake. Would you like to talk?" she said softly.

Ethan nodded to her, the excitement beginning to build, then carefully stepped over the snoring Pete into the aisle. He followed her to some seats several rows back. He sat down next to Victoria, smelling her perfume and feeling her breath. The airplane was dark and everyone else in the cabin was asleep. Ethan could see her face in the dim light of the cabin, just enough to outline her glowing face. *Damn, wish I had a breath mint.*

"How are you holding up?" she asked, sitting with her knees almost touching his.

He felt the dryness of the cabin air in his mouth. "Okay, I guess. It's still sinking in."

She looked at him with her big, round, dark eyes. She tilted her head slightly as she looked at him carefully.

"I heard you gasp a moment ago," she said, a worried look on her face. "Is everything okay?"

Ethan felt his face getting hot as he rubbed his red and splotchy eyes. "I was thinking about my daughter when she was young," he said, a weak smile on his face. "I used to tell her stories about bad men and how they would try to lure little girls and boys into their cars, and to be careful . . . ."

Vicki's eyes became moist. "I'm so sorry, Ethan. I didn't mean to . . . ."

"No. No. It feels good to talk to someone about it. I've been keeping it bottled up and it's driving me crazy."

"You must be a mess on the inside, but you seem so calm on the outside," she said.

He laughed softly. "Yeah, well, it's all smoke and mirrors right now."

"Smoke and mirrors? I'm sorry, I . . . ."

He smiled. "An American term. It means I don't know how I'm holding together—magic, maybe?"

"Yes, I think I have heard the term before. I think, though, that it's more than just magic, as you say. You seem like a very calm, confident man."

He was beginning to regain his confidence. "In business, I guess I am. But I've never faced anything like this before. I feel like I could turn into a blubbering idiot at any time."

"Well, my father is very impressed with you, and he doesn't impress easily. He is a tough businessman and he requires the utmost discipline and order in his world. If he sees something in you, then there must be something there."

Ethan felt his face turning a deeper shade of red. *What was it about this woman?* "Was it difficult growing up with such a disciplinarian?"

"Sometimes. He demanded our best effort and pushed us very hard. But he always backed it up with love . . . and my mother kept him in line," she laughed, quietly.

"It must have been very difficult when your sister died."

Victoria pursed her lips tightly and nodded. "It was hell for a few years. Daddy blamed himself for her death and still hasn't forgiven himself. He sometimes falls into melancholy for days and ends up drinking a lot, but it's happening less and less now. Time is beginning to heal the wounds."

Ethan saw her eyes growing moist. "It had to be hard on you, too."

She nodded, blinking a tear away. "I miss my little sister. She would have been twenty-five now. I was twenty when she was killed and I also went into a shell for several years. But life goes on . . . ."

He stared at the beautiful woman sitting next to him and wanted to reach out and hug her, but held back. Instead he reached over and put his hand on her hand. "I'm sorry, Vicki."

She didn't pull her hand back, as he thought she might. Instead, she put her other hand on top of his.

"I'm so sorry about your wife. So recent . . . ."

Ethan's shoulders sagged. "That was hard. Hard on my children, hard on me . . . just very hard."

"Did she suffer?"

Ethan took a big gulp of air. "Yes. She did," he said. "She was a strong woman, but the cancer won."

She continued to hold her hand on his, drawing a little closer to him. He felt the touch of her leg on his and it felt good.

"You have a difficult few days ahead of you, Ethan. Are you ready?"

He turned and stared off into the darkness for a few seconds. Turning back to her he said, "I don't know. I guess I have to be."

Victoria leaned over and put her arms around his shoulders, her cheek next to his. Ethan felt the electricity run through his body. They hugged silently for several minutes, nothing being said. He wanted to remain like this forever, the warmth, the touch, the smell.

She released him and sat back in her seat. "I'm glad I met you, Ethan." Her eyes met his and they looked at each other for several seconds. "I want to help you . . . in any way I can."

He took a deep breath. "You already have helped, Vicki. Just listening has helped a great deal."

Their heads jerked up as the cabin lights came on. They blinked several times at each other as their eyes adjusted to the light, giggling like two school children.

"Well, I guess I'll see you on the ground," she said, standing up.

Ethan stood and moved into the aisle, letting her pass. "Thank you, Vicki."

She leaned in and gave him a kiss on his cheek, then walked back to her seat.

CHAPTER 30

"When was the last time you slept?" Jake asked Charlie, who was beginning to show signs of heavy eyes. "We're approaching Tijuana."

"What?" Charlie said as he glanced at Jake. His eyes were half way closed.

"Pull over, son. I'm driving."

Charlie pulled over to the shoulder of the highway, almost side-swiping a passing car.

"Jesus, kid!" Jake said.

He climbed out of the van and walked around to the driver side. Charlie crawled into the passenger seat and his eyes immediately closed. Jake glanced over and was about to say something, saw the kid's head fall to one side, and decided to let him sleep. He felt sorry for the poor kid. He shouldn't have to go through what he's going through at his age. Life is tough enough without having a nightmare like this thrown at him.

Jake pulled out onto the highway that led into Tijuana, with traffic beginning to get heavy. It had been a few years since he had driven in TJ, so he tried to remember how to get to *Avenida Revolucion*. It was near the border so he watched for signs. Ten minutes went by before he began to recognize the area.

Lilly's was a small bar in the middle of the tourist zone and *Avenida Revolucion* was the main drag. Horns were honking everywhere and there was no consideration for lanes or stop lights. Jake fought the traffic for a few miles, then ran smack into *Avenida Revolucion*, a big, wide thoroughfare. He got his bearings, turned right onto the *Avenida* and spotted the small bar two blocks down. He didn't want to park the school van in the street, so found a parking lot close by and paid fifty *pesos* to the attendant. He woke Charlie up with a soft shake of his shoulder.

"Let's go, kid."

"Huh? What?" Charlie mumbled, rubbing his eyes.

"We're here. No sleeping on the job, son."

Jake climbed out of the driver's seat and walked over to the passenger side. Charlie stumbled out and almost fell on his face.

"You okay, kid?"

"Yeah. And stop calling me kid, damn it!"

Jake smiled at him. "Whatever you say, boss." The kid was getting grumpy.

Jake began walking down the *Avenida* and stopped in front of a small bar. Lilly's was a hangout for Americans, especially cops and ex-cops, with a sprinkling of regular folk. Jake had spent many hours in the little club when he was on the SDPD but hadn't been back since he left the force five years before.

As they walked into the dark bar, Jake looked around but didn't recognize anyone at the bar. He looked to his right and in the dim light saw Manny Fernandez sitting at a table, smiling at him. He had a beer and a glass of bourbon in front of him, half empty.

"Bull, you old sonofabitch!" the man exclaimed, rising to his feet. "How the hell are ya?"

Manny was in his late fifties, still in good shape. He had short-cropped gray hair on top of a tanned face. He was almost a foot shorter than Jake and had a middle-aged gut developing.

"Thirsty," Jake said, reaching over and shaking his hand. "Good to see you, Manny."

Charlie was standing behind Jake, almost hidden from sight. He stepped to the side and looked at Manny.

"Who's this?" Manny asked.

"Charlie Paxton. He and his family are the reason I'm down here," Jake said, pulling a wooden chair out and sitting down.

"Hi, Charlie. I'm Manny," the gray haired man said, holding out his hand. "Have a seat."

Charlie frowned as he shook Manny's hand, then pulled a chair out and sat down.

Manny looked at Charlie then back at Jake. "Quiet type, huh?"

"Sometimes," Jake answered. "He's pretty tired. Been through a tough twenty-four hours."

Manny nodded. "You guys want something to drink?"

"Yeah, Bushmills straight and a Corona for the ki . . . for Charlie," Jake said.

Manny yelled to the bartender. "*Mamacita*! A bottle of Bushmills and one Corona!"

Manny furrowed his brow as he looked at Jake. "Still drinking the Bushmills, Bull?"

"Why do you call him Bull?" Charlie asked.

"That's what we called him when we were on the force together. You know, I can't remember why we called him Bull. You remember?" he said, looking at Jake.

"Yeah, I remember. But let's get to the point, Manny." He looked at Charlie. "The stories can wait." Jake noticed Manny staring at his scar.

"Jesus, Bull. Is that from that night?"

"What night?" asked Charlie.

"Yes. And the stories will come later, damn it." He looked at Charlie, then Manny. "Okay?"

"No problem. How was the border?" said Manny.

"Piece of cake," Jake answered. "It'll be a different story when we try to return."

"No shit. It's a complete mess at the TJ border," Manny said, glancing at Charlie.

"We crossed at Otay Mesa and backtracked on the same road the school kids took," Jake said, trying to get to the point.

"How'd that go?"

"We found the spot where Charlie's sister and the other girls were abducted. About a mile from the border on a dirt road just off the main road."

Manny looked at Charlie. "What's your sister's name, son?"

"Molly."

The bartender brought the drinks over to the table. Charlie smiled when she didn't ask him for his identification.

"Thanks, Rosa," Manny said, handing her two hundred *pesos*.

Jake poured himself a glass of Bushmills and threw it down while Charlie took a long gulp of the Corona. They both let out a satisfied sigh when they finished.

"You two must have been thirsty," Manny said, chuckling. "So how many girls were with Charlie's sister?"

"Two other girls and a female teacher. All taken at the same time," Jake said, throwing down another glass.

"What else did you find in Tecate?" Manny said.

Jake told him about the tire tracks on the dirt road matching the tracks on the hilltop, about the young kids talking about a boy named Rafael, and about the fact that the kidnapping had been planned.

"Definitely sounds like it was planned," Manny said. "I'll have my TJPD contact run the name Rafael, see if he comes up with anything. Pretty common name down here, though."

Jake leaned across the table and looked at Manny. "You trust this TJPD guy?"

"Yeah, I do. I've worked with him for a few years. His brother was killed by one of the cartels, so he has a grudge against the gangs down here."

Jake continued to look at Manny. "I don't want some Mexican asshole screwing this up, Manny. But if you trust him, okay."

"Have you had any contact with the SDPD?" Manny asked, changing the subject.

"Not today, but they told Charlie and his principal yesterday that they had to be missing for twenty-four hours before they would make a report."

"How long's it been?"

"Twenty-four hours."

"Anyone talking to the SDPD right now, filing a report?"

"Probably the principal of the school, a Mister Sizemore. He's a dick," Jake said, looking at Charlie. "Charlie just about took his head off this morning."

"Really?" Manny said, staring at Charlie. "Why was that?"

"Long story, I'll tell you later. Right now we have to go on the premise that we have to find Molly and the others on our own. You know how it works down here, Manny. SDPD can only do so much and the TJ cops are useless."

"What about the FBI? This is a federal crime, across a border."

"Haven't talked to them, but I'm sure the SDPD will get them involved. I don't think they'll be much help with this terrorist stuff going on."

"Yeah, you're probably right." Manny glanced at Charlie, then back at Jake. "Any ransom demands yet?"

"No, not that we know of. We need to check with your principal, Charlie, as soon as we're done here."

"You've talked to Charlie about the possibilities?" Manny said.

"Yeah, we've talked about it. He knows it may not be a kidnapping for ransom. We're going with that until we hear different."

Charlie suddenly stood up. "I'm going to call Mister Sizemore, to see if he's heard anything."

Jake looked at him and nodded. "Stay in front of the bar, don't go wandering off," Jake told him.

Charlie walked out of the bar, holding his cell phone.

"How's he holding up?" Manny asked Jake once Charlie was gone.

"Not bad for a nineteen year old kid. He's smart. But he's headed for a crash—soon."

"He looks worn out. Has he slept since this all started?"

"Don't think so. I need to find a place for us to crash tonight. He's not going to make it much longer."

"You can stay at my place over at Rosarito Beach. It's only ten miles from here. I won't take no for an answer. Plus, it'll give us a chance to talk and plan while he's crashed out."

"Thanks, Manny."

"Why don't we finish these drinks then head on over. Get the kid some shut-eye and we can figure this thing out. It sounds like a tough one, Bull."

"Okay. Good idea. The kid's dad is trying to get here from Europe, so he may or may not make it by tomorrow. Probably won't know until we see him. I'm not counting on him making it." Jake leaned in close to Manny. "The girl doesn't have much time, Manny. We've got to find out where she is if she's gonna have any chance at all."

"Yeah, if she's not gone already."

"That's why we've got to move fast," Jake replied. "We could use some help on this, Manny. Got anyone in mind?"

"Yeah, a couple of guys. All ex-cops that live down here. They all remember the raw deal you got from the SDPD. I'll make some calls tonight."

"How about...weapons," Jake said, looking around the bar.

"I can get my hands on some automatic stuff. Ex-military. And a couple of nine millimeter Glocks."

"You'll be sticking your neck out, Manny. I don't want you to screw up your retirement."

"You need some help, Bull. Besides, I'm bored as hell, so this gets my blood going!"

Jake smiled and clasped hands with his old friend. They both chugged another glass of whiskey.

"I heard you've been hitting the booze pretty hard since you got canned," Manny said.

Jake's smiled faded. "Yeah, I guess you could say that. You been talking to Tiny, right?"

"I call him every now and then, just to check up on you. You sure you're up to this?"

"Don't know. We'll see," Jake said as he downed another shot of Bushmills.

"You're gonna have to ease off the Bushmills a little bit over the next couple of days, Bull."

Jake shot Manny a look. "Don't worry about me, Manny. I'll be ready."

Charlie came back into the bar with a glum look on his face. "Nobody's heard a word. No ransom demands, yet," he said, sitting down at the table.

"You talk to that prick, Sizemore?" Jake said.

"Yes. He's pissed, Jake. He asked where we were and I told him to go to hell," Charlie said, a defiant look on his face.

"Damn," Jake said. "That dick can cause us some trouble if he files a complaint with the SDPD."

Manny stared at Jake. "You want me to make some inquires, Bull?"

"Yeah, try to find out where we stand. I don't want some cowboy arresting us when we try to cross back over."

"Okay," Manny said, standing up. "Let's get out of here and go to my place. Charlie, you need some sleep, son."

Charlie stared at Manny, then at Jake, the dark circles around his eyes growing darker. "I could use some, I guess."

Jake looked at Manny, the smile gone from both of their faces. They knew the clock was ticking.

CHAPTER 31

The huge, lumbering jumbo jet set its wheels on the runway without so much as a bump. It took a long time to taxi to the end of the runway, then it turned around onto a side runway and taxied back to the terminal, heading for the cargo terminal. It finally came to a stop in front of a large metal building with a sign that said '*Estafeta Carga Aerea*'. Ethan saw several men roll some metal stairs up to the door. He looked at his watch. Seven-fifteen in the evening.

"Would you gentlemen mind if my wife and daughter go first," Arturo Calderon said as he joined Ethan and Pete in the front of the cabin. "You see, she's wearing a dress, and . . . well, you understand."

"Of course. Please," Ethan replied. "It's your plane, Arturo," he smiled.

"Thank you. I'll go down first."

Arturo climbed down the steep stairs and looked up. Ethan helped Alexandria onto the stairs and then Victoria. Pete followed her, then Ethan. Before he descended the stairs, Ethan thanked Jan and shook his hand. Once down, Jan dropped their carry-ons to a baggage handler at the bottom of the stairs.

"Good luck, Mister Paxton," Jan said through the opening. "God bless you."

Ethan looked up and waved to the flight attendant. "Thank you, Jan."

As they grabbed their luggage, Pete said, "Your horses took the landing pretty good, Arturo. I didn't have to hold my nose this time."

"Landings are always better than take-offs. They don't get as nervous," Arturo replied, smiling.

"Are they thoroughbreds?"

"No. Quarter horses. We attended several shows in Europe, trying to create a market for my breed. It was quite successful."

"I don't want to get personal, but what did it cost you to charter this plane? I'm in the logistics industry and I know how expensive chartering a 747 can be."

"Oh, I only paid for part of it," Arturo replied. "I guess you would call me a sub-contractor. Someone else paid for most of the charter, I just tagged along."

"That's good. You'd have to sell quite a few horses to pay for this baby."

"Yes, and I'm afraid I don't have that many," he laughed.

They began their walk down the metal stairs, with Victoria leading the way. The air was heavy and humid. Even at seven in the evening it was stifling hot. A blanket of smog was covering the sky, the smell overpowering them as they walked off the airplane.

"Holy cow! I forgot how hot and humid it got down here!" said Pete as they descended the stairs.

"It's only going to get worse when we fly to Chihuahua, I'm afraid," said Arturo. "Chihuahua is close to the Sonora desert, so we get very high temperatures."

Ethan and Pete looked at each other and shrugged their shoulders. Welcome to Mexico.

They walked across the tarmac to the cargo terminal. By the time they reached the building they were all soaked in sweat. A man in light blue overalls opened a door for them and they walked into the building, which thankfully was air conditioned.

"Damn, that feels good!" exclaimed Pete, wiping the sweat from his forehead.

A dark-skinned man with a shirt that said 'ECA' and name tag that said 'Ramirez' greeted them. "*Buenas tardes,*" he said politely, bowing toward Vicki and the Calderons. "Welcome back to Mexico."

"Thank you, Esteban," Arturo said. "These are our friends from America. Can you take care of them?"

"*Sí,*" he said, turning to Ethan and Pete. "Please follow me."

He led the two Americans to a small office where a Mexican customs official was waiting for them. The gruff-looking man frowned at them and held out his hand, obviously waiting for their passports. After looking at each of their passports, he finally stamped them and waved them into a waiting room, where they would wait for their luggage. No words, no pleasantries were spoken.

"What bug crawled up his a— "Pete began to say, stopping when he saw Arturo walking up to them.

"We arrived a little late," Arturo said to Ethan and Pete. "The customs official was kept overtime to wait for you. I apologize for his curtness. He is probably hungry for his dinner."

"No problem, Arturo. I'd be grumpy, too," Ethan said, frowning at Pete.

"Our charter is scheduled to depart at eight forty-five, from this same area. It is a King Air 200 turbo-prop and will seat all of us easily."

"What about your horses?" Ethan asked.

"Oh, they will go coach class—by truck," he smiled. "They will arrive tomorrow afternoon after an overnight ride in a horse trailer. I've spoiled them too much already."

"We can't thank you enough for this," Ethan replied. "We would probably be stuck here in Mexico City until tomorrow if it wasn't for your generosity."

"As I said before, it is our pleasure and our sincere desire to help you in any way we can. It is not costing us any more for you and Pete to fly with us."

The luggage was brought into the building by a cargo attendant, who checked each piece against the luggage tags. The grumpy customs official had each person open their luggage so that he could inspect the contents.

"This is standard procedure for arriving charters," Arturo said, seeing the discomfort on the American's faces. "Mexico is trying to do her part on the war against drugs."

When the luggage process was completed, Ethan turned to Arturo and said, "I have to make a call while we're waiting, to find out what is happening in Tijuana."

"Absolutely. Please do."

Ethan looked at his watch. It was seven forty-five, making it five forty-five in California. He pulled out the cell phone that Henrik had given him and turned it on. He hadn't used it yet so had to become familiar with it. Once he was comfortable he dialed his son's cell phone number. After three rings a man answered.

"Yeah," the voice said.

"Hello? Who's this?" Ethan said, not recognizing the voice immediately.

"Ethan? This is Jake."

"Jake? I didn't recognize your voice. Where's Charlie?" Ethan asked.

"He's sleeping. We're at a friend's house in Rosarito Beach."

"Where's that?"

Jake coughed. "Mexico, near Tijuana."

"You're in Mexico? With Charlie?"

Several seconds of silence. "Yeah, we're in Mexico. Where are you?"

"I just landed in Mexico City. We're waiting for our charter flight to Chihuahua, so I don't have much time. What's going on?"

"Well, like I said, we're in Rosarito Beach at a friend's house. We crossed the border today and drove to Tecate this afternoon to check the build site."

"Charlie went with you?"

"Yeah, Ethan. I needed him. He's been a big help."

"Damn, Jake, I didn't want Charlie going back there. It's too dangerous."

"I know, Ethan, but—"

"Jake, damn it! What the hell is going on?"

"We're looking for your daughter, Ethan."

Ethan took a deep breath. "Okay. Sorry, Jake. What else? Have the kidnappers called?"

"No. No one has called."

"Shit!" Ethan said into the phone. His worst nightmare was coming true. "How about the other parents?"

"Nothing. No one has heard a thing, according to the school principal."

Ethan put his hand over the cell phone and closed his eyes. After several seconds he put it back to his ear. "What are you doing now? Have you talked to the police?"

"No, we haven't. Do you want to know what's going on or not?" Jake said.

Ethan took a deep breath. "Okay, Jake. Sorry, I've been flying for the past twelve hours. Fill me in."

Ethan listened to Jake as he recapped the day's events, from the meeting with Charlie at the El Toro, the altercation with the principal, finding the tire tracks near Tecate, all the way up to arriving at Manny's house a few minutes earlier.

"Charlie passed out as soon as his head hit the bed," Jake said. "The poor kid was exhausted."

Ethan rubbed his temple, trying to digest this new information. "What's the deal with the principal? Why did Charlie almost take his head off?"

"The guys a prick, Ethan. He screwed up and that's why Molly and the other girls were abducted. Charlie just lost it."

Ethan's mind was going a million miles an hour. "Is everything okay? I mean, is Charlie in trouble?"

"Nah," Jake said. "We've got it under control. Don't worry about him, Ethan. He's a good kid."

After a couple of deep breaths he said, "Jake, are you going to find my daughter?"

"I'm doing everything I can, Ethan. I'm going into Tijuana tonight to dig around while Charlie is sleeping. But it's not looking good, Ethan."

Ethan rubbed his temples again. "Why, Jake?"

"Because we're not dealing with a normal kidnapping here. I have some people helping me that know what they're doing, you have to trust me."

Ethan took another deep breath and blew it out. "Okay, Jake. I'm flying to Chihuahua tonight, but it's still another eight hundred fifty miles to Tijuana from there. I'm not sure if I'll have to drive or if I can find a flight, but either way it will be tomorrow afternoon before I can get to TJ."

"I'll do what I can until you get here. Ethan, prepare for the worst."

Ethan's stomach tightened and he felt the nausea filling his head. "Jake?"

"Yeah?"

"Find my daughter."

"I'll see you when you get here," Jake said. *Click.*

CHAPTER 32

Cindy and Jenny had been awake for an hour. All three girls had been allowed to take a shower and put on clean clothes out of their own duffle bags. They sat on their mattresses with their hands tied in front of them, their wet hair dripping down on the mattresses. Molly was pacing back and forth in the dark room, glancing at Missus Caldwell, then at Cindy and Jenny. Missus Caldwell was still breathing, but her breaths came sporadically. Molly knew that without a doctor she would die soon. She had been trying to figure a way out of this for the past hour, but her mind was still foggy from the drug that Natalia had injected into them. Natalia was not in the room, having gone out thirty minutes before.

"Molly, what are we going to do?" asked Cindy, who had been watching her friend pace back and forth. Cindy was sitting with her legs crossed, brushing her long, blond hair.

"I don't know, Cindy. I know people are looking for us, but I don't know what happened after we were taken. I don't know if Charlie got my voicemail. Even if he did, how would he know where to look?" Molly was agitated, the bitterness oozing out of her when she looked at Cindy.

"My parents have to be looking for me. And Mister Sizemore, he must have talked to the police, right? They have to be out there looking for us," Cindy said.

"It's your fault we're here, Cindy," Molly said suddenly. "You took so long to get ready, we were the last car . . . ."

Cindy stared at her friend, tears welling in her eyes. "But I didn't—"

"You didn't what? Think for once?" Molly was staring at her, her nostrils flaring.

"I'm sorry, Moll," Cindy said.

Molly's shoulders sagged as she walked up and held her friend tightly. "No, I'm sorry, Cindy. It wasn't your fault, it just happened."

Molly looked at Jenny, who was lying down on the mattress again. Molly was concerned about her because she hadn't said a word since they were kidnapped. She just stared off into space. Now she was rocking back and forth, her legs tucked up to her chest in the fetal position, her wet hair a tangled mess.

"Jenny, how are you doing?" Molly asked the girl.

Jenny glanced at Molly but didn't respond. Molly glanced over at Cindy and shook her head. Molly knew they had to get Jenny some help soon, or she would end up like Missus Caldwell.

"What about the woman?" Cindy said. "She likes you, Molly. Will she help us?"

"I think so, but I don't know how much she can do. She's controlled by that freak outside. There are lots of men on the other side of that door, and only one way out. I don't know."

Molly thought about the white van. They must have it because Natalia brought in their duffle bags, which were in the van. Then it hit her. *The cell phone! It might still be in the van!* She remembered kicking it under the driver's seat when she was being pulled out of the van. She would have to get Natalia to look for it. She could call Charlie and tell him where they are! Suddenly, Molly had energy, she had hope. *Hope!*

The girls heard the dead bolt beginning to open.

"Lie down!" Molly said to Cindy.

The door slid open wide, showering the room with light from the outside area. It was the first time Molly could see anything outside. She saw several men standing around, one or two looking at her. Before the door was closed she thought she saw the white van. *It's still here!*

"¡*Buenas noches, señoritas!*" Angel said as he walked into the room, followed by Natalia.

Angel told another man to close the door part way. Angel and Natalia were the only ones in the room with the girls and Missus Caldwell.

"It's so nice to see you awake, finally. Did you have a good sleep?" Angel said, a broad smile on his face.

Molly and Cindy just stared at him, not saying a word. Jenny continued to rock back and forth, not looking at anyone.

"What's wrong with her?" Angel asked, looking at Natalia and pointing to Jenny.

"She hasn't talked since she's been here. She just rocks back and forth in that position," Natalia replied.

Angel walked over to Jenny and bent down to look into her eyes. When he stood up he shook his head. "She is distant, not all here. I think she has checked out. . Too bad."

Molly was surprised to hear the man speak almost perfect English, and intelligently. This was not good. It made him more dangerous.

Angel looked at Cindy. "I see you got cleaned up, even washed your beautiful hair. Very pretty."

He bent down and touched her hair, then rubbed the back of his left hand across her cheek. "Very smooth skin. Very nice."

He pinched Cindy's face together, looking into her eyes. "This one's alert, nice blue eyes. They like that." He looked at Cindy's legs in her tight jeans. "She's a little skinny, but not bad." He patted her on the rear and smiled.

For the first time, Molly noticed his right arm hanging at his side, a black glove on it. He used his left arm for everything.

Angel then turned his gaze to Molly. He shook his head back and forth. "Yes, you are the prize, little one." He walked over to Molly and said, "Stand up."

Molly didn't move. She continued to lie on her side, staring at the man.

"Did you hear me?" he said, louder. "I said stand up!"

Natalia reached down and helped Molly to her feet. Molly stood and stared at him, defiance in her eyes. She jerked her arm from Natalia's grasp, giving her a defiant look also.

"Well, well. It looks like we have an angry one here. Are you not happy to be here?" Angel said, pursing his lips as though he was pouting.

"Screw you!" Molly said, her eyes bulging, her courage coming from knowing the white van was just outside.

"Yes! Yes! I like the spirit! You are definitely a *Latina*. A hot tempered *Latina*."

Angel walked over to her and put his hand close to her hair. Molly took a step back. He reached out quickly and grabbed her hair in his left hand and yanked her to him. He had his face only inches from her face. They were staring into each other's eyes.

"You ARE a *Latina*? Yes or no?"

"Screw you!"

Angel twisted her hair and forced her down on her knees. Molly grimaced in pain. Then he pulled her back to her feet. "Turn around."

Molly stood still, breathing hard, staring at him.

"Then I will turn you around." Angel grabbed her shoulders and forced her to turn one hundred eighty degrees. "Very nice. Very, very nice," he said seductively.

Natalia had seen enough. She reached over and grabbed Molly's arm and pulled her to her side.

Angel reached out and slapped Natalia with the back of his right hand, the gloved hand. Her head twisted to the side and blood spurted out of her mouth. He grabbed Molly and forced her from Natalia's grip.

"You *puta loca!* You want to go where they are going? *¡Pinche perra!*" He put his foot on Natalia's rear end and pushed. She fell to the floor, sprawled out on her stomach.

"You ever do that again I will kill you!" His eyes flashed and his breath seethed out between his teeth.

After he settled down, Angel turned his attention on Molly. He put his face next to hers and licked her cheek. He turned her head so that she was face to face with him. She looked into his eyes and saw evil and pure animal lust. She looked away quickly.

Angel forced her down on the mattress. "They like spirit, so you will bring some good *dinero*. Too bad I can't keep you for myself. I would break you and have you begging for more. What's your name?"

Molly continued to lie on her side, not moving. He reached down and turned her over on her back, squeezing her face with his left hand. "What . . . is . . . your . . . name?"

"Molly."

"Molly? What kind of *Latina* name is that? No, no. From now on you will be Rosalinda. My beautiful rose," he said, looking at Natalia, grinning. "You like that name, don't you my love?"

Natalia stared up at him, fear and loathing in her eyes.

"Yes, Rosalinda," he said, smiling at Natalia again. "You will hear that name from many men." He turned and put his lips next to Molly's right ear. "Rosalinda. Rosalinda," he whispered. "Get used to it."

Angel stood up and looked at the other girls. Then he saw Missus Caldwell lying motionless in the corner. "Is she dead?"

"No," Natalia said.

"She looks dead. We'll get rid of her."

He looked at Jenny, still rocking back and forth on the mattress. "Maybe we should get rid of this one, too."

"No!" Molly said. "She'll be fine. I'll take care of her."

Angel looked at Molly in surprise. "Rosalinda is a nurse? Just like my sweet Natalia." He walked to Natalia and picked her up. "You like the name Rosalinda, don't you my love?"

Natalia turned her face away, tears streaming down her blood-smeared cheeks.

Angel pushed her away. "Clean yourself up."

As he walked to the metal door he looked back at Molly and smiled as though nothing had happened. "Have a good night's sleep, Rosalinda." He glanced at Natalia and laughed as he walked out and slid the metal door closed.

CHAPTER 33

Everyone was in shock, including Natalia. Molly stared at her as she washed the blood off of her face and stopped the bleeding from her nose.

"You hate him, don't you?" Molly said.

Natalia hesitated. "Yes, I hate him. I despise him . . . and I fear him."

"How long have you been with him?"

Natalia looked at the teenager with sadness in her eyes. "Three years."

"Why? Why stay with him so long?"

"You are so young, and so innocent. I was like you when I was young. So full of hope and spirit. We were poor, but we had love and a strong family." Natalia peered at Molly, the sadness etched on her face. "When I was sixteen, I got pregnant by a boy in our village. He raped me."

Molly held her gaze. "I'm sorry," she whispered.

"My father was ashamed of me and sent me to live with an aunt in the United States. Being Catholic, abortion was not an option. So I had the baby in the U.S. I gave it away." She wiped a tear from her eye. "When I came back to Mexico, my father would not let me live in our home, so I was forced to live with a friend in Tijuana. One thing led to another and I started working in the bars, just to survive. I had been working in the bars in Tijuana for ten years when I met Angel. He was very handsome, very macho, and he was nice to me. He bought me things and treated me like his girlfriend."

"Why did he call me Rosalinda?"

Natalia stared at her and then hung her head.

"I found out later that he had many girlfriends in the bars. I was so naïve and so stupid. I thought I could get away and tried several times, but he found me and beat me." She closed her eyes.

Molly suppressed a gasp. "You have no one to help you?"

"No. My only friends are other bar girls, and they are controlled by men also. Once you get into this life, it is impossible to get out . . . alive."

Molly looked at her differently, with pity instead of hatred. "Did you ever try to contact the child you gave up?" Molly asked.

"No. I lost all contact once I came back to Mexico. She was adopted by an American family and my aunt kept in contact with them for a year or so. I have never spoken to her."

"Was her name Rosalinda?"

Natalia looked up and stared at Molly. "That's the name I gave her when she was born, but the American family changed it."

"So he called me Rosalinda to hurt you?"

Natalia nodded her head, wiping a tear from her eye.

Molly saw the absolute sorrow in Natalia's face and felt sorry for her, in spite of her own circumstances and in spite of Natalia's involvement with her abduction. She was about to say something to comfort the woman when Natalia suddenly spoke.

"Are you adopted, Molly?" Natalia asked, out of the blue.

"Why would you ask me that?" Molly said, shocked and defiant.

"I can see it in your eyes, your face."

Molly turned her head, then looked back at Natalia. "It's none of your business," she hissed.

"It's okay, Molly. I hope that the little girl I gave away grew up like you have."

Molly glared at the woman, the fire in her eyes slowly going out. "I love my family. They've given me a wonderful life, a full life. I have no desire to know who my birth mother was." There, she said it.

Natalia didn't hesitate. "Because she might be someone like me?"

Molly turned away, the tears welling up.

The woman and the teenager sat silently for several minutes. Molly wiped her face with the back of her hand. She looked over at Cindy, who had been silently listening to her. She crawled to Cindy and the two girls hugged each other in silence, both of them crying softly.

"Molly, I'm so sorry for what happened to you. I have to find a way to get you and the other girls out of here." Natalia was staring at her. "I'm not smart, but you are. You have to help me."

Molly glanced at Natalia, wiping her eyes. "The van. I saw it on the other side of the door. My cell phone is under the driver's seat. I kicked it under the seat when the man grabbed me out of the backseat."

Natalia stared at her wide-eyed. "I . . . I can't. They're outside, watching . . . ."

"You have to get inside the van to see if it's still there," Molly said.

"Angel's men are outside . . . there is always someone on guard in the other room."

Molly saw the fear in Natalia's eyes. "We need a diversion of some kind, so that you can check the van."

"Even if it's there, it won't have power," Cindy said, joining the conversation.

"I know, but the power cord is in my duffle bag." Molly dug it out and held it up. She then looked around the room to see if there was an electrical outlet. She spotted one above them, next to the dangling light bulb. "And there's the outlet."

"If we can create a diversion, get the men out of the other room, you may have time to get my cell phone. Can you do that, Natalia?"

"I don't know . . . ."

"It's our only chance," Molly said. "He's going to kill you, Natalia."

Natalia jerked her head up, glaring at Molly. "He wouldn't . . . do that," she said.

"Natalia, the way he treats you . . . ."

"No! He loves me! He gets mad sometimes . . . ." Natalia's voice trailed off as she lowered her face, the tears beginning to run down her cheeks. "He still loves me," she whispered.

Molly walked over to the woman and held her, brushing her hair and whispering. "He's using you, Natalia. He doesn't care about you. You have to help us, all of us, get out of here."

Natalia cried quietly in Molly's arms. "*Mija* . . . ."

CHAPTER 34

The Pacific Ocean continued to roll in, wave after wave, the rhythmic sound of water hitting the beach soothing Jake's rattled mind. He leaned on the balcony ledge of Manny's condominium, an empty glass of Bushmills in his hand, feeling a million miles away from the nightmare that was facing him and the Paxton's. He closed his eyes and felt the ocean breeze on his face, the smell of salt water filling his nostrils, the sound of the waves cascading in his ears.

"He's still out cold," said Manny, from behind, interrupting the silence.

Jake opened his eyes and turned to see Manny holding a bottle of Bushmills. *Ahh. His old friend.* He reached out with his empty glass.

"Yeah, he'll sleep until tomorrow," Jake said. "The kid was running on fumes. Thanks for letting us crash here, Manny," Jake said, holding up his full glass.

"Cheers, Bull," Manny said, clinking glasses with Jake. "Good to see you after all these years. Didn't know if I'd ever see you again."

"Yeah, well, I wouldn't be here if it wasn't for that kid in there, and his sister." Jake took a drink. "I knew their dad back in my military days. We were stationed in Japan together in seventy-eight and seventy-nine. He's a good man."

"How'd he find you?"

"He told me he got my number from one of his Air Force buddies. Don't know how his friend had my number. He called me last night out of the blue. I was still in the El Toro, watching all the crap about the terrorist attacks. I'd been drinking all day, so doubt if I was very coherent."

Jake took another swig of Bushmills, glancing at Manny. "He told me about his daughter and the fact that he was in Europe and couldn't get home. I remembered him as a decent, honest guy when we were in the service and, I don't know, I just felt sorry for him. I agreed to take his case and here I am."

Manny shook his head. "It's a lot to take on when you've been out of the game as long as you have. There are some bad people out there, Bull, and they won't just sit still while you try to take this girl away from them."

"I had some serious second thoughts when I woke up this morning, but getting to know his son over the past few hours has...." Jake took another drink. "I'll do whatever it takes to get this family back together."

"I'm not questioning your commitment, Bull, but it's been five years."

"I know, Manny. I know," Jake said, turning to look out at the crashing waves.

"That's if we can even find out where she is," Manny said, walking up next to Jake and looking out at the Pacific.

"They're here in TJ, Manny, I know it. It's probably some small-time local gang, wanting to make a quick payday."

"My guy at TJPD is pretty reliable for the most part. Some of them are connected to the local gangs and corrupt as hell, but my guy can be trusted." Manny looked at Jake. "When are you going to go into TJ?"

"It's going be an all-nighter for me, I'm afraid," Jake said, still staring at the crashing waves. "I'd welcome some help if you know someone that knows TJ."

"Already done. His name is Amos Stillwater. He'll be here in a few minutes," Manny said. "I'll stay here and watch over the kid and make some phone calls while you two are out beating the bushes. Take some time and enjoy your drink, eat some food. I'll be back in a few."

Jake grabbed a burrito from the patio table and peered out at the ocean. The Bushmills was starting to make him feel normal again, just like every other night over the last five years. He knew he was an alcoholic and he made no bones about it, but he also knew that he could function just fine with Bushmills running through his veins. *The alcoholic's theme song. You damn drunk.*

He heard Manny on the phone in the kitchen. He thought about when he was a rookie on the SDPD, when Manny was his training officer in the early days, teaching him things that he wouldn't have learned from anyone else. They formed a strong friendship, until Jake got kicked off the force in 1996. Manny tried to keep in touch, but Jake didn't return his phone calls, didn't want anything to do with anyone connected to the SDPD. Manny was there the night he got his scar. Jake reached up and felt the six-inch ribbon of raised red flesh, the result of another drunken night.

After a few minutes of relaxing on the balcony, watching the sun slowly sink in the western sky, Jake's quiet time ended abruptly.

"Bull, bad news. I just talked to my contact at SDPD, to see what they knew," Manny said, then hesitated. "They have a warrant out for your arrest, and one for the kid."

"God damn it!" Jake said. "That prick!"

"The principal?"

"Yeah, the goddam principal."

"They say you stole a car and threatened the guy. And the kid is wanted for assault. That have anything to do with the kid almost taking the guy's head off this morning?"

"Yeah - shit. I didn't think the prick would do anything, he was so scared. I guess I misjudged him. He really screwed up yesterday when he organized the school kid's return to the U.S. He rushed and didn't take his time, which meant a car full of girls and one female teacher were in the last car, unprotected. Made them an easy target for a kidnapper if he was watching, which he obviously was. He let the security guys go ahead to the border, leaving the entire convoy vulnerable. Plus, he lied about someone seeing the probable kidnapper's trucks at the scene. That's when Charlie lost it."

"What about the stolen car?"

"First of all, we borrowed it, we didn't steal it. I figured it would be easier to get back and forth across the border in one of the school vans, since it was registered with Mexican customs already. I didn't think the asshole would press charges, but I guess he grew some balls after we left. Shit!"

"Well, the good news is that you're in Mexico, so they can't touch you until you go back over the border. The bad news is that they'll nab you at Customs when you try to return," Manny said. "Plus, they've probably contacted the TJPD, so you'll be radioactive if you try to talk to them."

Jake nodded, looking out at the ocean. "Let's not tell the kid about this. He has enough to worry about."

"Okay," Manny said. "So this changes things a little. You go shake some trees in TJ, along with a friend of mine that will be here in a few minutes. Name is Amos Stillwater, a retired cop who lives down here. He spent a few years in drug enforcement so knows the territory and most of the local gangs. In the meantime, I'll call my contact at TJPD and work that end. I won't mention your name or Charlie's, since they've probably heard about you already from SDPD."

Jake just nodded, staring out at the ocean.

"This is getting more and more complicated, Bull," Manny said, shaking his head. "You never do anything the easy way."

Jake turned and smiled weakly at his friend. "Story of my life, Manny. I seem to be my own worst enemy most of the time."

"You'll need some protection while you're running around TJ. I have a nine millimeter Glock that you can take with you."

"No thanks, Manny. If I get stopped by some gung-ho TJ cop that may recognize me or my picture I don't want to be packing anything. Like you said, I may be radioactive down here. This Stillwater, will he be carrying?"

"Yeah."

"That's good enough. I know how to take care of myself, or at least I used to. Does Stillwater have your cell phone number, and you got his?"

"Yep. We'll stay in touch. I'll let you know if anything shakes loose."

"Watch the kid and if he wakes up, keep a lid on him, okay? I'll leave his cell phone with you." Jake handed Manny the phone. "There's a slim possibility that the kidnappers may call this phone number, but I doubt it. The kid's dad might call again, too."

"Got it. You be careful out there, Bull. Sure you don't want that Glock?"

"Yeah, I'm sure."

They heard a knock on the downstairs door.

"That's Amos," Manny said. "I'll introduce you."

Jake turned and shot one more glance at the ocean, took a deep breath of sea air and threw down a final swig of Bushmills. It was time to go to work.

CHAPTER 35

The sun was setting as they passed through the dense smog layer and broke through to the clear sky. Ethan looked down at the huge city below, which stretched for many miles, and saw thousands of lights filtered through the gray haze. The King Air 200 turbo-prop had a distinctive whir as opposed to the giant 747's hum. Ethan felt every little bump in the smaller plane until they reached cruising altitude. He closed his eyes, enjoying the quiet buzz of the propellers on each wing until the cabin lights came on.

"Ethan," said Arturo Calderon from across the aisle, "I couldn't help but overhear your conversation before we took off. Is the situation with your daughter any better?"

Ethan opened his eyes and looked at Arturo. "No, it's worse, I'm afraid. There have been no ransom demands from the kidnappers. Usually they contact the families within the first twenty-four hours." He turned and looked out into the darkening night.

"Does Jake have any leads?" Pete asked, sitting next to him.

"Not much, just a name. He said he's going to be working all night to find someone that knows something. Tijuana is a large city, so he didn't sound too hopeful."

"How about Charlie? Is he holding up okay?" said Pete.

"Jake said that he was ready to crash from lack of sleep and the emotional strain. Jake's going to let him sleep at a friend's house while he goes out and does his thing. It sounds like he has help from some ex-cop friends that live in TJ."

"That's good, Ethan," replied Arturo. "What about the police? Are they involved yet?"

Ethan rubbed his forehead. "Not yet. Jake thinks they would just slow things down. We're up against the clock now so he doesn't want red tape dragging him down. I have to trust him, not that I have much choice right now."

"He's probably right, Ethan. The U.S. police can't do much in Mexico, and the Mexican police . . . ." Arturo had a grimace on his face. "Maybe it's best that he takes care of this on his own, in his own way."

Ethan glanced at the older man, seeing the concern on his face. "I guess so."

"I wish I would have done that ten years ago, when my daughter . . . ." Arturo turned his head towards his wife, unable to finish the sentence. He wiped his eyes and turned back to Ethan. "It has to be difficult for you to have to put your entire trust in someone that you haven't seen in so long." Arturo reached over and put his hand on Ethan's knee.

Ethan smiled weakly, nodding his head. He tried to lighten the mood. "I can't believe your daughter is flying this airplane."

Arturo laughed. "We're very proud of Victoria. Actually, she became interested in flying after Gabriella..." His mood darkened again. "She was so distraught about her little sister that she dove into flying as a diversion. She is a horse woman and helps Alexandria and me with our business, but her true passion now is flying. She was so excited when she landed this job as a charter pilot."

"Is she gone a lot?" Ethan asked.

"So far she flies to major Mexican cities only, such as Mexico City, Guadalajara, Hermosillo. They are all just a few hours away, so normally she is not gone overnight, unless she has to wait for a client."

"It must be tough on her social life," Pete said.

"She is not on the ground long enough to meet anyone," Alexandria said, leaning around Arturo to look at Pete. "She just turned thirty, so I am worried about her. She's such a beautiful woman, so much to give."

"Spoken like a concerned mother," Pete smiled.

Alexandria smiled at Pete, then looked at Ethan. "She has a very big heart, my Victoria."

Ethan smiled at Alexandria and felt the heat creep up his neck. He looked at Pete, who had a mischievous grin on his face.

"Ethan, I've been thinking," Arturo said. "Chihuahua is still a long way from Tijuana, by car. If you drive, it will take you close to twenty hours. Plus, you will have to drive through mountains, desert, and some very dangerous country, and at night."

"What choice do we have?" Ethan responded.

Arturo smiled widely. "How about letting Victoria fly you to Hermosillo tonight? It will cut a good chunk of the distance off of your trip. You will still have close to five hundred miles to Tijuana from Hermosillo, but you will eliminate the mountains and much of the desert."

"I couldn't ask her to do that, Arturo," Ethan said, shaking his head. "You've all done so much already."

"She's the one that suggested it. She got approval from the charter company to use this aircraft for the flight to Hermosillo. All you have to do is gas up in Chihuahua and you should be in the air by midnight."

"But the cost . . . ."

"Cost is not your concern."

Ethan frowned at Arturo and then at Alexandria. "No, I can't ask you to take on the expense. I have to insist that I pay for the charter to Hermosillo."

Arturo reached across and put his hand on Ethan's knee again. "Getting your daughter back is the only payment we want, son."

Ethan looked at Arturo and saw the look in his eyes. The man had made up his mind. "I understand why you feel so strongly about this..."

"Good. Then it's settled," Arturo said, smiling.

Ethan shook his head. "No question it would get us much closer to Tijuana, but . . . ."

"It's settled. And don't even think about trying to talk Victoria out of this," Arturo said, chuckling. "She's as stubborn as her mother."

"I beg your pardon," Alexandria said sternly, poking her husband in the ribs.

Ethan and Pete laughed at the older couple. Turning serious, Ethan asked, "Do you know how long it would take to drive from Hermosillo to Tijuana?"

"It's nearly five hundred miles, but fairly good road all the way, and no mountain passes. With light traffic, you should be able to make it in ten hours. You'll be in Hermosillo by two in the morning, and on the road shortly after that," Arturo said. "Victoria has already arranged a rental car for you."

"Then we could possibly make it to TJ by noon or shortly after," Ethan said.

"Victoria also did some checking of flights between Hermosillo and Tijuana to see if there was an early morning flight, but unfortunately they still are canceling most flights into TJ due to the terrorist activity."

Ethan nodded, looking at Pete. "If we can get to TJ by early-afternoon . . . ."

Pete slapped him on the back. "Let's do it!"

"You still have to rely on your friend and son to do what they can," Arturo said, "but at least you have a chance to get there by tomorrow afternoon."

Ethan nodded his head. "Thank you, Arturo."

"One more thing, Ethan," Arturo added. "And this was not my idea, but Victoria's. She wants to drive with you from Hermosillo to Tijuana. She has driven that road several times going to horse shows and knows it well. She can help you with any problems along the way and with the language. It can be dangerous on those roads at night."

This took Ethan by complete surprise. "Whoa. I can't ask your daughter to take that risk, Arturo. No."

"I'm afraid you don't have much choice, my friend. Her mind is made up and once it is made up, there is no changing it." He smiled as he looked at his wife.

"He's right, Ethan. You're stuck with her until you get to Tijuana," Alexandria said, smiling.

Ethan shook Arturo's hand and held Alexandria's hand for a few seconds. "I promise I will make sure Victoria gets home to you safely."

"And God willing, your daughter will get home safely, too," Arturo said, his eyes growing moist.

Ethan looked at the older man. "Thank you."

"Now," Arturo said, clapping his hands, "let's have one more bottle of wine and enjoy our trip to Chihuahua."

"I'll second that!" exclaimed Pete, a broad smile on his face.

CHAPTER 36

Jake stared at the road ahead, every now and then glancing at the driver. Amos Stillwater was a tall African-American man with handsome features, dressed casually in tan khaki shorts, sandals and a red polo shirt, as though he was going to a beach party. Jake still had on his faded jeans, yellow aloha shirt and tennis shoes.

"When did you retire, Amos?" Jake said.

"Last year," Amos replied, staring straight ahead. "Got my thirty years in and said *adios*."

Jake glanced again at the youthful-looking man. "Damn, you must have been a kid when you joined the force."

"Twenty-two, right out of USC," Amos said, a slight smile on his face. "I played football with OJ Simpson."

"No shit? What position?"

"Split end. My blocks made him a big ass star," Amos said, laughing. "Then he goes and pulls that crap up in L.A."

"You mean the murders . . . ."

"Yeah, the murders. Makes me sick to think about it."

Jake nodded, changing the subject. "Manny said you were on the drug enforcement task force for a while."

"I got out just as the drug trafficking started to escalate down here. I think it's going to get a lot worse before it gets better, and Tijuana is going to be the epicenter of it all."

"Why's that?"

"The border. All the border towns will be hotspots. A lot of blood is going to be spilled in the coming years, mark my words."

"What about kidnapping? Is it becoming more of a problem down here?"

"Just starting to become a major problem. It's a way for the cartels to generate money, scare the locals, and keep the politicians under control."

"What about kidnappings of Americans and foreigners?" Jake said.

"That hasn't been too bad up to now, but it's the next step. With this terrorist stuff going on in the U.S., it's anyone's guess what will happen next."

"Did Manny fill you in on my case?" Jake asked, looking at Amos.

"Yeah, somewhat. A couple of American teenage girls were grabbed off the highway over near Tecate yesterday. That's brazen, even for down here."

"Any ideas?"

"It could've been any number of local gangs. With the drug trafficking starting to grow down here, they all want a piece of the action and the only way to get inside is to have money and a name. Kidnapping is one way to do it, but it takes someone with a lot of balls. I have a couple of locals in mind, but need to do some checking first. How about you, any leads?"

"Only one," Jake said. "A kid named Rafael. The local kids in Tecate told us some city kid was asking a lot of questions around the American's camp the last couple of days. He wasn't from the Tecate area, so probably TJ. This was planned, no doubt about it. They hung around the American's camp until the day they left, which was yesterday."

"Damn, Rafael's a pretty common name, so not much of a lead, unless I can tie him to a particular gang. As far as being planned, that's not a surprise." Amos finally looked over at Jake. "You ready for a long night?"

"Pour a Bushmills into me every now and then and I'll be okay," Jake said.

Jake felt Amos staring at him.

"What do I call you? Jake, or Bull?" Amos said, continuing to stare.

"Hell, I don't know. I was called Bull on the force."

"Okay, Bull it is." Amos was silent a few seconds. "I don't have to worry about you do I, Bull?"

Jake glanced at him sharply. "What the hell do you mean?"

"Drinking," Amos replied. "I don't want to be hitched to a drunk tonight."

Jake turned and looked at the road ahead. "No, you don't have to worry about me."

"Good. We're going to be spending a long night together in some pretty raunchy places, so we need to keep sharp."

Jake nodded. "Whatever it takes."

Jake and Amos sat quietly until they hit the outskirts of Tijuana. The traffic was beginning to get heavy as they approached *Avenida*

Revolucion, the center of the tourist area. Jake was already missing the quiet of Rosarito Beach, the crashing of the waves.

"I have to ask, Amos. Why are you doing this?" Jake said, looking at the man. "You're retired, obviously living the good life now. Why jump back into the shit?"

Amos sat silent for a few moments, glancing at Jake.

"Manny, for one. He vouched for you. He and I are good friends, worked together on the SDPD a few years. He said you needed help."

"What's the other reason?"

Amos cleared his throat. "He also said that you drank a lot. The lives of these American girls shouldn't hinge on a drunk. I have two young daughters myself."

Jake stared at Amos, his face growing red, his breathing getting heavier as his temper took hold.

"Sorry to be so blunt, Bull, but our main priority has to be those young girls."

Jake started to blurt something out about his drinking, then relaxed his shoulders and dropped his head. He nodded, knowing that what Amos said was the truth. "You're right, Amos. It's about getting those girls home."

Amos glanced at Jake again, a slight smile crossing his face. "So we good?"

Jake held out his hand to Amos. "We're good."

Amos reached over and grabbed his hand. "Sorry for the blunt answer, but it is what it is."

"I won't let you down tonight, Amos."

Amos smiled. "That's what I wanted to hear, Bull," he said.

"So where do we start?" Jake said.

"We'll start at the center and work our way out. The biggest clubs are on *Constitucion*. The prostitutes down there hear everything, so we'll start with them. Throw this name Rafael around and see what comes back. Just listen for something that we can tie in."

"I used to spend quite a bit of time down here when I was still on the force, so I know how the game is played."

"You get that down here?" Amos asked, pointing to Jake's scar.

Jake looked straight ahead. "No. I got this in San Diego."

"It doesn't look so bad. Gives you character," Amos said.

"I should call you 'Bull', as in bullshit," Jake replied.

They both laughed as they turned onto *Avenida Constitucion*. The long night was about to begin.

CHAPTER 37

The two men pulled the white Tahoe into a nearby parking lot, just off of the *Avenida*. After paying the attendant, they began walking toward the main bar area, the sounds and smells reaching them before they arrived. The smell stirred something in Jake that had been buried for a long time. The two years he spent in Japan, they had open sewers called '*benjo* ditches'. The smell in Tijuana was very similar, only stronger. Strong enough to get your attention.

"Did you ever get used to the smell down here?" he asked Amos.

"No. It's like walking around in a toilet all night. Which is basically what it is."

Jake laughed, nodding his head. "That it is."

They reached the main area where most of the big clubs were. They looked around, then Amos pointed right and began walking quickly. He was almost as tall as Jake, but much thinner. He walked with a confident gait, his long arms swinging in a fluid motion. Jake walked a half step behind Amos, working hard to keep up with him. Everyone kept a wide berth when they walked by.

"Let's start with The Bronx," Amos said. "It's in the middle and usually gets rolling pretty early."

They walked into the loud bar, Bruce Springsteen's 'Dancing in the Dark' blaring from a jukebox. It was eight o'clock but the club was already crowded. They walked to the bar and stood in between two ladies in short, skin-tight skirts. The men standing next to them looked at the tall Americans and beat a hasty retreat.

"You want that Bushmills?" Amos asked Jake.

"Yeah, if they have it. If not, just a beer."

"You got Bushmills?" Amos said to the bartender.

"*Sí*," he replied as he grabbed a bottle from behind the bar.

"One Bushmills for my friend and one *cerveza* for me," Amos said.

As the bartender poured the Bushmills into a dirty glass, Jake looked down at the woman standing next to him. She looked to be in her early twenties. Attractive, but worn.

"What's your name?" Jake asked her, taking a gulp of whiskey.

She smiled as she looked up at him. "Desiree," she said, touching his arm. She frowned when she saw his scar.

Jake acted like he didn't notice. "A nice, Spanish name," he said, chuckling, looking at Amos. "How long have you worked here, Desiree?"

"I don't know," she replied, still frowning. "You buy me a drink?"

"Sure, I'll buy you a drink. Can you get your friend over there to join us and we'll buy her one, too?"

"Okay." Desiree motioned to the girl standing next to Amos as they walked to a nearby table.

"This is Monica." Monica was older than Desiree, by a good ten years or more. She looked tired and weathered, but gave Amos her best come-on smile.

"Hi Monica." Amos nodded, pulling a chair out for her.

The girls ordered their watered down drinks and when it came time to pay, the waitress asked Amos for a hundred and fifty *pesos*, about fifteen dollars. "The price of water keeps going up," he said, smiling at Jake.

Jake nodded. "Can we ask you ladies a couple of questions?"

The older woman leaned back, frowning as she looked at Desiree. "Why? Are you cops?"

"No. We're not cops," Jake replied.

"You look like cops," Desiree said. Then she pointed to Jake's scar. "How did you get that?"

Jake put his hand to the scar. "This? I cut myself shaving."

Desiree and Monica looked at each other and they started to get up from the table. Amos slid two hundred *pesos* across the table at them. "We just want to ask some questions. Won't take much of your time."

Desiree looked at the money and grabbed it, looking around quickly. "Okay, but we don't have much time."

"Have you heard anything about a kidnapping of three American girls?" Amos asked, getting right to the point. "It happened yesterday afternoon. Any rumors around?"

The women looked at each other nervously and shook their heads. "No. Nothing," Desiree said.

"How about the girls here? Has anyone not shown up the last day or two?" he asked.

"I don't know. I only worry about myself," said Desiree. "You need to talk to her," she said, nodding at an older woman standing at the end of the bar.

Jake took a drink as he looked at the woman that Desiree had pointed to. She was staring back at him.

"How about you, Monica? Any of your friends miss work the last day or two?" Amos said.

She shook her head, glancing at Desiree and then at the woman at the bar.

"All we want is information, nothing more," Jake said.

Both women chugged their colored water down and got up to leave. "Talk to her," Desiree said, nodding again at the woman at the bar. They walked away, quickly glancing at the woman.

"Okay, let's talk to her," Amos said, looking at Jake. They walked over to the woman at the bar, who had been watching them closely.

"Are you the manager?" Amos asked her.

"*Sí.*"

"Can we ask you a couple of questions?" Amos asked her. "We're not cops, but we are private investigators working on a kidnapping case of three American teenagers. You hear anything about this?"

The woman, who appeared to be in her forties and looked like she could handle herself pretty well, shook her head.

"You've heard nothing about any kidnapping?" Jake said. "It happened yesterday, so you must have heard something."

"No. I've heard nothing," she said, frowning. "You want another drink?" she said, looking at Jake's empty glass.

"Yeah, sure," Jake said, glancing at Amos.

"Okay. How about your girls? Anyone been missing or not shown up for work the past day or two?" Amos said.

"Girls don't show up all the time. I only worry about the ones that are here."

"How about a young guy named Rafael? Anyone by that name come in here?"

She shook her head, obviously getting nervous about talking to the two men. "Please, don't bother my girls," she said as she handed Jake a fresh Bushmills.

Jake and Amos looked at each other. Jake pulled out a five hundred *peso* bill and held it so only the woman could see it. "Will this help you remember anything?"

She looked at the bill, worth fifty U.S. dollars, glancing around to see if anyone was watching. She saw the bartender staring at her. "No. Please go." She motioned towards the door.

Jake gulped his Bushmills down and the two men left, on to the next round.

CHAPTER 38

As the King Air 200 taxied to the small terminal, a familiar voice came over the cabin intercom.

"Welcome to Chihuahua. I hope you enjoyed the landing, and enjoy your stay in our beautiful city. It has been a pleasure flying with you this evening. And Dad, have a glass of wine ready for me."

Everyone laughed at the last comment, clapping in their appreciation of the smooth landing.

The aircraft came to a stop a few feet from a small passenger terminal. The twin turbo-prop engines ramped down and then shut off. Ethan and Pete unfastened their seatbelts, stood up and stretched, trying to get blood flowing after flying for nearly fifteen hours.

"You've had a long trip already, gentlemen," Arturo said from behind them.

Ethan turned and smiled. "I'm used to it, but not under these circumstances."

Ethan heard the cockpit door open and turned to watch Victoria Calderon walk out, a big smile on her face. She bowed in appreciation as everyone clapped politely.

"Wonderful job, Vicki," said her dad. "You made an impression on our American friends."

Ethan saw the beautiful olive skin under jet black hair pulled back in a ponytail. Even with the uniform on, he could see the curves of her body. He couldn't take his eyes off of her.

"Looks like she really made an impression on Ethan," said Pete, chuckling. "And I don't think it was all about her flying."

Ethan looked at his friend in mock anger. "Thanks, Pete."

"So, Vicki, how about that glass of wine?" said Arturo. "You have some time before you take off again."

"I was just kidding, Dad. I can't drink and fly. But please feel free to have one while we talk a bit. We have an hour before we take off for Hermosillo."

"Here, have a seat," said Pete, motioning to the seat next to Ethan.

"Thank you," she said, glancing at Ethan.

Arturo poured the last of the red wine into the two American's glasses and topped off his wife's glass. "I told Ethan and Pete about your offer."

"Oh. Good! I'm so glad that I can help," she said.

Ethan cleared his throat. "First of all, I can't tell you how wonderful your parents have been. And now, with your offer to fly us to Hermosillo, it's a little overwhelming," Ethan said. "But I can't ask you to drive all the way to Tijuana with us in the middle of the night. That's above and beyond, to use an American expression."

Victoria looked at Ethan closely. He could feel her looking into his eyes, almost as if she was trying to look into his soul. He felt the eyes of Arturo and Alexandria on him, making him feel uncomfortable.

She took his hand. "My father said that you are a good man, and my mother agrees. I love my parents, and trust their judgment. I know what it's like to lose a loved one at a young age. If I can help you avoid that pain, I would like to do it. Please let me help."

Ethan stared back at her. "Thank you. All of you." He smiled at Arturo and Alexandria. "If Pete and I get to Tijuana in time . . . in time to find my daughter, then we will have the Calderon family to thank."

Victoria cleared her throat. "Also, Ethan . . . ." She stopped and looked at her father. "I think I have a small plane reserved for us in Hermosillo that I can fly all the way to Tijuana."

Ethan stared at her, his mouth hanging open. "But I thought we couldn't fly into Tijuana."

"Larger planes are banned, but small private aircraft are allowed with notice." She shook her head. "But it's not for certain yet. We may get there and find out the Cessna never arrived in Hermosillo. It's always questionable in the early morning hours, so I don't want you to . . . ."

"Vicki," Ethan said. "It's a shot, and that's all I'm looking for." He grabbed her hand. "Thank you for even trying."

He turned to Arturo and shook his hand, clasping his left hand over the man's right arm. They looked at each other in silence, each knowing what the other was thinking. Then he stood and hugged Alexandria, who whispered something in his ear. He looked into her eyes and said, "I will. I promise."

"Well, my dear," Arturo said, looking at Alexandria, "it's been a very long day and we need to get some sleep before we drive to the ranch."

"How far is your ranch from here?" asked Ethan.

"It's about eighty miles due south, in the small town of Hidalgo del Parral. Our ranch is just outside of the town. We'll be staying at Vicki's townhouse here in Chihuahua tonight and then depart early. Our world-traveling horses will be arriving around noon, so I want to be there when they arrive. They're going to be grumpy after that long ride from Mexico City."

"On that note," Ethan said, "I have to make a couple of phone calls before we take off again."

Looking at Arturo and Alexandria, he said, "Someday I'd like to come back here and visit your ranch . . . and I'll bring Molly with me." His stomach tightened as he mentioned his daughter's name.

"You have an open invitation, son," Arturo said. "And we can't wait to meet your beautiful daughter." His eyes grew moist as he reached out and hugged Ethan tightly.

As Alexandria hugged Ethan, she said, "God bless you, Ethan, and your daughter." Her voice was cracking. "Our prayers will be with you until you bring her home safely."

They shook hands with Pete, with Alexandria giving him a hug. "You be careful, Pete. And keep your eyes on these two," Alexandria said, pointing at Vicki and Ethan.

"I will. Thank you for your kindness," Pete said.

Arturo and Alexandria hugged Vicki and then turned and began walking down the aircraft stairs to the tarmac. As they reached the ground, they turned and looked at the two men, and their daughter behind them.

"*Vaya con Dios,*" Arturo said, and they turned and walked into the small terminal.

"I have to do some prep for the flight to Hermosillo," Vicki said, wiping a tear from her cheek. "I will let you know when we are ready for takeoff." She walked to the cockpit and closed the door.

Ethan and Pete stood in the open doorway of the small plane, staring at the cockpit door.

"Well, partner, let's make those phone calls," Ethan said, reaching down and pulling out his cell phone. "Time to find out what's going on in Tijuana."

CHAPTER 39

It was eleven o'clock when Jake and Amos entered a nightclub called *El Californian*, a few blocks away from *Avenida Constitucion*. It was smaller than most of the others, with fewer women and fewer customers. They'd been at it for three hours, with no luck in any of the bars. No one had heard anything and no one knew anything. Jake was beginning to feel the effects of too many Bushmills.

"Think you should slow down on those Bushmills?" Amos said as they approached the bar in the small club.

Jake didn't acknowledge him, ordering another shot from the bartender.

"You made me a promise, Bull. We still have a long night ahead of us."

Jake threw back the shot of Bushmills, turning to look at Amos with eyes that were turning red. "That's the last one, Mom," he said, slamming the shot glass on the bar. He turned and began to raise his hand for another one, then stopped. *Shut it down, Jake. For Molly's sake.*

Amos walked up beside Jake and clapped him on the shoulder. "I need you, Bull. Thanks."

Jake stared at the bartender, who seemed to be taking an interest in them. Putting his elbows on the bar, he said "*Buenas noches, amigo.*"

The bartender nodded at Jake, his eyes on the scar.

Jake pulled out a one hundred *peso* bill and put it on the bar. "One question. Give me a straight answer and this is yours."

The bartender looked around nervously, then looked back at Jake. "You want another drink?"

"No, I just want some information," Jake said. "Any of your girls missing last night or tonight?"

"What do you mean, missing?" the bartender said.

"Your regular girls. Any of them not show up?"

The bartender looked nervously at Jake while he dried a beer glass with a towel. He glanced again at the money. "Five hundred."

Jake didn't hesitate as he replaced the hundred *peso* bill with a five hundred bill. He held his hand on the bill as he stared at the bartender.

"Natalia," the bartender said, barely audible.

Jake leaned in. "Natalia who?"

"Natalia, that's all."

Jake held on to the bill and asked him again. "Natalia who?"

The bartender looked down at the five hundred pesos. "Blanco. Natalia Blanco."

"You got an address on her?" Jake asked, keeping his hand on the bill.

"No, señor. Ask Jessie. She's her friend."

"Which one's Jessie?"

The bartender pointed to a girl standing at the end of the bar, talking to a customer.

"Ask her to come over here," Jake said.

The bartender walked to the end of the bar and whispered in the girl's ear while pointing to Jake. She hesitated, then walked over slowly. She was wearing a very short, skin-tight skirt and had on a tight, sleeveless blouse that showed lots of cleavage. She looked to be in her late twenties, still attractive, but painted up.

Jake slid the five hundred *pesos* toward the bartender. "*Gracias*," he said.

Jake glanced back at Amos, who was looking at him, nodding his head.

"Hello, Jessie," Jake said to the girl as she approached. His eyes went down to her cleavage then back up to her face.

"Hello," she said, glancing at the bartender. "Do you want to buy me a drink?"

"Sure," Jake said, sliding a hundred *peso* bill over to her.

Jessie looked at Amos nervously. "And your friend?"

"No. He doesn't drink," Jake said, not taking his eyes off of the girl. "Do you know Natalia Blanco?"

Jessie looked at Jake and then at the bartender. "*Sí*, she works here."

"But not last night, or tonight?"

"*Sí*."

"Why?" Jake bent down and put his face close to hers, looking into her eyes. "Do you know why?"

She backed away, looking at Jake nervously. "Are you *policia*?"

"No," Jake said. "Do you know why she didn't show up last night or tonight?"

Jessie took a drink of colored water, looking around to see who was watching. "No."

Jake pulled out several hundred *peso* bills from his wallet and put them on the bar.

"Have you heard anything about a kidnapping of three American girls?" Amos said, joining the conversation.

The girl suddenly got very nervous and backed further away, glancing to her right and then to her left. She began to walk away, but Jake grabbed her arm. He pulled her next to him gently, pressing her body up against his. The bartender stared at him.

"Jessie, this money is yours if you answer the question," Jake said in her ear. "What have you heard?"

Jessie's eyes were wide open as she looked to the bartender for help. None came.

"Just you and me, honey," Jake said softly. "What have you heard?"

She put her mouth close to Jake's ear. "Natalia's boyfriend," she whispered.

"What about her boyfriend?" Jake whispered back, his heart beginning to beat faster.

"She told me about him. He's the leader of some gang."

"What's his name?" Jake said, glancing at Amos.

"Angel."

"Angel what?"

"That's all I know. She never said his last name."

"Where does she live?"

"She lives with me. We share an apartment."

Jake looked at Amos, the hope flickering in both of their eyes.

"Has she been home the past few days?" Amos asked, leaning close.

"No, not since Monday."

"Can you take us to your apartment, right now?" Jake asked the girl.

"How much?" She said, loud enough for the bartender to hear.

"One thousand *pesos*," Jake said, glancing at the bartender and smiling.

"Give it to me now and meet me outside."

"I'll give you five hundred now, and five hundred when we get to your apartment," Jake said.

The girl looked around and nodded. "Okay."

Jake slipped her the five hundred *peso* bill and she put it in her cleavage. She reached up and kissed Jake on the lips and smiled at him. She said something to the bartender, then sauntered out the front door.

Jake and Amos waited a minute or two at the bar, looking around to see if anyone was interested in them. Only the bartender noticed them, glancing at them quickly as he went back to drying his beer glass.

Jessie was waiting for them outside the bar. She took Jake's arm to make it look like he was a customer. It drew little attention from the people on the street. Amos walked several yards behind, trying to act inconspicuous. They walked two blocks and turned down an alley. It was dark, with nothing but trash cans along one wall. It smelled of rotting garbage and piss.

"Whoa! Where are we going?" Jake said, looking down the dark alley.

"To my apartment," Jessie said. "This is just a shortcut."

Jake turned to Amos, who took the lead and began walking down the alley slowly, his hand on his Glock nine millimeter in his back holster. Jake and Jessie followed a few feet behind, Jake glancing behind them. When they reached the end of the alley, Amos took his hand off of his gun.

"All clear," he said.

"No more dark alleys," Jake said to Jessie. "Got it?"

"*Sí*. But we are here." She pointed to a dilapidated three-story building across the narrow street. It was dirty, with laundry hanging from most of the balconies. There was no foot traffic and no cars on the dark street.

"What floor do you live on?" Jake asked her.

"Second. Apartment two-one-one."

"Stay here while I check it out," Amos said, walking across the street and entering the building. Two minutes later he stood in the entrance way and waved them over.

"You are not trusting me?" Jessie asked.

"Just being careful, darlin'," Jake said. "Nothing personal."

They walked into the building and up the stairs to the second floor. The walls were made of gray brick, the graffiti everywhere. Noises were coming from several of the apartments, the sound of a bed squeaking in the apartment next to her room. Jake looked at Amos, who had his Glock out of its holster and pointed up, at the ready.

"Okay, Jessie. Open it slowly," Jake said. "Slowly," he said again.

Jessie put her key in the door and slowly opened it, the door creaking. Jake put his arm in front of her and blocked her way while Amos slipped into the dark apartment, his gun pointing in the direction he was looking. Jake turned on the lights, looking around the dingy, sparsely furnished living room.

"Which bedroom is Natalia's?" Amos asked the girl.

She pointed to the room on the left. Amos slowly opened the door and turned on the light. The room was messy, with clothes strewn all over the floor and bed. Jake and Jessie waited in the doorway and watched as Amos began rummaging through her clothes, papers and personal effects.

Jake turned and began looking at the living area. A worn green sofa, a wooden chair and a small TV were the only items in the room. He moved to the kitchen, looking for something on the refrigerator, like a note or address. He pulled out drawers and rummaged through normal kitchen items.

"How long have you two lived together?" he asked Jessie.

"About one year," she said. "What are you looking for?"

Jake didn't answer her, but kept an eye on her while he was looking for any kind of clue that could tell them where Natalia was.

"Did Natalia tell you where she was going?" Jake asked.

"No, only to see her boyfriend."

"Have you ever met him?"

"Yes, one time. He came into the bar."

"What does he look like?" he asked, still rummaging through the kitchen.

"Very nice looking, well dressed. He is short."

Jake looked at her. "How short?"

"As short as me," she said.

Jake looked at her and guessed that she was five foot five inches.

"Shorter than Natalia?"

"Yes, by a couple of inches at least," she replied.

"How did he treat her?"

"Like shit, with no respect. I didn't like him."

"Jake! In here!" Amos yelled from the bedroom.

Jake grabbed Jessie and rushed into the bedroom. Amos was holding up a city map of Tecate.

"A map? So what?" Jake asked.

"Look what's circled," Amos said, pointing to an area on the map.

Jake looked closely at the map and saw an area south of Tecate circled in red. It also had the road out of Tecate marked in red, including the side road that Jake and Charlie had found that morning. An arrow was drawn in red, pointing to the entrance to the side road.

"Damn!" Jake exclaimed. "That's the road I saw this morning!"

"Looks like Natalia Blanco is our girl and her boyfriend Angel is our guy," Amos said, smiling at Jake.

Jake smiled broadly, then turned to Jessie. "I need to know where Natalia is and where Angel lives. Can you help us?" He handed Jessie the second five hundred *pesos*. "There're more of those if you can get us an address."

"Is she in trouble?" Jessie asked, looking at the money.

Jake took her by the shoulders and looked her directly in the eyes. "Listen, Jessie. This boyfriend of Natalia's is a bad man. He's going to do bad things to these American girls, and probably to Natalia. She's a witness and he won't leave her alive to talk. Do you understand?"

Jessie's eyes began to well up. "I don't know where he lives. But his gang is called . . . ." She stopped and stared at Jake.

"What?" Jake said. "What's the name of his gang?"

"*La Mano Negra.*"

Amos looked at Jake and nodded. "The Black Hand. I've heard of it. Small time drug runners, strictly nickel and dime. I can get an address from the SDPD."

Jake looked at Jessie and hugged her. "You've made my day, Jessie." He reached into his pocket and pulled out a one thousand *peso* bill. "Use this to get a new apartment. Don't stay here. It's not safe. Okay?"

She nodded. "*Gracias.*"

As they walked out of the apartment, Amos reached for his cell phone. "We finally have a lead," he said to Jake.

"And not a minute too soon," Jake answered.

CHAPTER 40

Ethan sat back in the King Air 200 turboprop as it rose into the night sky, the lights of Chihuahua below them twinkling goodbye. Somewhere down below were Arturo and Alexandria Calderon, probably asleep already after a seven thousand mile trip from Europe. Victoria was at the controls of the small twin propeller aircraft that was carrying Ethan and Pete to another Mexican town, this time Hermosillo, in the Sonora desert. It was a little bit closer to their ultimate destination of Tijuana, but still five hundred miles away.

Ethan was beginning to feel the strain of the past forty eight hours, the lack of sleep, the worrying, the wondering. He was getting closer to his daughter, but didn't know any more about her situation than he did when he started the long journey in Amsterdam. He had called his son's cell phone while they were still on the ground in Chihuahua, but there was no answer and it went to voicemail. He told his son that he was about to take off from Chihuahua, headed for Hermosillo, and he would call him when he landed around 2 a.m., which would be midnight in Tijuana. Another flight, another two hours of not knowing.

Ethan looked at Pete, who was asleep in the seat across the aisle from him. They were alone in the passenger cabin of the aircraft. He peered out the small window at the night sky, which was black now, the stars hidden by clouds. He felt alone and wanted to wake his friend up, to have someone to talk to, but knew that Pete needed his sleep. He needed sleep too, but he couldn't shut his mind down.

His thoughts turned to his daughter again. She had just turned sixteen the week before. He and Charlie had thrown a party for her at a local lodge, inviting all of her school friends. She was queen of the ball, dressed up in a new dress and looking radiant. Molly was so happy that night, so proud to be the center of attention. Ethan felt the sting of tears in his eyes as he thought about that night, just one week ago. Everything had changed in the blink of an eye. The ugly thoughts began to invade his mind again. He wouldn't allow himself to think about what may be happening or what might happen in the next few days. He would only think of finding her, alive and safe, and taking her home. This is what was driving him and keeping him sane.

He thought of his son, Charlie, who would turn twenty in April. How was he getting along with Jake? Was he safe? Why didn't he, or someone, answer his cell phone? The uncertainty was eating at Ethan as he stared out into the black sky, the hum of the propellers finally lulling him to sleep.

CHAPTER 41

The teacher's breathing was becoming more and more shallow, her face barely visible in the dark room. Molly brushed Missus Caldwell's hair and talked to her softly, not knowing if she could hear her or not. Tears streamed down Molly's face as she tried to comfort the dying woman, who had been her friend as well as her teacher. Now she was lying almost lifeless in a shabby, stinking warehouse in Mexico, beaten nearly to death and almost unrecognizable.

"Molly, is she dying?" a voice said nearby.

Molly looked over at Cindy, who had just woken up from yet another drug-induced slumber. Her eyes were bloodshot, with dark bags underneath. She was sitting up, staring at Molly and the teacher. Molly could see the confusion and fogginess in her face, brought on by the drug and by too much sleep. She looked so helpless, so fragile.

Molly's voice trembled. "Yes, she's dying."

Cindy began to whimper, slumping back down on the dirty mattress. Her whimpers became louder, then became sobs.

Molly rushed to her side and lay down next to her friend. Throughout the ordeal the two had not talked or comforted each other. Molly glanced at the big metal door and saw Natalia sitting on the wooden chair next to it, her head propped back, asleep. She began to untie Cindy's wrists, as Natalia had done with hers earlier.

"Cindy, there's nothing we can do. They won't send in a doctor. She'll be gone soon." Molly said this softly, brushing away her friend's tears. Cindy looked like a little girl, rolled up in a fetal position, tears flowing out of her red, bloodshot eyes. Molly began to cry herself, holding her face next to Cindy's.

"What's going to happen to us?" Cindy said, sniffling.

Molly raised her face to look at her friend. She saw fear and hopelessness in her eyes. She glanced over at Jenny, who was still in a fetal position, not moving.

"We have a plan, Cin, me and Natalia. We talked while you were asleep. She's on our side and is going to help us," Molly said. "We're going to get out of here."

Cindy looked over at the woman sleeping next to the door. "Why would she help us?"

"She doesn't want us to get hurt. And she hates the man that is doing this to us."

"Molly? What if we don't get out? What's going to happen to us?"

Molly held her friend's head next to her chest and brushed her hair softly. "We're going to be okay, Cin. I promise, we're going to get out of here—soon."

Molly wondered if she even believed those words. Hope was slowly slipping away, along with the life of her teacher. For the first time, Molly wondered what her life would be like if they couldn't find a way out of this mess. She shook the thought from her head, instead thinking of her family. They would find her and save her. Her daddy was on his way, she knew it. He wouldn't let her die in this place. *Daddy!*

As the two teenage girls hugged each other, their tears dropped onto the filthy mattress and formed little pools beneath them. Molly suddenly heard a noise and looked up to see Natalia sitting up and stretching her arms, looking at her. Molly didn't know whether to despise the woman or trust her. To love her or hate her.

"Natalia, what did they do to her?" she asked, nodding towards the teacher.

Natalia looked at the dying woman and shook her head. "She was fighting against them, trying to save you. They hit her many times . . . and then . . . ." Natalia hung her head, the shame and guilt weighing heavily on her. She looked up at Molly and said, "She was a brave woman, but she had no chance against those animals."

The thought of her teacher enduring the horror of a beating and rape was almost more than Molly could take. She began to shake, the fear and hatred welling up in her. Her sixteen year-old mind could not take much more of this madness.

Cindy reached for Molly, fear and terror in her eyes. "Molly, I want to go home," she cried. "I want to go home."

Molly put her arm around her friend and rocked back and forth. "We will, Cindy. We'll get home." She glared at Natalia. "We're going to get out of this hellhole."

Molly looked up at the skylight in the ceiling and, through the small opening, saw the moon. It was a quarter moon and made her think of her parents, how they used to call it Molly's Moon. She dropped her head and began softly crying.

CHAPTER 42

It was close to midnight and Jake was on his second glass of root beer at Lilly's bar. Amos had talked to his contacts at the SDPD, asking them to check on a Tijuana gang called *La Mano Negra*. They were waiting for the response.

"A good night's work, Amos," Jake said, throwing back the rest of his root beer.

"How's that root beer, Bull?"

Jake shot a glance at Amos. "Tastes like piss."

Amos smiled. "We got lucky tonight, Bull. Real lucky."

Jake nodded. "Yeah, well, there's still a lot to do and not much time to do it."

Amos stared at Jake. "So how about the scar? You ever going to tell me how you got it?"

"Yeah, someday, if we get through this," Jake said. "What did your contact at SDPD say?"

"They're running down *La Mano Negra* now. Shouldn't take long. We should have something within the hour."

"Then what? We gonna John Wayne it or wait for back-up?" Jake was getting antsy, starting to miss the Bushmills.

"Depends on the intel. If they show up as having lots of firepower we probably want back-up. What do you think?"

"I think the clock is ticking on our teenage girls and we can't afford to wait too long," Jake said. "What are the chances they have the girls somewhere else?"

"High. Especially since it involves Americans. They may be small time, but they aren't stupid, especially the leader, Angel. They've watched enough American movies to know we get pissed off when someone takes one of our women. They'll be holed up somewhere in TJ, though."

"You ever run across this gang when you were on the task force?"

"Once. Don't remember that much, except for the leader. He was a short, macho asshole. He'd cut your head off and piss down your neck if you looked at him crooked. He wore a black glove on his right hand."

"Why a black glove?"

"Not sure. Something about hurting it in a fight years ago. Or maybe it's just a symbol, who knows."

Suddenly, two men walked into the bar wearing the tan uniforms of the Tijuana Police Department. Even though Lilly's was a hangout for off-duty SDPD and ex-cops, the TJPD liked to come in and act tough. Jake had seen it many times when he was on the force. The two men walked to the bar and sat down.

"TJPD. Think we should leave?" Jake said.

"No, we're okay. They're just beat cops taking a break. Shouldn't be a problem," Amos said.

"Maybe they know this Angel dude."

"Maybe, but these cops can't be trusted. Lots of them are linked to the local gangs. You never know who's legit. If we mention the little prick it could get back to him and then we'd never find him. I think it's best if we handle it on our own."

"Your call," Jake said. "We'll probably run up against the TJ cops at some point, though."

"You could be right, but now's not the time," Amos replied. "Let's see what the SDPD comes up with first."

Jake heard Amos's cell phone ring and watched as he answered it.

"Stillwater," Amos said into the phone.

Jake watched Amos's eyes grow wide as he listened to whoever was on the other end. After a few seconds, Amos looked at Jake and gave him a thumbs up.

"Thanks, Ditch. I owe you one." Amos hung up and smiled at Jake. "We got an address. But we're gonna need some manpower. *La Mano Negra* has grown some since I messed with them. The leader is still the little sonofabitch, Angel Rojas."

Jake stared at Amos. "What'd you say his name was?"

"Angel Rojas. Why?"

Jake looked down at the table. He lifted his hand and felt his scar, then looked up at Amos. "That's the name of the asshole who gave me this."

"Pretty common name down here," Amos said, staring at Jake. "How do you know?"

"Short prick, mean as a rattlesnake, with balls the size of coconuts."

"So? There's lots of short pricks in Tijuana."

"*La Mano Negra*," Jake said. "The Black Hand."

"Yeah, so what?"

Jake rubbed his scar again. "After he slit my face open, I fucked up his right wrist pretty good. Felt some bones break."

Amos stared at Jake. "Damn, Bull. You think this could be the same guy?"

"It's the same guy. This just got very personal."

CHAPTER 43

Jake and Amos got back to Manny's townhouse around one in the morning. Jake didn't say a word on the drive back, his thoughts on the man who carved him up and who now could be the animal that was holding Molly Paxton.

"Is Charlie still asleep?" Jake asked Manny as they walked in.

"Yeah, out like a light. Poor kid was exhausted," Manny responded. "How about you? You must be running on empty, too."

Jake rubbed his eyes and yawned. "Yeah, guess I am. I need some shuteye before this day gets going. It's gonna be a long-ass day, Manny."

"Sure. You can sleep in the den—"

Jake interrupted him. "I've got some news, Manny," Jake said as he walked to the kitchen and poured a shot of Bushmills.

Manny looked at Jake, then shot a glance towards Amos.

Jake threw the glass of Bushmills down and put it on the table. "Remember the little prick that gave me this?" he said, looking at Manny.

"Hell yeah. I was there," Manny said.

"You were there?" said Amos, staring. "You never told me that."

"Me and Sandowski. Remember him? Biggest asshole on the force back then. We were having a beer in the back of the bar—"

"It's the same guy," Jake said, cutting in. "The prick kidnapped Molly."

Manny stared at Jake in disbelief. "How do you know? He disappeared a few years ago before we could get him in a courtroom—"

"It's him, Manny," Jake said. "He wears a black glove on his right hand. Remember his right arm?"

"Hell, yes. You fucked his wrist up pretty good," Manny said. "He'll never use that hand again."

"*La Mano Negra.* The Black Hand. That's the name of his gang," Amos said.

"Yeah, I've heard of 'em, but how do you know—"

"Angel Rojas. It's him," Jake said.

Manny stared at Jake. "I'll be goddamned," he said. "The little prick ran to Mexico. That's why we couldn't find him back then."

"Yep. And he formed his own little piss-ant gang," Jake said. "Only it's not a piss-ant gang anymore."

Manny continued to stare at Jake, then at Amos. "I'll be goddamned," he said again.

"We need some manpower, Manny," Jake said. "We have to strike fast if we have any chance of finding those girls."

"Damn, it's the middle of the night, but I'll do what I can."

"It has to be early, before sun-up," Amos said. "We have to use the element of surprise."

Jake looked at Manny. "You sure you trust your guy at TJPD?"

"Yeah, I do. He's solid."

"We can't afford to have anyone tipping Rojas off before we get there," Jake said, downing another shot.

Amos looked at Jake, a frown on his face. "You'd better put a lid on that bottle, Bull."

Jake stared at Amos with fire in his eyes. Amos stared back, standing his ground. Then Jake softened, his shoulders sagging noticeably.

"You're right," Jake said. "I'm gonna get some sleep." He stood up and stretched. "Wake me up in three hours, Manny."

"Okay, Bull. I'll make some calls and have everyone here by five. We should be able to hit 'em by six, before the sun comes up. You sure you know where they are?"

"We got their location. I just hope they're there," Jake said, rubbing his eyes.

Amos continued to stare at Jake. "You gonna be okay with three hours sleep, Bull? You put a lot of that shit away tonight," he said, pointing to the bottle of Bushmills.

Jake began walking out of the kitchen towards the den. "Don't worry about me, Mom," Jake said. "I'll be ready."

After Jake had been gone a few minutes, Amos asked Manny the question that had been burning in his mind for the past hour.

"What happened that night, Manny?" Amos said, leaning over the table.

Manny got up and closed the kitchen door, sat back down and poured himself a Bushmills. "I'll tell you the story, but don't let Bull know I did."

Amos nodded, waiting for Manny to begin.

"It was about five years ago, in October of ninety-six. Me and Sandowski had dropped by the El Toro for a beer. Got there around ten o'clock after pulling a twelve-hour shift at HQ. Bull was already drunk, really pissed drunk," Manny said, shaking his head. "Me and Sandowski took a table in the back of the bar. I didn't want to be anywhere near Bull that night and started to leave but Sandowski pulled me back down. He hated Bull with a passion."

"Why?" Amos asked.

"Long story. Bull made some enemies on the force back then with his tactics and give-a-shit attitude. Sandowski was waiting for a chance to nail his ass."

"He was a dick," Amos said. "Never liked the man."

"Yeah, me neither, but he was a Lieutenant and I was working for him back then, so I had to put up with his bullshit." Manny shook his head. "Anyway, I heard Bull at the bar..."

"Hit me again, Tiny," the big redhead said.

"Hey, Bull, I think you've had enough," the bartender replied.

"Screw you! Hit me again!" Bull smashed his massive hand on the old wooden bar, his eyes blazing and bloodshot after several hours of downing shots of Bushmills.

Tiny walked down and poured another shot into Bull's glass and walked away, shaking his head. "That's the last one, Bull," he said over his shoulder. "The last damn one."

"Here's to you, Tiny!" Bull yelled as he raised his glass above his head. He rocked his head back and downed the Irish whiskey in one motion, slamming the glass on the bar. *Whop!*

"Keep it down, Bull, or get the hell out," Tiny said from the other end of the bar. "Matter-of-fact, just get the hell out." The big black bartender's patience was at an end.

"One more, Tiny," Jake slurred. "One more and I'll go." He followed this with a big sigh and a belch.

"Manny, your old partner is fucked up," Sandowski said. "The guy's a mess."

I nodded silently. I'd seen Bull Delgado drunk many times, but never like this. I felt sorry for my old partner. I noticed Bull's Glock nine millimeter handgun holstered behind him, his badge sitting on the bar in front of him.

"I'd better try to calm him down and get him home," I said, sliding my wooden chair back quietly.

I froze when the door to the shabby, hole-in-the-wall bar flung open and four men stumbled in, talking loudly. Two of the men were huge and brawny, with tattoos covering their exposed arms. One had a long ponytail, the other one a shaved head. The third man was shorter and skinnier, with long stringy blond hair and a wild look in his eyes. The fourth man was short and wiry, but well-built, with jet black hair and brown skin. He was staring at the huge man at the bar. They took a table next to the bar and sat down heavily, scraping their chairs across the floor.

"Four beers, barkeep!" the skinny blond yelled. "And four shots of Patron!"

Tiny looked at the men and nodded, shooting a glance down the bar at Bull.

"Bull, why don't you get on home and sleep it off," Tiny said.

"Hey, Tiny," Bull said loudly, "my old man was buried today. Whadaya think of that shit?" He pounded the bar again. "The goddamn sonofabitch!"

I was still standing in the back of the bar. "Damn it, his old man died. There's gonna be trouble," I said quietly to Sandowski. "I better try to get Bull outta here."

Sandowski grabbed my arm. "Wait a sec. Let's see what happens."

I jerked my arm away, frowning at Sandowski. "That's my friend up there, asshole," I said.

"And I'm your superior officer," Sandowski said, staring up at me. "And I say sit the fuck down."

I continued to stand as I stared at the scene in the front of the bar. I moved my hand behind my back and gripped my nine millimeter, ready to bolt to the bar if there was any trouble. I watched as Tiny carried the shots and the four beers to the table, setting the shot glasses down in the middle of the table and placing a beer in front of each man.

"That'll be twenty bucks," Tiny said.

"The sonofabitch!" Bull yelled again, slamming the bar. He was oblivious of anyone else in the bar, including me.

"Hey asshole! Why don't you go home and sleep it off?" the man with the ponytail yelled.

The short, dark-haired man paid Tiny and continued to stare at Bull.

"Thanks," Tiny said as he moved quickly back to the bar. He walked down and stood in front of Bull. "Take it easy, Bull. I'm sorry about your old man, but you gotta go home before . . . ."

"Before what?" Bull asked, looking up at Tiny through bleary eyes.

"Fuck your old man!" yelled the skinny blond man, laughing loudly. "And fuck you!"

The two burly men began laughing, pointing at Bull. The man with the ponytail put his fist to his eyes and began chanting, "Boo hoo. Boo hoo." The short dark haired man sat quietly, watching the man at the bar intently. None of the four men seemed to notice me and Sandowski sitting in the dark in the back of the bar.

"C'mon, Bull. It ain't worth it," Tiny pleaded. "These dickheads ain't worth it." He glanced at me and Sandowski, pleading with his eyes for our help.

I took a step forward but Sandowski held me back. "Stand down, Fernandez," he said. "That's an order."

I looked up as Bull put both hands on the bar and slid his barstool back with a loud, scraping noise. He slowly stood up and turned to face the four men.

The men at the table stopped laughing when they saw Bull stand up. They recoiled when they saw the look in his eyes.

"You fucks got a problem with me?" Bull said, slurring his words. "Hey Tiny, why they call me Bull?"

Tiny let out a long sigh and shook his head. "C'mon, Bull. These dickheads aren't worth it, man." He looked at the four men and said, "You know who this is?"

There was nothing but silence from the four men as they stared at Bull. For several seconds the bar was as quiet as a church on Tuesday morning.

I continued to stand in the darkness in the back of the bar, slowly pulling my pistol out of its holster, getting ready for whatever was about to happen. I looked down at Sandowski and saw a grin on his face. The asshole wanted Bull to hang himself.

"Why they call me Bull, Tiny?" Bull said again, still staring at the four men.

"'Cause you're as big as one and just as mean," Tiny muttered, reaching for the telephone. As he held the phone he looked over at the four men. "You assholes know he's a cop?"

Before the four men could say anything, Bull said, "Not tonight, Tiny." He took off his holstered gun and slid it on the bar towards Tiny. He picked up his detectives badge and slid it down the bar. "Tonight it's just me and my old man."

I held my nine millimeter at my side, watching and waiting.

"Hell, he don't look so tough!" said the burly man with the ponytail as he stood up. He was almost as tall and almost as big as Bull. The man with the shaved head stood up, flexing his muscles.

"Shit man! Look at his eyes! He's crazy!" said the skinny blond man as he stumbled to his feet, his chair crashing to the floor.

The dark-haired man continued to sit quietly, watching Bull intently, his right hand under his black leather jacket.

"Yeah, but his old man's still dead," the burly ponytail said, laughing.

"That's it, dickheads!" Tiny said, pointing at me and Sandowski in the back of the bar. "There are two cops . . . ."

Tiny stopped in mid-sentence as Bull shot across the bar as though he were spring-loaded. Bull grabbed the big man by the ponytail and smashed his huge fist into the man's face, the sound of breaking bone echoing throughout the bar. Blood spurted everywhere as the man crumpled to the floor, screaming in pain. The other big man lunged at Bull, grabbing his arm. Bull shook him off as he would a fly, grabbing the man's shirt and smashing his face into the table three times. The man slumped to the floor, out cold.

I started to leap forward but was held back by Sandowski. "Delgado's got it under control," he said.

Click! Bull turned around at the unmistakable sound of a switchblade opening. The short, dark haired man was standing, waving the knife in front of him.

"What now, big man?" the man said with a slight Spanish accent. His gleaming white teeth showed through his smile. "Skinny, get behind him!" he said to the skinny blond man.

"C'mon, Angel! He's a cop!" Skinny screamed.

"I don't give a shit, get behind him!"

Skinny moved slowly to his right as the man with the knife moved to his left, cornering Bull against the wall. Bull put his back against the wall and lowered his arms to his side, staring at the man with the knife.

"What now - Angel?" Bull said slowly.

The man lying on the floor with the smashed nose reached out and grabbed Bull's right leg, pulling him off balance. As Bull stumbled, Angel lunged forward and caught him on the cheek, just missing his left eye. He slashed down with the knife all the way to Bull's chin, slicing his skin like an apple, blood spurting out of the open wound. Bull dropped to one knee and put his hand on the huge gash in his face, blood seeping through his fingers. Before the knife could strike again, Bull sprang up and grabbed the man's right wrist, twisting with all his might. There was the sound of bone breaking as the knife fell harmlessly to the floor. Bull then brought his knee up into the man's groin and pulled the man's head down into his knee. The man dropped backwards to the floor in a bloody heap.

As Bull put his hand back to his face, the man with the ponytail, blood gushing out of his nose, stood and grabbed Bull from behind, clutching at his throat. Bull pushed backwards with all his strength, pinning the man against the wall. A loud *swoosh* escaped the man's lungs as he fell to the floor, gasping for air.

The man named Skinny looked in horror at his three friends lying on the floor. He looked up to see Bull staring at him with the look of a wild animal, blood streaming from his face. Skinny suddenly pulled a gun from behind his back and pointed it at Bull.

"Back off, man!" he yelled. The gun was shaking in his hand.

I lifted my gun and pointed it at Skinny, my finger ready to squeeze the trigger. "Drop it!" I yelled. It was too late.

Skinny closed his eyes and fired, hitting Bull in the left shoulder. Bull stumbled backwards, catching himself before he fell. Skinny fired again, this time hitting Bull in the right side, spinning him around. Bull hugged the wall, screaming in pain. Skinny pulled the trigger again, but heard only a *click*.

"Drop it, asshole!" I yelled from the back of the bar.

Skinny turned and pointed his gun towards me.

I fired two shots, both of them ramming through the skinny man's chest. He dropped to the floor, dead.

I watched Bull drop to his knees and let out a scream that shook the walls. His blood was forming small pools on the barroom floor, continuing to gush out of his open wound. He sat with his back against the wall, staring at the four men on the floor.

"Bull! Hang on," I yelled as I rushed to his side. "Tiny, call an ambulance!"

"On its way," Tiny yelled back.

"You sonofabitch!" Bull screamed, looking up at the ceiling, the blood pouring out of his left cheek. "You goddamned sonofabitch!"

"Then he passed out cold," Manny said. "He was on life support for a few days after losing half his blood."

"Damn," Amos said, staring at Manny. "So the man with the knife was this Angel Rojas?"

"Well, Bull seems to think so," Manny replied. "He fits the description, and with the screwed up right hand . . . yeah, makes sense."

Amos stared out at the black sea. "Sounds like Bull might become a loose cannon when everything goes down."

CHAPTER 44

The King Air turboprop bounced around like a leaf in the wind. Ethan's eyes were open wide as he gripped the sides of his seat. He glanced at Pete, who had woken up at the same time, eyes red and mouth wide open.

"Holy Shit!" Pete cried. "What the hell is going on?"

"We must be passing through one helluva storm," Ethan replied.

"Gentlemen, please make sure your seatbelts are securely fastened. Once we get below these clouds the turbulence should ease up a bit. We'll be landing in Hermosillo in about fifteen minutes. Sorry for the rough ride."

Ethan smiled when he heard Vicki's voice over the intercom. He looked at Pete and began to laugh. Pete's hair was disheveled and sticking straight up in front. The usually perfectly groomed man looked like a little boy that had just crawled out of bed.

"What the hell's so funny?" Pete said, frowning.

"You look like you just came out of a blender," Ethan said, laughing. It felt good to laugh. He felt the tension ease.

"Well, you don't look so hot yourself," Pete retorted just as the airplane took another dip.

The airplane continued to bounce around in the dark clouds for several minutes. At one point it made a steep dive, pinning the two men back against their seats. Once the aircraft leveled off, the turbulence subsided.

Ethan looked out the window, streaked with rivulets of water, and saw the lights of a good-sized city. They were beneath the storm clouds. It was a welcome sight. He was four hundred miles closer to his daughter, but with a long way yet to go.

Pete let out a long breath once he realized they were out of danger. "That was some scary shit," he said to Ethan.

Ethan nodded. "Well, old buddy, you ready for the next leg of our journey?"

"Just get me on the ground. I'll tell you then."

Ethan smiled at his friend. He was glad Pete decided to come along, but worried about the next twenty four hours. The doubts about what they would be facing on this new day, September thirteenth, were gnawing at Ethan unmercifully.

"What are you thinking about?" Pete asked, seeing the tension in Ethan's face.

"I'm thinking about what this day is going to bring. And it scares the hell out of me."

Ten minutes later the airplane made a smooth landing and taxied to the end of the runway, stopping in front of a small terminal. When they heard the engines power down, Ethan and Pete unhooked their seatbelts and stood up, bending and stretching their tired, tight legs. They were feeling the strain.

Victoria Calderon opened the cockpit door and walked towards them, looking as though she had just exited a spa, her perfectly brushed hair swept back in a ponytail. She had a smile on her face, gleaming white teeth surrounded by beautiful bronze skin.

"So sorry about that turbulence, gentlemen. Unfortunately, the only way to get down is to pass through a cloud or two, and these clouds were angry."

Ethan stared at her, amazed at her beauty and composure. "That's okay, Vicki. You got us down and that's all that matters," he smiled.

"Nice wake up call, though," Pete said as he patted down his hair. "Sorry about my appearance, Vicki." Pete's face was red, with lines across one cheek where he had fallen asleep.

"You look fine, Pete. You guys can freshen up in the terminal while I complete some paperwork with the charter supervisor. I'll check on the Cessna to see if it's available. If not, we have a car waiting for us in the parking lot, so whenever you're ready we'll get on the road to Tijuana."

"I need to stretch my legs before we cram into another small space," Ethan said. "And I need to make a phone call."

"I'll be about thirty minutes. It's one thirty now so we'll meet at two. See you in the terminal," Vicki said, opening the door of the aircraft, releasing the stairs to the tarmac. "Be careful going down the stairs. It's raining and they're slippery. Just enter through the door over there," she said, pointing to the terminal about twenty feet from the airplane.

Ethan and Pete grabbed their computer bags and slowly made their way down the metal steps. They were both stiff and sore and moved slowly. The air was heavy with humidity from the passing storm. Even though it was early in the morning, the temperature was in the low nineties. They walked through a light rain towards a door with a single light above it.

It was dark inside the small terminal except for an office to the left where a man sat over a computer. Ethan knocked on the open door, poking his head inside. When the short, stocky man saw them, he stood up and held out his hand.

"Hello. Welcome to Hermosillo," he said with a thick accent. "My name is Tomas."

"Pete Cruz," Pete said, shaking the man's hand.

"Ethan."

"Where is Victoria?" Tomas asked, looking behind them.

"She'll be here in a few minutes," Ethan answered. "She said that you have a restroom where we can freshen up?"

"Of course. Right over there," he said, pointing to a door next to the office. "I'm sorry, but we don't have showers. Only latrines and a sink."

"That's fine. Thank you." Ethan smiled.

"A shower would feel great right about now," said Pete as they walked to the latrine. "I'm embarrassed to get into a car with Vicki, smelling like this."

Ethan shrugged. "Maybe we can at least get the stink off in here. Not much choice."

After fifteen minutes of scrubbing and brushing and washing, the two men walked out of the latrine, feeling a little fresher than before. The smell of after shave filled the small terminal.

"Think you overdid it on the after shave, buddy?" Ethan said, smiling at his friend.

Pete sniffed the air. "That's just my natural body odor, Ethan. Don't I smell pretty?"

"I just hope Vicki doesn't change her mind about driving with us," Ethan responded.

"Ah, she'll have a hard time keeping her hands off of me, more like it," Pete said, slapping Ethan on the back.

Ethan rolled his eyes. "I have to call Charlie to see what's going on."

"You think he's going to be awake this time of night?"

"Don't know, but I've got to try." He sat down in a wooden chair in the terminal and dialed his son's number. After several rings a man answered.

"Hello."

"Hello. Who's this," Ethan said.

"Manny. Who's this?"

"Manny? Who the hell are you? Where's Charlie?" Ethan said, his voice rising.

"Is this Ethan Paxton?"

"Where the hell is Charlie?" Ethan repeated.

"He's asleep. So's Bull. They're staying at my place," Manny said.

Ethan let out a long, slow breath. "Sorry, Manny, but I was expecting to talk to my son."

"No problem, Mister Paxton," Manny said. "Where are you?"

"Just landed in Hermosillo. We're going to start the drive to Tijuana in a few minutes, unless we get lucky with a small plane. What's going on there?"

"Well, not sure where to start," Manny said. "We know who the kidnapper is and where he's located . . . ."

"What?" Ethan said, his voice rising, his heart beginning to beat rapidly.

"We know who kidnapped your daughter," Manny said slowly. "We're going after them in a few hours."

Ethan held his head as he tried to digest the news. *They know where Molly is!* He put the phone back to his ear. "What time?"

"Sorry?"

"What time are you . . . going after them?"

"Six."

Ethan stood up and shook his head as he took the information in. "Are you sure about this?"

"Yeah, we're sure," Manny said. "Listen, I think you should talk with Bull, Mister Paxton."

"You said he was asleep."

"He is, but I can wake him up."

"No, don't do that. Let him rest. I'll be on the road for the next few hours so have him or Charlie call me before you do anything."

"Your son was awake for a few minutes but I sent him back to bed about half an hour ago" Manny said. "The kid was still exhausted from the ordeal. Do you want me to wake him up?"

Ethan thought for a second. "No, have them call me as soon as they wake up."

"You doing okay?" Manny asked.

"You tell me, Manny. Are you going to get my daughter?"

There was silence. "We're going to do our best, Ethan."

Ethan stared out the window into the darkness of the Sonoran night. "Manny, don't let anything happen to my son, and please get my daughter back safe."

"Goodbye, Ethan."

Ethan stood still, staring at the night sky, feeling the humidity, smelling the oil from the King Air mixed with Pete's aftershave. He rubbed his eyes, said a silent prayer again, and walked out into the night.

CHAPTER 45

Natalia watched as the teacher took her last gasp of life, her chest heaving up, then down, her mouth open, her eyes closed. Then it was over. Julie Caldwell was dead.

Natalia sat on the chair near the door, watching Molly and Cindy huddle together as they cried softly. Natalia was shedding her own tears as she watched the woman die. She knew that she was now an accomplice to murder and her own life was over. But she had known that for some time. It was over the moment she met Angel Rojas.

She stared at the young girls in the middle of the filthy room. She wanted to help them, to comfort them, but she was paralyzed with fear. Angel was going to kill her anyway, she knew that. She didn't know when, but it would be soon. Once the girls were gone, he wouldn't need her anymore. She would be irrelevant, but worse, she would be a witness. A witness to murder and a witness to sending three innocent girls to a life worse than death.

Natalia blinked when she saw Molly staring at her, the tears streaming down her young face. She saw the sorrow in her eyes, but also saw the hate. Natalia hated herself for what she had done and for what she had not done. She allowed the devil to complete his plan without so much as a fight. She was a coward and she deserved a life in hell. Her entire life had been going in that direction ever since she gave her child up for adoption so many years before. She was now getting what she deserved. She watched as Molly stood up, fire in her eyes.

"You did this! You killed her!" the girl said, her face just inches from Natalia. "I hate you more than I hate that animal out there. You are a gutless, worthless whore!" Molly spit in her face and slapped her across the face so hard that Natalia fell off of her chair.

Natalia hit the floor hard and lay there, simpering like a scorned child. She rolled up into a ball as Molly stood over her. The teenage girl, who was much smaller, towered over her.

"Molly, don't!" said a voice from across the room.

Molly, shocked, jerked her head towards the voice. Natalia opened her eyes and stared at Jenny. Natalia had not heard her utter a word since they had abducted the three girls. She had been a vegetable for the last twenty four hours, lying on her mattress either asleep or in a fetal position, rocking back and forth.

"Jenny?" Molly said.

"Don't hurt her anymore, please," Jenny said quietly. "I can't bear to see anyone else get hurt." She was standing next to Molly, weaving back and forth, looking like she would fall over any minute.

"Jenny, you're okay? I was so worried about you," Molly said, hugging the pudgy girl.

"Please don't hurt her anymore, Molly."

"I won't, Jen. I'm okay now. I'm so glad you're back."

Jenny cried softly and dropped down to Natalia and brushed the hair out of her eyes. "Are you okay?" she said.

Natalia gazed at the girl as though she was a ghost. "I'm . . . I'm okay," Natalia said, staring at Jenny.

Molly blinked back tears as she looked down at the woman. "I'm sorry. I didn't mean to hit you," she said. She bent down and offered her hand to Natalia.

Natalia took her hand and struggled to her feet, blood and tears merging at the corners of her mouth. "I'm so sorry about your teacher," she said, blinking back more tears.

Molly looked at her with sad eyes. "We have to talk about getting out of here," she said quietly.

Natalia nodded as she watched the two girls stagger to their mattresses. She walked over to them and sat down on the mattress where the dead teacher was lying. Natalia reached over and closed her mouth and then made the sign of the cross. She turned to the three girls who were watching her.

"The men will be asleep by now. There will be a guard asleep on the other side of the door. If I can get his attention and tell him that the woman is dead, he will have to come in and look at her and probably take her outside. While he does that, one of you can sneak out and check the white van for Molly's cell phone. It is just on the other side of the metal door."

"I'll do it. I know where it is," said Molly.

"You have to do it quickly, before he notices that you're gone," Natalia replied.

"What will they do with Missus Caldwell's body?" asked Cindy, still crying softly.

Natalia looked at the blond girl. "I don't know."

Molly reached over and held Cindy. Jenny joined them as they wept for their friend and teacher. Natalia watched them cry softly together, holding each other, wanting to join them, but knowing she couldn't.

Molly wiped the tears from her face and turned to Natalia. "Let's do it."

CHAPTER 46

Vicki was standing in the terminal office, a serious look on her face. Ethan had reentered the terminal and was standing next to her.

"I'm sorry for the limited facilities, but maybe we can stop somewhere along the way so you can properly clean up." She held up some keys. "I have bad news," she said, looking at Ethan. "The Cessna never arrived so there is no airplane for us here. We'll have to drive to Tijuana, unless I can arrange something between here and TJ."

Ethan felt the air release from his lungs, the hope in his heart going with it. He looked at Vicki and saw how disappointed she was.

"Well, it was worth a shot," he said. "Can we wait for a while in case it arrives?"

"The person that was supposed to deliver it never left Santa Ana, because of the storms. We'll have a better chance of driving through the night and I can work on getting a plane somewhere up ahead."

Ethan pursed his lips and nodded. "Thanks for trying, Vicki."

"Our car is waiting, whenever you are ready," she said, glancing at Ethan.

Ethan and Pete followed Vicki to the front of the small terminal, dragging their luggage behind them. She opened a door and they immediately felt the sticky heat. They walked in the early morning darkness to a blue Ford Explorer sitting in the empty parking lot. A solitary lamppost was the only light in the parking area.

"This is our home for the next five hundred miles," she said. "I will drive first, if that's okay."

Ethan nodded as they threw their luggage into the back of the SUV. Pete got into the backseat and Ethan took the front passenger's seat.

"I don't know about you, but I am starving," Vicki said as she put the Explorer into gear. "I know a great little cantina a couple of miles outside of town if you want to stop. They make great Chorizo and eggs. A little coffee would help, too."

Pete immediately said, "Chorizo and eggs, my favorite."

"Is that okay with you, Ethan?" Vicki said.

Ethan glanced at her without smiling. "We need to get on the road."

Vicki looked at Ethan, concern on her face. "It will only take a few minutes, Ethan. We need to eat something."

Ethan nodded his head as he stared off into the night.

Vicki drove out of the small parking lot onto a surface street. There were few street lamps and very little traffic as they drove around the outskirts of Hermosillo towards the west side of the city. The rain had stopped but the streets were still wet as Vicki drove slowly until they hit the main road that took them north on Sonora state Highway 15.

"This is a toll road, so we will have to pay a toll every thirty miles or so," Vicki explained. "It's the quickest route north to Highway 2, which will take us west, all the way to Tijuana. It's not as good as your interstate highways in the U.S., but at least it's drivable."

"How long?" Ethan said.

"To Tijuana? Barring any problems, about ten hours, maybe eleven," she said. "But on Mexican highways, problems are always a possibility. And the tolls slow us down some. We should be in TJ around one or two p.m."

Ethan sat silent, staring straight ahead.

"Are you okay?" Vicki said, looking at him, the concern growing on her face.

Ethan continued to stare straight ahead. "Yeah, I'm fine."

She took the next exit off of the toll road and several minutes later they were parking in front of a small, rundown building that had a neon sign blinking 'Consuelo's Cantina'. Just one other car was parked in front.

"Here we are," Vicki said, putting the Explorer into park and turning off the engine. "It's not much to look at, but the food is good and the place is clean. I would recommend drinking anything out of a bottle. Don't drink any tap water."

"Don't worry. I learned my lesson on my first trip to Mexico City a few years ago," Pete said. "I won't make that mistake twice."

They got out of the truck and entered the small cantina. There was one other person sitting at a table in the corner. The bartender was sleeping at the counter, his head in his arms.

"*Buenas noches*," Vicki said loudly, waking the man up.

The man behind the bar lifted his head. "*Buenas noches,*" the man said, grumbling and rubbing his eyes.

"*Tres chorizo con huevos,*" Vicki said. "*y tres cervesas, por favor.*"

The man nodded, walking back to the kitchen, scratching his rear end.

They took a table close to the bar and sat down. The man in the corner glanced at them and went back to his food.

"Most of the people outside the big cities don't speak English," Vicki explained. "That's another reason I thought you needed someone with you. It's hard to get around if you don't speak Spanish."

Ethan sat silent as Vicki and Pete made small talk. He noticed Vicki glancing at him nervously every so often.

"Are you sure you're okay, Ethan?" she finally said. "You look a thousand miles away."

Ethan forced a slight smile. "Make that about five hundred miles away."

Pete was looking at him. "What's bothering you, buddy?"

Ethan glanced at Pete, then at Vicki. Leaning forward, he said, "They know where Molly is."

Pete's mouth dropped open. Vicki put her hand to her mouth.

"They're going in after her in a few hours," Ethan said.

"Oh, my god," Vicki said, reaching for his hand. "Ethan . . . ."

"They know where she is," Pete said. "That's great news."

Ethan sat silent, his mind racing. "I need to be there."

Vicki blinked back her tears. "I'm so sorry about the Cessna . . . ."

Ethan stared at her. "I need to be there," he said again.

CHAPTER 47

After twenty minutes, their stomachs full of chorizo and eggs, Ethan, Vicki and Pete left the cantina. The storm clouds had passed and the night sky was full of stars. The stifling heat had gone down about ten degrees, but the air was still heavy with humidity.

"I'm going to make some calls," Vicki said as she excused herself and walked back to the cantina. "Maybe I can find a plane in Santa Ana or somewhere up the road."

Ethan stood next to the blue Explorer, looking up at the clear Sonoran sky. He felt Pete's gaze.

"What are you thinking, Ethan?" Pete said.

Ethan paused. "I'm thinking that my daughter is going to live or die on what happens in the next few hours, while we're driving on some god forsaken road in the middle of the Mexican fucking desert."

Pete nodded. "Vicki will get us there."

Ethan looked at his friend in frustration. "How, Pete. How is Vicki going to get us there?"

"I don't know, but she'll do whatever she can do," Pete said. "We know that much about her, Ethan. But she can't work miracles."

Ethan hung his head. "That's what I need - a miracle."

"She's a remarkable woman, Ethan," Pete said. "If there's a way, she'll find it."

Ethan paced back and forth for five minutes, waiting for Vicki. He saw her approaching them, a smile on her face.

"We've got a small plane reserved," she said. "But it's in Puerto Penasco, about a four or five hour drive from here. We can fly directly into Tijuana from there."

Ethan's heart sank. "That's too late, Vicki."

"That's the best I can do, Ethan. They have no planes available here in Hermosillo, or in Santa Ana. It's the middle of the night . . . I'm sorry."

Ethan breathed a deep sigh, swinging at the air with his fist. "Damn it!"

Vicki grabbed his hand. "It will get us there by nine o'clock."

He jerked his hand away. "Don't you understand? It's going to happen at six o'clock. She could be dead by then!"

Vicki stepped back. "It's . . . it's the best I can do, Ethan," she said. "I'm sorry."

Ethan looked at her and realized what he had done. He reached out for her but she backed away, the hurt evident in her face.

"I'm sorry, Vicki."

She stared at him, wiping a tear from her cheek. "I tried, Ethan."

Ethan reached out again and took her hand, bringing her slowly to him. They embraced in silence.

Pete cleared his throat. "Well, we'd better get on the road. Every minute counts now."

Ethan glanced at his friend. "Pete's right. Let's go."

They climbed into the Explorer, Ethan in the front passenger seat and Pete in the back, and began the drive north on Highway 15, towards the United States. The road was nearly deserted, with an occasional car passing them going in the other direction.

After ten minutes of silence, Vicki said, "You were thrown into a horrible situation, Ethan." She rubbed her hand up and down on Ethan's forearm.

"So many thoughts keep running through my mind," he said, feeling the electricity of her touch. "Why did it happen to her and not any of the other three hundred kids in that convoy? Why did her principal allow a car of all girls to bring up the rear of the convoy? Why wasn't a man in the car with them? It's driving me crazy thinking about it."

"Would that have made a difference?" Vicki said. "Having a man in the car?"

"Maybe. Maybe not," Ethan replied. "Maybe the kidnappers would have thought twice about it if they saw a man in the car." Ethan shook his head. "Who knows?"

He felt Vicki looking at him but didn't want to meet her gaze. There was more silence as they drove through the dark night. Pete began to snore in the backseat, breaking the silence.

"I bet this wasn't something you thought you'd be doing tonight," he said quietly. "Driving two Americans through Mexico in the dead of night. Sounds like something out of a horror novel."

She grinned and said, "You're right. This was NOT in my plans for this evening. Life has a funny way of getting in the way of our plans." She looked at Ethan, who was staring at her again. "But I'm glad I'm where I am right now."

He looked at her in the dim light of the truck. She was a beautiful woman and so confident and accomplished. At any other time and under different circumstances he would be immensely attracted to her. In fact, he was attracted to her now, but his mind and his heart were focused on his daughter.

"I just wish the circumstances were different," he said softly.

"So do I, Ethan, but it's all about finding Molly and taking her home. That's all that matters."

Ethan felt his eyes growing heavy as they drove through the darkness of the Sonoran desert. The highway was straight and endless, with few cars or lights anywhere, just long stretches of nothing but desert and black sky. Just as he was closing his eyes once again, he noticed a light in the distance.

"What's that?" he said, pointing ahead.

"It's a toll booth," she replied. "We went through one about fifteen miles back but you were asleep." She smiled at him as she saw the look of surprise on his face.

"Really? I don't remember dozing off. Guess I'm more tired than I thought."

"You need to get some sleep, Ethan. You have a very long day ahead of you and you're going to need to be alert," Vicki said with a worried look on her face. "Why don't you try to sleep for a while. The road is long and boring so I'll be fine. As a pilot I'm used to long stretches behind a wheel."

Ethan looked at her. "Where would Pete and I be without you and your family? We'd probably still be in Mexico City, waiting for a flight to somewhere."

"We'll talk more as we get closer to Tijuana," she said. "But right now, try to get some sleep."

"Yes, ma'am," he said, leaning back and closing his eyes. He opened them when he felt the Explorer slowing down at the toll booth. Vicki slowed the car to a stop as she handed the money to the toll booth operator, then sped up and continued down the desolate road.

"There's no way I can sleep right now," Ethan said, looking at Vicki.

She returned his glance. "Then let's talk."

"Okay," he replied, sitting up. "You know, I don't know anything about you, other than that you're a damn good pilot and have great parents."

"Well, let's see. I graduated from university with a degree in economics. My father wanted me to become a lawyer so I could help him run his business. I went to one year of law school in the U.S., and—"

"You lived in the U.S.?" Ethan asked, surprised.

"Yes, for one year. I went to Law School at the University of Texas, in Austin. I dropped out after the first year because it bored me to tears. My dad was disappointed, but he never tried to talk me out of it."

He looked at her and shook his head. "So how did you go from law to being a pilot?"

"I used to travel with my father to many different places for horse shows and fell in love with flying. I thought by being a pilot I could help the family business, since I sucked at being a lawyer."

"Your father seems very proud of you, so I guess that worked out. You're a damn good pilot, the way you maneuvered that plane through the thunder clouds in Hermosillo."

"I love it, I really do. Except that it makes it very hard to develop a relationship with anyone. I'm always flying somewhere, which doesn't help the dating process."

"No serious relationships?" Ethan asked.

"There was one, but he couldn't handle my schedule so it didn't work out."

"You still think about him?"

"No, that was several years ago," she answered.

Ethan noticed her glancing at the rearview mirror, a worried look on her face.

"What is it?" he said, looking back through the rear window.

"Probably nothing," she said, glancing again in the mirror. "The car behind us is coming up very fast."

Ethan looked at the side mirror and saw the headlights several hundred yards behind them, but closing fast. Looking back at Vicki, he said, "Why does it worry you?"

She glanced at him and then at the mirror. "This time of night, the chances are very good that it is one of two things. Trouble—or the police. Neither one is good."

"Why would the police be a problem?"

"In Mexico, the police can be very corrupt. Getting stopped in the middle of nowhere, in the middle of the night, is not good." Her tone had changed. She was obviously very nervous, glancing every few seconds at the headlights behind them.

Within several seconds the headlights were on top of them and then passed them quickly. Ethan saw the logo on the side door.

"Sonora State Police," he said, glancing at Vicki.

The brake lights came on as the brown truck slowed down in front of them. A blue light began flashing from inside the front cab.

"What's happening?" said Ethan, seeing the fear in Vicki's eyes as she pulled up behind the truck and put the Explorer in park.

"Do you have your passport handy?" She said, staring at the truck in front of them.

"It's in my computer bag in the back," he answered, his stomach beginning to tighten.

"What's going on?" a voice from the backseat said. Pete was sitting up, rubbing his eyes.

"Pete, get your passport and my computer bag from the back," Ethan said.

"What the . . . ."

"Do it. Now." Ethan gave his friend a no nonsense look.

Ethan turned to Vicki. Her knuckles were white as she gripped the steering wheel tightly. The fear tumbled out of her eyes as the police officer approached the car. He was wearing a brown uniform and was carrying a machine gun. Another man approached on the other side, his machine gun hanging at an angle. Three other men were standing outside of the brown Suburban, machine guns hanging at their sides.

Vicki stared at Ethan, afraid to look at the man approaching the car. He knocked on the window and gestured for her to roll it down. Ethan looked into her frightened eyes.

"Vicki, you need to roll the window down."

She turned and looked up at the man standing outside the car. She hit the button and the window began to slide down. The man bent down and peered inside the Explorer, both of his hands on the machine gun.

"*El permiso, por favor,*" he said to Vicki.

She turned to Ethan and said slowly, "He wants our passports."

Ethan and Pete handed them to Vicki, who handed them, along with her driver's license, to the officer. The officer signaled another man to join him at the car before he looked at the documents. The other officer held his machine gun pointed down, but ready to go into action if required. The first officer began to read the documents, starting with Vicki's driver's license. He looked at it, then at Vicki, and back to the license. Seemingly satisfied that it was valid, he began looking at one of the foreign passports. He said something to the other officer and then bent down and looked inside the Explorer, first at Ethan, then at Pete. He glanced at the passport and back at Pete.

"*Americano*," he said.

He did the same thing with Ethan's passport, looking at the picture, then at Ethan, and then back to the picture. All the while, Vicki was staring straight ahead, not saying a word.

"Get out of the car, please," the man said, bending down and speaking to Vicki.

Ethan looked at Pete and then at Vicki. She was shaking, the terror obvious on her face. Ethan reached over and touched her arm. "Vicki, are you okay?"

She looked at him, the fear in her eyes startling him. *Why is she so terrified*, he thought? He looked up at the officer, who was standing to the side so that Vicki could open her door. He noticed the name tag sewn into his shirt: Gomez.

"Vicki, we need to get out of the car. It will be okay," Ethan said, trying to hide his own fear.

The two men opened their doors and stepped out of the Explorer. They walked around and stood in front of the truck. Ethan glanced at Vicki and saw her slowly open her door and step outside. She quickly walked over to him and stood next to him.

Officer Gomez looked again at the passports and then at the two Americans. "Why are you traveling in Sonora so late at night," he said in English. He had a heavy Spanish accent, which made Ethan and Pete strain to understand him.

Vicki had calmed down enough to answer him, but didn't look at him directly. "We are traveling to Baja, to Tijuana. I am taking this one," she nodded at Ethan, "to see his daughter, who is ill in Tijuana."

Officer Gomez looked at Ethan, then at Vicki. "Why are you driving instead of flying?"

"Because of the terrorist attacks in America," she said. "Both of these men have flown all the way from Europe to Mexico because they cannot fly into their country."

Gomez was silent, staring at the two Americans. He looked at their passports again.

"Your *permiso de tourista* says you landed in Mexico City last evening," he said, looking up. "How did you get all the way to Sonora so quickly?"

Ethan spoke first. "Victoria is a charter pilot. Her and her family allowed us to fly from Mexico City to Chihuahua, and then to Hermosillo, on their charter plane."

The officer glanced at Vicki. "Do you have your pilot's license?"

"Yes," she said, as she went to the truck to get her purse. She showed her pilot's license to the officer. Gomez looked at the license, then at Vicki. He handed the license to another man and said something in Spanish. The other man walked to the suburban and began talking into the radio.

"Where do you live in America?" Gomez asked Pete.

"Oregon," he replied.

"And you?" he said to Ethan.

"California," Ethan said.

Gomez turned to Vicki and said something in Spanish. She nodded and looked at Ethan. "They want to check your luggage."

Ethan looked at the officer and nodded.

Ethan and Vicki walked to the back of the Explorer, with Gomez following them. The other officer stood in front of Pete, holding his machine gun down at the ground. Vicki unlocked the rear cargo door and lifted it up. Ethan grabbed his suitcase and laid it at the feet of the officer.

"Please open it," he said politely.

Ethan opened the suitcase on both sides and lifted the top up, then stood back.

The officer motioned for another man to come over and check through the bag.

A dog began sniffing the contents of Ethan's bag. They lifted Ethan's clothes and looked at the bottom of the suitcase, feeling for something out of the ordinary. They then opened his toiletry case and looked through the contents, opening the toothpaste tube and smelling it, holding it down for the dog to smell. The same thing with the shaving cream. They then zipped the toiletry bag up and replaced it in the suitcase.

"*Nada,*" the man said to Officer Gomez.

"Okay, you can close it and return it to the truck," the officer told Ethan.

Gomez turned to Pete and said, "Now you."

Pete followed Ethan's example and the dog sniffed and checked the contents. "*Nada.*"

"And your bag, *señorita,*" Gomez said to Vicki, looking at her closely.

Vicki was still holding Ethan's arm. She didn't want to let go.

Officer Gomez saw her hesitate and saw the fear in her eyes. "*Señorita*, your bag?" he said, glaring at her.

She released Ethan's arm, nodding her head to Gomez without looking at him. She reached into the Explorer and came out with an overnight bag. She dropped it at the officer's feet without looking at him. She quickly returned to Ethan's side.

The officers and the dog went through the same scenario. "*Nada*," they said, looking at Gomez.

Satisfied, Gomez told Vicki to close the cargo door and return to the front of the truck. Vicki, Ethan and Pete walked to the front and stood silent, waiting for the officer's instructions.

The man who had been checking on Vicki's pilot's license returned and handed it to Officer Gomez. They spoke quickly in Spanish.

Gomez handed the license back to Vicki. "Pardon my English, it is not so good. We stopped you because this highway is a main artery for drug dealers."

Gomez stared at Vicki. "You must be very careful on this road, *Señorita* Calderon. Do not stop where there are no lights. Be wary of other people, especially this time of day. It could have ended badly for you and your American friends if we happened to be the wrong people." He had a strange smile on his face. "*¿Comprende?*"

"Yes, I understand," Vicki answered without looking at him.

Gomez looked at her carefully and said, "Please, be on your way, and be careful." He shifted his gaze to Ethan. "Señor, I hope your daughter is well. Good luck." He bowed slightly to Vicki and nodded at Ethan and Pete, then walked to the Suburban. The men climbed in and drove off on the dark highway.

Ethan, Vicki and Pete continued to stand in front of the truck.

Ethan turned to Vicki. "Are you okay?" he asked her.

She looked at him and then grabbed him around the waist and put her head on his chest. Ethan could feel the wet tears on his shirt. They stood next to the Explorer for several seconds before anyone spoke.

Pete stood several feet away, watching the two. Finally, he said, "My heart rate is going bonkers."

Vicki continued to hold Ethan tightly until the tears stopped. Ethan looked over at Pete and said, "Mine, too, Pete."

Ethan grabbed Vicki's chin and held her face up to his. "You okay, now?"

She nodded and smiled weakly at him, glancing at Pete.

Ethan wiped away a tear from her cheek. It made him feel better to see her smile. He saw her eyes begin to soften, the tenseness in her face lessening. "That really shook you up, didn't it?" he said.

She slowly pushed herself away from him, an embarrassed look on her face. "I'm sorry."

"Are you okay now?" he asked her.

She didn't respond. She turned and walked to the driver-side door and opened it. "We need to get back on the road."

Ethan continued to stare at her. He walked to the passenger-side door, shaking his head. Pete was climbing into the back seat.

Suddenly Ethan saw headlights coming their way at a high speed. "Now what?" he said.

Within seconds a gun-metal gray SUV pulled up behind them. A man got out of the driver's side door and walked up to the van. He had a uniform on, a different color than the Sonora State police. He rapped his knuckles on Vicki's window, indicating that she should roll her window down.

Vicki looked at Ethan with panic in her eyes. "Ethan?"

Ethan peered at the man at the window. "It's okay. Go ahead and open it."

Vicki hit the button and the window opened.

"Is everything okay here?" the man said in Spanish.

Vicki nodded, looking up at the man in the gray uniform. "Can you speak English?"

"I am Officer Mendez, of the Federal Police. We patrol this area for drug smugglers." He peered into the van and looked at Ethan and Pete. "Americans?"

Ethan nodded. "Americans."

Officer Mendez stared at Ethan for several seconds. "Why are you on this highway so late at night?" He spoke in perfect English.

Vicki cleared her throat. "I am taking them to Tijuana. His daughter is . . . ill," she said, nodding at Ethan.

Officer Mendez looked at Ethan again. "Can I see your passports, please."

Ethan and Pete handed their passports to Vicki, who gave them to Mendez.

He backed off several steps while he looked at the passports, peering inside the van to look at Ethan and Pete.

"And you, *Señorita?* Your identification, please."

Vicki handed him her driver's license. She was much calmer than she had been with the Sonora police.

"Victoria Calderon, from Chihuahua," Mendez said, looking at the license. "Are you related to Arturo Calderon?"

She stared at him in surprise. "Yes, how did you know?"

"I know your father . . . I assume he is your father. He is a good man."

She continued to stare at him. "But how did you know . . . ."

"I noticed that you had been stopped by the Sonora State police," Mendez said quickly. "Is everything okay?"

Vicki nodded. "Yes, we're okay," she said, continuing to stare at the man.

"Where are you headed?" he asked.

"To the airport at Puerto Penasco. We're chartering a private plane to fly to Tijuana," Vicki said.

"Why so early in the morning?"

"Because we just flew from Amsterdam to Mexico City tonight," Vicki said. "I flew these men from Mexico City to Chihuahua, then to Hermosillo." She looked at Ethan. "This man is trying to get to his daughter in Tijuana."

Officer Mendez gazed at Ethan again, squinting his eyes. "Why didn't you fly directly to Tijuana from Mexico City?"

Vicki was now in control, confident. "Because of the terrorist attacks in the United States, they wouldn't allow anything other than small, private aircraft to fly into Tijuana." She grabbed Ethan's hand and squeezed it. "That's why we have to fly from Puerto Penasco."

Officer Mendez bent down and spoke directly to Ethan. "And what is your daughter's condition?" he asked.

Ethan stared at the man, not knowing what to say. He coughed and said, "She is very ill and I have to get to her as soon as possible."

Mendez peered at Ethan, the compassion showing in his face. "Okay, señor. Be on your way." He put his hand on Vicki's shoulder. "Be careful, Victoria. It is dangerous on this highway at night."

Ethan stared at the man, wondering why he called her by her first name.

Vicki smiled at the officer."Thank you. We will be careful." She rolled up the window as Officer Mendez walked back to his SUV.

"Do you know him?" Ethan asked her.

"No, but he was a kind man, which is rare for a policeman in Mexico," she said, turning the key to the ignition and pulling out onto the highway, spitting gravel everywhere. "Very rare."

CHAPTER 48

Molly turned on the shower as high as it would go, closing the shower curtain from the outside. Then she walked out of the bathroom. Everyone was looking at her, the fear evident in their faces. Cindy and Jenny sat on their mattresses, their hands tied loosely behind their backs. Natalia was standing next to the metal door, nervously shifting from side to side.

"They'll think I'm in the shower. You guys lie down..." she said. "You guys lie down and act like you're asleep," Molly said to Cindy and Jenny. "Don't make any noise when they take Missus Caldwell out, okay?"

The two girls nodded. "Be careful, Molly," Cindy said quietly.

"I will. I'll be back in here in no time—hopefully with my cell phone." She hugged Cindy, then Jenny. "We're getting out of here."

She walked to the door and nodded to Natalia. Molly stood behind a corner near the door, so that she would be hidden when the man came in to look at Missus Caldwell. Natalia was standing in front of her to shield her from sight.

Natalia made the sign of the cross and then took a deep breath, looking at Molly one last time. She knocked loudly on the metal door several times. There was no response. She knocked again, this time saying loudly, "*¡Abre la puerta!*"

She waited with her ear to the door. She heard a noise on the other side, the sliding of a chair.

"*¡Abre la!*" she said again.

"*¿Quien es?*" a raspy voice said.

"Natalia," she responded. "*¡Abre la!*"

She heard mumbling and then someone fumbling with the lock. Finally, the dead bolt began to slide against the metal loudly. Molly held her hand to her mouth, hoping that the noise wouldn't wake the others on the other side of the door. She heard the familiar *click* when the dead bolt was clear of the lock, then the big metal door began to slide open. The head of a man appeared, but the door didn't open all the way.

"*¿Que?*" he said, looking at Natalia.

Natalia pointed to the body of Missus Caldwell. "*Se muere*," she said.

The man looked over at the body of the dead woman, then back to Natalia. He shrugged his shoulders, as if saying 'so what?'

"*¡Apesta!*" she said, waving her hand in front of her nose, indicating the decomposing body and the distinctive smell of death enveloping the small room.

The man opened the door a little more and sniffed. He crinkled his nose when the odor of death reached his nostrils. He slid the door open wide and walked into the room holding his nose. He looked at the girls lying still on the mattress and noticed the empty mattress.

"*¿Donde esta?*" he said, pointing at the empty mattress.

"*La regadera el chubasco,*" Natalia replied, pointing to the bathroom. "Shower," she said in English.

The man walked to the bathroom. Molly held her breath as he poked his head into the small room. Natalia moved over slightly to make sure Molly was hidden from the man's sight. Evidently satisfied that someone was in the shower, he walked back to Natalia.

"*La cobija,*" he said, pointing to a blanket and motioning towards the dead body.

Natalia walked to Missus Caldwell's body, picking up a blanket from Molly's mattress. She turned and motioned for the man to join her. He hesitated for a second, then walked slowly towards the body.

Molly saw Natalia glance at her, the signal to move. Molly slid around the open door and moved to the other room, which was dark except for a light near an office on the other side of the warehouse. She saw the white van not more than ten feet away. She glanced back at Natalia and the man, who were covering the dead body. Molly looked around the large warehouse and, not seeing any movement, walked quickly to the white van. She knew the interior light would come on so she had to move fast, and quietly. The door lock was up, so she lifted the door handle gently, hoping it wouldn't make any noise when it opened. She heard a soft *click*, and then the door was open. She opened it just enough to slide her upper body through the opening and felt under the driver's seat. She moved her hand around until she felt something. She clamped her hand on the piece of metal and pulled it out - her cell phone. She shoved it into her jeans pocket and closed the door quietly. The small *click* was all that was heard. She quickly walked the ten feet back to the metal door and peered inside. The man had his back to the door, picking up the feet of the dead body. Natalia was holding the head, looking at the door. Molly quickly moved back to the spot behind the corner, out of sight. She watched as Natalia and the man carried Missus Caldwell's body through the open door, the man walking backwards. Once they were in the warehouse, Molly ran to the bathroom and quickly took her clothes off and walked into the shower.

After several minutes Natalia and the man came back into the room. The man told Natalia to pick up Missus Caldwell's mattress and take it outside. Molly heard footsteps walking towards the shower and saw through the shower curtain a head poking into the bathroom. Her heart stopped when she saw the shadow of the man walk towards the shower. She stood under the water to make sure she was wet. The man pulled the shower curtain open, glaring at Molly. She hid her private parts as he looked her up and down, a smile on his face.

"*Muy linda,*" he said, leering at her.

The man's gaze and gold teeth sickened Molly. She thought that he was about to walk into the shower, so she reached up and closed the curtain. The man opened it again, staring at her exposed breasts.

"*¡Pendejo!*" Natalia said loudly as she pulled him backwards. "*¡Deja la!* Get out!"

The man backed out of the bathroom, glancing at Molly, cursing at Natalia. "*¡Ay, puta loca!*"

Molly stared into Natalia's eyes, then turned her back to her.

When Molly turned back around she noticed Natalia still staring at her. "What are you staring at?"

Natalia, eyes wide and moist, looked at Molly. "You have a birthmark on your back."

"So?" Molly said.

Natalia backed away, wiping her eyes. "Nothing."

Molly closed the shower curtain, letting the water run over here. *What was Natalia talking about?*

"*¡Pendejo!*" she heard Natalia say again. Molly opened the curtain so she could hear better. She heard the metal door begin to close and the familiar rasp of the dead bolt sliding into place. She breathed a deep sigh, then stepped out of the shower and peeked outside to make sure the man was gone. Natalia was looking down, shaking her head. Molly dried herself and put her clothes back on.

"Did you get it?" Natalia asked her as she walked out of the bathroom.

Molly nodded, looking over at Cindy and Jenny, who were sitting up, staring at her.

"We're getting out of this hellhole," she said to them. For the first time since they were abducted, they had hope. Molly pulled the cell phone out of her jeans pocket and tried to turn it on. Nothing would work. She tried again, nothing.

"It's dead, Cin. It was on the entire time it was in the backseat, which has been thirty six hours. These batteries will only last a few hours. I need to charge it."

Molly walked quickly to the duffle bags in the corner and opened her bag. The charger was beneath her clothes.

Molly looked at the outlet in the ceiling. It was at least ten feet high.

Molly walked quickly to the chair and put it directly under the outlet. She stood on the chair and reached as high as she could, but was over a foot from the outlet.

"Cindy," she said. "You're taller, you try."

Cindy slowly stepped onto the chair and reached up but she was only slightly taller than Molly. She came closer, but was still eight or nine inches short of the outlet.

"We can use the chair and you can stand on my shoulders," said Jenny. "It will be close but I think you can reach it."

Molly thought about this. "It'll have to work. We have no other option," she said, grabbing the wooden chair.

Jenny walked over and stood on the chair to see if it would hold her weight. She nodded to Molly.

"Jenny, since you're the strongest and Cindy is the tallest and weighs the least, Cindy should get on your shoulders and plug the charger in," Molly said, looking at Cindy.

Cindy nodded in agreement.

"Okay, Cindy you need to get on Jenny's shoulders before she climbs up on the chair."

Molly and Natalia stood on either side of the two girls to catch them if they fell. Jenny bent down and Cindy climbed onto her shoulders. Jenny slowly raised up until she was standing upright.

"Natalia, hold the chair steady so it doesn't move," Molly said.

Jenny slowly raised her and Cindy onto the chair and then moved her other leg up so that they were standing solidly on the chair.

"Cindy, see if you can reach the outlet," Molly said.

Cindy was wobbly at first but caught her balance with Jenny's help. When they were at the full height, Cindy reached up with the prong end of the charger in her right hand, fumbling with the charger but finally getting the prongs in place. She pushed them into the outlet.

Molly handed Cindy the cell phone and watched as Cindy connected it to the charger. She stared at the cell phone, waiting for the charging light to come on. She saw a red light blink.

"Got it!" she said softly.

Cindy and Jenny climbed down from the chair. The three girls hugged each other and danced a silent dance. Natalia watched them and smiled.

"Come here, Natalia," Molly said to the woman.

Natalia joined them in their group hug.

"Great job, everybody. Thanks for your help, Natalia," Molly said, smiling at her.

Natalia smiled back, her grin as big as her face would allow.

"We have to make sure no one comes in here in the next hour, to give the cell phone a chance to charge," Molly said. "Natalia, what time is it?"

Natalia looked at her watch and said, "Two-thirty."

"Good," said Molly. "We should have plenty of time before the others wake up."

She glanced up at the cell phone, hanging in mid-air above them. The little red light kept blinking. *That light is my life*, thought Molly. *As long as it's blinking, I have hope.*

CHAPTER 49

As they drove past a small town named Querobabi, Ethan thought about the sight of automatic weapons being pointed at them. He was worried about Vicki, about the way she had acted when they were stopped. He glanced over at her, wanting to ask her about it, but decided to leave her alone with her thoughts for now.

Ethan turned and looked at Pete in the backseat. He was awake but staring off into the night. Finally, Ethan broke the silence.

"Anyone up for a cup of coffee?" he said, looking at Vicki, then Pete.

Vicki continued to look straight ahead at the road, not answering. Pete yawned, stretched and said finally, "Sounds good."

Ethan reached over and put his hand on Vicki's shoulder. "How about you, Vicki? You must be getting tired."

She glanced at him and said, "I'm okay. We'll be in Santa Ana in thirty minutes so we can stop there."

Ethan continued to look at her, his hand resting on her shoulder.

"You haven't said anything for quite a while."

She smiled slightly, barely looking at him. "Just thinking, that's all."

Ethan removed his hand. She glanced at him again, then returned her eyes to the road. Her demeanor had completely changed since they had been stopped. She seemed much more nervous, almost cold. He decided to try to lighten the mood.

"Pete, you get enough sleep?" he asked his friend.

"I never get enough sleep," he replied. "I couldn't sleep once we got back on the road, too much adrenalin. You must be tired as hell."

"You'd think so, but I have the same problem. Too much adrenalin, too much going through my mind right now." He glanced at Vicki quickly, but no reaction.

"Well, I can understand that," Pete said.

"We'll be in Santa Ana in half an hour," Vicki said. "From there, Puerto Penasco is less than an hour. Why don't you get some sleep now, Pete, then we can wake you up in about half an hour, when we reach Santa Ana?" she replied.

Pete yawned and said, "That sounds good to me. Will you guys be okay?"

"Sure, Pete," Ethan said, looking back at his friend. "We'll wake you when we stop for coffee."

Ethan watched Pete close his eyes and rest his head on the window. He glanced at Vicki, hoping that he would have a chance to talk to her while Pete was sleeping. She looked straight ahead, not returning his glance. Within two minutes they heard snores coming from the back seat.

"Wish I could fall asleep that fast," said Ethan. "That guy can sleep anywhere, through anything."

Ethan was looking out his side window at the dark desert night. Suddenly, he felt Vicki's hand on his arm. He turned and looked at her. Her hand was trembling and tears were forming in her eyes. He put his right hand on her hand and felt it shaking.

"Vicki, what's wrong?"

She continued to tremble, enough that Ethan became worried about her driving.

"Why don't you let me drive to Santa Ana," he said. "It's only half an hour and—"

"No, I need to drive, to concentrate on something."

Ethan had to know what was bothering her. "Was it the Police? You seemed so frightened back there."

She looked at him and nodded her head. "I need to talk about it. Is that okay?"

"Sure. I've wanted to talk about it since we got back on the road, but I didn't know if you did, especially in front of Pete."

She glanced back at Pete, then at Ethan. Her shaking subsided somewhat but her eyes were moist.

"It happened three years ago, right after I got my charter license. I was driving on this same road, between Hermosillo and Nogales, which is on the U.S. border." She wiped her eyes. "It was late at night, around eleven o'clock, and I was very tired. I had flown a charter into Hermosillo that evening and was driving to Nogales to meet my father at a horse show. It's about a three hour drive normally. I wanted to get to Nogales by midnight because it's a dangerous city at night. I had stopped in the town we just passed, Querobabi, for a cup of coffee and to go to the bathroom. As I was walking out of the cantina to my car, a truck, very similar to the one that stopped us, pulled up next to me. It was the state police."

Ethan remembered that the sight of the brown Sonora State Police truck had struck fear into her.

She brushed some tears away. "One of the policemen stood in the path to my car, not letting me pass. I said 'excuse me' and tried to walk around him. He moved back into my path. I asked him if there was a problem and he said, 'No, as long as you give me a kiss.' I could smell the alcohol on his breath. His eyes were red and they scared me. The other policeman just looked at us and walked into the cantina. We were all alone in the parking lot, standing between his truck and my car."

"You don't have to continue—"

"No, I have to tell you while I have the courage," she said. "The man grabbed my arm and pulled me to his truck, pinning me against the side. He tried to kiss me but I turned my head. I struggled against his grasp, but he was too strong. He reached under my blouse and grabbed my breast and squeezed very hard. He was breathing in my face, the smell of the alcohol and smoke making me sick to my stomach."

She looked at Ethan, then glanced back at Pete. Satisfied that Pete was asleep, she continued.

"I tried to knock his hand away but he just squeezed harder. Then . . . then he grabbed my hair and pulled my head back and kissed me so hard it made my lip bleed. I tried to scream but he kept his . . . tongue in my mouth. Then he said in my ear, 'If you scream, I'll kill you.' He opened the door to the back seat to my car and shoved me inside. When he climbed in after me he reached up my leg and . . . and grabbed me." She stopped talking and looked away. Her lips were trembling.

"Vicki, you don't—"

"I haven't told anyone about this—not even my father. He would have done something stupid. The state police are untouchable. They can do anything they want and no one can do a thing about it. That's the way it is in Mexico. Please, I need to finish this," she pleaded.

"Okay."

"He got on top of me and raised my skirt. He . . . he ripped my panties off of me and groped me." The tears were streaming down her face again, this time in torrents. "Then he entered me. It took just a couple of minutes, and he was finished." She again wiped the tears from her eyes so that she could see the road. "He left me in the backseat. I couldn't move, I was so terrified. I heard their truck start up and leave. I was alone in the backseat of my car for what seemed to be a long time. No one was around. I finally got the courage to move and sat up. I put myself together and got out of the car and went to the bathroom in the cantina. I cleaned myself up as best I could and then got back in my car and left."

"Vicki, I'm so sorry," Ethan said, putting his hand on her arm.

"That's not the end," she said, choking.

Ethan saw the pain and the guilt in her eyes. He let her continue.

"Six weeks later I found out I was pregnant," she said, glancing at Ethan. "I had it aborted. I never told my father or mother. You are the first person I have ever told."

Ethan sat in stunned silence, staring at her. He reached over and wiped her cheek with his hand, brushing her hair back from her wet cheeks.

"I'm sorry you had to go through that alone, Vicki. Now I understand why you were so frightened tonight." He cleared his throat. "Was he there tonight?"

She began to tremble again, the car lurching to the right, spitting gravel and dirt as the car drove off the road slightly. She pulled it back onto the road and continued driving.

Ethan stared at her, then glanced back at Pete to see if he had woken up. He was still snoring in the back seat. "Vicki, was he the one—named Gomez?"

She stared straight ahead and nodded, the tears running down her cheek.

Ethan just stared at her, the anger beginning to boil inside of him.

"What can I do?" he said.

She shook her head and wiped away some more tears. "Nothing. You need to concentrate on your daughter," she answered.

"Vicki, you need to tell your father. You can't live this nightmare by yourself."

She shook her head again. "No, I know my father. He would not let it go. He would get himself killed. You cannot go up against the Police in Mexico. It's suicide." Her face crinkled into a frown. "I shouldn't have told you. You have too much to think about already. It wasn't fair of me to burden you with this."

"You haven't burdened me with anything. I'm deeply honored that you felt you could tell me about something so personal, and so devastating." He touched her arm. "You didn't do anything wrong, Vicki. You were a victim."

She looked at him, the fear and emotion draining from her face. "I thought that I had it buried deep inside of me, but seeing him tonight brought it all back."

Ethan wanted to hold her, to let her know she was safe. He looked ahead and saw lights in the distance. "Let's stop up ahead, where the lights are."

As they got closer they saw that it was a gas station and cantina. No cars were around except one parked on the side of the gas station. Vicki pulled into the gas station and pulled the car to a remote part of the lot. She turned off the key, still shaking.

Ethan got out of the car and walked around to the driver's side and opened the door. Vicki looked up at him and unhooked her seat belt. She got out of the car and fell into his arms, sobbing. He held her tightly, brushing her hair and not saying anything. He felt the wetness of the tears through his shirt, felt the trembling and listened as the sobs turned to sniffles. He continued to hold her in silence.

Vicki finally looked up at him, her eyes red and puffy, mascara smudges on her cheeks. He pulled out a handkerchief and wiped her face. They stared at each other for a lingering moment before she said, "Thank you, Ethan."

He smiled and kissed her forehead. "You're not alone with this nightmare anymore, Vicki."

She reached up and put her hand behind his neck and pulled him to her. They kissed softly and held each other until they heard sounds from the backseat.

"We there already?" Pete said, yawning.

Ethan smiled at Vicki. "Yeah, we're getting there, Pete."

CHAPTER 50

Within fifteen minutes they passed through the town of Santa Ana, where the highway forked. State Highway 15, which they had been traveling on since leaving Hermosillo, continued north to Nogales, on the U.S. border. Vicki turned left onto State Highway 2, which ran west, eventually ending in Tijuana.

"At least we're getting closer to the good ol' U.S.," Pete said from the backseat, unaware of what had happened.

"Nogales is about sixty miles north on Highway 15, and Tucson, Arizona is another sixty miles past Nogales," Vicki said, finally under control.

Pete thought about this. "We're only sixty miles from the border," he said absently, more to himself than anyone else.

Ethan turned to his friend. "You want to get off here, Pete? You could take a bus or maybe even a taxi to the Nogales border crossing and be in the U.S. in an hour or so."

Pete turned to look at Ethan. "I'm with you till the end, old buddy. I signed up for the entire tour, so let's go," he said, smiling.

Ethan grinned back at him, but then turned serious. "Listen, Pete. I know you want to get home and see your family, and this trip hasn't been the easiest. I wouldn't think any less of you or our friendship if you wanted to get off now and head home."

For once Pete turned serious, too. "I'm all in, Ethan. Tijuana or bust. End of story."

Ethan slapped him on the knee and nodded. He turned to Vicki and said, "How about that coffee you promised us?"

"I know a place just up ahead, just off the highway. We'll be there in a few minutes," she said, glancing at Ethan. "Good, strong coffee."

Ethan looked out the window and saw the outskirts of a small city. It was still dark out, but there were lights on the side of the road and on the hillsides. It felt good to be around people again after driving through the dark and isolated desert for several hours.

"How big is Santa Ana?" Ethan asked, looking at Vicki.

"Not big, maybe ten thousand people. It's mainly a crossroads for the two highways, so it gets lots of traffic. Not much to the town, mostly agricultural."

Vicki exited Highway 2 and stopped at another small restaurant. It was bigger than the one in Hermosillo and had several cars parked in front. She pulled into the parking lot and parked close to the café. It was nearly five o'clock in the morning.

"Do you want to get the coffee to go or drink it here?" she asked Ethan.

"Let's sit down and drink it here," he said. "I have to go to the bathroom anyway. We can afford ten minutes or so."

They all got out of the Explorer and walked into the café. The smells hit them immediately. The smell of tortillas frying on a grill, of chorizo and other meats sizzling in the kitchen, and the unmistakable smell of brewing coffee. They took a table in the corner in the back, away from anyone else. There were six tables in the café. Two of them were occupied when they walked in.

"*Buenos dias,*" a man said as he approached the table.

"*Buenos dias,*" Vicki answered. "*Tres café Americano, por favor.*"

"*Sí.*"

Ethan got up, excused himself and walked to the restroom. He entered the dingy restroom and immediately looked at himself in the cracked, dirty mirror. *Good God, how can Vicki stand to look at me?* He splashed water on his face and combed his hair, which was badly in need of shampoo. He took a whiff of his clothes and pinched his nose as he relieved himself. He glanced in the mirror one more time as he washed his hands, then headed back out into the café.

As he approached the table he saw Vicki and Pete staring at the front of the café. Turning to see what they were looking at, he saw three Sonora State Police officers standing at the counter ordering coffee. He froze when he recognized Gomez, the man who had checked their luggage earlier and the one that Vicki had said raped her three years before. He walked to the table and sat down, putting his hand on Vicki's arm.

"Stay calm, okay? They probably didn't see us back here in the corner." His words were hollow, since he knew that they probably recognized their blue Explorer in the parking lot.

Vicki was looking down at her coffee, afraid to look up at the three policemen. Pete glanced at Ethan and raised his eyebrows. Nothing was said for several minutes. They stirred their coffee and drank slowly, not wanting to draw any attention to their table.

Ethan looked at the front of the café and saw Gomez looking in their direction. He was holding a Styrofoam cup of coffee, blowing on it to cool it down. Staring at the three people in the corner, Gomez began walking slowly towards them. Ethan felt Vicki's muscles tighten as he held her arm.

"*Buenos dias,*" the policeman said, smiling. "The *Americanos,*" he said in a friendly manner, looking at Ethan, then Pete.

"*Buenos dias,*" Pete said, looking at Vicki and Ethan. "You on a coffee break?"

Gomez looked down at his coffee. "*Sí, señor.* Coffee break. My English is not so good," he said, smiling at Pete. He turned his gaze towards Vicki. "*Buenos dias, señorita.*"

Vicki looked up at him and nodded, then looked back down at her coffee.

Ethan continued to look at Gomez to see if there was any hint of recognition when he looked at Vicki. He didn't notice anything.

"You are traveling to Tijuana, no?" Gomez said.

"Yes," Ethan replied, not smiling.

"You have a very long drive," Gomez said. "You must be very tired."

"We're okay," Ethan said.

"Is the señorita going to be driving?" he said, looking at Vicki. "It is a dangerous drive along the border. Many bad people."

Ethan didn't respond as Vicki continued looking down at her coffee.

Gomez now concentrated his gaze on Vicki. He tilted his head to get a better look at her.

"What is wrong with the señorita? She no look at me," he said, the smile gone from his face. "Am I ugly?"

"Excuse us, but we have to get back on the road." Ethan stood up, drinking the last of his coffee.

Vicki stood up and slowly raised her head, looking directly into the policeman's eyes.

"The señorita is very beautiful," Gomez said. "She should smile more." The man ran his gaze down Vicki's body and back up to her face. "Very beautiful." He squinted his eyes while staring at her, shaking his finger. "You look very familiar."

"Yeah, well you just saw us less than an hour ago," Ethan said. "Excuse us, but we have to go." He began walking past the man.

As Vicki walked around the table, Gomez grabbed her arm.

"I know you from somewhere," he said, his face just inches from hers. "Somewhere before tonight."

"I don't think so," Vicki replied, trying to remove her arm from his grasp. She looked into his eyes. "I'd remember you."

Gomez's eyes widened as though he suddenly remembered. He began to smile and pulled her closer to him. She resisted and tried to pull her arm away. Gomez pulled her to him roughly.

Vicki let out a groan.

"Get your hands off of her," Ethan said, grabbing at the policeman's arm.

One of the other officers reached out and pulled Ethan away from Gomez, holding him in a bear hug.

Gomez looked at him, still holding Vicki's arm in his left hand and reaching for his gun with his right, his eyes blazing. "Fucking *yanqui*," he said, seething. "You dare touch me?"

As Vicki tried to pull away from Gomez, Pete grabbed the policeman's arm.

"Let her go," Pete shouted as he tried to wrench the man's arm away.

Gomez turned his gaze on Pete. "You are a dead *gringo*," he said, pointing his pistol at Pete.

Ethan tore away from the other man and lunged at Gomez. He hit the policeman's arm as the shot rang out. The sound of shattered bone echoed throughout the restaurant.

Pete groaned and fell backwards, hitting a table and sending chairs flying.

Gomez tore his arm from Ethan's grasp and pointed the gun at him. "Fucking *gringo*," he said as he pointed his gun at Ethan.

Everyone heard a shot ring out, but it was from the front of the restaurant.

"Gomez! Back away! Now!" a voice yelled.

Everyone jerked their heads to the front of the restaurant. Standing in the doorway was Mendez, the Federale officer. His gun was pointing directly at Gomez. Two other *Federales* were aiming their pistols at the other state policemen.

"Drop your gun," Mendez said, walking slowly towards Gomez. "*¡Vamanos!*"

Gomez released the grip on his pistol, dropping it to the floor. He was staring at Mendez, rage in his eyes.

"Step away, Gomez," Mendez said. "You, too," he said, looking at the other two officers with Gomez.

Gomez turned and glared at Ethan, a scowl on his face. "You are *muerte*, *Americano*." He said it quietly so that only Ethan and Vicki could hear him.

"*Muerte*." Gomez drew his hand across his throat. When he looked at Vicki he smiled. "I remember you now."

"Señor and Señorita, walk towards the door," Officer Mendez said loudly. "Gomez, stay where you are."

Ethan bent down and picked Pete up by the shoulders, walking quickly to the front of the restaurant. The blood was flowing from Pete's left arm, so Ethan held the wound tightly, trying to stop the flow. They stopped at the door and looked back. Ethan stood frozen as he saw Vicki standing in front of Gomez, her face just inches from his. The look on her face shocked him.

"Vicki!" Ethan yelled. "He's not worth it."

Vicki was trembling with rage as she spat at Gomez, the spittle dripping from his face. "I remember you, too. Fuck you!"

Gomez raised his clenched fist, ready to strike her.

"Gomez! It's over!" Mendez yelled five feet away from the man, his gun aimed at his temple. "Back away now!"

Gomez looked at Mendez with hatred in his eyes. He dropped his arm and stepped back. The two other *Federales* grabbed his arms and cuffed him immediately.

Ethan sat Pete on the floor and ran to Vicki, catching her as she began to fall. She was shaking uncontrollably. He held her to his chest tightly.

"It's over," he said, looking into her eyes. "It's over."

Vicki slumped into his grasp, the adrenaline rushing out of her body. Ethan held her until he felt her strength returning. They walked slowly toward the front of the restaurant and saw Pete slumped on the floor next to the door. A man from the restaurant was kneeling next to him, holding a white cloth on the wound.

"Pete!" Ethan yelled as he bent down, seeing the blood seeping through the towel. "Mendez, we need help here!"

Mendez ordered one of his officers to apply a tourniquet to Pete's arm and bandage the wound, all the while keeping his gun pointed at Gomez.

Ethan continued to kneel next to his friend. "Stay with us, Pete. You'll be okay."

"I don't know, buddy," Pete said. "I can't feel my arm."

"We'll get him to the local hospital," Mendez said to Ethan as one of the *Federale* officers walked Pete outside.

"Thank you," Ethan said, looking at Mendez while still holding Vicki close.

Gomez, hands handcuffed behind him and walking toward them, smiled at Vicki. It was a wicked, suggestive smile.

Ethan took a step toward the policeman, stopping just inches from him. Gomez smiled at Ethan, mocking him. Ethan rocked back with his right arm and slammed it into the policeman's face with all the force in his body. Gomez stumbled backwards, blood spurting from his nose, shock on his face. He stared at Ethan with wide eyes as he tumbled to the floor.

"Señor Paxton, go wait outside," Mendez said, holding his gun on Gomez. "Now!"

Ethan stared at Gomez with a hatred he had never experienced. "You are *muerte*, asshole," he said, drawing his hand across his throat, this time mocking the policeman. Ethan turned and walked out of the restaurant with Vicki.

"Are you okay?" he asked her, as they got outside.

Vicki looked up at him, still shaking, and nodded. "Ethan, you shouldn't have hit him."

"Yes. Oh, yes, I should have," he said. "I wanted to do more than that."

Ethan walked Vicki to the blue van and put her in the passenger seat. He kissed her on the cheek and said, "I'll be right back."

He walked quickly to the *Federale* van where Pete was sitting. "You doing okay, Pete?"

Pete opened his eyes slightly and looked at Ethan. "I'll make it, buddy," he said, closing his eyes again. "I think."

"We'll follow you to the hospital, Pete. Hang in there."

"No, you and Vicki get to the airport. Molly needs you more than I do," Pete said weakly. "I'll be fine."

Ethan stared at his friend, the stress of the last few moments beginning to hit him. He saw Mendez walking out of the restaurant. "I'll be right back, Pete."

"Officer Mendez, can I talk to you?" he said, walking toward the *Federale* officer.

Mendez looked at Ethan and nodded.

The two men walked over to the Federale Police suburban, out of earshot of Vicki. No one else was around. Mendez stopped and turned to Ethan.

"Are you okay, *señor* Paxton?"

Ethan took a deep breath as he looked at Mendez. "I'm okay," he said, shaking his hand.

"That was a very stupid thing to do, *señor*," Mendez said. "He is a state police officer and has many friends."

"Gomez raped Victoria Calderon three years ago," Ethan said, looking at Mendez.

Mendez stared at Ethan, not saying a word.

"Vicki never told anyone, not even her father, until she told me right after they stopped us tonight," Ethan said, waiting for his reaction.

"*Señor* Paxton, that is a very serious accusation. Unless *Señorita* Calderon is prepared to press charges and face the accused, there is very little I can do."

"She just faced the accused," Ethan said. "It was Gomez. She will not press charges because she is terrified, as you can see. She knows that she can't go up against the police." Ethan looked into the *Federale's* eyes. "How many others has he raped?"

Mendez continued to stare at Ethan, choosing his words carefully. "The State Police in Sonora have much power, I admit," he said. "But rape is not something that they would condone." He stopped and looked towards the café, then back at Ethan.

"She would not lie about something like this," Ethan said. "She is terrified."

Mendez nodded his head. "Thank you for telling me, *Señor* Paxton. Tell *Señorita* Calderon that if she wants to press charges against the officer, I will make sure she is protected and not harmed. If she does not want to press charges, there is little I can do - legally."

Ethan looked around to make sure no one was close, then turned back to Mendez, leaning in close. "But there is something you can do about it, correct?"

Mendez looked towards the café, then back at Ethan. He had a smile on his face. "Yes, there is something I can do about it. Maybe not as dramatic as what you did, but we have our ways."

Ethan smiled back at him. "Thank you, Officer Mendez. You are a decent man. I will not mention this conversation to anyone other than Victoria Calderon."

"One more thing, *Señor* Paxton," he said, again looking around to make sure they were alone. "I know *Señorita* Calderon's father. He is a well-known person in the Chihuahua and Sonora area, with acclaim as an excellent businessman. I met him ten years ago when his daughter was kidnapped in Juarez. I was just beginning my career then and I worked on the case. I also met Victoria Calderon, but she would not remember me. She was very young then, a very beautiful girl, but devastated about her sister. It was the first time I experienced how death affects the victim's family."

Ethan looked at the man and could tell there was more to the story.

"*Señor* Calderon called me earlier tonight and asked me to check on his daughter." Mendez glanced at Vicki sitting in the Explorer. "He knew that I was stationed in Hermosillo." He waited to let the information sink in. "That's why we were so close when you were stopped by Gomez on the highway, and why we got here just in time."

Ethan was speechless. "You were following us?"

"Yes."

"For how long?" Ethan said.

"Since you left the airport in Hermosillo."

Ethan stared at the officer, not saying a word.

Mendez took Ethan's hand and shook it. "Tell *Señorita* Calderon that the matter will be taken care of immediately." He smiled at Ethan. "You had best be on your way to Puerto Penasco. You have an airplane to catch." He reached into his shirt pocket and pulled out a business card. "If you run into any trouble on the way, give me a call."

"I have to make sure my friend is okay," Ethan said.

"We will make sure he is taken care of. When he is strong enough, we will escort him to the border in Nogales. Your friend will be okay, but you must take care of your daughter."

Ethan let a long breath escape. "My daughter is not ill, she was—"

"I know about your daughter," Mendez interrupted. "*Señor* Calderon informed me of your situation."

Ethan's eyes grew wide in amazement. "You knew that she has been kidnapped?"

"Yes. We will give you an escort to Puerto Penasco," Mendez said. "And we will have officers waiting for you in Tijuana, to help you in any way we can. As a matter-of-fact, two Federal officers are meeting with the Tijuana police this morning."

Ethan's eyes grew moist as he grabbed Mendez' hand and shook it. "Thank you."

"*Vaya con Dios*," Mendez said. "And don't worry about Gomez. He will be taken care of, the Mexican way."

Ethan nodded to Mendez and turned and walked to the car where Pete was sitting. He opened the door and looked down at his friend.

"Pete, we have to go . . . my daughter."

"Go," Pete said. "Go get her."

Ethan bent down and shook his friend's hand. "Thank you, Pete. Mendez will make sure you get across the border okay." Ethan felt the sting of tears.

He looked up when someone touched his shoulder. It was Vicki. He moved out of the way so that she could talk to Pete.

"Pete, I'm so sorry," she said, the tears glistening in her eyes. "Thank you for protecting me."

Pete smiled through the pain. "A damsel in distress, that's what I do."

Vicki bent down and kissed him on his cheek. "You are a very good man, Pete Cruz."

For the first time, Pete blushed. "Thank you, Vicki. Take care of the big lug behind you."

She nodded and moved out of the way for Ethan, who bent down and held Pete's hand.

"Ethan," Pete said weakly, "I'm sorry I can't make it to Tijuana with you." He coughed roughly. "Get Molly and take her home."

Ethan felt the lump in his throat. "I will, Pete. I will."

"And Ethan," Pete said, his eyes beginning to get heavy. "Don't let Vicki go, she's a . . . ." He drifted off, his eyes closing.

I know, old friend. She's a keeper.

Ethan closed the door and watched the Federale cruiser pull away from the restaurant. He walked slowly back to the blue Explorer.

As he climbed into the driver's seat, he looked at Vicki, who was staring at him, waiting for an explanation.

"I'll explain later. Let's get out of here."

As he started up the Explorer Ethan shot one more glance towards the café. Gomez was standing in the doorway in handcuffs, staring at the blue Explorer, blood running from his nose. Ethan watched as Officer Mendez and the two other Federales walked the man to their van. Gomez continued to stare back at Ethan, the smile gone from his face.

Ethan pulled out of the parking lot, following the gray Federale cruiser with its lights flashing. He grabbed Vicki's hand as they pulled onto the highway.

"What did you say to Mendez?" Vicki said, staring at him intently.

"Just that he had some business to take care of," Ethan replied. "And from the looks of it, he's about to take care of it."

CHAPTER 51

Jake couldn't sleep, the thoughts of what was about to happen running through his head like a runaway locomotive. He hadn't been in a situation this critical in years, and he was beginning to doubt his abilities, his will, and his confidence. For all the bluster on the outside, he was a jumbled mass of nerves and insecurity on the inside. He walked out of the den and onto the balcony. Manny and Amos were evidently trying to get a couple of hours of sleep in other rooms, so he had the balcony to himself.

Jake looked out at the dark ocean, listening to the crashing waves. He was comforted by the knowledge that the waves flowed in and flowed back out, regardless of what was happening on the land beyond. They were consistent, reliable. You could count on them doing what they do, crashing in and out. Jake wondered if he could be counted on today, when people were depending on him. He had lived the past five years in a cocoon, hiding from people and from responsibility. He drank to numb the pain and loneliness, but every morning when he woke up they were both still there. *Would he be able to help these innocent girls?* He stood staring at the waves crashing against the sand for several minutes.

"Jake?" he heard behind him.

He turned and saw Charlie standing in the doorway, rubbing his eyes and yawning.

"Good morning, sunshine. You get enough sleep?"

Charlie walked out on the balcony and stood next to Jake. He put his hands on the railing and looked out over the black ocean, listening to the same crashing waves. He yawned again and stretched his arms in the air.

"How long was I out?" he asked Jake.

"Only about half a day," Jake said, chuckling again. "It's nearly five in the morning and you went down around five last night."

"Really? Did I miss anything?" Charlie said, stifling another yawn.

"We've made some progress. Manny and Amos will be up in a few minutes and we'll start talking about what we're gonna do then."

Finally starting to wake up, Charlie said, "Anyone call me on my cell phone while I was out?"

"Your Dad called from Mexico City. He's on his way to TJ as we speak."

"That's great," Charlie said, a slight smile on his face. He was quiet for a few minutes, looking out at the ocean. His young mind was still trying to catch up with everything from the day before. Looking at Jake, he said, "Did you find out where Molly is?"

Jake continued to look out over the sea, letting the cool salty breeze wash over him. He turned square to Charlie, making sure the kid was looking at him.

"We know who took her. And we know where their hang out is, but we don't know where he's keeping her and the others yet. Hoping to get some answers this morning."

Charlie's eyes widened. "Who kidnapped her?"

Looking at Charlie, he pointed to his scar, which was purple and pronounced in the cool early morning air. "The man who gave me this, if you can believe that. A punk named Angel Rojas."

Charlie stared at the scar. "Who is he? Some big time drug dealer?"

Jake shook his head. "Nope. Just a small-time punk with big balls. He's a gang leader of some nickel and dime gang here in Tijuana." Jake glanced at Charlie and saw the fear on his face. "We'll get him, son. And your sister."

Jake watched as Charlie stared out at the ocean, tears beginning to glisten in his young eyes. "You ready for what's going to go down today, son?"

His eyes wide and wet, Charlie nodded his head. "Damn right! When do we go?"

Jake smiled and patted him on the shoulder. "Soon, kid. We have a ways to go yet."

Jake heard sounds from inside the condo so looked back through the balcony door. He saw Manny in the kitchen next to the coffee pot. Amos was just walking out of the living room where he'd evidently slept on the sofa.

"Morning, gents," Jake said loudly.

Amos looked out at the balcony and waved. After talking to Manny, he walked outside.

"Morning. I see young Paxton is finally awake," Amos held out his hand to Charlie. "Amos Stillwater."

Charlie grabbed the man's hand and shook it. "Charlie Paxton."

"Don't know if Bull told you, but I'm ex-SDPD, too. I'm really sorry about your sister, son."

Charlie nodded as he wiped his eyes, saying nothing.

"Bull, you ready for the day?" Amos said, rubbing his face and stretching.

Jake glanced at Amos and then returned to gaze out at the waves. "Yeah. I'm ready."

"Coffee's ready, gentlemen," Manny said as he walked out onto the balcony. Seeing Charlie, his face brightened. "Hey, look who made it! Good morning, Charlie."

Charlie mumbled something, looking embarrassed.

"I don't think I've ever seen anyone quite as tired as you were yesterday," Manny said. "You get enough sleep, son?"

"Yeah," Charlie said sheepishly.

Jake glanced at Charlie and grinned. "A man of few words, as always."

"Well, let's get our coffee and start talking," Manny said. "We have a very big day ahead of us."

Manny, Amos and Charlie walked into the kitchen to get a cup of coffee. Jake continued to stare out at the crashing waves, wondering what the day would bring, and wondering if he would have what it took to save Molly Paxton. Taking a deep breath and exhaling, he walked into the kitchen. Amos was pouring himself a cup of coffee from the glass coffeepot. Charlie was sitting at the large kitchen table, staring at Jake.

"You okay, kid?" Jake said, looking at Charlie. He grimaced when he realized what he'd said.

"Damn it! Stop calling me kid!" Charlie said, glancing at Manny and Amos, an embarrassed look on his face.

"Sorry, Charlie. Just habit," Jake said, looking at Manny and shaking his head. "Won't happen again." Charlie sat back in his chair, a sullen and angry look on his face.

Kid's still grumpy from all that sleep. Jake stared at the young man and wondered how the day would end.

Manny handed Charlie a cup of coffee and patted him on the shoulder, glancing at Jake. "This'll help wake you up," he said.

Amos sat across from Jake and took a sip of the hot coffee. Looking at Manny he said, "Did you hear from your TJPD contact?"

Manny sat down next to Charlie and stirred his coffee. He took a long sip before answering Amos. "Yeah, I did."

Jake stared at him. "And?"

Manny looked up from his coffee and shook his head. "Nothing yet. They're still working on the location. Jorge said they have a couple of leads."

Jake slammed his hand on the table, causing a couple of spoons to jump. "Damn it! We can't trust those assholes!" he said loudly.

Charlie sat up straight in his chair, staring at Jake, then at Manny.

Manny's face turned red, slowly sipping his coffee before responding to Jake's outburst. Putting the cup down, he said, "Listen to me, Bull." His face was stern, serious. "Like it or not, we need their help. We're in their country, their town. We have no chance of finding the girls without them. Are you listening to me?"

Jake stared at Manny, the scar turning purple. He glanced at Charlie when Manny mentioned the girls. This helped him calm down.

Jake nodded his head. "Yeah, sorry. I had some bad experience with the TJ police and it's tough to forget."

"Okay," Amos said, trying to bring the conversation back to a positive level. Looking at Manny he said, "What do we do until we hear from them?"

Jake took a long drink of coffee and sat the cup down on the table. "We hit the streets. Someone in that shithole knows something," he said, staring at his coffee.

"You and Amos, and Charlie here, can go back to Tijuana and see what you can find. In the meantime, I'll call my contacts at SDPD to see what they know. Probably nothing but I gotta check," Manny said.

"I want to meet your TJPD contact. What's his name?" Jake said.

"Jorge Morales. I can set it up, but you've got to promise to hold your temper, Bull. I'm not screwing around here," Manny said. "We need Jorge on our side."

Jake stared at Manny. He nodded his head in silence.

"Good. Charlie, you might want to call your father and let him know you're okay and to fill them in on what's going on," Manny said, patting Charlie's shoulder.

Charlie nodded at Manny, glancing nervously at Jake.

"Let's go out on the balcony and call your dad," Jake said, standing up from the table. "Amos, it's five-thirty now. Let's plan on leaving here at six."

"No problem."

Jake and Charlie walked to the balcony, Charlie reaching for his cell phone.

CHAPTER 52

Molly stared at the fully charged cell phone. It wasn't getting any reception. The girls had retrieved it from its hanging position after an hour of charging. She tried again, dialing Charlie's number, but nothing happened.

"Damn!" she exclaimed a second time. "The walls must be too thick or something. We have to get out of this room and outside somehow." She looked at Natalia. "Natalia, you'll have to do it. You can take it out of the room and see if you get reception."

Natalia stared at Molly, shaking her head. "No, I don't know about those things. I can't."

"Yes you can," said Molly. "I'll show you. It's easy. Just push a few buttons."

"But they will be watching me," Natalia said, a frown on her face.

"Natalia, please. You have to try," said Jenny. "It's our only chance."

Molly saw the fear on Natalia's face. She knew that Natalia would be a long shot and would probably freeze and they would lose the cell phone forever. She knew then that she had to do it herself, had to somehow get out into the main warehouse and make the call to Charlie.

"Natalia, what time is it?" she asked the frightened woman.

"It is a little after five o'clock. They will start waking soon."

Molly thought about how they had lured the man inside the room before and how she had retrieved the cell phone from the van. It may work again, but they needed a reason to get him into the room.

"Natalia, we have to get the man back in here so that I can sneak out. What can we do to get him in here again?"

Natalia looked at Molly and shrugged her shoulders. "I don't know. He was mad when he left the last time. I'm worried that he will wake the others."

Molly began to panic, knowing that they only had a few hours. She dropped down on her mattress, staring at the wall. The tears began streaming down her young face and she let them run. She began to cry softly and her thoughts went to her family. She would never see them again, would never feel her father's hug. She looked over at Cindy and Jenny through her tear-filled eyes. They were lying on their pathetic mattresses, staring at her.

No! No, she would not give up! Not when they were this close.

"Natalia, get him in here now!" she said, her voice low and menacing. "Tell him Jenny is sick and needs medicine. Tell him anything, but get him in here and keep him here until I can get outside and make my call. Do it, now!"

Natalia gazed at her and began to tremble. "But Molly . . . ."

Molly stared directly into her eyes and said, "Do it. Now." She walked to the spot next to the door where she had hid before. It had to work, or they were dead. Worse than dead. "Call him," she said softly.

Natalia took a deep breath and knocked on the metal door.

"Harder," Molly said, standing next to her.

Natalia knocked on the metal door harder until they heard movement on the other side.

"*¿Que quieres?*" the man said, sounding tired.

"*Abre la puerta,*" she said loudly.

Suddenly, Natalia reached out her hand to Molly. "Give me the cell phone", she mouthed silently. Molly hesitated, then handed the cell phone to her. Natalia jammed it into the pocket of her jeans. Natalia motioned for Molly to get on her mattress.

Molly heard mumbling on the other side of the door and then heard the familiar sound of the dead bolt sliding back. She saw the same man poke his head into the room and look around.

"I have to come outside for a few minutes to use the bathroom," Natalia told the man in Spanish. She was looking directly at him. "The one in here is not working."

He slid the metal door open slightly to allow Natalia to step out. He then looked back inside and swept the room with his eyes. Satisfied that everything was okay he closed the metal door and slid the dead bolt closed.

Molly looked at Cindy and Jenny and saw their mouths hanging open in shock. No one said a word. Molly stared at the big metal door, wondering what was happening on the other side. Her life and the lives of Cindy and Jenny were now in the hands of this Tijuana prostitute. She closed her eyes and began to pray.

CHAPTER 53

Jake and Charlie were on the balcony, looking out at the ocean, Charlie's cell phone in his hand. Suddenly it began to ring, startling Charlie. Almost dropping the phone, he looked at the screen. It said 'Molly'! Charlie looked at Jake with eyes as big as saucers.

"Hello?" he said excitedly into the phone.

"*Hola*," a female voice replied. Jake leaned in to listen, barely able to hear the weak voice.

"Molly?" Charlie replied, his voice cracking.

Jake's heart was beating so fast he could hardly keep it in his chest. He held his breath as he stared at Charlie. He put his head next to the phone so he could hear.

"No, no Molly—*amigo*," said the voice softly, as though she were whispering. She spoke with a heavy Spanish accent.

"Who is this? Where's Molly?" Charlie replied loudly, startling Jake. By this time both Manny and Amos had joined them on the balcony, staring at Charlie and Jake.

Charlie heard the woman take a deep breath before saying, "We are at a warehouse called Tijuana Ve . . . ." She stopped in mid-sentence. Charlie and Jake heard shouting and what sounded like scuffling.

Charlie yelled into his phone. "Hello? Hello? Molly? Molly!"

They heard heavy breathing on the other end. "Wrong number," a male voice said with a heavy accent. The cell phone went dead.

Jake looked at Manny and Amos, shaking his head.

Charlie stared at Jake as he redialed Molly's number. There was no connection, only silence.

"What happened?" Manny said, staring at Jake.

Jake put his hand on Charlie's shoulder and said, "Whoever called you was found out. They probably destroyed the phone."

"But it wasn't Molly. Who was it?" Charlie said. "Who the hell was it?"

The three men looked at each other. "Someone that probably risked her life to call you," Amos said. "Maybe one of the other girls?"

"No," Jake said. "It was a heavy Spanish accent. And older." Jake rubbed the stubble on his jaw. "I think she was trying to tell us where Molly is being held."

"Did she say anything?" Amos asked, leaning in.

"Can we trace the call?" Charlie said, ignoring the question.

"No, cell phones are untraceable," Amos replied.

Charlie stared at the three men. "But Molly's alive—right? She's alive?"

Jake glanced at Manny and Amos. "It's hard to tell from that call," Jake said. "Whoever it was that called said she was Molly's friend. But she was whispering, like she didn't want anyone to hear her."

Charlie's face contorted in fear and anger. "Let's go get her!"

"Whoa, slow down son. We have to figure out where she is first." Jake turned to Manny and Amos. "She said 'we are at a warehouse. Tijuana something. Then she was cut off. Any ideas what that means?"

"That's it? A warehouse in Tijuana?" Manny said. "Talk about a needle in a haystack."

"No, she said Tijuana Ve . . . Tijuana Ve," Charlie said. "The second word was cut off before she could finish."

"I think we need to get a phone book and yellow pages and start looking," Amos said. "Maybe something will stand out."

"I'll go get one. Be right back," Manny said, walking into the kitchen.

Jake put his arm around Charlie's shoulders. "This is good news, Charlie. It means that Molly and the girls are alive somewhere in Tijuana."

Amos looked at Jake and Charlie, a grim expression on his face.

"What's wrong with you?" Jake said when he noticed his frown.

"They caught the woman who called us. They'll be worried that she gave their location away, so they could be packing up as we speak. We need to move fast."

Jake nodded. Their timeline to save Molly just got shorter.

CHAPTER 54

Ethan followed the Federale squad car and watched as the sun brought early morning light to the desolate desert as they drove up Highway 2. The sun felt good, warming his face, but the glare was beginning to burn his eyes.

"Damn, I wish I had some sunglasses," Ethan said, squinting.

He saw Vicki reach into her purse and pull out a pair of designer sunglasses, with gold trim on the stems.

"Here, these should work," she said, handling them to Ethan.

Ethan stared at them and began laughing. "Are you serious? I can't wear these things while I'm following a Federale squad car screaming down the highway."

Vicki looked at the golden swirls on the sunglass stems and began laughing, too. They both laughed out loud, until tears began streaming down their faces.

"Ethan, I don't think anyone will care what you look like," Vicki said between laughing fits. "It may improve your appearance."

Ethan took the sunglasses and put them on his face. They blocked the harsh rays of the emerging sun so he kept them on, laughing along with Vicki.

"Hey, not bad," he said as he looked at himself in the rearview mirror. "I may start a whole new fashion trend for the American male."

Vicki held her stomach as she continued laughing. Ethan watched her and for the first time in three days felt at ease. They were on their way to Tijuana, with an escort, and he finally allowed himself to hope.

"Thank you, Vicki," he said as the laughter quieted. "For everything."

Vicki released the last few chuckles and then stared at Ethan. "We're going to make it, Ethan. We're going to save your daughter."

"For the first time I have hope," he said, smiling at her.

She smiled back at him, then burst out laughing again. "But you need to get another set of sunglasses soon," she said. "Those look ridiculous on you."

They both continued to laugh as they drove towards Puerto Penasco airport. The laughter stopped when Ethan heard his cell phone ring. He glanced nervously at Vicki before he answered it.

He punched the talk button and said, "Hello?"

"Dad?"

"Charlie!" Ethan exclaimed, breathing a sigh of relief. "Damn, it's good to hear your voice. What's going on, son?"

"Dad, where are you?"

"We're heading for a small airport to catch a plane to Tijuana. We should be there in about two or three hours." Ethan heard nothing but silence. "Charlie? What's happening?"

"Dad," Charlie said excitedly, "we got a call from Molly's cell phone!"

"What? When?"

"About half an hour ago."

"Was it Molly?" he asked, a cold shudder caressing his neck.

"No. It was someone else using her phone. She said she was Molly's friend."

"One of the other girls?"

"No. She had a Spanish accent."

Ethan frowned as he looked over at Vicki. "What did she say?"

After several seconds of silence, Charlie said, "She was trying to tell us where Molly and the girls were."

"What? Do you know where she is?"

"She got cut off before she could finish."

Ethan's stomach tightened. "And?"

"And then a man, with an accent, came on and said 'wrong number'. Then the phone went dead."

Ethan pulled the sunglasses from his face and slumped, putting his right hand to his face. He knew what was coming.

"Ethan, this is Jake."

Ethan sat back. "Jake. What's going on?"

"We're running down leads right now. The woman on the phone was trying to tell us where the girls are being held. We've narrowed it down to an empty warehouse owned by Tijuana Verduras, meaning Tijuana Vegetables. The TJPD is sending a SWAT team over there right now to check it out."

"Where are you and Charlie?" Ethan said.

"We're headed there now, but we're half an hour away. We think they know we found out their location and are probably moving the girls. We may be too late."

"What!" Ethan shouted. "Too late? What do you mean?"

"Just what I said," Jake answered. "They'll move them as fast as they can if they think we know where they are. We'll know in a few minutes when the TJPD calls us."

Ethan's head was swimming, trying to digest the information. His heart was beating through his chest and sweat was beading on his forehead.

"Ethan, how far away are you from TJ?" Jake said.

Ethan cringed at the question. "About two to three hours," he said.

Silence. "We can't wait for you, Ethan. We have to move fast."

"I understand. Go get her, Jake. Don't worry about me, just keep me informed."

"We'll call you back." The phone went dead.

Ethan dropped the phone from his ear and sat, stunned, staring at the road and the *Federale* cruiser in front of them.

"Ethan, are you okay?" Vicki said, her hand on his shoulder, a worried look on her face.

"Someone called my son from Molly's phone and tried to give him their location. The Tijuana police are headed to an empty warehouse where they think they're being held."

Vicki's face brightened. "That's great!" She looked at Ethan's ashen face, realizing he was worried. "Isn't it?"

"Jake and Charlie think the kidnappers found out and are moving the girls. They might be gone before they get there."

Vicki held her hand to her mouth. "But there's still a chance . . . ."

Ethan looked at her and tried to smile. "Yeah, there's still a chance, but it doesn't look like I'll be there to help."

"It means she's still alive and in Tijuana. That's a positive."

Ethan stared at the *Federale* car in front of them, the blinking lights reminding him of the life and death situation ahead of him. *Please be alive, Molly.*

CHAPTER 55

Molly had her ear to the big metal door, trying to hear anything, but the door was too thick. She heard faint noises that could have been someone talking, but she couldn't be sure. Then she heard the unmistakable sound of a car door slamming, and then shouting. The voices were getting closer to the metal door so she moved quickly back to her mattress.

Suddenly she heard the familiar grinding of the dead bolt as it slid open. She felt her stomach tighten as she realized what was happening. *They found the cell phone!* The metal door began its slow slide to the left. She saw Natalia standing in the opening, but her eyes were closed and blood was running from her mouth. She was being held up by one of the men. Molly put her hand to her mouth to keep from screaming when Natalia was thrown into the room, landing on the hard cement with a thud, out cold.

Molly looked up and saw Angel Rojas standing in the opening. He was glaring at her, a frown contorting his face. He walked into the dark room and looked around. Seeing that the girls were all there, he walked up to Molly.

"I think this is yours, Rosalinda," he said, sarcastically. He threw several pieces of her cell phone in front of her. "That was a good try, but sadly, unsuccessful." He bent down and grabbed Molly's hair and pulled her to him, his face just inches from hers. "Whoever the *puta* tried to call will now think you are alive, so this changes our plans. Now we must move you to another place, pronto." He let her go.

Molly saw several other men walking into the room and knew that they were about to be gagged and tied up again.

"*¡Vamanos!*" Angel yelled at the men.

The man with the gold teeth bent down and roughly slapped duct tape on Molly's mouth, then flipped her over and tied her wrists and ankles tightly. He stood her up, holding a black hood over her head. Molly glanced at Cindy and Jenny, the same thing happening to them. She didn't know if she would ever see them alive again. Then everything went black once more.

She felt someone picking her up and carrying her. She was thrown into the back of an SUV, or was it the van? She felt another body thrown in next to her, then heard the grunts of a third person. *Cindy and Jenny.* She heard shouts in Spanish and within a couple of minutes the car was started up and began to back out of the warehouse.

She heard voices in the front of the truck, speaking in Spanish. One of them was Angel Rojas. She made out several words but not enough to make anything sound coherent. Molly tried to count the minutes and turns, but it became too confusing as they made turn after turn. After what seemed like fifteen to twenty minutes they came to a stop. Angel shouted something and then the truck inched forward slowly. Molly felt the change in light through the dark hood and she knew they were inside another warehouse.

Suddenly, the door opened and someone grabbed her, picked her up and roughly carried her and dropped her onto a cold, cement floor. She laid there and heard the moans of Cindy and Jenny as they were dropped next to her. Several minutes went by. She heard talking and shouting several yards away and then another body was dropped next to her, but there was no moaning, only silence. *Natalia . . . or Missus Caldwell,* she thought in horror.

Molly heard a door close and the voices became faint. She began to whimper as she thought about what was going to happen next. Angel said that whomever Natalia called knew she was alive. That meant she got through to Charlie or someone in her family. They knew she was alive! There was still hope, but it was fading. Everything would move fast now, including her fate. The blackness under the hood became like a coffin. *She may never see the light of day again.*

CHAPTER 56

Jake and Charlie drove the SEA van, following Manny and Amos. They left Manny's condo in Rosarito Beach at six a.m., knowing that the TJPD was en route to the Tijuana Vegetable warehouse and would arrive before they got there. Manny was trying to convince them to wait until they arrived before storming the warehouse. His contact at the TJPD, Jorge Morales, said that he would do his best but he couldn't promise anything.

"How'd they narrow it down to the Tijuana Vegetable factory?" Charlie asked Jake as they weaved in and out of traffic in Tijuana.

"It was the only warehouse that was empty that fit the name," Jake said. "When the TJPD called the owner he said he'd rented it to someone for a month, but didn't have a name. It may be a wild goose chase, but we've got to run it down."

"Will the TJPD wait for us?"

"Probably not. Especially if they see any activity. They'll barge in like Mexican cowboys and screw everything up."

"What about Molly and the girls?" Charlie asked, looking at Jake.

Jake glanced at him, feeling an ache in his heart for the kid. Jake knew his sister was probably already moved but he didn't want to take the hope from Charlie.

"Let's wait and see. We're only a few minutes away."

Suddenly, Manny's truck turned into a narrow alleyway in an industrial area. Jake followed him down the alley. Manny screamed to a stop in front of a large warehouse with the faded name of Tijuana Verduras stenciled above the large sliding door. Several TJPD cruisers were parked in front, with about ten men congregated outside the warehouse. The sliding door was open, not a good sign.

Jake parked next to Manny and watched him approach a TJPD officer. Jake hurried up to find out what was going on.

"Charlie, wait in the van. Do not get out until I call for you. Understood?"

Charlie stared at Jake, nodding his head.

Jake walked up to Manny, Amos and the TJPD officer.

"Bull, this is Jorge Morales," Manny said when Jake approached. "Jorge, this is Bull - Jake Delgado."

The two men shook hands, looking at each other warily.

"What happened? The door is open," Jake said, pointing at the warehouse.

"It was open when we got here," Morales said. "We've reconned the area and no one is around," he said in excellent English. "We waited until you got here before going inside."

While the two men were talking, Manny slowly walked into the warehouse.

"Any activity inside?" Jake asked.

"Nothing. There's a van parked inside," Morales said.

"The kidnapped girls were driving a white van when they were abducted," Jake said.

Jake walked to the open warehouse door, with Morales and Amos right behind. Manny had already walked inside and was standing next to the van, about to open the passenger door. Suddenly, Jake felt someone fly by him, running into the warehouse. It was Charlie.

"That's Molly's van!" Charlie yelled as he approached the van.

"There's a body in here!" Manny yelled.

"Charlie! Wait!" Jake yelled. "Manny, don't open the—"

Boom! A ball of fire exploded from the van, hurtling Manny backwards. Charlie was right behind Manny and was thrown backwards onto the cement floor, Manny landing on top of him. Pieces of the van flew in all directions, hitting several of the TJPD officers. Jake just missed being hit by a flying piece of white metal when he ducked behind the door. Smoke immediately filled the warehouse and the fire scorched everything within twenty feet of the van.

Jake peered inside the smoke and fire-filled warehouse, searching for Charlie and Manny. He couldn't see anything because of the smoke that was billowing out of the door. The van was a ball of fire, spewing out smoke and heat. He heard a scream from inside and waded into the warehouse, covering his face with his shirt.

"Charlie!" he yelled. "Charlie, where are you?"

Jake heard a moan and inched towards it, his hands in front of him to deflect anything in his path.

"Charlie!" he yelled again.

"Over here," a barely audible voice said about ten feet in front of Jake.

Jake waved his hands in front of him to try to clear a vision path through the smoke. He barely made out two bodies lying on the floor, one of them waving his hand. Jake walked cautiously towards the two bodies until he was standing over them. The heat from the burning van was overwhelming, making Jake back off.

"Charlie?" he said.

"Yeah. Down here," Charlie said weakly.

Jake bent down and reached for the first body he saw. As he got closer he saw Manny lying on his back on the scorched cement. The clothes were burning. Jake took his shirt and patted the flames out. Then Jake looked at his face. It was unrecognizable. Jake grabbed for the man's arm and felt for a pulse. He was dead.

"Jake, I can't move," he heard Charlie say. He was lying several feet behind Manny.

Jake stepped over the dead body of his friend and bent down to look at Charlie. He was sitting up but he was clutching his leg. His face was black from the smoke and soot.

"I think my leg's broken," Charlie cried, coughing uncontrollably.

"Okay, son. Hold on, I'll get you out of here," Jake said, picking Charlie up gently.

They were both choking and coughing from the thick smoke. They walked out of the warehouse into the bright light. Jake set Charlie down against a police cruiser and took a deep breath. He looked at the boy's leg. It was a bloody mess, with bone sticking out of his right leg. Charlie's face was contorted in pain.

"Amos! Amos!" Jake shouted, looking around.

"Right here, Bull," Amos said. He saw Charlie's leg. "Oh, shit! I'll call for an ambulance."

"Amos! Wait!" Jake said loudly. "Manny's inside. Go get him out of there."

Amos' face fell as he looked at the smoke pouring out of the warehouse. Jake saw him run into the warehouse, waving his hand through the smoke. A minute later he walked out, carrying Manny. Jake blocked Charlie's view so that he couldn't see the gruesome sight.

"Is Manny okay?" Charlie asked, the pain obvious in his voice.

Jake stared down at him. "He's dead."

Charlie looked up at Jake, tears welling in his eyes. "No!"

Jake held the boy in his huge arms, hugging his head to his chest.

Charlie pulled back, his eyes wild. "Molly? Where's Molly?"

"She's gone, son," Jake said. Then, realizing how this must have sounded to Charlie, he said, "They've already moved her and the other girls." Jake said this, knowing that there was a chance they were in the van or somewhere in the warehouse.

Jake saw Jorge Morales walk out of the warehouse, looking at Jake and Charlie. He walked up to them, his face ashen. He turned to look at Manny's body, then turned away when he saw what was left of the man's face.

"What is it?" Jake asked him.

Morales coughed several times from the smoke and the shock of seeing the dead man. "The remains of a body were spotted in the van," he said, coughing again.

Charlie stared up at him, then looked at Jake. "Jake?"

"That's why Manny opened the van door. He saw the body. He went against all of his training because he saw someone in the van," Jake said softly.

"All the other rooms are empty," Morales said. "They moved the girls, except for whoever was is the van."

"Is the body identifiable?" Jake asked Morales.

"Not until the fire and heat go down. But it appears to be a woman."

Jake looked at Charlie and saw the fear in his eyes, the pain in his face. He didn't know what to say to comfort him.

"Let's get you to a hospital, son."

"Ambulance is on its way," said Amos, standing over Charlie, tears streaming down his face. "Manny's gone."

"One more thing," Morales said to Jake. "We found something in one of the rooms you might want to see."

"Amos, stay here with Charlie." Jake followed the TJPD officer into the warehouse. The smoke was still heavy, the heat from the blast almost suffocating. They walked around the smoldering van and entered a dark, smelly room. It was filling with smoke but Jake was able to make out several dirty mattresses on the floor. This is where they kept the girls, he thought.

"Look up at the light," Morales said.

Jake looked up at the ceiling light and saw something hanging down. He wiped his eyes and reached up and grabbed it and pulled it down. It was the cell phone charger.

"This belonged to one of the girls," he said to Morales. "That's how we found out about this place. She must have gone through hell trying to charge her cell phone, and . . . ."

His voice trailed off as he thought about Molly's fate. He put the charger in his pocket and began to walk out of the room. Suddenly something caught his eye underneath one of the mattresses. It was sticking out slightly, barely visible. He bent down and pulled it out from under the mattress. He held it close to his face, the smoke getting thicker. It was a girls tee shirt. It said 'Santa Elena Academy' on the front. The letter 'M' was written in ink on the inside collar.

As Jake walked out into the warehouse he peered into the still smoldering van. He saw the burnt body in the backseat. It was unrecognizable, but he could make out the general shape and size of the body. Jake walked out into the daylight, breathing in the fresh air in gulps.

He bent down to show Charlie the 'SEA' tee shirt. "Is this Molly's?" he said.

Charlie's eyes opened wide. "Yes," he said excitedly.

Jake pulled out the cell phone charger and showed it to Charlie. "Does this match her cell phone brand?"

Charlie nodded, and tears filled his eyes. "That's hers."

Jake nodded, anticipating both responses. "By the way," he said, speaking softly. "The body inside the van was a big woman. Probably the teacher. That means Molly's still alive."

Charlie jerked his arm up, pointing at something on the rooftop. Jake turned to look, but saw nothing.

"What did you see?"

Charlie mumbled something, his eyes beginning to close.

"Charlie, what did you see?" Jake said, shaking him.

"Baby . . . face," Charlie said before he passed out..

CHAPTER 57

They had been traveling in silence since the phone call. The laughter from before was a distant memory. Ethan focused on the *Federale* car in front of him, not looking right or left, or at Vicki. His mind was on his daughter and how this day would end. He blocked out the ugly thoughts and tried to concentrate on the positive ones, the ones that ended with Molly rushing into his arms.

Vicki reached over and grabbed Ethan's hand. "When this is all over, Ethan, we need to sit down and talk." She kissed his hand and held it to her chest. "But we need to find Molly and get her home."

Ethan looked at her for a long moment and nodded. "Okay."

Suddenly, the *Federale* cruiser slowed down and made a right turn onto a narrow, paved road. Ethan saw a small white sign ahead that said, "*Aeropuerto.*"

"We're here," he said, glancing at Vicki.

"They should have the Cessna all gassed up and ready for us," Vicki said. "We can be in the air in a matter of minutes."

Ethan followed the *Federales* through a security gate and out onto the small tarmac, where a single-engine Cessna was sitting. They pulled up close to the airplane and got out of the car. Ethan opened the truck and grabbed their bags while Vicki climbed into the cockpit. As Ethan threw the bags into the back of the airplane, he heard the small engine rev up and the propeller begin to whir.

Ring!

Ethan fumbled for the phone in his pocket and looked at the incoming number. *Charlie!*

"Charlie. What's happening?" he said into the phone, his breaths coming in spurts.

"Ethan, it's Jake."

"Jake? Where's Charlie?"

After a moment of hesitation, Jake said, "He's in the hospital, Ethan."

"What?" Ethan stiffened, grabbing the door of the Cessna.

"There was a bomb at the empty warehouse. Charlie was close to the blast when it went off. He's alive, but he has a pretty banged-up leg."

Ethan, trying to digest what Jake had just told him, shook his head and said, "A bomb?" Then he thought of Molly. "Is Molly . . . ?"

"They'd already moved her and the other girls, so I assume they're still okay," Jake said. "But there was a body inside the van that got blown up. We think it's the teacher."

Ethan closed his eyes. "How do you know it wasn't . . . Molly?" he said.

"Body type, mainly. She is obviously unrecognizable, but she was a bigger woman, too big for Molly or the other girls."

"Jesus," Ethan exclaimed. "Was it intentional, the bomb?"

"Oh yeah. It was a statement. It killed a friend of mine and injured several Tijuana cops, as well as Charlie."

"Why was Charlie so close . . . ?"

"He ran to the van when he saw it was the one Molly and the girls were riding in. I couldn't stop him. He was actually pretty lucky. My friend, Manny, was in front of him when the bomb went off and sheltered Charlie from the full blast. He fell on Charlie when they were thrown backwards and that's what broke Charlie's leg."

"Christ almighty," Ethan whispered. "Where is Charlie now?"

"At a hospital here in TJ, but they're transferring him to a hospital in San Diego soon. He's okay, Ethan. Pretty shaken up, but except for the leg, he's okay."

"What about the warrant out for Charlie and you?"

"The SDPD canceled it for Charlie, but I don't know about the one on me," Jake said.

Ethan held his face in his right hand. *How much more can I take? My daughter, now my son . . . .*

"Ethan? You there?"

"Yeah, I'm here. I'm sorry about your friend, Jake. Was he the ex-cop?"

"Yeah. He made a rookie mistake that cost him his life. He shouldn't have opened the van door, but he saw the body . . . ." Jake's voice trailed off.

"Jake, you said it was a statement. What did you mean?"

"They knew that we would open the van when we saw the body so they trip-wired the door. It caused one helluva blast. Charlie is one lucky kid, Ethan."

"What about Molly? Do you know where they took her?" Ethan said, his voice starting to crack.

Ethan felt Vicki touching his arm. She had shut off the engine so that Ethan could hear.

"Not yet, but I have some good news. Charlie recognized one of the kids that was hanging out at the camp. He was at the blast site. We ran him down and have him in custody now. He'll know where they took Molly and we'll get it out of him."

"How did Charlie . . . ?"

"He's a brave kid, Ethan. Just before he passed out he whispered to me, 'baby face' and pointed to a rooftop across the street from the warehouse. The guy must've been watching so he could report back to Angel Rojas."

Ethan felt the nausea as he thought of his son lying in the hospital. "How bad is Charlie's leg?"

"Compound fracture, but they'll fix him up. He'll be okay, maybe even play hockey again someday."

Ethan was silent, waiting for the emotions to subside. He glanced at Vicki and tried to smile.

"Ethan?" Jake said.

"Yeah."

"When are you going to get here?"

"We're at the airport now and will be flying out of Puerto Penasco in a few minutes. We should be in Tijuana around nine or ten."

"That's good. That's very good. We'll be running down the leads and hopefully will find out where they're holding Molly. Ethan, one more thing," Jake said.

"What's that?"

"When I said they made a statement with the bomb, it doesn't stop there. They may be looking to make a name for themselves."

"Meaning what?" Ethan asked.

"Meaning they may do something outrageous, something that will draw the attention of the world, or at least this corner of the world. I know the little prick that kidnapped Molly, and he's an egomaniac. He wants attention and he'll do anything to get it."

Ethan was dumbfounded and didn't know how to respond. He stared at Vicki, shaking his head.

"Find Molly, Jake," he said. "Goddamn it! Find her!"

After several seconds of silence, Jake said, "Call me when you land in Tijuana. God speed." Jake hung up.

Ethan dropped his arm, the cell phone falling to the tarmac. He leaned forward and put his face in his hands. He felt Vicki rubbing his back. *So close, but so far away.*

CHAPTER 58

Jake was nervously pacing back and forth in the waiting room of Tijuana General Hospital, still holding the cell phone. He glanced at Amos Stillwater, who was sitting in the waiting room watching him.

"You okay, Jake?" Amos said.

Before Jake could answer, they heard a voice from down the hallway. Jake looked in the direction of the voice and saw George Sizemore walking towards him.

"That's him," Sizemore said to a policeman walking beside him. "That's the man that stole our van and accosted me."

Sizemore had a peculiar look on his face, a combination of concern and satisfaction.

Before Jake could respond, Amos walked calmly up to Sizemore and introduced himself.

"I'm Amos Stillwater," he said. "I'm working with Jake on the kidnapping."

Sizemore stopped and looked at Amos. "Well, that man stole our school van and needs to be arrested. He . . . ."

"I'll take it from here, Mister Sizemore," the Tijuana policeman said in perfect English. "Hello, Amos. I remember working with you on the task force a few years ago."

Amos looked down at the cop's name tag. "Perez. Yeah, I remember you."

"Amos, I have to talk to Mister Delgado . . . ."

Amos put his hand on the officer's chest. "Be careful, Perez. We both lost a close friend today."

Perez nodded. "Mister Delgado, I need to ask you a few questions. My name is Jose Perez of the Tijuana Police Department."

Jake ignored the policeman and turned to Sizemore. "Do you even give a shit about the three girls that were kidnapped? About whether they're alive or dead?"

Sizemore stepped back when Jake approached him. "Well, I, of course I do."

"Did you know that one of your teachers, Missus Caldwell, is dead? Died protecting those three girls?"

"Julie?" Sizemore stuttered. "She's dead?"

"Yes, and unless you let me and Amos do our job, the three girls that you—YOU—were supposed to protect, may be next. Now get out of my face, you prick."

Jake stared at Sizemore, his face just inches from the frightened principal's face.

"Back off," the policeman said.

Amos stepped up and gently took the arm of the policeman and walked him down the hall. "Let's talk, officer."

"Are . . . are they okay?" Sizemore said, staring at Jake, fear in his eyes.

"That remains to be seen. Get the hell out of my sight," Jake said, seething.

Mister Sizemore backed away and began walking down the hallway, glancing nervously back at Jake.

Amos sidled up next to Jake and said, "That went well."

"That cop an old friend of yours?" Jake said.

"I knew him before I retired. Good man. He understands the situation and will cancel the warrant on you."

Jake glanced at Amos and broke out in a big grin. "Thanks, Amos. Let's make sure Charlie's okay then head back to the TJ police headquarters," Jake said. "I don't trust those assholes."

The two men walked into the hospital room. Charlie was lying on the bed with tubes running from each arm. His eyes were closed.

"Charlie," Jake said, shaking Charlie's shoulder. "You awake?"

Charlie slowly opened his eyes, blinked, and looked at Jake.

"Jake . . . ."

"Don't try to talk, son. I just need to know you're okay," Jake said as he looked at the big white cast on his leg. "You in any pain?"

Charlie shook his head back and forth. "Molly . . . ?"

Jake glanced at Amos. "It's still up in the air, kid—er, Charlie. We're heading back now, but I wanted to make sure you were okay."

Charlie nodded slightly, opening his eyes long enough to meet Jake's gaze. "Find Molly, Jake."

Jake nodded. "We'll find her, son."

CHAPTER 59

Jake and Amos drove the short distance from the hospital to the Tijuana police precinct where Jorge Morales was holding Rafael.

"How in the hell did Charlie recognize Rafael on a rooftop in the pain he was in?" Amos asked off-handedly as they maneuvered through the Tijuana traffic.

"He's a tough kid. A smart kid. His instincts took over, lucky for us," Jake answered.

"How'd he know it was him?"

"Not sure. Charlie just mumbled 'babyface' before he passed out."

"Babyface?" Amos said.

"That's what the kids in Tecate called Rafael."

"And you told Morales before heading to the hospital?" Amos said.

"Yep. Morales called me right after Charlie went into emergency, said that they caught Rafael and were holding him at a local precinct house."

"We have to hope that it's him, and that he knows where Rojas is hiding," Amos said as they pulled into the Tijuana police station. "The clock is ticking on this mad man."

Jake and Amos parked the van and strode into the building, stopping at the front desk.

"Jorge Morales. Where can I find him?" Jake asked the desk sergeant.

The dark-skinned desk sergeant said something in Spanish to the man sitting next to him, then turned to Jake.

"He's busy," the man said, dismissing them with a wave of his hand.

Jake slammed his hand on the desk and said, "Where the fuck is Morales?"

Startled, the desk sergeant sat up straight and stared at the big man in front of him. Jake was leaning over the desk, his face just a foot away from the sergeant.

"Delgado—over here," they heard a voice say from a side door. They glanced over and saw Morales waving them over.

Jake glared at the desk sergeant as he and Amos followed Morales through the door and down a long hallway. They entered a small, windowless room and saw a young boy sitting behind a wooden table, his hands shackled to a steel ring in the middle of the table. Jake noticed a one-way mirror in the rear of the room and wondered who was looking at them from the other side. Morales' partner was sitting across from the boy, staring at the two Americans.

"Is this him?" Jake said, looking at Morales.

"*Sí*. This is Rafael," Morales answered.

"You find out anything?" Jake said.

"Not yet. This is my partner, Hector Gonzalez," Morales said, pointing to the man sitting at the table.

Jake and Amos nodded to Gonzalez then looked at Rafael. He looked so young, so innocent. He barely looked fourteen years old. Jake noticed a welt on his left cheek. Jake grabbed a wooden chair and turned it around, with the back facing the table. He was sitting directly across from Rafael.

"Does he speak English?" Jake asked.

"*Sí*, very good," Gonzalez answered.

"Hey kid. You know who I am?" Jake said.

Rafael looked up at Jake. "No," he said defiantly.

Jake leaned across the table and grabbed the kid's face in his massive hand. "Look at this scar, kid. You know where I got it?"

"No," the boy said, visibly shaken.

"Your boss gave it to me a few years back. Anyone that gets in the way of me finding the prick is gonna wish he was never born. Are you gonna get in my way, kid?"

Rafael swallowed quickly as he stared at Jake's eyes. The scar was turning purple and was bulging. "Fuck you," he said, with not much commitment.

Gonzalez reached over and slapped the kid across the face with the back of his hand. Rafael's head snapped left and blood spurted out of his nose.

Jake stared at Gonzalez, then at Morales. "I'll handle it from here," he told them.

Jake leaned down and put his face a few inches from Rafael's. "Are you gonna get in my way, kid?"

Rafael, blood running from his nose, looked into Jake's eyes and backed away. "N..no."

"Good. Where is Angel Rojas?"

"I don't know," he said, the blood continuing to run down from his nose.

Jake slammed his fist on the table, startling everyone in the room. "Where are the American girls?" he seethed.

Morales and Gonzalez glanced at each other and then at Amos. Amos stood expressionless behind Jake, staring at Rafael.

"I don't . . . I don't know," Rafael said. "Angel didn't tell me where he was taking them."

"Bullshit! You were watching the warehouse. How were you gonna contact him?"

Rafael began to shake, rattling the chain around his wrists. "I was to call him on his cell phone," he said.

Jake glanced at Amos, then back at Rafael. "Have you called him yet?"

Rafael shook his head back and forth. "No."

Jake stood up and motioned for Amos and Morales to join him outside. They walked out of the room and huddled in the hallway.

"You think he's telling the truth?" Jake asked Morales.

"Yes. He's too scared not to tell us the truth. We caught him before he could call Rojas."

"How do you know?"

"He didn't have a cell phone on him, so he would have to make the call from a pay phone. He didn't have a chance before we caught him."

Jake looked at Amos. "What do you think?"

"I think it's time the kid calls his boss," Amos said matter-of-factly.

Jake nodded. He looked at Morales and said, "Did you notice anyone else around when you caught the kid?"

"No, he was alone," Morales answered.

"You sure?"

"We caught him in a small alley and no one else was around."

"How about the rooftop? Did you have someone check it?"

"Gonzalez checked all the surrounding rooftops. No sign of anyone."

Jake nodded. "How much do you trust Gonzalez?"

"He's been my partner for three years."

Jake glanced at Amos, then nodded. "Did you bring the kid in in a squad car?"

"No, he was put in the backseat of my car and laid flat so no one could see him," Morales said.

A slight smile crossed Jake's face. "Guess Manny was right about you."

Morales didn't smile, just stared at Jake.

"Okay, but before we make the call we need to make sure he isn't being watched by anyone else. Do you have a secure phone in here?"

"Why?" Morales asked.

The smile on Jake's face disappeared. "Because I don't trust anyone in this building and I don't want Rojas to know we caught the kid." This made Jake think about when they brought Rafael into the police headquarters. "Who saw you bring him in here?"

"We brought him in through the back and put him in the room he's in now. No one but me and Gonzalez saw him."

Jake looked at Morales, suddenly remembering the one-way mirror in the interrogation room. "What about the one-way mirror in there? Who has access to the other side?"

"No one. It's locked and used as a storage area. No one uses it. That's why we picked this room."

"That makes it easy then," Jake said. "If Rojas knows we have the kid, I know who to blame. You understand?"

Morales scowled at Jake. "Don't worry about me, *Señor*. Manny was my friend. I want Rojas as bad as you do."

"Good. Then let's go make the call."

They re-entered the room and Jake sat down across from Rafael. He glanced over at Gonzalez, still not sure about him.

"Kid, we're gonna call your boss and you're gonna give the performance of your life—or it will cost you your life. *¿Comprende?*"

Rafael nodded as he stared at the scar on Jake's face. "Yes."

CHAPTER 60

Ethan strapped himself into the passenger seat of the Cessna and watched Vicki flick switches, making the small plane come to life, all the while speaking to the control tower in Spanish. When the plane began to move forward he felt his heart beating faster, knowing that when they landed he would be so close to his daughter and son. They taxied out to the runway and waited for instructions from the tower.

"Next stop, Tijuana," Vicki said to Ethan. "We should land in about an hour, around nine-thirty Tijuana time."

Ethan felt the tightness in his stomach again as he smiled at Vicki. Out of the corner of his eye he noticed a gray SUV speeding towards them. As the truck got closer, he recognized the markings of the Federal Police. He glanced at Vicki, who had seen the SUV approaching, too. He saw the fear return to her eyes.

"What do they want?" Ethan said.

Vicki didn't respond, and she didn't wait to find out. She pushed the lever down and the Cessna began to move faster and faster down the small runway. The gray SUV sped up and pulled alongside the plane on Ethan's side. He glanced down and saw Mendez waving at him wildly from the SUV.

"Vicki! Wait! It's Mendez. He wants to talk to us."

"Are you sure it's him?" she said.

"Yes, I'm sure."

Vicki pulled back on the stick and the Cessna rolled to a stop on the runway. Ethan looked down at the SUV parked next to the plane, opening his door when he saw Officer Mendez approaching them. Vicki let the propeller idle.

"*Señor* Paxton. I'm glad I caught you before you left," the Federal officer said.

"How the hell did you get here so fast?" Ethan asked, stepping down from the plane.

"Federal Police, *Señor* Paxton," he said, smiling. "I took a helicopter from Santa Ana to here, hoping that I would be able to talk to you before you took off."

"Why did you go to all that trouble?" Ethan asked as Vicki walked around the plane and stood next to him.

"*Señorita* Calderon, thank you for stopping," Mendez said as he bowed to Vicki as she approached.

"You scared the hell out of me," she said, still shaking. "You people."

"I am so sorry. I didn't mean to frighten you, but I felt it was important to talk to you and *Señor* Paxton before you took off. Please forgive me."

Ethan grabbed Vicki's hand and squeezed. "Again, why did you go to all this trouble? We're in sort of a hurry, here."

"I won't hold you much longer. I wanted *Señorita* Calderon to know that Gomez is behind bars and will be brought up on multiple charges of rape and assault. With some help, he admitted to his crimes, which have been going on for some time."

Ethan looked at Vicki and saw a mixture of relief and confusion in her eyes.

"And I felt it important to let you know that your name did not come up and you will not be brought into it unless you want to be. We have enough evidence and testimony from other victims to convict him many times over."

Vicki stared at the Federal Officer. "Have you told anyone else about what he did to me?" she said weakly. "And how did you know that he . . . ?"

Mendez glanced at Ethan, clearing his throat.

"I told him," Ethan said, turning to Vicki. "He needed to know that Gomez was dangerous and had hurt you. I'm sorry I didn't tell you."

Tears welled in Vicki's eyes as she backed away from Ethan, turning her back on both men.

"Vicki, I wanted him caught and to pay for what he did to you." Ethan reached out to touch her but she brushed him away. "I'm sorry I didn't talk to you first." Ethan felt the bile rising in his throat, the guilt covering him like a quilt.

"*Señorita* Calderon, I know you went through a very traumatic experience with Gomez, but you are now safe from him, thanks to *Señor* Paxton. He acted out of concern and affection for you. No one will ever know, it will remain between us. No one else will ever know unless you want them to."

Vicki choked back tears. "My father, does he . . . ?"

"No, *Señorita*. He does not know and he will never hear anything about it unless you tell him. That is a promise from me."

Vicki turned and looked at Mendez. "Thank you," she said quietly. Then she turned to Ethan, tears beginning to tumble out of her eyes. "You should have told me."

Ethan reached for her hand. This time she didn't brush him off. They held each other close, nothing being said for several seconds.

Mendez cleared his throat. "When you land at Tijuana airport, we will have a car waiting for you. And we will have several Federal officers accompanying you."

Ethan stared at Mendez, nodding. "Thanks. You told us that earlier."

"The Tijuana police and two Americans, whom I assume are working with you, have a lead and they are pursuing it now. Two of our Tijuana officers are on their way to help them."

"There was an explosion, my son was hurt . . . ."

"Yes, we know. I'm deeply sorry about your son, but we understand he is being well-cared for." Mendez cleared his throat again. "They have one of the kidnappers in custody and are questioning him now."

"I know. I just talked with the private investigator, Jake Delgado. "

"I'm hoping that this boy will provide the information they need to find your daughter. Our two officers will help your man in this regard."

Ethan frowned. "I wish your Federal Officers the best of luck with Jake Delgado. I don't think he'll take kindly to the Federales coming in this late in the game."

"I understand, but kidnapping is a federal crime in Mexico, as it is in the United States. Our involvement is required."

"And I thank you for that, Officer Mendez. I sincerely do."

"I won't keep you and the *señorita* any longer. Good luck, señor. I hope you get your daughter back safely."

"Thank you, Officer Mendez," Ethan said. "What about Pete Cruz? Is he okay?"

"He is resting in the local hospital in Santa Ana. I have two officers with him until we can transport him to Nogales. We have someone on the other side of the border that will drive him to Tucson, where he can arrange transport home. Maybe by then the air traffic will be open in the U.S. He's in good hands."

"Thank you," Ethan said. "That's very kind of you."

Vicki reached out for Mendez' hand and held it tightly. "Thank you for everything. You are a good man."

"You are welcome, both of you. Now, go get your daughter, *señor.*"

Ethan and Vicki climbed back into the airplane. As Vicki revved the engine up, Ethan opened the side window.

"By the way, what's your first name?" Ethan yelled to Mendez.

"Angel," he yelled back. "Angel Mendez."

Ethan smiled. *Of course it is.* He waved goodbye to the officer as the Cessna began to pull away. *An angel on my shoulder.*

"¡Vaya con Dios!" Mendez yelled after them.

The Cessna quickly became airborne and began the left turn towards the Pacific Ocean and Tijuana.

CHAPTER 61

Molly and the other two girls had been lying in the darkness for nearly two hours with their mouths taped and the black hoods covering their heads. All Molly had heard since they were dumped onto the cold, cement floor was sobbing and whimpering from Cindy and Jenny. The fourth person that was dumped next to her had made no sounds. Molly wondered if it was Natalia or Missus Caldwell. She moved closer to the body and craned her head to hear if there was any breathing. She thought she heard slow, shallow breaths coming from the body, but she wasn't sure.

Suddenly a loud scraping noise startled her. It sounded like a door opening! She heard footsteps coming towards her. There were at least two people speaking softly in Spanish. Then she felt someone untying her hood and lifting it off of her head. The light overhead was blinding, causing her to shut her eyes. The man then ripped the duct tape off of her mouth. The pain was harsh, but ended quickly.

"Rosalinda. How do you feel?" she heard Angel Rojas say.

Molly opened her eyes and squinted at the smiling man standing over her. Rojas had a strange look on his face, one that frightened her more than ever before.

Molly coughed several times. "Water," she choked.

"*Agua*. Get some *agua* for my *chica*," Angel said to the man next to him. He leaned down and brushed Molly's hair away from her eyes. The man brought a bottle of water to Angel, who lifted Molly's head and put the bottle next to her lips.

"Drink," he said.

Molly slurped as much water as she could from the bottle before Angel took it away. She ran her tongue over her lips, trying to get them wet. The duct tape had dried them out and they were chapped and cracked.

"More . . . please," she said.

Angel put the bottle back to her lips and she drank as much as she could before he pulled it away again.

Molly then glanced next to her at the fourth body. It was still motionless. "Is that Natalia?" she asked Angel.

"Yes. What's left of her," he said. "She is still alive, but not for long."

Molly raised her head and looked at the other two girls. Both of them were moving, struggling against their bindings. Both of them still had the hoods over their faces.

"Can you give them water?" she asked, looking up at Angel.

Angel smiled. "Still playing the nurse, Rosalinda? Sure, we will give them water."

Angel motioned for the other man to give Cindy and Jenny some water. Molly watched the man as he took off the hoods and tape and let them sip from a bottle of water. He left the hoods and tape off, but kept them hog-tied.

Angel rubbed the back of his hand across Molly's cheek. "It won't be long now, my little *chica*."

Molly stared up at him, her eyes filled with fear. "What will happen to us?" she said, her voice cracking from dehydration.

"Oh, I wish I could tell you that, but I'm going to have to make that a surprise," he said, smiling widely. "I have big plans for you and your two friends."

Molly's fear was palpable. The tears began to well up in her eyes, stinging like crazy.

"Please, I want to know," she choked.

The smile faded from Angel's face as he stood up. He turned and told the other man to leave the room. After the man left and closed the door, Angel bent back down so that his face was close to Molly's.

"My plans have changed, I'm afraid. You will not be sold and you will not have to live the rest of your life as a prostitute," he said quietly, almost nonchalantly. "I hope that pleases you."

Molly stared up at him, eyes wide. "You're letting us go?"

Angel shook his head slowly. "That I can't do, I'm afraid."

"Then what, ransom from my parents?"

"Sadly, no. I will not be getting any money from anyone."

Molly continued to stare at him, the fear growing uncontrollably in her mind. She glanced at Cindy and Jenny. They were staring at her with the same fear in their eyes.

"What are you going to do with us?" she said, choking each word out slowly.

"That's the surprise, Rosalinda. You must wait just like everyone else. But it will be soon—very soon." He smiled and stood up and began walking towards the door.

"Wait! Please!" Molly shouted.

Angel turned to look at her.

"Please . . . I'll . . . do anything you ask," she said haltingly. "But let my friends go. Please."

Angel stared at her. "It's too late for that. Too bad, it would have been fun. Goodbye, Rosalinda." His eyes turned dark, darker than normal. He smiled at Molly. "And say goodbye to your mother." He glanced at Natalia as he said this, then walked out the door.

Molly stared after him and then turned and looked at Natalia. *My mother? Could she be . . . ?*

CHAPTER 62

Jake and Amos watched as Morales and Gonzalez set up the phone. Jake wanted them to be able to trace the call in order to get a reading on where Angel Rojas was located. But Rojas couldn't know that Rafael was making the call from the TJPD precinct, so a special outside line was used. When they were ready with the phone set-up, Morales gave the thumbs up.

Jake looked at Rafael and went over again what he was going to tell his boss. He would be speaking in Spanish so Jake would have to rely on Morales to interpret the conversation.

Right before they made the call to Angel Rojas, Jorge Morales was called to the front desk. He had some visitors.

"Shit," cursed Jake. "We wait any longer, Rojas will get suspicious. He's probably suspicious already. How long's it been since the blast?"

"Almost two hours," said Amos. "What time were you supposed to call him?" he asked Rafael.

"He didn't give me a time. He just told me to call him after the bomb went off."

"Damn it," said Jake. "The little prick's gonna know something is wrong."

Just then, Morales walked back into the room. Two men were behind him and entered the room and shut the door.

"What the hell?" said Jake. "Who are these guys?"

Morales stepped back and allowed one of the strangers to introduce himself.

"Special Agent Diaz and Special Agent Fuentes. We are with the Federal Police," the man said, nodding to Jake and Amos.

Jake looked at Amos in bewilderment. "What the hell is going on here?" he said, throwing his hands in the air. He looked at Morales but got only a shrug of the shoulders from the TJPD officer.

"*Señor*, we understand your confusion," Agent Diaz continued. "Let me explain."

"Yeah, please do," said Jake in exasperation. "And fast."

"We were called about thirty minutes ago by a Federal Officer named Mendez in Sonora. He has been in contact with the father of one of the kidnapped girls. *Señor* Ethan Paxton," Diaz said. "He advised us of the kidnapping and asked us to assist you in any way we can."

Jake's jaw dropped as he stared at Diaz. "Ethan Paxton is the man that hired me to find his daughter," he said, still flabbergasted. "He didn't say a word to me about the Federal Police being involved. What the hell are you, anyway, like our FBI?"

"Yes, more or less we are like your FBI, as you said. Mister Paxton didn't know himself until thirty minutes ago. Officer Mendez advised him of our involvement right before *Señor* Paxton and his friend took off from Puerto Penasco. We have agents meeting him at Tijuana airport when they land in about one hour." Diaz said this matter-of-factly, without emotion.

Jake on the other hand showed lots of emotion. "What the hell are you gonna do to help us at this point? Do you know where Angel Rojas is located?"

Agent Diaz cleared his throat before speaking. "No, *señor*, we do not know where Mister Rojas is located—"

"Mister Rojas! The prick kidnapped three teenage American girls and killed an American woman, as well as a good friend of ours! He is not MISTER Rojas! He's a cold-blooded killer!" Jake was getting red-faced and his scar was turning purple.

Agent Diaz once again cleared his throat. "*Señor*, we are here to help, not to impede your investigation. We can give back-up and advice but once the perpetrator is located we will take over, as kidnapping is a federal offense, as it is in the United States."

This sent Jake over the edge. He slammed his fist down on the table, making the telephone jump and startling everyone in the room.

"No one is taking over this 'investigation,' as you call it. That prick is mine and I will make sure he pays for what he did to the American woman and my friend. *Comprende, Señor* Diaz?"

Diaz took a step back and stared at the wild American in front of him. His partner, Agent Fuentes, stood behind Diaz, trying to look as inconspicuous as possible.

"Do you understand?" yelled Jake.

Amos finally stepped in and tried to calm the situation down. He put his hand on Jake's shoulder. "Calm down, Bull. They're only trying to help."

Jake looked at Amos and let out a long breath. His face began to return to normal and the purple scar became less noticeable. Amos seemed to be the only person that could have this effect on Jake.

Amos looked at the two Federal agents. "This is very emotional for us, as you can see," he said. "We just witnessed our friend being blown to bits, and the son of Mister Paxton almost killed by the bomb blast. This is very personal to us."

The presence and calmness of Amos seemed to let the tenseness out of the room. The two Federal agents breathed a sigh of relief.

"We understand and we apologize for saying that we would take over," Diaz said. "Of course, this is your investigation and we will help in any way we can. But," he said, looking at Jake, "we must insist that the perpetrator be taken alive if at all possible. This is not negotiable."

Jake, both hands on the table and his breathing under control, looked up at Diaz. "If at all possible. Now, if we can move forward, we have three young girls to find and a madman to catch."

Jake looked over at Rafael. The boy was shaking, his eyes wide open, staring at Jake.

"Are you okay, kid?" Jake asked him.

"I think we need to give him a minute to compose himself, and maybe change his shorts," Amos said.

This lightened the mood and everyone laughed. Everyone except Rafael.

CHAPTER 63

Ethan stared at the water below as the Cessna cut through the clouds toward Tijuana. His thoughts were rampaging around his mind like a wild mustang. The events of the last hour were clouding his single-minded goal of finding Molly. He hoped that he hadn't ruined his relationship with Vicki, but he had to put that out of his mind and concentrate on his daughter. He glanced at his watch again, then returned his gaze to the water below.

"We're flying over the Gulf of California," Vicki said loudly, glancing at him. "Nice to see some water, huh?" She glanced at him again, a worried look on her face.

Ethan continued to stare at the water below. He slowly turned his head and looked at her. It was difficult to hear because of the roaring propeller just in front of them. Vicki handled the small Cessna flawlessly, flying at ten thousand feet.

"I've never been in a small plane before," he yelled. "Didn't realize how loud they were."

"This one is louder than normal because of a hole in the dash." She pointed to a small opening below the controls. "It lets in much more noise than it should. Sorry we have to scream at each other."

Ethan nodded and gave her a quick smile.

"We'll be in Tijuana in about thirty-five minutes," Vicki yelled. "Are you okay?"

He nodded again. "It's just all rattling around in my brain. I know we're getting close, but not knowing what's going on with Molly is getting to be more than I can take. I want this to be over, Vicki. I want to hold my little girl in my arms and tell her it's all behind her, just a bad nightmare."

Vicki took her hand off of the small steering wheel and grabbed his hand. She held it tightly, then released it.

"Not much longer, Ethan. Hang in there, okay?"

He nodded and stared vacantly at the blue sky ahead of them. He thought about the last forty-eight hours, about the long flight from Amsterdam to Mexico City, about the generosity of Arturo Calderon, about the beautiful woman sitting next to him right now. He was almost at the end of this long, stressful journey, but he didn't know how it was going to end and that was what bothered him the most. Not knowing how it was going to end.

"Vicki," he said suddenly. "I don't know what's going to happen when we land in TJ. It could, and probably will be, chaotic."

"I'm sorry, Ethan, you need to talk louder," she yelled.

"I said," he yelled, looking at her, "that it will be chaotic when we land."

She nodded that she heard him and understood.

"And in case we don't have a chance to talk later," he said, stopping to rid himself of the lump in his throat, "I want to tell you something."

She glanced at him nervously. "Okay."

"First of all, I want to thank you for everything that you've done for me and my family." The lump in his throat returned. "I wouldn't be anywhere close to my daughter right now if not for you."

She nodded again, smiling weakly.

"And," he said, then stopped again as he swallowed hard. "And, I want you to know that I've..." He couldn't finish the sentence. He gently put his hand on her arm.

Vicki looked at the blue sky in front of them, then slowly turned her head towards him. She had tears forming in her eyes, wiping them with her sleeve.

"Your timing really sucks," she yelled.

He gazed at her, watching the tears form in her eyes. "It does, doesn't it?"

She nodded vigorously, starting to laugh.

They both broke out in laughter at the absurdity of the situation.

The calm before the storm, Ethan thought to himself. *If Molly and I get out of this alive . . . perhaps.*

CHAPTER 64

Jake stared at the young boy in front of him and shook his head. Rafael was shaking like a stalk of corn in the wind. Fear covered his face, his eyes big as saucers.

"He's not gonna be able to do this," Jake said to Amos. "He's scared shitless."

"What choice do we have? He's gotta call Rojas, and soon. It's probably already too late," Amos replied.

"Are you guys ready?" Jake said to Morales and Gonzalez, who were setting up the tracing.

"Ready," said Morales.

"Okay, remember—no noise."

Jake leaned over the table and spoke softly to Rafael. "Just relax and try to act normal, babyface. Take a deep breath, let it out."

Rafael took a big gulp of air and released it. He nodded to Jake.

Jake pointed to Rafael and said, "Call him."

Rafael picked up the receiver and began dialing the number he had been given by Angel Rojas. The receiver shook in his hand as he held it to his ear. Jake thought the kid might throw up when Rojas answered. Jake had a second phone to his ear so that he could listen in on the conversation. The phone began ringing—once, twice, a third time. Finally, on the fourth ring, someone picked it up on the other end.

"Who is this?" a male voice said in English.

"It's Rafael," the kid said, sweat running down his cheek.

There were several seconds of silence before anyone answered him.

"Where the hell have you been?" the voice on the other end said.

Jake looked at Rafael and mouthed "Rojas?"

Rafael nodded. "I—they, the police, were all over the place and, uh, I couldn't get past them right away," Rafael said.

Jake shook his head, knowing that Rojas would pick up on the kid's nervousness. He grew nervous himself after another second or two of silence. He motioned for Rafael to take a deep breath.

"Where are you?" Rojas finally said.

"I—I'm in a cantina." Rafael looked at Jake with wide eyes.

"Really, kid? Funny looking cantina."

Rafael almost dropped the phone, looking at Jake with absolute fear in his eyes.

"I know exactly where you are," Rojas continued. "Say hello to the big guy with the scar on his left cheek."

Rafael stared at Jake. Jake stared back, yanking the phone from the boy.

"Hello, Rojas. It's been a long time," Jake said, glancing at Amos. "How'd you know I was here?"

"That's my secret. How's the scar feeling today?" Rojas said sarcastically. "A little more purple than usual?"

Jake put his hand up to his scar and felt the bulge. "Cut the bullshit, asshole. You know what we want. Where are the girls?"

"Girls? What girls?"

"Listen, you piece of shit. You harm one hair on their heads and you are a dead man, *comprende?*"

"Ah, it's too late for that, *señor*. I've already had my fill of them. You can have them back." Rojas laughed into the phone.

Jake's face began to turn red. He tried to calm himself before speaking.

"Where are they?" he said calmly.

"You're tracing this call so you should know in about twenty seconds," Rojas said. "But unless you are right around the corner, you'd better hurry."

"What are you gonna do, you little prick?" Jake said, seething.

"Everyone is asking me that question lately. It's a surprise, Delgado. Watch TV and you will find out."

Agent Diaz grabbed the phone from Jake. "Rojas, this is Special Agent Diaz of the Federal Police."

"Oh, the *Federales* have joined the party?" Rojas said. "It must be crowded in that room."

"Release the girls now and you might live through this," Diaz said.

"Who says I want to live through this," Rojas said. "I just might take the girls and a few other people out with me," he said.

"What?" Diaz glanced at Jake. "What are going to do?" Diaz stuttered.

"Again, the same stupid question! Watch TV, just like I told the big asshole with the scar!"

Jake grabbed the phone from Diaz, a menacing scowl crossing his face. "Listen, Rojas, I—"

Click!

Jake stared at the table as he heard Rojas hang up. He stood up and threw the receiver against the wall, almost hitting Diaz.

"Goddamn it!" he yelled. "Thanks for the help, Agent Diaz," he said, staring at the Federal Agent. "You sure put the fear of God into him."

Diaz glared at Jake, not saying a word.

Amos once again tried to calm things down. "Did we get a trace?" he asked Morales.

Morales shook his head. "Not enough time."

Jake and Amos looked at each other. They both knew that something big and something horrible was about to happen.

Rafael was slinking in his chair, shaking uncontrollably.

"What do you know, kid?" Jake said, his voice low and menacing. "Tell us now!"

Rafael shook with fear at the sight of Jake hovering over him. "Nothing. He told me nothing," the kid said.

"Did you hear anything, anything at all about what he was planning?" Amos said calmly. "Think kid. You might save a lot of lives if you can remember anything."

Rafael stared at Amos, then back at Jake, who was balling his hand into a fist.

"The border."

"What do you mean the border?" Jake said quickly.

"I..I heard Angel ask someone about the border crossing this morning."

"Like he was going to cross?" Jake said.

"No. No. Like he was asking how many people would be there."

"Which border? Tijuana?"

Rafael nodded.

Jake stared at Rafael, then glanced at Amos. "He's gonna do something at the border. He said that maybe he would take a few other people out with him. Where would a lot of Americans be right now?"

"At the border!" said Amos loudly. "That sonofabitch wants to be a martyr, just like the terrorists in New York!"

Jake shook his head. "No, he wants to be the mastermind behind it, but he doesn't want to die. He wants the glory too much."

Jake sat down slowly, his mind racing. He stared at Rafael for several seconds.

"Wait a minute," he said slowly. "How did Rojas know you were here with us? And how did he know I was here?"

"He must have had another spotter at the blast scene," said Amos.

"Maybe. Or maybe there's someone in this room feeding him information," Jake said, looking around the room. He glanced at Morales, then at Gonzalez. Gonzalez diverted his eyes just slightly. Jake knew it was him.

"Why are you looking at me?" Gonzalez said. "I am a Tijuana police—"

"You and Morales were the only TJ cops at the blast scene that knew about Rafael," Jake said, interrupting him. "You said you checked the roof tops for anyone else. I trust Morales," Jake said matter-of-factly, looking at Morales. "But I don't trust you."

Jorge Morales stared at Jake, then at Gonzalez. "You are the only one, other than me, that had an opportunity to call Rojas," he said. "I know I didn't call him."

Jake noticed a bead of sweat forming on Gonzalez' forehead.

"Why so nervous, Gonzalez?" Jake said, standing up slowly. "You have something to tell us?"

Jake turned his attention back to Rafael, who was staring wide-eyed at Jake.

"Kid, did you ever see Gonzalez before today?" Jake said, looking directly into his eyes. "And I better hear the truth coming out of your sorry mouth."

Rafael started breathing heavy, his breaths turning to pants. "Yes. He was at the warehouse several times." Rafael didn't look at Gonzalez.

"He's a liar! A fucking liar!" Gonzalez yelled. He took a step back and pulled his revolver, pointing it at Jake, then at Morales, then back at Jake.

Morales stepped towards him and put his hands out, palms down. "Put the gun down, Hector. It's over."

"Back off, Jorge!" Gonzalez yelled, pointing the revolver at his partner.

In a flash, Amos threw himself at Gonzalez, knocking the gun from his hand. The two men fell to the floor, a loud gasp escaping from Gonzalez as the breath left his lungs.

Jake walked over to where the two men were lying and grabbed the gun from the floor and handed it to Morales.

"Goddamn TJPD," he said. "This asshole knows what Rojas is planning."

Morales nodded at Jake. "We'll get it out of him." Staring at Gonzalez, he said, "Won't we, Hector?"

Jake bent down, his face just inches from Gonzalez' face. He grabbed the man's hand and bent it backwards until it was about to snap. "You gonna talk?"

Gonzalez stared at Jake, wincing in pain, then spit in his face.

Snap! The bone between the hand and arm cracked. Gonzalez screamed out in pain.

"How about now?" Jake said, wiping the spit from his cheek..

"Si, si, I will talk," Gonzalez said, sweat running down his face.

Jake stood up and looked at Morales. "I think he's ready."

CHAPTER 65

As the Cessna touched down on the runway, Ethan pulled out his cell phone and dialed his son's number. Vicki taxied the small plane down the runway and pulled it over to a small terminal where a Federal Police car was parked.

"The *Federales* are here waiting for us," she said, glancing at Ethan.

Ethan nodded as he waited for Jake to answer.

"Hello?"

"Jake—Ethan. We just landed."

"Just in time, old buddy. Are the *Federales* there?"

"Yeah, we're pulling up to them right now."

"Get in the car and get your ass to the San Ysidro border crossing. It's going down."

"What? What's going down?"

"A shit storm. The *Federales* will fill you in. See you in a few."

Click!

Ethan stared at his phone, his mouth hanging open.

As Vicki pulled the plane to a stop, she looked over at Ethan. "What's going on?"

"Evidently all hell is about to break loose," he answered. "Let's go."

"I'll grab our luggage," Vicki said.

"No time. We'll get it later," he yelled behind him as he ran to the *Federales* car.

Ethan approached the Federal Officer standing next to the car. "I'm Ethan Paxton," he said, holding out his hand.

"Special Agent Torres of the—"

"I know," Ethan said. "We need to go—now."

Ethan and Vicki climbed into the backseat of the Federal Police cruiser and the driver sped off, burning rubber.

"What the hell is going on?" Ethan asked as they sped out of the airport onto a surface street.

"The kidnapper is heading for the border crossing, with your daughter and the other girls," Agent Torres said from the front passenger seat. "All we know is that he is not going to give up quietly."

Ethan's eyes narrowed as he stared at the officer. "What does that mean?"

Agent Torres glanced at Vicki, then back to Ethan. "We're being told he has a bomb."

Ethan stared at Torres. He felt Vicki grab his hand. He turned and looked at her. She had one hand on her mouth, her eyes wide with fear.

"God, no," Ethan said under his breath. "Molly . . . ."

"We're only ten minutes from the border, and we have both Federal and Tijuana police at the scene," Torres said. "Your friends are at the scene, too."

Ethan stared at the man, unable to speak. The long nightmare was coming to an end, but not the end Ethan was hoping for.

Ethan heard sirens and horns blasting as they got closer to the San Ysidro border crossing. The traffic was backed-up as they approached the border.

"We'll have to get out and walk from here," Torres said.

Ethan and Vicki climbed out of the car and followed the two *Federales* as they weaved their way through the crowd of people. There were hundreds, if not thousands of people walking toward the border to cross over to the United States. There were also ten lanes of traffic, filled with cars headed for the U.S.

"How the hell are we going to find anyone in this mess?" Ethan said, huffing and puffing to keep up with agents.

"Just follow us. Stay close," Torres said.

Ethan reached for Vicki's hand and gripped it tightly. She glanced up at him, her eyes wide with terror. They had no time to talk or discuss the situation. Ethan kept his eyes on the two *Federales* as they made an opening through the crowd of people.

Finally they approached a large, gray building next to the line of cars. The agents stopped and waited for Ethan and Vicki to catch up to them. Standing next to them were several other men. Standing head and shoulders above the group of men was a huge red-haired man. Without seeing his face, Ethan knew it was Jake. The man turned around just as Ethan arrived.

"Ethan Paxton, I presume," Jake said. "I'd recognize that baby face anywhere."

Ethan was breathing hard. "Jake, it's good to see you, finally."

The two men grabbed each other and hugged. Jake pushed back quickly, the smile gone from his face.

"We can catch up later. Right now, we have a madman to deal with," Jake said. "This is Amos Stillwater," he said, pointing to the tall black man next to him. "Amos, this is Charlie and Molly's father, Ethan Paxton."

Amos held out his hand to Ethan and shook it vigorously. "Glad to finally meet you, Ethan. I wish it was under better circumstances."

Ethan nodded, then turned to Jake. "What's going on, Jake?"

"It's a long story, but I'll cut to the chase. Molly's kidnapper, Angel Rojas, is planning something big here at the border. And our information is that he'll have Molly and the other girls with him." Jake looked at Ethan and grabbed his shoulder. "And we think he has a bomb."

Ethan just stared at Jake, trying to digest everything he said. "But why can't you stop them?"

"Because we don't know where he is, or what he's driving, or when he's planning to . . . do it . . . or how."

Ethan looked around at the hundreds of people standing in line waiting to cross the border. "He would kill all these people?"

Amos stepped forward and leaned in so that Ethan could hear him above the noise. "He's not just a kidnapper anymore, Ethan. He's crossed that line and now he wants to be famous, or infamous. The terrorist attacks in New York showed him that all he has to do is blow up a lot of people to make that happen."

Ethan shook his head. "But what about Molly and the girls?"

Jake stared at Ethan before speaking. "They're collateral damage as far as he's concerned." Jake hesitated, then continued. "He may even use them to carry out his plan."

Ethan's eyes grew wide, the fear growing by the second. "How . . . ?"

"Ethan, we don't know. We won't know until right before it happens, if then," Jake said. "He knows we won't fire on him or his men if Molly and the girls are with them and he'll be using that knowledge as a weapon. How, we don't know yet."

Ethan's breathing came in spurts now. Vicki reached over and grabbed him by the waist.

"Who are you?" Jake said, looking at Vicki.

"Victoria Calderon. I helped Ethan get here from Mexico City," she said, staring at the big man with the hideous scar.

"Oh, the charter pilot," Jake said. "Ethan didn't tell me you were a knockout," he said, smiling.

Ethan grabbed Jake's arm. "What the hell do we do now?" he said loudly.

"We wait."

"For what? This madman to come barreling at us with a bomb?"

"Something like that," Jake said. "We have Tijuana police and Federal police working on getting more information. Hopefully, they will find out what the little prick is going to do before he actually does it. But we know it's going to be here at the border somewhere, so we wait."

Ethan turned and looked out at the crowd of people walking toward the border and exiting from the border. They were all oblivious to what was about to happen. To them, it was a normal day and they were just going about their business. Until a madman decides to change everyone's plans.

CHAPTER 66

Molly was lying on the cold, concrete floor, her hands and feet still hog-tied together. She had been listening to the other two girls whimpering, no one speaking to each other. They knew that they were going to die soon and each one was alone with her thoughts and their silent prayers.

Molly heard someone move next to her and looked over at Natalia, who had been out cold since they arrived. Blood had dried on her face where Angel had hit her. It was caked around her nostrils where the blood had dripped out. Molly saw the woman's eyes open, then shut again.

"Natalia," Molly said softly. No response. "Natalia!" she said, louder than before.

Natalia opened her eyes and blinked several times. She lifted her head and looked at Molly.

"Natalia, are you okay?" Molly whispered, trying to move closer to the woman.

Natalia blinked again, then laid her head back down on the cement, about to pass out again. Molly moved her legs and kicked her in the shin.

"Natalia, wake up," she whispered loudly, glancing at the door.

This time Natalia opened her eyes wide and stared at Molly. Both eyes were swollen and purple, but she could open them enough to see the teenage girl.

"Can you talk?" Molly whispered.

Natalia moved her lips, running her tongue along them. They were cracked and dry, dried spittle caked on the corners. She stared at Molly and tried to talk. A sound came out of her mouth.

Molly noticed that her hands were not tied together.

"Natalia, can you untie me?" Molly whispered, kicking the woman gently.

Natalia opened her eyes again, in obvious pain. She blinked at Molly, glancing at her hands behind her back. She nodded.

Molly turned on her side, her hands facing Natalia.

"Hurry," Molly pleaded.

Natalia rose up on her elbow, grunting in pain. She moved her hands slowly to Molly's tied wrists. The knot was too tight. She fell back down, already out of breath.

Molly looked over at her and rolled onto her back, lying right next to Natalia. "Natalia. You have to try. Please, you have to try or we're all going to die." Molly saw a solitary tear forming in the corner of Natalia's swollen left eye. "Please, Natalia. Try."

With immense effort, Natalia rose up again on her left elbow and pushed Molly onto her side. She continued to blink while she worked on the knot in the twine that was holding Molly's hands together. She grunted in pain several times, but continued to work on the knot.

Molly, lying on her left side, glanced at Cindy and Jenny. They were both looking at her through dried tears. Molly nodded to them, as though everything would be okay. She felt Natalia working the knot slowly. Finally, she felt the tension around her wrists ease. *She's doing it!* She felt the knot open and she could move her wrists. She waited until Natalia had the twine completely untied, then moved her arms free. She rolled onto her back and rubbed her wrists. Natalia was staring at her, a slight smile on her bloody and caked lips.

"Thank you, Natalia," Molly said, reaching over and hugging her. Then she sat up and began working on the knot around her ankles. She glanced at Cindy and Jenny and smiled for the first time. They stared at her, the fear frozen on their faces.

"We're going to get out of here," she whispered loudly so that they could hear.

She glanced at the door as the knot around her ankles loosened. She tossed the twine off and moved quickly to Cindy and began untying her wrists. Once Cindy's wrists were free she moved to Jenny and did the same thing.

Once their bindings were off they sat up next to each other, holding each other tight. Cindy began crying softly.

"Cindy, we need to move. Don't cry, we can't risk them hearing us," Molly said softly.

Molly stood up. Her head was dizzy from lying down for so long. She stood still for several seconds while her equilibrium returned. Then she looked around the dark room. It was similar to the warehouse they had first been in. It was dark, with just a glimmer of light coming from a window high up on one wall. She walked to the door and put her ear to it, trying to hear any activity or voices. She heard nothing. Then she walked along each wall, feeling for a door or an opening. Nothing. It was an enclosed room, with just the one door as an escape. She looked up at the window but it was too high and too small. She moved slowly back to the other girls.

"There's no way out except the door," she whispered. She saw Cindy's shoulders sag. Jenny just stared at her with no expression.

"What are we going to do?" Cindy said.

Molly stood up again and walked quietly to the door. She put her ear to it again and again heard nothing. She put her hand on the handle and began to move it down slowly. It stopped moving, so she knew it was either locked or it was at the position to open the bolt. She pressed down harder on the handle, hoping for some movement. She felt something moving and suddenly heard a *click!* She glanced at Cindy and Jenny and put her finger to her lips. She slowly pulled on the handle and the door began to open. So far it made no noise other than the click. When it was open a few inches she looked through the slit and peered out. She saw nothing, so she opened the door a few more inches, enough to put her head through the opening. She looked out into the empty warehouse. No one was around. She opened the door far enough to walk through. She took a step into the warehouse and looked to her left and right. Still nothing. She saw a large warehouse door in the distance. It was closed. She looked for movement anywhere but saw nothing. She motioned for Cindy and Jenny to join her. They quickly got up and tiptoed to the door. Molly glanced at Natalia, who was lying still, her eyes closed.

"Stay here. Keep looking for any sign of movement," she said to Cindy and Jenny.

Molly walked quickly to Natalia, bent down and shook her shoulders. Natalia slowly opened her eyes.

"Natalia, we're getting out of here. Come on," she whispered.

Natalia looked up at her and shook her head slowly. "I can't."

"Yes, you can," Molly said, putting her arms under Natalia's armpits and lifting the woman to a sitting position. "I'll carry you if I have to," she said.

Natalia tried to stand but fell back in pain. "My ankle is broken," she said, gasping.

Molly looked down at her ankles and saw the bone sticking out of her right ankle. Blood was seeping out of the wound. She looked at the woman, who was staring back at her.

"I'm sorry, Natalia." Molly grabbed her and hugged her. She felt Natalia brush her hair softly.

"Go, *mija*. Save yourself and your friends," Natalia said into her ear.

Molly laid her back down, the tears stinging her eyes. "Thank you, Natalia," Molly choked. "We'll send someone for you."

"Molly, I'm sorry," she said, coughing. "I...I wish you were my own . . . ."

Molly bent down and kissed her on the forehead. "I know, Natalia."

"Go," said Natalia, smiling weakly. "My daughter."

Molly stared at her and was about to say something, but the woman's coughing became worse. Molly saw blood running out of the corner of her mouth. Molly got up and ran to the door, looking back at the dying woman.

The three girls quietly tiptoed out into the empty warehouse, looking around in all directions. They moved quickly to the large sliding metal door.

"If there's anyone outside, it's over," Molly said.

"Molly, look over here," Jenny said, waving them to a small door several feet away in the corner. It was an entrance door to the outside, with a metal bar that had to be depressed to open it.

Molly put her ear to the door, listening for any noise or someone talking. She couldn't hear anything.

"Here goes nothing," she said as she pushed down on the metal bar. It made a loud noise as it reached the bottom, but the door opened slightly, sunlight streaming into the dark warehouse.

"Stand back," Molly said. "I'll peek outside to see if it's safe."

Molly opened the door slightly, the hinges squeaking loudly. She opened it just enough to stick her head through the opening. She looked right and saw an empty alley. She looked left and froze in terror. Standing two feet away was Angel Rojas, pointing a gun at her.

He grabbed the door and opened it wide. Molly went careening backwards onto her back. Rojas stood in the open doorway, pointing his gun at the three girls.

"Rosalinda, Rosalinda," he said, shaking his head. "Were you thinking of leaving me?"

Molly stared at him, seeing the devil himself staring back at her.

CHAPTER 67

As Jake and Amos watched the street below, Ethan and Vicki stood on the gray concrete platform above the immigration center where hundreds of people walked by on their way to the United States. Ethan searched the crowds for any familiar face, hoping beyond hope that his daughter might be amongst the hordes passing by. Suddenly he heard his cell phone ring.

"Hello?" he said into the phone.

"Dad?"

"Charlie? Where are you?"

"I'm about to leave the Tijuana hospital. They're transferring me by ambulance to a hospital in San Diego."

Ethan exhaled a big sigh. "How are you feeling, son?"

"They have me drugged up pretty good. My leg's a mess. What's happening? Are you still traveling?"

Ethan closed his eyes, trying to decide what to tell him. "I just got into Tijuana, about half an hour ago," he said.

"Really? How'd you get here so fast?"

"A good friend chartered a small plane and we flew the last couple hundred miles," Ethan said, looking at Vicki.

"Dad, what about Molly?"

Ethan couldn't bring himself to tell Charlie about the dire situation they were in. "They're still looking for her, son." He blinked back a tear. "We'll find her and get her home, don't worry."

Suddenly, Ethan thought about what Charlie had just told him. "Charlie! When are you crossing the border to go to San Diego?"

"They're just about to wheel me down to the ambulance now, why?"

Ethan stopped to think. He wanted his son to get the care he needed in an American hospital but he didn't want him anywhere close to the border right now.

"Charlie, I can't explain, but don't come near the border right now," he said, his voice strained.

"What do you mean? They have to get me to San Diego so I can have my leg operated on. What's wrong? Dad, what's wrong?"

Ethan cleared his throat. "There's a bomb threat at the border and they're closing it. You won't be able to get through."

Jake had been standing close by, listening. He asked Ethan for the phone.

"Charlie? Jake. Have them take you across at Otay Mesa, son. It's not safe at the Tijuana crossing."

"Jake? What's going on, really? Is Molly in danger? Is my Dad in danger?"

Jake heard the panic in Charlie's voice, but he had to make sure he didn't come anywhere close to the border. "We don't know, Charlie. Everything is happening fast right now and the border is not a place to be. Put the doctor on the phone so I can talk to him."

Jake waited while Charlie found his doctor. Finally, a man with a heavy accent came on the line. "Dr. Gutierrez, what is this about?"

"Dr. Gutierrez, this is Jake Delgado. There is a bomb threat at the San Ysidro border crossing so you can't take Charlie Paxton through—you must go across at Otay Mesa."

"Who are you? I have no news of a bomb threat."

Jake pulled Agent Diaz over. "Tell this doctor not to take Ethan's son across to San Diego through San Ysidro—please."

Jake and Ethan listened as Agent Diaz explained the situation to Dr. Gutierrez in Spanish. After several minutes Diaz handed the phone back to Jake, nodding it was okay.

"Dr. Gutierrez?" Jake said into the phone.

"No, it's Charlie. Whatever you said convinced them to take me across at Otay Mesa," Charlie said. "Jake, is my Dad safe? Tell me the truth."

Jake pursed his lips and shook his head at Ethan. "Charlie, it's a complicated situation here but you have to trust me that your Dad is safe. Believe me, son."

"And Molly? What about her?"

Jake held the phone away from his ear for two seconds. *Damn pushy kid!*

"Charlie, we don't know yet. All we know is that she's still alive. We'll do everything we can to bring her home, your Dad and I. Just trust us."

Jake handed the phone to Ethan, shaking his head. "He reminds me of you when you were his age."

Ethan smiled weakly at Jake and put the phone to his ear. "Charlie? You have to trust us. Get to San Diego, get your operation and get some rest. We'll take care of everything here. Okay, son?"

"Okay, Dad," he said, his voice choking. "I love you, Dad."

Ethan's voice wavered. "I love you, too, son. See you in San Diego."

Ethan pushed the button to end the call, bending over at the waist, holding his face in his hands. Vicki put her arm on his shoulders, leaning over to console him.

"He's a great kid, Ethan. He's strong, tough. He'll be okay," Jake said.

Ethan stood up straight, his eyes red and puffy. "I'm not worried about him, Jake," he said haltingly. "I'm worried about my little girl."

Vicki put her hand on Ethan's face, but didn't say anything.

Ethan tried to smile. Her touch was soothing. He and this woman he hardly knew had already been through so much together. He stared at her and realized that she was in danger, too.

"Vicki, you have to get out of here," he said, grabbing her hand. "It's too dangerous."

"No. I'm not leaving you."

"Vicki," he said, pulling her to him. "I'd never forgive myself if anything happened to you. Please . . . ."

She looked up into his eyes. She kissed him lightly on the lips and stepped back.

"Whatever happens to you happens to me," she said. "You're stuck with me, Ethan."

Ethan pulled her to him and hugged her tightly. He saw Jake staring at them.

"Looks like you two have some explaining to do," Jake said, a smile wrinkling his scar.

Ethan and Vicki stepped apart, the embarrassment obvious on their faces.

"Don't want to break up this Hallmark moment, but we have some news," Jake said, turning serious.

Ethan's eyes narrowed as he stared at the big man. "What?"

"We know where Rojas is hiding."

Ethan's face lit up. He was speechless.

"The TJPD and Mexican Feds are on their way there right now," Jake continued.

"Let's go!" said Ethan, excitedly.

"No," Jake said, putting his hands up. "We need to wait here in case they've left already."

"I thought you said—"

"We know where he's been hiding, but there's a good chance he's left already."

"But I want to be there when they find Molly."

"I know, Ethan, but she might already be on her way to the border. We can't take that chance. Let's let the TJPD and Feds do their job. They'll contact us as soon as they have information. It's best if we just sit tight here."

Ethan's shoulders sagged and he let out a sigh. "I can't stand waiting anymore, Jake. I've been flying for two days to get here and now you're telling me to just wait?"

Vicki grabbed his arm. "He's right, Ethan. What if they aren't there? We need to be here if and when they arrive."

Ethan stared at Vicki. The pent up emotion he'd been holding in for two days was about to explode. His eyes filled with tears again as he grabbed her and held her.

"I'll give you guys a moment," Jake said. "Sit tight, Ethan."

Ethan nodded. *That's all I've been doing is sitting tight.*

CHAPTER 68

"Cover them up good," Rojas said. "I don't want anything showing."

Molly, tape on her mouth and hands tied behind her back, sat motionless as the man with the gold teeth finished his job. She stared at him, the fear inside of her ripping her apart. She glanced at Cindy and Jenny, who were sitting next to her. They also had their mouths taped and their hands tied. Tears were streaming down Cindy's face. Jenny sat motionless, staring ahead. The life seemed to be ebbing out of her.

Rojas sauntered up to Molly and patted her head. "The final act is about to begin, Rosalinda," he said . "I'm going to miss you. I wish it could have ended differently, but it wasn't to be."

Molly stared up at him, trying to hold back the tears that were fighting to get out. She tried to show contempt for the man, but all she could muster was total fear.

"Oh, by the way. I hear your father made it to Tijuana. Make sure you give him a big hug when you see him." Rojas patted her on the cheek and laughed as he walked away.

Molly stared at him, wanting to scream, but the tape was like a dam, holding it back. The tears began to flow as the man with the gold teeth draped a white jacket over her. He zipped the jacket up to her neck and smiled at her one last time.

Molly looked over at Cindy, who was being covered with a blue jacket, zipped up to her neck. Jenny already had on a red jacket. *The son of a bitch! He's mocking our country!* Molly squirmed and fought against the twine on her wrists. She moved her mouth back and forth, trying to dislodge the duct tape. It was hopeless. Then she glanced behind her in the direction that Rojas had walked. She saw him bending over Natalia, whose eyes were wide and filled with tears. She was staring at her. *Please don't hurt her anymore.*

She watched as Rojas stood up and walked away from Natalia, who was still staring at her. Molly nodded her head at Natalia, who blinked and turned her head away.

"Load them into the taxi," Rojas said loudly. "Red first, then white, then blue."

Molly felt herself being lifted up by her armpits and walked towards the green taxi, which was sitting outside the warehouse. Jenny was put in first, in her red jacket. Then Molly was shoved in, next to Jenny. Cindy was last, in her blue jacket. Molly looked at both girls. Cindy still had tears streaming down her face and Jenny sat motionless and expressionless. *She's back in her shell*, thought Molly. *I wish I was that lucky.*

Rojas leaned down and looked at Molly through the window. "Remember, say hello to your father," he said. "He flew a long way to see you." He laughed loudly, the evil and contempt flowing out of his mouth.

He said something to the driver and the man with the gold teeth, who was sitting in the passenger seat, and the taxi sped off. Molly looked behind them and saw Rojas and four other men getting into a black SUV. She turned forward. She thought about her father, who had made it all the way from Amsterdam—to see her die.

CHAPTER 69

Jake heard his cell phone, actually Charlie's cell phone, start to buzz. He was an amateur with the things so fumbled around until he heard a voice on the other end.

"Delgado?" the voice on the other end said.

"Yeah," he answered, recognizing Jorge Morales's voice.

"We're at the warehouse, about ten minutes from the border."

Jake motioned for Ethan to join him. "What's the story?"

"It's empty, almost."

"What do you mean, almost?"

"There's a woman here, lying inside. It's not one of the girls, she's older, and Mexican."

"Is she alive?"

"Yeah, but I've instructed everyone to stay back until we can check it out. Don't want the same thing to happen as last time."

Jake nodded. "Good thinking. Do you have your bomb squad there with you?"

"Yeah. They're working it now."

"No traces of anyone else?" Jake asked.

"Just some duct tape, some twine and a shoe."

"What kind of shoe?"

"A small shoe, for sports. What do you call it? A tennis shoe," Morales said.

"Any idea how long ago they left?" Jake said.

"Just a minute or so."

"How do you know?" Jake asked.

"Because the woman told us."

"You're talking to her?" Jake said, surprised.

"Yeah, from a distance. We can just barely make out what she is saying. She's beat up pretty bad, especially her face."

Jake remembered the prostitute. "It's probably Natalia Blanco, the girlfriend," he said, looking over at Ethan. "Sounds like she got the worst of it."

"Hold on. She's trying to tell us something," Morales said.

Jake heard Morales walking and then heard a female voice that sounded far away. She was saying something to Morales in Spanish.

Morales came back on the line. "She said 'green taxi'."

"Green taxi? That's it?"

"Yeah. Maybe she saw them put the girls in a taxi," Morales said. "Hold on, she's saying something else."

Jake put his hand over the phone and repeated the word to Ethan. "They're in a green taxi."

He put the phone back to his ear just as Morales said, "Border. They're headed for the border."

Jake nodded to Ethan. "They're on their way here."

"Ask her if Rojas is with them," Jake said.

There was silence for several seconds before Morales came back. "Too late."

"Why is it too late?"

"She's dead."

Jake dropped the phone to his side and rubbed his eyes. He put the phone back to his ear. "Okay. Thanks, Morales."

Jake hung up and looked at Ethan . "It's happening. They're in a taxi headed for the border. They should be here in five, maybe ten minutes."

Ethan stared at Jake, then looked out at the crowd of people.

"Let's get the word out to everyone. We have to spot them before they . . . ." Jake stopped in mid-sentence. He motioned for Ethan and Vicki to follow him.

Jake ran down the steps of the immigration building and found the Federal agents. He told them what was happening and they immediately got on their walkie-talkies and began barking instructions to other agents. Jake saw six men run across the wide boulevard to the other side. Another six to eight men were on his side of the street, all in plainclothes.

Ethan and Vicki were standing next to him. "We need all eyes on every green taxi that comes close," Jake said. "We're looking for the three girls, probably in the back seat."

"What do we do when and if we spot them?" said Ethan.

"We try to find out what we're dealing with," said Jake. "We'll know it when we see it. The earlier we spot them the better chance we have of diffusing the situation."

"There are hundreds of cars and dozens of taxis out here right now. How the hell are we gonna spot them in this mess?" Ethan said, his breathing coming in spurts.

"We start looking for green taxis. You, Victoria and I will walk up the street so we can see any taxis approaching. You're the only one that knows what Molly and the other girls look like," he said, looking at Ethan. "I know what Rojas looks like, so I'm gonna be looking for him."

Jake turned to Amos, who was talking to one of the Federal Agents. "Amos, stay here with these guys. Ethan and I are gonna walk up to the entrance and try to spot them before they make the turn."

"Okay, Bull. Should we clear everyone out?" Amos said, pointing to the mass of cars and people in front of them. "I would think the Federal Police could give the evacuation order."

"I don't think there's time. You got a walkie-talkie?" Jake asked him.

"Yeah."

"Amos, I don't know what this prick has up his sleeve, but God knows it's not good."

Amos nodded.

Jake motioned to Ethan and Vicki. "Let's go."

CHAPTER 70

Molly watched the traffic become heavier as the taxi they were riding in got closer to the border. She looked behind her again and saw the black SUV right behind them. She knew what was about to happen and she was powerless to stop it. She heard a phone ring and watched the man with the gold teeth pick up his cell phone.

"*Sí*," he said into the phone.

Molly watched him nod his head as he looked back at her and the other two girls.

"*Sí*," he said again, putting the cell phone down on the seat next to him. He turned again to look at Molly. He smiled his gold tooth smile, but this time it was tinged with sadness.

Molly looked at Jenny sitting on her right. She was staring vacantly straight ahead. Molly put her head on Jenny's shoulder, knowing she would get no response. Jenny was somewhere else, her mind shut down from the terror. She looked at Cindy on her left. Cindy looked at her with red, swollen eyes. The tears had stopped, but the terror in her eyes was still there. Molly put her head on her best friends shoulder. Cindy leaned her head against Molly's. They knew that their time was just about up, that they were careening towards a violent death. They stayed in this position until Molly looked out the front window and saw what she had been dreading. A sign said 'Tijuana Border Crossing straight ahead'. They were almost there.

She thought about her family, how they would take her death. Her father had flown thousands of miles from Europe to try to save her and now he would have to watch her die. Charlie. Her brother would be an only child, no sister to pick on. The tears began to well up in her eyes once again, but she fought them off. She would not give these animals the satisfaction of seeing her cry.

Molly got a sick feeling in her stomach when they approached the street that would take them to the border. The traffic was heavy. So many people walking towards the border. *Would they be walking to their deaths too?* She looked down at her waist, where he had taped the explosives. They were wrapped around her waist with duct tape. The white jacket covered them up so that no one would know she was a walking bomb. *How would he do it? Just let them drive into the crowd of people and detonate the bomb?* She felt sick to her stomach, the bile and acid climbing up her throat.

As the green taxi started to make the turn onto the main avenue that led to the border crossing, she gazed out at the mass of people on the sidewalks, all with their heads and eyes towards the border. She looked at the faces, mostly Mexican, and felt sadness for them. They knew nothing about what was about to happen.

Suddenly she saw a face in the crowd on the sidewalk, looking out at the cars driving by. Her heart leaped into her throat, a scream rose up from her soul, suffocated by the duct tape. *Dad! Dad!* It was him. Her father was in the crowd, searching for her.

The taxi slowed down almost to a stop as it joined the long line of cars heading for the border crossing. Molly kept her eyes on her father, who continued to search the cars with his eyes. She didn't take her eyes off of him, for fear that he would be gone. *Daddy! Look over here!* She watched his eyes as they moved towards the taxi that she was riding in. *Here I am, Daddy! Over here!*

Suddenly their eyes locked. She stared at her father, who was staring back at her. She saw him point to her, a lady next to him looking in her direction. Then another man, a tall, red-headed man, looked in her direction. She watched as they began to move towards her. Suddenly fear gripped her as she thought of the explosives around her waist. *Daddy, go back! Go back!* She began to kick and thrash about in the backseat. She screamed as loud as she could through the duct tape, only muffled sounds coming out.

She froze as she saw her father stopped in his tracks, just ten feet away from her. The big, red-headed man had a phone to his ear. He was holding his arms out in front of her father, keeping him from going any further.

Daddy! Daddy!

She felt the car begin to move, slowly inching toward the border. She watched as her father got further away. He was still staring at her, reaching out his hands to her. He was yelling something to her but she couldn't hear because of all the noise. He was crying.

CHAPTER 71

Ethan stared at his daughter's eyes, her face tilted toward him, peering out the back window of the green taxi.

"Molly! Molly!" he screamed. He fought against Jake to get free, but he was too strong.

"Stay back!" Jake yelled over the noise of the cars and people. "She's strapped with explosives."

Ethan kept staring at Molly, who was peering back at him as the green taxi inched forward. He was overcome with emotion and fear.

"Molly!" he screamed, reaching his arms out to her. "Molly!"

"Rojas is behind them," Jake yelled to Ethan and Vicki. "He told us to stop or he would blow them up. He's in the black SUV several cars behind them."

Ethan looked at the ominous-looking black SUV that was three cars behind the green taxi. He saw the window slowly go down and saw a man smiling, looking directly at them. He was holding a black device in his hands. Then the window slowly closed.

"Is that Rojas?" Ethan yelled.

"That's him," Jake answered. "And he's calling the shots."

Ethan returned his gaze to the green taxi and his daughter in the backseat, who was still staring at him. The taxi had not moved more than a few feet. Ethan glanced in front of the taxi and saw that at least twenty cars were ahead of them before they reached the border.

"What are we going to do?" Ethan said, absolute panic in his voice.

Jake was on the walkie-talkie, talking to Amos. "He's in the black SUV, three cars behind the girls who are in a green and white taxi. He has a detonator in his hand. The girls are carrying the explosives on them." Jake glanced at Ethan, then returned his gaze to the SUV.

Ethan stared at Jake, his knees beginning to buckle. Vicki grabbed his arm. He looked back at the green taxi and his daughter, who was not looking at him. Fear gripped him like a vice and began to crush the life out of him.

Just then, Ethan saw the green taxi stop. The front passenger-side door opened and a man got out and walked to the right rear door and opened it. A young girl got out. She was wearing a red jacket, zipped up to her neck.

"Jake! Look!" Ethan yelled, pointing to the taxi.

They watched as another girl got out and stood next to the girl in the red jacket. She was wearing a white jacket, zipped up to the neck. *Molly!*

"Molly!" Ethan screamed, starting to run to her.

Jake grabbed him and pulled him back. "He'll kill her if you run to her," he yelled.

Ethan yanked his arm away from Jake and started towards the green taxi. Vicki grabbed his left arm and held on, with Jake grabbing his right arm.

"Ethan! Stop!" Vicki yelled.

They all watched in horror as the third girl got out of the taxi. She was wearing a blue jacket, zipped up to the neck. Suddenly, music started blaring from the green taxi. "America, the Beautiful" was the song.

The crowd of people pulled back when they heard the music and saw the three girls in red, white and blue, forming a semi-circle around them, everyone standing and staring at the strange sight.

Ethan tried to pull away, but Jake was too strong. Amos came up to them and grabbed Ethan from behind.

"Cool down, Ethan. Let us do our job," he said.

Ethan stopped straining and stared at his daughter, who was staring back at him, tears streaming down her face.

Two men got out of the black SUV and walked up to the three girls. They ripped the duct tape away from the girls' mouths, then stood next to them, looking at the black SUV.

"He's giving the finger to the U.S.," Jake said. "Red, white and blue, America the Beautiful. That prick."

Ethan heard Jake's cell phone buzz again.

"You're crazy, you little prick," Jake yelled into the phone.

Ethan stared at his daughter, who was standing in the middle of the crowd of people, staring back at him. He saw her mouth the word, "Daddy."

Jake put the phone back in his jacket and turned to Amos. "Tell the Feds to back off."

Amos got on his walkie-talkie and told the Federal agents to stand down. They were going to let Rojas play it out.

"They're all strapped with explosives," Jake said, looking at Ethan. "He wants us to clear a path for them so they can walk toward the border."

"But why? It's suicide!" Ethan yelled.

Jake nodded. "He wants to go out a martyr, and take as many people as he can with him."

Jake and Amos huddled together, talking rapidly.

Ethan looked at them and then back at Molly, fighting the urge to run to his daughter. "Jake, what the hell do we do?" he yelled.

Jake motioned for Ethan to join him and Amos. "We can't let him call the shots—too many people will die," Jake said. "Are you willing to risk your life and your daughter's life to save her?"

Ethan stared at Jake, his eyes wide, his heart beating wildly in his chest. He glanced back at Molly, still standing in the middle of the street, still looking at him.

"Yes," he answered. "Yes!"

"Amos, you have that extra Glock on you?" Jake said.

Amos pulled out a handgun, keeping it under his jacket.

"Okay, give it to me." Jake took the pistol and slid it under his belt, zipping up his jacket to keep it hidden.

"Ethan, I want you to circle around this crowd and get lost amongst them. They'll be watching me and Amos, not you. I want you to get in that crowd of people standing near the girls. We'll have two Mexican Feds standing next to you. When you see me and Amos walk to the SUV, get ready to grab Molly. The two Feds will grab the other girls. Get them away from the street as far as you can."

"But the explosives . . . ."

"Me and Amos will take care of that . . . God willing. Just get Molly and the girls away from the crowd and away from the street." Jake looked directly into Ethan's eyes. "But you have to wait for my signal."

"What's your signal?"

"When I fire my gun. The crowd will panic and start running everywhere. That's when you grab the girls. Got it?"

Ethan nodded, the panic written over his face.

"Tell your friend to get out of here, away from this area. No need to put her in danger."

"She won't go," Ethan said.

"It's up to you, but she's at risk if she stays here. Okay, start circling around behind the crowd. Just fade in so Rojas can't see you." Jake grabbed Ethan's hand. "Ethan, if this doesn't work, I'm sorry. I tried."

Ethan turned to Vicki and grabbed her arm and started walking down the crowded street. Everyone was staring at the three girls in red, white and blue, with America the Beautiful blaring, and didn't notice them.

"I want you to get as far away from here as you can," he said to Vicki as they continued to walk through the crowd. "Don't look back, just keeping walking."

"No, I won't leave you," Vicki said, the fear evident in her voice.

"You have to, Vicki. I promised your father that you'd return to him safely. I may not make it through this, but I need to know you're safe." He stopped and held her face in his hands. "Please."

Vicki looked at him and slowly nodded her head. "I love you."

"I know. I love you, too." He leaned in and kissed her softly on the lips. "Now go."

Vicki began walking quickly down the street, further and further away from the crowds and the border crossing. Ethan watched her get lost in the crowd of people, then he quickly began walking across the street, lost amongst the crowd of gawkers and onlookers.

CHAPTER 72

Jake watched Ethan get lost in the crowd of people and then he turned to Amos.

"I'm going to walk over to the SUV and try to get Rojas to roll his window down. I need you to make sure his goons are covered when this all goes down. Drop them as soon as you hear me fire."

"All he has to do is press a button and this whole area is a wasteland," Amos said, shaking his head.

Jake nodded. "Yeah, you're right. But I think he wants to talk a little before his big moment. If I can get him to roll down his window, we have a shot."

"Bull, you've been out of the game too long. You aren't fast enough to keep him from pushing that button."

"I don't have to be, as long as the Feds have a sniper that can take him out for me."

Amos grinned at Jake. "Got it. Give me two minutes to get someone in place. When does he fire?"

"When he sees my gun, he fires his. Just make sure he misses me and hits Rojas."

"It's a big risk, Bull. If we don't pull this off, lots of people, including you, me and the girls, will die. You sure you want to risk it?"

"What choice do we have? The prick in that car is planning to blow everything up anyway. I just don't want it to be on his schedule."

Amos nodded. "Give me two minutes to get the shooter in place." He faded into the crowd and began talking into the walkie-talkie.

Jake looked at his watch and then at the black SUV. He began slowly walking toward it, holding his cell phone up so Rojas could see it. Right on cue, it began to ring.

"You willing to talk?" Jake said into the phone.

"Fuck you," Rojas answered. "I'd rather shoot your ass."

"You're calling the shots, Rojas. I just want to know what we can do to save a few lives here."

Jake was ten feet away from the SUV when the window began to come down.

"That's close enough, big man," Rojas said.

Jake stopped. "I don't want to talk into this thing," Jake yelled, holding up the cell phone. "Let's talk face to face."

Rojas now had the window all the way down and was staring at Jake, who began walking slowly toward the SUV. Jake saw two men get out of the truck and stand next to the window. They had their hands inside their jackets, ready to pull their weapons.

Jake put the cell phone in his pocket and stopped when he was three feet away from the SUV. He glanced at the two men and then back to Rojas.

"Get your hands where I can see them," said Rojas.

"What the hell are you doing, Rojas?" Jake said, raising his hands. "Stop this madness before it's too late."

"I'm doing the same thing those terrorists did in New York, except that I have the balls to do it in person," he replied. "I'm not sending someone else to kill for me."

Jake felt his heart pounding as he glanced at his watch. The two minutes were up.

"You late for something?" Rojas said, the smile fading from his face.

"Let the girls go. Strap me with the explosives, you pussy."

Rojas let out a loud laugh. "Pussy? Who gave you that scar, you ugly bastard? You're going to die anyway, so what difference does it make?"

Jake glanced in the direction of the three girls and searched for Ethan in the crowd behind them. He didn't see him but had to trust that he was in position. Amos had his two minutes and should have the shooter in place.

"You holding that detonator with your left or right hand, Angel? Seems I remember you couldn't use your right so good after I mangled your wrist."

Angel smiled and nodded. "Yes, but all I need is one little finger. One little finger and it all goes boom!"

Jake slowly reached behind him and grabbed the Glock. "I only need one little finger, too, asshole."

He quickly pulled the Glock with his right hand and shot one of the goons in the head. In a split second Jake heard two rifle shots, one hitting the other goon in the forehead and the second hitting Rojas in his left arm.

Jake lunged forward, grabbing Rojas' right arm before he could push the button on the detonator. He saw the detonator fall harmlessly to the floor. Rojas, blood gushing from his left arm, grabbed Jake by the neck and held him. Jake fought to get free but the wiry Mexican had the leverage on him. Rojas had the knife in his right hand, the one with the black glove. Jake heard the sound that had filled his nightmares for the past five years. *Click!*

Rojas held the knife to Jake's jugular vein. "My hand is working fine now, isn't it asshole. You won't live through this one," he said into Jake's ear as he pressed the knife into Jake's flesh..

Jake heard another rifle shot and felt the hiss of the bullet pass next to his ear. As Rojas's grip loosened, Jake felt the knife scrape his neck and felt the warm blood begin to seep out. As Rojas fell backwards, Jake looked into his lifeless eyes and saw the bullet hole in his right temple.

The crowd was screaming, running wild in every direction. Jake pulled his head out of the SUV and looked in the direction of the girls. He couldn't see anything, so he climbed up on the hood of the SUV and gazed at the spot where the girls had been standing. They were gone, but two bodies were lying on the ground.

He scanned the crowd of people and then spotted them. Ethan and Molly were hugging each other as people scurried around them. The other two girls were standing close by, being held up by two Mexican Federales.

Jake slumped down on the hood of the SUV, putting his hand on his neck and feeling the blood. It was gushing between his fingers, just like five years ago. Exhausted, he laid back on the windshield, listening to the screams and shouts of the people running by, America the Beautiful still blaring. He gazed up at the blue gray sky as the blackness engulfed him.

EPILOGUE

Ethan woke up groggy, his eyes opening slowly as he arched his back to ease the stiffness after falling asleep on the small chair. He felt someone staring at him. Molly was sitting up in bed, a big smile on her face. She had an intravenous needle stuck in her arm, giving her the vital nutrients and fluids that she had been deprived of during her captivity.

"Hi, Princess," Ethan said, standing, stretching and walking to the bed. "How you feeling?"

"A little groggy, but okay," she said, hugging her father tightly. "How long have I been here?"

Ethan looked at his watch. It was seven o'clock on the evening of September fourteenth. "About twenty four hours. You were out cold when we rode across the border in the ambulance last night."

"What happened, Dad? I remember lots of people and noise and then nothing until now."

Ethan tried to smile as he thought of the events of twenty four hours earlier. "You passed out right before the ambulance arrived. I think you were just so weak and exhausted."

Ethan kissed his daughter on the forehead. "But it's over now." He looked up and winked at someone on Molly's left.

"Hey, Moll," a voice said.

Molly turned and saw Cindy sitting up in the bed next to her, an IV tube running from her left arm.

"Cindy!"

Cindy smiled at her best friend. "You okay, Moll?"

"Yeah, I think so. How about you?"

"I slept a long time, but I guess I'm, like, okay," she said. "My parents will be here tomorrow, I'm so excited."

Ethan watched the two girls talk. He laughed when he saw their smiles, fighting back the tears at the same time, trying to be strong one more time.

"How's Jenny?" Molly said.

Cindy shook her head. "Still not responding much. They said it was, like, mental trauma or something. She's here in the hospital."

Ethan sat back down in the chair and watched the two girls chatting and giggling, as though the nightmare they had just been through had never happened. He couldn't help but smile at the sight that just twenty four hours before he thought he would never see again.

He heard a squeak of a wheel and noticed someone in the doorway. Charlie, in a wheelchair, his right leg extended out in front of him, a white cast covering his leg up to his waist, was sitting there smiling his big smile.

"Hey, sis," he said. "I thought I heard voices from your room."

"Charlie!" Molly yelled, as she broke out sobbing. "Charlie," she said again weakly.

Ethan walked over to him, bending down and hugging his son. "How are you feeling today, son?"

"Better, now that my baby sister is here," he said.

Ethan wheeled him over to the side of the bed, in between Molly and Cindy.

"Hi, Charlie," Cindy said softly, tears forming in her tired eyes.

"Hey, kid. How're you feeling?" Charlie said, reaching over to take her hand.

"Better. Much better. How's your leg? Is it, like, broken or something?"

"Yeah. Or something. I'll be playing hockey by November though."

Charlie reached out his hand to his sister. "Hey, sis," he said, fighting back tears. "You look a helluva lot better than when they brought you in last night."

"You were here?" she said, eyes red and swollen.

"Yeah. You and Cindy were drugged up pretty good so I'm not surprised you don't remember."

Molly put her wet cheek on his hand and kept it there for several seconds. No one said a word for a few minutes as they just let the silence and the moment speak for them.

Ethan sat in the chair and gazed at his family. It was the first time in three days that he felt like he could relax. He had flown thousands of miles and endured many sleepless hours, but it was behind him. He smiled as he looked at his son and daughter, who both seemed older now.

"Hey, Paxton's. Why's it so quiet in here," a voice said from the doorway.

Ethan looked up and saw the big redhead standing there, filling up the doorway. Jake had a huge piece of gauze on his neck, covering the wound, and was dragging an IV stand.

Ethan stood up and walked quickly to his friend and, without speaking, they hugged each other. Ethan finally stood back and looked at the man that had saved his daughter's life.

"You look good, Jake," Ethan said.

"Thanks, Ethan."

"Dad, it's not Jake, its Bull," said Charlie, who had wheeled himself over, grinning from ear to ear.

Jake reached down and grabbed Charlie's hand. "How you doing, kid?"

"I'll be playing hockey by winter," Charlie said. "And don't call me kid."

Jake reared his head back and laughed, holding his neck. "I wouldn't bet against you, Charlie," Jake said, patting him on the shoulder. "And that's the last time I call you kid. You are definitely not a kid anymore."

Ethan heard someone cough behind Jake. Amos Stillwater poked his head into the room. "Is this a private party?" he said.

Jake stepped aside as Amos walked into the room. Ethan saw his daughter and Cindy staring at the two men and realized that they had never met.

"Jake and Amos," he said, "this is my daughter, Molly, and her friend, Cindy."

Jake looked at Molly and walked over to the side of the bed and took her hand. "It's a pleasure to finally meet you, young lady. You caused us more than a little concern over the last couple of days."

She grabbed his arm and pulled him down and kissed him on his cheek, right on the scar. "Thank you," she whispered, choking. "Jake, did you see the Mexican woman?"

"The one with your dad?" he said.

"Who? No, the one with Angel Rojas . . . his girlfriend."

"Oh, Natalia Blanco. No, sweetie, I never met her or talked to her."

"Is she . . . ?"

"She died, Molly," Jake said, squeezing her hand. "But she helped us right before she died. She told us you were in a taxi and the color, so we could spot you when you got to the border. She was a brave woman."

Molly stared at Jake as the tears dripped from her eyes onto the bed. "Thank you, Jake."

Jake stood up and wiped his own tear away. "You're welcome, Molly."

Jake turned and saw the other girl staring at him. "So this is Cindy," he said, grinning. "Very nice to meet you."

She nodded, the tears flowing down her cheeks. She reached out and hugged the big man. No words were spoken.

Jake cleared his throat and turned to look at Ethan. "Well, Ethan, we did it. We brought them home."

Ethan nodded, his eyes becoming moist again. "You did it, Jake. You and Amos—and Charlie."

Jake smiled, glancing at Charlie and Amos. "And a good man named Manny . . . ." Jake's smile faded as he thought about his old partner. He looked at Charlie, who was fighting back tears.

Amos leaned over to Ethan. "Ethan, can we go out into the hallway and talk a second?"

"Sure. Jake can stay here and get to know my family." He looked at his children. "I'll be back in a minute."

He left the room and entered the hallway, Amos right behind him. They walked down the hall to the waiting area and sat down. Ethan heard laughter coming from the room, warming his heart.

"How you holding up, Ethan," Amos asked.

"Everything's good now," he answered, smiling. "How about you?"

"I'm good as gold, not a scratch. The doctor said the knife just nicked Jake's jugular vein, enough to cause some serious blood loss, so they want him to stay in the hospital a day or two. Guess it could've been a lot worse."

Ethan looked at the man closely for the first time. "Thank you for your help, Amos. I heard you kept Jake in line the last couple of days. I'm sorry about your friend, Manny."

Amos pursed his lips. "Manny was a good friend, a good cop, but he made a rookie mistake." Amos stared off into space for several seconds. "I'm going to miss him." He looked up at Ethan. "I'm glad Charlie's going to be okay."

Ethan nodded. "I guess Manny saved his life by taking the brunt of the blast."

Amos nodded. "Yes, he did. Yes, he did." Amos looked away.

"Amos, who took the shot that killed Angel Rojas? Was that you?"

Amos glanced at Ethan. "The last kill shot, that was mine," he said. "The first two shots were Mexican Federal agents, snipers."

"Tell them thank you for me, will you?"

"I will, Ethan," Amos said. "By the way, I talked to your friend after everything happened."

"Vicki?" Ethan said, his heart racing.

"Yeah, Vicki. She wanted me to tell you that she—"

"Thanks, Amos, but I can tell him myself," a voice said behind them.

The two men turned around quickly and saw Vicki standing there, flowers in her hand. She was dressed in a flowery summer dress, her hair down around her shoulders. Ethan felt the familiar charge run through his body.

"I'll leave you two alone," Amos said, a smile creasing his face. He stood up, nodded to Vicki, and walked back down the hall to Molly's room.

Ethan's eyes locked onto Vicki's. They looked at each other for a couple of seconds before Ethan walked to her. She trembled as he held her in his arms.

"Are you okay?" he said.

"I didn't know if I would ever see you again. Amos told me that you and your daughter were rushed to the hospital. I didn't know what to do." She was crying softly.

"Vicki, I'm so sorry. Everything happened so fast and they rushed us out of there—"

"I know. Amos told me everything. At first I thought about flying home right away because I knew you'd be with your family." She wiped away a tear. "But then I realized I couldn't leave without talking to you, so I crossed the border and took a taxi to the hospital."

"I'm so glad you did."

"I wanted to make sure you and Molly were okay, and . . . ." She buried her face in Ethan's shoulder.

Ethan held her and let her cry. When she was done, he kissed her gently. "You look beautiful. Vicki, I—"

"Shhh. We have plenty of time for that. Just hold me," she said. They embraced each other tightly, silently.

Finally, Ethan looked at her and said, "I want you to meet Molly. Without you, I wouldn't be here and she probably wouldn't be alive."

"I'd like that," she said.

Holding hands, they walked down the hallway to where the laughter was coming from. When they walked into the noisy room everyone fell quiet. Everyone was staring at the beautiful woman by his side.

Ethan cleared his throat. "This is Victoria—Vicki—Calderon," he said. "She's the one that got me all the way from Mexico City to Tijuana."

Molly stared at her, not taking her eyes off of the mysterious woman. Ethan realized that he hadn't told Molly anything about Vicki and how he got to Tijuana.

"I'll tell you the whole story when you get stronger, Princess," he said. He smiled at Cindy. "And you too, Cindy."

Charlie wheeled up to Vicki and stuck out his hand. "I'm Charlie. Thank you for helping my dad," he said as they shook hands.

"Nice to meet you, Charlie," Vicki said. "Are you doing okay?"

Charlie hit his cast with his knuckles and nodded, embarrassed.

Finally Molly was able to speak, her voice wavering. "You remind me of my mom," she said, the tears once again filling her eyes. "You're so beautiful."

Vicki put her hand to her mouth. She walked to Molly's bedside and took her hand. "Thank you, Molly. You're a beautiful young woman yourself."

Ethan bit his lip, trying to keep his emotions under control. He watched as Vicki turned and hugged Jake.

"Good job getting Ethan here in time," Jake said, smiling. "I can see on his face that it was torture spending so much time with you."

Vicki stared at his neck, then at his scar just above the gauze. "You've had a rough time, Jake. Thank you for making this a happy reunion."

"Daddy?" Ethan heard his daughter say. "Can we talk on the balcony for a minute?

She hadn't called him Daddy in a long time. "Sure, Princess."

He helped her out of bed and they walked to the balcony together, Molly dragging her IV stand with her. As they walked out onto the balcony, Ethan looked back and saw everyone talking and laughing. It was a sight that he had dreamed about many times over the past seventy two hours.

"Are you okay?" he asked his daughter once they were on the balcony.

Molly was wiping her face. "I miss Mom, Dad. I miss her so much," she choked.

Ethan put his arm around his daughter and they hugged tightly for several moments. He never knew what to say when one of his children talked about their mom. He felt so inadequate, her death so recent and so fresh . . . .

"I know, sweetheart. I miss her, too."

"Dad, do you remember the name of my birth mother?"

Ethan stared at her for a moment. *Where did this come from?* "Yes, why?"

Molly lips began to tremble. "I think I met her."

Ethan took a step back and looked at his daughter carefully. "The woman you asked Jake about?"

Molly nodded. "Natalia Blanco. Is . . . is that my birth mother's name?"

Ethan put his hand on her face, brushing her hair. He shook his head. "No, Princess, that wasn't her name."

Molly stared at her father for a long time, wiping the tears away. "Are you sure?"

"Yes, I'm sure." He took a breath. "Your birth mother's name was Rosalinda."

Molly began to tremble as the tears tumbled out of her eyes. Ethan held her tightly and let her cry. They were silent for several minutes, listening to the laughter in the hospital room. He saw Charlie at the sliding door, ready to come out onto the balcony, but Ethan put his hand up and shook his head. Charlie backed away, staring at them.

"Angel Rojas called me Rosalinda," Molly said, choking.

"Why?"

"I . . . I think because he knew that Natalia was . . . ."

"Your birth mother?" Ethan said.

"She mentioned the birthmark on my back, like she had seen it before."

Ethan stared down at his daughter, not knowing what to say.

"Could it have been her?" Molly said, looking up at her Dad. "Could she . . . ?"

Ethan held her tightly. "We'll never know, Princess," he said, a tear forming in his eye.

Ethan looked up and saw a sliver of white in the night sky.

"Molly, look at that," he said, pointing to the moon. "Remember what your mom used to call that?"

Molly looked up at the twilight sky, tears dripping down her face. She sniffled. Then she smiled. Finally, she giggled as she hugged her father tightly.

"Yeah, daddy," she said. "She called it my toenail moon."

"That's right, Princess. It's Molly's Moon."

Ethan waved Charlie to come out and join them. They stood on the balcony, staring at the night sky and the toenail moon. At that moment, Ethan knew everything would be okay.

ACKNOWLEDGEMENTS

I wish to express my eternal gratitude to several people for their support, expertise and knowledge in the creation of this novel: J.B. Hogan, who without his expertise and editing prowess, this book may never have left my hard drive. He was invaluable in the editing of *Molly's Moon*, giving me undying support during those inevitable periods of doubt. He also introduced me to Duke and Kimberly Pennell of Pen-L Publishing, who took a chance on a rookie writer. "Hogie" and I met while in the U.S. Air Force in Misawa, Japan, and is a published author himself; Paul Pfeifer, my good friend who was the inspiration for the character of Pete Cruz. Paul was with me in the Netherlands during the chaos of 9/11, and, yes, we really did stay in the city of 's-Hertogenbosch; Jonathan Parham, my chiropractor-to-be son, who read the early stages of the novel, in the days when my spirit and determination lagged. He also provided valuable information about the Baja California area, the school missions that he was part of, and the border crossing process; Rick Parham, my late brother, who actually lived in Tijuana for several years and helped me understand the sub-culture of the Avenida Revolucion area. He was also an early reader of the novel and gave me much support and encouragement. He died suddenly of a massive coronary while I was beginning my second novel, Copperhead Cove. Rest in peace, little brother; Terry Curley, my closest friend in the world, who encouraged me every day, usually with a glass of Chardonnay in his hand; Adan Martinez, boyfriend of my daughter Kelli, who helped me with some of the Spanish terms used in the novel. The gang's name, La Mano Negra, the Black Hand, was his idea; Kelli Parham, my beautiful daughter, who gave me unconditional love and support during the entire two-year process of writing the novel; thanks also to my editor, Staci Troilo, who did a terrific job of cleaning up some of my messy writing, making it look more professional and clean; and finally the aforementioned Duke Pennell, owner of the indie company Pen-L Publishing, based in Fayetteville, Arkansas, who saw something in my writing and offered me a contract, enabling me to share my book with you.

ABOUT THE AUTHOR

 After thirty years in the global logistics and high-tech industries, Ron Parham retired on his birthday in 2011 and immediately began penning his first novel, *Molly's Moon*. He hasn't looked back and will soon finish his second thriller, *Copperhead Cove*. His novels incorporate his many *unusual* experiences while traveling around the world on business. He writes in the seaside town of Carlsbad, CA.

Dear Readers,
If you enjoyed this
book enough to review
it for Amazon.com
or Pen-L.com, I would
appreciate it!
Thanks, Ron

**More great reads at
Pen-L.com**

www.ingramcontent.com/pod-product-compliance
Lightning Source LLC
Chambersburg PA
CBHW071231250626
47163CB00001B/127